THE FISHERBOY'S BLUES

ISBN: 9798684270512

Alan Alfredo GEDAY

THE FISHERBOY'S BLUES

a novel

Translated into English by Adam Wilson

For my father, Andréa

For my mother, Viviane

For my sister, Anna Karina

With thanks to Coralie Rolin

"Writing a novel is a lot of work," she'd warned me when we first met. That first encounter was in Paris, in a café in the Latin Quarter, where we would see each other again a few times before feeling the need for change. Just long enough to become regulars; not long enough to tire of the place. I appreciated that she always wanted to meet out in the world; writing comes to me more easily when I can become detached without realising it. If only I had known how right she was — writing a novel is a truly herculean task — I would probably never have allowed myself to begin, but she was there to support me every step of the way, and now my ambition and my inspiration are limitless. "I want to write until the end of my days," I concluded after two years of work. She smiled, realising that she'd instilled in me the same love of literature and creative desire she herself felt. "There's no greater gift you could give me," she answered. I could not have wished for a more able teacher. Today, I can only thank her from the bottom of my heart.

Part I

The Fishermen of Livorno

1.

Along the quays of Livorno harbour, children scamper and splash in the water, their small feet slipping over cobblestones worn smooth by the tide and polished with seaweed. The bambinos flit back and forth like baitfish, returning to seek warmth in the arms of their *mamma*, who wrap them in soft, warm, white towels. Far off, the dock workers are stacking barrels of fuel oil near the portside cafés. Ignoring the nauseating odour of the oil, the old men drink their coffee at the Aragosta, sheltered from the sun by a broad awning of red canvas. Earlier in the day, these *vecchio* had settled in to discuss the rebuilding of the town. Their precious Livorno may have been torn up by American air raids, but the place was too old and too stubborn to disappear. It was being rebuilt stronger than ever. The port's lamplighter chuckles to himself as he listens to the ramblings of the *vecchio*. He lights the gas lamps that illuminate the café's terrace, casting a purplish hue over the windows and cobblestones. Sitting around small tables covered with chequered cloths, some play at dice while others sit lost in thought, watching the surf gather on the surface of the water or the sailors loading and unloading their boats. All this movement serves as a distraction. *Il fotografo* ambles from one café to another, taking pictures with his Sanderson, trying to capture the expressions of the old boys in their pensive dazes or the innocent smiles of children heading home to their mothers' arms. Artists are painting the island of Gorgona, as passers-by stop to admire their canvasses. Alongside the usual picturesque landscapes are charcoal portraits of Gina Lollobrigida, Valentina Cortese or Anna Magnani, displayed on wooden easels. The cobbled streets around the port have become a creative space for young people, too, who make charcoal sketches of Christ in his crown of thorns or the nativity of baby Jesus. Then they let the wind carry off their drawings, a sort of religious offering to the infinite expanse of the water. Only the sea survives, uncaring and eternal.

The father of the Valci family and his son, Giovanni, were sailing around the outskirts of the port in their Neapolitan skiff. The little rounded boat, known as a *gozzo*, is used only by the fishermen of Livorno. Each one is painted with a protective eye to watch over its occupants, and the vessels carry an almost sacred status. Each *gozzo*'s name is carefully chosen: theirs was called Nina, named after *mamma* Valci. When he was still a child, Giovanni had wanted his mother's name to go with him, for her comforting presence to follow them everywhere. It was he who had the honour of christening the *gozzo* when they went to collect it from the workshop. On that day, the old woodworker had been making a statue, and sitting in admiration before the outline of the Madonna, Giovanni watched the woodworker level the base with his plane. His rugged hands moved expertly, with tender, precise strokes. The child observed the sawdust suspended in a ray of light and was briefly entranced by this moment of grace. The workshop was imbued with a fresh, musky odour; a smell that was gentler than the acrid salt of the sea. The boy stared in wonder at the saws that hung from the walls, their blades gleaming in the dim light, their dangerously sharp and strange edges instilling in him a lust for adventure. He was suddenly able to conceive of a life where people didn't fish but were busy building unknown countries and cities. It was at this moment that Giovanni had begun to dream. Now, his wide, melancholy eyes were lost in the horizon. The island of Gorgona was absorbing the last light of the day. Beside him, Valci senior was getting impatient. He cursed the sea at whose mercy he laboured: "The old wench is holding out on me today." He'd sifted the water a hundred times and brought in nothing but sugar kelp and seaweed, clogging up the holes of his nets. The hulking old man rowed with angry strokes. He'd have to find a new spot. Giovanni seemed unaware of his father's bad mood.

"Stop daydreaming, we haven't caught a thing since this morning!" sputtered the old fisherman through his cough.

"Well, that's not my fault, is it?" his son answered nonchalantly, hands idle in his pockets.

"Do some rowing then, at least pretend to be helping!"

"We'd be better off heading in – the wind's picking up."

"Scared of the wind, are you? How are you ever going to be a fisherman thinking like that?" his father said angrily.

"Do I really want to be a fisherman?" sighed Giovanni as he took the oars and began pulling towards himself.

Valci senior was not a cruel man, but at this, he gave his son a hard look. The boy spent too much time thinking and not enough wiping his brow under the hot sun.

"Don't you want to become a man, and provide for your family?"

"There are other things out there. You don't understand."

"I understand that you're ashamed of your father and that you don't want to end up like him," grunted Valci senior.

"I'm not ashamed. I'm just...bored. That's no way to live."

"And just how do you have time to be bored? Being bored is for rich people, who have money and don't have anything else to do. Are you a bourgeois? Are you a parasite? No! You're my son and you have some pride, you have dignity, and you're not going to let your poor mother go without supper!"

What could Giovanni have offered in response? He knew his father was worried. His illness tormented him more than he dared to admit, so he lost his temper instead. His lectures were exhausting. The poor man had toiled his entire life; now he was an old dog, so long in the tooth that he barked just to make sure nobody forgot he was there. Giovanni was overcome with pity for his father. He would end his days here in Livorno, knowing nothing of the rest of the world. The boy, meanwhile, thought of nothing but getting out of this town as he watched the old man cast his net with furious energy.

"Nothing! Not a single damned fish!" cried Valci senior.

"We should head in; it's starting to get cold," warned Giovanni.

"No, we're going to keep trying!"

The old man was stubborn. He made it a point of pride to always bring fish home to his wife, Nina. However much she begged him, Giovanni's father refused to let the boy go fishing alone. Staying home was out of the question. A little bout of tuberculosis wasn't going to get the better of him, and nobody could tell him otherwise. He would not be reasoned with. The father began to cough. Giovanni patted him affectionately on the back and wrapped a blanket around his shoulders to warm him up.

"I'm fine! I'll be OK. I'll get better soon," the father said impatiently.

Giovanni sat down in the bow. The nets had been cast; now there was nothing to do but wait. A heavy silence settled upon the little boat.

The old man drifted off to sleep. His white hair rustled against his nut-brown forehead. Giovanni entertained himself by counting the creases between his father's two eyebrows. These were the wrinkles of a worried man. His father had never taken a day's rest in his life. All of a sudden, the boat rocked. Valci senior awoke with a jump.

"It's moving! Pull in the net!"

The young fisherman did so quickly:

"Two mullets!" he exclaimed.

"Ouffa! And a dreamfish!"

Valci senior was satisfied. His wife Nina would be happy. This sliver of joy seemed to restore his strength, and he manoeuvred the boat back towards the harbour. Giovanni took advantage of this fleeting jubilation to take out his harmonica. He wanted to play the blues, the music that let him dream. The father did not like to see his son getting all moody like he did, but was too busy rowing to put a stop to it. So Giovanni began to play, and in his mind he waded into another world, the one that made him feel alive. It was a world of emotion, filled with hope and memory. He knew that this interlude would be short, and that back on dry land he would have to live among his own kind once more. But in the meantime, he'd let his thoughts wander. The wind whistled in his ears like a seashell; the cry of the blues was lost in the lapping of the waves.

It was Benjamin — Giovanni called him 'Ben' — who'd taught him to play the blues. When the Americans were rebuilding the port, Giovanni liked to go swimming with them. One day he'd left his harmonica on the dock, hidden inside a moccasin. But while he was immersed in the warm water of the late afternoon, swimming among the fish and the green seaweed that caressed his legs, he heard a smooth tune wafting through the air. Afraid that someone had stolen his harp, he hurried back and saw that a small crowd had gathered around a mysterious musician. It was a sailor, playing something the captivated crowd had never heard before. He wore a khaki jacket, pale mustard trousers and laced boots. The local boys gazed covetously at the knife strapped to his right leg. It was a black American in Livorno, treating the locals to the sound of the Chicago blues. Giovanni approached the man, who was enjoying the encouragement from the fishermen yelling *"è mio, è mio!"* The soldier met Giovanni's gaze and stopped playing:

"Hey man! This yours?"

Giovanni didn't understand but pointed to the instrument. The sailor went on:

"Name's Benjamin. From Chicago. You like the blues?"

The teenager nodded, and the solider grinned. From then until the Americans went home, Ben taught Giovanni the slow, sultry rhythms of the blues. Every night after the fishing was done, Giovanni would run to the army barracks and interrupt their card games. For a boy who'd only ever known sea shanties and Neapolitan *tarantellas*, the sound of the blues conjured tantalising images of skyscrapers and the American dream. Benjamin was impressed with his diligence and taught him a few songs by Sonny Boy, which Giovanni practised on his *gozzo*. The music soothed his father's moods, even if he did wonder where this flight of fancy came from. He asked his son no questions; it was not his way. "What's that your son's playing? It's not from around here, anyway," curious onlookers would say. A wry smile would form on Valci senior's face. It made him feel a certain pride, knowing his son wasn't like the other teenagers. Giovanni looked up at the Livorno lighthouse rising majestically from the water. Valci senior manoeuvred his *gozzo* between the other boats, shaking hands with their owners as he passed. They docked the *Nina*, and Giovanni tied the rope around a bollard. Valci senior nervously shooed away the gulls that were making their way towards the boat, eyeing their catch with covetous intent. Giovanni watched the old man as he stood up shakily on the *gozzo* and thrashed at the air like a rickety windmill. A song went up over the port: *"Oh catch! Oh miraculous catch! Oh millions of stars caught in my net!"* It was a fisherman singing happily as he spread his net over the bollards, its cork floats unfurling like giant rosary beads. Giovanni and his father greeted the net mender, whose great rugged hands were plunging damaged nets into a bucket of scalding water infused with pine bark and ground oak; the tannins in the mixture would stop the nets from rotting. Beside them, a diver was flagging down the oyster sellers, who were looking for crab and shrimp for tomorrow's market stalls. "Live shellfish! Live shellfish!" he yelled at the top of his lungs, holding up his basket of prawns and green crabs. Valci senior and Giovanni made their way over to the lemon seller. They each squeezed a slice between their fingers to remove the stubborn odour of the fish. The juice stung their cracked skin, but it smelled fresh and marked the end of their day's labour.

"Valci, my friend!" called out another fisherman sitting on the quay.

"Marcello! Your wife will complain if you come home smelling like fish. How was today's catch?"

"I got four sea bream on my own! Quite the miracle. Come and celebrate at the Aragosta with me!"

"Marcello, I can't...you know I'm not well."

"Come on, Valci — one drink won't kill you!"

The Aragosta was a timeless, simple place where everyone felt at home. Even the oldest patrons couldn't tell you how long it had been around. Everything there was reassuringly ordinary, preserving an almost mythical sort of Italian-ness, from the photographs pinned to the wall to the music crackling from behind the counter. Its customers mainly drank coffee, but the bar also served wine and a few local spirits. The owner was a fearsome sort who seemed to have been born within its walls; a part of the furniture and a part of its charm. His main clients were the *vecchio*, but they were often joined by the fishermen coming back into port at the end of the day. Marcello and Valci walked in, greeting the regulars and sitting down beside two old-timers deep in conversation:

"I tell you, coffee fairly puts you to sleep if you don't drink it."

"Ma daaaai! Are you saying that if I drink coffee I'll fall asleep?"

"No, that's not what I said! I said that if you drink coffee, you won't sleep at night."

"Well, coffee makes me sleep."

"How can you sleep when you drink coffee at this time of the day?"

Marcello flashed his friend a knowing smile. He took off his rubber boots and extended his legs lazily:

"How is Nina?"

"She can't sleep at night with all my coughing. And Valentina?"

"She's well! She's well, thank you. Still waiting on her gifts from the 'States."

"Are your sons still sending her presents in the post? That must cost a lot."

"Yes, and they don't always get to us. And when they do get here, they've been opened and looted by the customs people."

"Marcello, I don't understand how you and Valentina can do it, living without your children," Valci senior blurted out suddenly.

"Well...you know as well as I do Valci, we Italians are an immigrant people. I mean, we're all over the place."

"Marcello, family means more than anything. You don't leave your parents, you take care of them until the end. It's a child's job to look after their elders, and it's the parents' job to pass on their wisdom to the younger generations. Without that, the world would go to pot. Young people will always have their wild ideas; they have all that energy but don't know what to do with it. Then there's old folks like us; all we can do is wish we still had the strength to act on those ideas. We all need to live together, not go off looking for happiness somewhere else."

"For someone who likes to talk politics and read the paper every day, you don't have the most progressive ideas. I'm happy that my children have made something of themselves, even if they did it without me."

"You didn't have much of a choice in the matter!"

"How many times have we had this conversation, and it always ends badly! How about we just don't talk about it?" concluded Marcello, before signalling to the barman to pour him another *limoncello.*

Marcello didn't have the heart of a patriot, and he'd always been too indulgent with his children, thought Valci, who didn't appreciate being cut off in this way. In the end he was right, though – there was no point in arguing when their opinions were fundamentally different, Valci told himself as he sipped his drink. But then there was his Giovanni – that boy would do well to stay loyal to his family and their traditions. Valci had raised his son according to the principles of the Christian Democratic Party: every man was a being in God's likeness and must serve his fellow. In Livorno, everyone was proud of the two sons of Marcello Creci, who had settled in New York's Little Italy, but Valci wasn't one of those simpletons whose eyes widened into saucers when people talked about America.

"The lira has no power anymore against the dollar," he grumbled.

"That's true! A hat costs a thousand lira, a coat fifteen thousand. A pair of shoes is five thousand lira. It's incredible."

"That's what you're worried about, Marcello? I barely have enough to buy peeled tomatoes for the *cacciucco*."

"What kind of peeled tomatoes?"

"San Marzano! They're expensive."

"How much does a can cost?"

"Ma daaaai! One can runs me two hundred lira."

"Don't worry, the lira will pick up again soon."

"Oh really? Well, I don't have the luxury of waiting. I'm angry. I can't afford to buy bread, and the politicians do nothing about it! Our mayor is more interested in looking after his wife than making decisions."

"Don't believe what you hear; I read in the *Tirreno* that the mayor has a new initiative to put five hundred empty olive oil barrels in the streets of Livorno as rubbish bins."

"Ma daaaai! Well, it's about time they did something...the streets are in worse shape now than they were during the war."

2.

Valci senior was staying at the Aragosta to talk politics, so Giovanni left the harbour. He headed up Via Grande, Livorno's main street that intersected the town from east to west in the Roman tradition. Shopkeepers were wrapping up their wares and bringing their shelves indoors; Giovanni revelled in the bright colours of the market as it wound to a close. He felt in himself the soul of an artist, like a child who finds inspiration in the slightest thing. His eye distilled the colours into nuances of light and shadow, shape and texture. He allowed his gaze to be drawn into the smallest details, losing himself in his lust for the new and unknown. Eventually, the young man awoke from his reverie: further up the road, a sign was swaying nonchalantly in the wind. It hung above the employment office, where Giovanni hoped to find his friend Luca. An air of dull idleness hung over the men gathered in the street; the unions mustn't have been able to place many of them today. The workers in their overalls looked bitterly at the ads posted on the wall of the rundown building. Their slogans spoke of courage and hope, but the waiting was like torture to the men. They rose in the morning with heavy hearts; with no work to go to, what was there to get up for? Then they came here to listen to the same old *merda* about how the crisis would soon be over. They're told that some get lucky and find work, but nobody knows who those men are. People said they must have been sent to jobs in the cities, but who knew what became of them? A man in a suit stood out from the rest of the herd, with the air of a bourgeois still hanging about him. He remained separate from the others, moping in silence. He did not dare to mix in their conversations. "I had a good job and workers who took orders from me..." he muttered to himself as he sat down on the pavement. Giovanni then spotted Luca, a strong, roguish lad with his cap perched casually sideways on his head, pulling a pack of cigarettes from his leather bomber jacket.

"Here, have a smoke!" he said to a sorry-looking man.

"No thanks, I don't smoke."

"Your loss; helps take the edge off."

Giovanni walked up to the familiar hustler, who turned to him with a smile:

"*Ciao Gio!* Did you catch something for your dear old mamma?"

"Sure did; enough for dinner with some left over to sell."

"You don't say! Good man. All this dead fish is making me hungry," teased Luca as he plunged his hand into the bucket.

"Come and eat with us if you like."

"I promised my 'ma that I'd keep her company. She drinks too much when she's alone, and I don't want to go home and find her dead drunk in god knows what kind of state. I need to sleep. All this doing nothing is exhausting!"

"Still no work?"

"Maybe something, in a garage on the north side of town."

"As a mechanic?"

"Yeah, who knows – maybe I'd be good at it! Speaking of cars, I saw the Palomis' big black sedan driving through town this afternoon."

"Stella must be back for the summer!" yelped Giovanni, unable to hide his excitement.

"Must be," answered Luca with a mocking grin. "But what's that little bourgeois got to do with us?"

"She's my friend."

"Your friend? Listen, I'm your friend. She's just a girl whose honour you want to corrupt," teased Luca as he tousled Giovanni's slick, unkempt hair.

"Quit that! You know I hate it when you do that. And don't talk about girls that way – especially not Stella," said the boy irritably as he pulled away.

"Alright, don't be so touchy!"

"She has class and character. She's educated. Give her a little respect."

"I'd rather find me a farm girl; a fresh young lass who smells like flowers and manure, a buxom dame with no airs or graces who kisses me like she's starved for it."

"Well, I'll leave those girls to you then. We're not hunting in the same deer park here."

"Now you're talking my language; we'll make a man out of you yet!" hooted Luca.

Giovanni felt a hearty slap on his shoulder. Sometimes this joking around got on his nerves. Luca definitely couldn't understand the sort of things that Giovanni felt. He played tough and liked to act like he was Don Juan or Casanova, living from one day to the next. He had feelings too, somewhere in there, but that air of detached bravado never let up long enough for them to show.

"I'm off, Gio. Got a few things to take care of before I head home to my old mama."

"What kind of things?"

"Just a couple of little rackets that could be big paydays. I'm not going to let all this get me down, hell!" exclaimed the young man, gesturing to the listless crowd of men seeking work.

Luca wasn't giving much away. What could he be plotting? He'd been accused of fencing, trafficking cigarettes and even pimping during the war. He had a bad reputation. Giovanni knew his friend would do anything to survive. He didn't judge Luca; his own family had taken refuge in the countryside when Livorno was being ripped apart by the air raids. He turned a deaf ear to rumours of what happened after the war. He trusted his instincts about Luca; his loyalty wasn't blind, but it was strong. Luca was a survivor, but he wasn't a coward or a cheat. Besides, he was Giovanni's only friend, and real friendship didn't exactly grow on the vines in this town. Having Luca was like having a wayward sibling – there was always room in your heart for them, even if it didn't swell with pride. Exhausted and sweating in the August heat, Giovanni finally arrived at the San Francesco cathedral. In front of the church, local kids were aiming at birds with their slingshots. He remembered how Luca had once broken one of the church's windows doing the same thing. The priest was furious and ran out to catch the little devil by the collar. Giovanni smiled. They'd have done anything to pass the time in those days. Today, children made their toys from debris left over from the war. It wasn't much further to the Valci house.

Nina was happy at her work, taking a package of marinated anchovies and a bunch of parsley from her basket. She opened up the little fish and spread them on a towel to soak up the liquid; the spiced oil formed a reddish halo around each one as she chopped the herbs into fine slivers using the edge of her knife. She liked to cook and knew she was good at it. In the kitchen she was an alchemist, patiently transforming and elevating the simple ingredients provided to her. Tonight she was preparing *cacciucco* for supper. It was peasant food, but poverty had honed this skill of hers: rich people didn't know how to be creative, because they didn't know the value of things. They had things handed to them. There was no joy in that; to truly savour something you had to make it yourself. Her two men would be home soon. They'd be tired and hungry, and the comforting aroma of the *cacciucco* would greet them like a warm embrace. To an outsider, her life might seem like mindless routine, but Nina did not share her son's dreams of adventure. Hers was a life woven from comforting habits that held her family together and kept their love intact. She never got bored. Nina always put her heart into her work, and it was a heart filled with both courage and tenderness. She heard a loud scuffling at the door; Giovanni had taken to kicking it open when his hands were full. She did not turn to greet him; she knew that her son would come and wrap his arms around her, and so he did. Nina stifled the joy she still felt as he pressed against her.

"Gio, you're not a boy anymore!"

"So?"

"And you smell like fish! Go and wash your hands!"

Nina took a quick look at the day's catch before rolling the fish in cloth and stashing them under the sink. She would sell them at tomorrow's market. She looked at her rough hands and their cracked skin; washing clothes every day had dried out the soft, pearly skin she had as a girl. "What a fine young man you are," she told her son. "Enjoy it while you can," she sighed as she caressed his neck.

Giovanni smiled at her but did not answer. He stirred the ladle around the pot while his mother poured in the canned San Marzano tomatoes. The smell of the anchovies made him hungry.

"Go and sit down son, let me finish. It's almost ready."

"I'm tired and I'm hungry," he told her as he sat down and buried his head in his arms.

Nina brought the pot to the table; they would eat without his father, as she would not make her son wait.

"Is your father at the Aragosta with Marcello?"

"Couldn't stop him."

"He only listens to himself. Doesn't know how to live at home," his mother sighed. "Let's start without him."

"When he's with Marcello he forgets he's sick; it's good for him to have a distraction."

"Marcello is his Luca. My oh my, you two...when you have a friend you swear by them."

"Oh yeah, I saw Luca at the employment office today."

"Slow down, you'll give yourself a stomach ache!" she nagged playfully as she watched him wolf down his meal.

"He's been looking for work for months."

"I know; I saw his mother at the market. She told me about it. The poor woman had already been drinking before the noon bells. Misery seems to follow misery around...ever since her husband died, things have been going wrong for them."

"Luca doesn't seem to mind that he's gone; he says all he did was gamble away their money."

"Your Luca's just acting tough! Do you really think a boy could forget his father just like that? You're lucky to still have yours!"

"Yeah, for now. Papa's really sick, you know...he can hardly pull the nets in anymore."

"Don't you invite the evil eye into this house! He's still alive from what I can see. And your father is stronger than you think. He's always been a fighter. He never gives up. He won't leave us behind."

Of course she was unwilling to face the truth. The Valcis had now been together for twenty-five years, facing poverty and hardship side by side. She couldn't be left alone; she wouldn't survive. She believed in her husband's invulnerability like she believed in God. Giovanni did not want to be the bearer of the news: Valci senior would be dead soon. For the young man, it was as if the death sentence was his. His life was slipping away from him at a terrifying pace. The noose felt tighter every day. Still a fisherman, and soon an orphan too. A sad, flat existence, like a cobblestone worn smooth by the waves. Politicians weren't doing anything for young Italians and even less for small villages. A lot of talk without saying much, taking big steps but getting nowhere. People here read the newspaper and listened to the radio because they wanted to hear where the world was going, but the truth was that it was leaving them behind. Who cared about the little people? Who would look after the fishermen? With the arrival of the big trawlers, their jobs would disappear. Most of the cod and sardine fishermen had already left Livorno; they, at least, were swimming away from the net.

Lying down on his bed, Giovanni blew into his harmonica. The blues rang out, and the young fisherman continued to dream of distant horizons. Maybe some heaven-sent stroke of luck would take him somewhere else. All of a sudden, a stone hit his window That must be Luca.

"What do you want?" he asked with a grin as he opened the window.

"Wow, you're quick. Any quicker and you'd have got a rock in the face."

"What about your 'ma?"

"She's out for the count. Come down, we're going out!"

Giovanni hesitated, but what else did he have to do but sit and be bored, staring at the same four walls that would still be there tomorrow? He slipped on his moccasins and faded old jacket, then stole out to join his cohort, who was amusing himself by spitting on the wall.

"What the hell are you doing?" cried Giovanni, repulsed.

"I'm watering the earth. I am the Lord, look ye upon the grape that shall groweth here!" Luca retorted, before aiming a huge ball of spit at the stunted vine growing along the stone.

"Have you been drinking?"

"Of course! Drinking steadies me and helps me win at dice. Let's go make some money!"

And so the two friends set off to find a café where they could gamble. They wandered deep into the labyrinth of little streets, dimly lit by the jaundiced halo of the streetlamps. Heat rose from the cobblestones and off the walls of houses. They passed a half-naked tramp sleeping on the pavement. Giovanni was filled with pity for the poor fellow, whose face was fixed in a dreamlike smile with a bottle of wine perched beside it. "That's how I want to leave this world," joked Luca. The few cafés in the centre of town were closed. The two lads frightened the rats that swarmed in front of the storefronts.

"You won't catch those little vermin dying of hunger. You and I could starve, but they'll always find enough to eat like kings," mused Luca with a grandiloquent air.

"You're talking like a poet tonight."

"And not just tonight — I've been drinking like a great Greek thinker!"

Giovanni laughed heartily and gave him a friendly slap on the shoulder; Luca was now busy counting stars on his fingers.

"So where to now?"

"Wherever life takes us! Or...we could ask those two old boys drinking coffee over there."

The two workers were finishing their meal at a table outside a cheap café and looked like they knew all there was to know about nocturnal activity in the town. If the boys wanted to play dice tonight, there was a joint on the north side they could go to. The two friends hurried off in that direction. The muggy night air excited their senses; Luca took off and Giovani bounded after him, whistling a carefree *tarentella*. The young fisherman felt suddenly free; he skipped through the deserted streets, unburdened by the heavy looks that were often cast his way in this small town. At this hour there was no-one to judge him, no-one to lecture him or tell him to shape up. "You're lagging behind, kid!" cried Luca, running like mad. Then he stopped abruptly, regathering his cool, playboy demeanour now that he could see the pink neon sign of the dice joint blinking in the dark. With a cigarette between his lips, he opened the door for his wingman and they stepped into the smoke. The air was heavy with the lingering, acrid odour of thick red wine, which in this joint was consumed with olives and by the litre. Giovanni stepped over a man who was scrambling about on the floor looking for his dice. Luca had already elbowed his way into the crowd that had formed around the players. Giovanni greeted a fisherman he knew who was a regular here, drinking brandy from a flask he'd brought in with him. Nobody seemed to mind. He showed off to the younger man by bragging and joking with the prostitutes. He held up his flask to the two girls leaning on the counter: "Bottoms up! Bottoms up!" he called to them hoarsely with a slow wink. They looked at him with suspicion, before turning away in silence. Not enjoying this awkwardness, Giovanni joined the crowd, where Luca was jostling for a place and asking:

"How much is a bet? How much to get in on this?"

"It's written on the board. Or don't you know how to read?" a man in the crowd answered.

Luca shot him a dark look. Who did that little runt think he was? A quick right hook would teach him some respect. But now wasn't the time for fighting; he wanted to play. The turn was over. An old man with a thick beard had won. He looked like he'd had plenty to drink already. "Next! Who's going to take me on?" he yelled. Luca crumpled up his ten-lira note and tossed it quickly onto the table. The crowd cheered this new challenger. Giovanni watched how the game progressed, wanting to ensure his friend didn't get taken for a ride. Luca had been drinking too, and being drunk gave him too much confidence. He'd lose the shirt off his back and wouldn't give a damn. What he was really playing for was the adrenaline; winning or losing barely seemed to matter.

"Well young fellow, are you ready to lose?"

"Don't get ahead of yourself, old-timer," replied Luca, sizing up his opponent.

"Play, then! Let's get on with it!"

"You'd be better off sitting this one out," suggested Giovanni as he took his friend by the shoulder.

"Who are you, my wife?" Luca replied angrily.

The other men guffawed; Giovanni fumed with humiliation. That would teach him to try and reason with Luca. Whether he won out or lost his money, it wasn't Giovanni's problem anymore. But he stayed to watch the end of the round with his arms crossed. The bearded man stared at Luca with a jeering expression. The dice rattled in the younger man's hand. Didn't look like the lad would last long. His face was already ashen. Luca held it together and threw the dice, paying no attention to his opponent's snickering laughter. He got two pair. Bad luck.

"You'd be better off giving up now, my lad," said the older man with feigned benevolence.

"The turn's not over."

Luca kept his cool. He wasn't going to give his opponent the satisfaction, even if the game seemed as good as lost.

"It's your turn, boy!"

"This is your last chance," Giovanni urged him worriedly.

Luca observed his adversary, slumped in the chair that might as well have been an extension of his body, fully at ease and wearing a hazy expression. This waste of space needed to lose. It was his destiny, as it was Luca's to win. He wouldn't cave; he'd rather lose everything than give up. He caught Giovanni's worried expression and gave him a reassuring grin. He tossed the dice in his hand, as was his habit. The ritual brought him luck. In his head he counted "one, two, three" and threw the dice. Five dice landed; the last one came to a stop a fraction of a second later. A 1-6 straight. The crowd roared, and Luca stayed calm. The older man was dumbstruck. He'd lost. Luca started howling with joy and disbelief. He swept up the money from the table, roaring: "Two hundred lira, all for me!" He gave his opponent a slap on the shoulder and left the game. Giovanni was delighted with Luca's victory but did not show it. Luca was ready to celebrate his luck, and made his way triumphantly over to the prostitutes.

"You with the leather jacket! What's your name? You're cute. Come over here," yelled the tall blonde as she applied a fresh coat of lipstick.

"I haven't enough to buy you a glass of wine," replied Luca coyly.

"You want to celebrate too, honey?" the second woman asked Giovanni, opening her coat.

"He's too young for that kind of thing," teased Luca.

"I'm not that young, I just don't like to waste my money," the young fisherman retorted with angry pride.

"I'm hurt! I really wanted you," she replied, blowing him a kiss.

The tall blonde took Luca's hand. Giovanni was about to turn and walk away when the woman in the coat held him back. "Don't you want to wait for your friend to finish, honey?" The young fisherman sat down at the bar and ordered a glass of *limoncello*. Luca and his lady of the night climbed the spiral staircase that led to a small bedroom, visits to which were carefully monitored by the owner as he washed the glasses. The door opened, and the prostitute showed Luca into a dirty little room crawling with mice and cockroaches. She lit the bedside lamp, startling the vermin and sending them scuttling under the iron bedframe.

"This place is disgusting."

"Don't worry, I'll take care of you."

She laid herself out seductively:

"Got something for me, honey?"

Luca took a hundred-lira note from his pocket, still sodden with sweat. The prostitute slid the money into her bra. The young man removed his leather jacket and threw it to the foot of the bed before sinking down onto his prize. He needed to forget, to lose himself. His orgasm would be the crowning glory of his victory at the table. Any doubts would evaporate in the intense concentration of his pleasure. Downstairs, the players listened with amusement to the creaking of the bed above them: "They're full of energy at that age!" At the bar, Giovanni remained pensive. He didn't really know why he was waiting. Out of loyalty? Or out of worry? It seemed to him that it was due to a dependence he only partially understood. Boredom meant that he needed the distraction; he was a moth to Luca's flame. Luca had a lust for life, and Giovanni needed that energy. But this friendship sometimes cost him, like when he found himself alone, and when the distance that separated the two became obvious. The prostitute was droning on about Livorno gossip. Giovanni wasn't listening; he didn't even know how long she'd been talking or how long he'd been waiting for Luca. He agreed with her out of politeness, and the hooker seemed satisfied with this response. She just needed to talk to someone; Giovanni's presence was her excuse. Why didn't he sleep with her? She was quite pretty, and there was something moving about her. But he was still beholden to his mother's sermonising. She'd see on his face that he'd sinned. "What's got you looking like that? What have you done?" she'd ask him with a suspicious eye. And he wouldn't have an answer. He was a useless liar, so he made sure he never had to do it. He feared his mother's judgement more than God's. He wasn't the most religious of sorts, but he feared the day of judgement the way some people feared disease. He looked at the hooker's bare legs as she crossed and uncrossed them under the bar. No, he would not be a sinner tonight. He lifted his eyes, and she met his gaze. She smiled at him. "Hard not to stare, isn't it kiddo? You can look, but you can touch as well..." He said nothing, but his eyes spoke for him. "Not in the mood, are you? You look so sad and thoughtful. That's OK, I'll just keep talking. I know you're not listening to me; I've been drinking, but I'm not drunk yet. But maybe you don't find my company too unbearable..." It was true – he was sad, or at least distracted. Stella was in Livorno, and he couldn't get her off his mind. He wanted to be rid of her, to clear his head and enjoy the warmth of the alcohol that was seeping through him. He ordered another *limoncello*. He looked at the barman as he opened the bottle and poured the hazy yellow liquid slowly into the glass. Even in his drink, he saw Stella. He knew that she was no angel, and sometimes he caught himself thinking of her in another man's arms. But tonight he could not; to do so would betray his feelings. Luca was keeping him waiting. Giovanni had lost his patience for sticking around. "Good-night, miss," he said to the pretty girl, who smiled warmly at him. Moments later he was back in the street, his evening having capsized under a stormy sky.

3.

As a young girl, Nina had received her schooling from the nuns of the Holy Order of the Visitation of Mary. Having retained a particular devotion to the Mother of God, to whom she prayed to watch over her household, Nina now lit a candle beside the icon of the Madonna as she cast a glance out the window. The silent flight of the gulls was a good omen for a day of particularly solemn worship: today was the fifteenth of August, the feast of the Assumption of the Blessed Virgin. Nina was preparing for the procession as Giovanni watched her fondly. His mother was steadfast, and unchanging. Her every habit was reassuring to him. She was predictable which was comforting. Valci senior read the headline from the *Tirreno* aloud: "The Prime Minister will address the nation with a speech!" Nobody was listening to him. Nina paid little heed to what happened beyond the physical and spiritual borders of her beloved little town. Giovanni seemed lost in a daydream. Valci looked up at his wife and son, who had not answered him. He observed Giovanni from the corner of his eye. The boy looked like him but had his mother's soft heart. Innocent souls sprouted up in the villages around this region. The young man knew nothing about the wickedness of the world; he didn't even know it existed. The boy buttoned his shirt as his father continued to observe him, unnoticed. Giovanni reminded him of his own youth before there was worry or anguish or politics. Back then, his only concerns were having fun and having big ideas. Giovanni dreamed about getting out of here, but where could he go? He was too naive. He mightn't be satisfied with the life of a fisherman, but he knew nothing about the brutality of life in a city.

"There he goes, daydreaming again! Always daydreaming! That boy's never even in the room half the time," he grumbled.

"Hush, leave him be," replied Nina.

"He can't even be bothered to read the paper."

"Ouffa! He's not interested in that. You and your politics!"

"That paper—," interjected Giovanni.

"Wait, Nina, the boy wants to speak!"

"Stop sniping. Leave him be."

"...that paper only gets read at the Aragosta. It's for old people."

"Ah! Nina, your boy reacts. He thinks. Perhaps he's a bit savvier than he lets on."

To amuse her son, Nina threw a flower at her husband's face and said with mock outrage:

"My son's a very smart boy. He just has better things to do on a holy day than to read the *Tirreno*!"

"You two are always ganging up on me, but I have nothing to fear: I'm still the most handsome man in Livorno," he added with a grin.

Giovanni caught his mother's eye, and their collusion gave way to a burst of laughter.

"Enough fooling around; we should be getting to the procession," said Nina, with one eye on the clock.

She didn't want to be late to meet Valentina and Marcello. And what would the priest think if they were late? Valci senior dove back into his paper. People here thought only of their piousness and their priest. This whole religious pantomime irked him, and being forced to take a day off from fishing was further insult. Looking enviously at his son, who was carefully combing his thick brown hair, he rose grumpily from his armchair to apply a dash of aftershave. All this sentiment wouldn't put fish on the table! Nina looked on with amusement at this man who was not used to getting ready for anything, and took the aftershave for her son. How handsome Giovanni looked today! Dabbing ambergris and lavender around his neck, the boy quickly forgot his lot as a fisherman and the fetid odour of fish that came with it. Everything seemed to delight him today, especially the fact that Stella was coming to the procession.

At the same time, in the hills above Livorno, Stella's brothers were waiting impatiently for her in the lounge. The two rich heirs had each taken a cigar from their father's smoke box and were sipping a cool brandy 'on the rocks', as they said in New York. Stella was almost finished getting ready in her room. Sitting at her dressing table, she dabbed a few drops of perfume behind her ear and adjusted her mantilla. She was perfectly elegant, perfectly bourgeois, and perfectly ready to be married. Her father spent all his time obsessing about finding the right match for her; after all, he had to think about expanding his business. Girls were to be married off;

they were not for the workforce. That's how these rich hypocrites did things, even though they made out like they worshipped hard work. She'd end up married to the Montinis' son, that pretentious little twerp. She was sure of it. The boys around here were different; they didn't have money to throw around, which meant they could understand what real love was. She liked Luca; he was brash and funny. She could love him. She could be one of those girls who fell head over heels in love, like the tragic heroine from some great folk tale. She could free herself from needing to be so respectable. No more obedience. No more submission. With Luca, she thought, or maybe someone else. Whatever his name was, for now he was a stranger. This summer would be decisive: it was to be her last before she was sentenced to death by boredom. She thought of all those women who'd been hanged for treason during the war as she caressed her beautiful head of silken, jet-black hair. How she would have loved to have been paraded like that in front of her persecutors. She'd have looked at them dead in the eye, offering only provocation instead of contrition: "And so what? I needed to do some living before I died!" Her dark eyes filled with tears. She'd never dare. Her sentence had already been handed down.

The Valcis arrived at the San Francesco cathedral and joined the crowd. Giovanni followed his father as he shuffled forward, muttering to himself, his cap fixed tightly on his head. He was eager for this to be over, and where was Marcello? Giovanni watched him getting jostled by the crowd but somehow managing to cut his way through, holding his handkerchief over his mouth as a precaution. The TB had robbed him of his haughtiness. Nina, meanwhile, walked in blissful calm, absorbed in the ambient piety of the occasion. Her quick, eager steps swung her from side to side like a gay little church bell. Her friend Valentina called to her. The two women greeted each other excitedly. Giovanni listened to them absent-mindedly, eager to show his disinterest. His mother shot him a disapproving look; Giovanni shrugged his shoulders and exhaled. He wasn't a child anymore; he could do what he liked, and he wasn't in the mood to make small talk. He still hadn't found Stella. Had he come here for nothing? He was bored without Luca around. His friend was probably still sleeping at this time of the day, the lucky sod. "Stop sulking, you look like your father!" Nina scolded him with a dig of her elbow. In truth, he had other things on his mind. Stella being in Livorno was an event of its own. He had been waiting to see her for so long, and she still wasn't here. Stella was like a foreign country waiting to be explored, full of mystery and so different from everything he knew. He needed to dream again; his memories of her as a girl were fading. He watched the priest leading the procession towards the Fortezza Vecchia. His solemn expression amused Giovanni, and made him curious. How could a man live solely for God? How could he be so convinced of his faith; so free from doubt? Beside him, Valentina was singing the praises of her two sons in New York as his mother threw a bunch of wolfsbane on the statue. Suddenly, a figure full of grace stood out among the simmering mass of people. Wearing a long black dress that flowed around her youthful body, the beautiful young woman gently lifted her veil to reveal her eyes. Walking behind, Giovanni hung upon the girl's every movement. It was her. His true icon, his goddess. He moved closer, desperately wanting to breathe in her sweet, delicate smell. She seemed to him like a flower that could never be picked; inaccessible, immaculate and sublime. He hoped to steal a glance from her. If only she would make it real, here and now. If only she would set his body and soul alight, plucking him out of this world and its banality. If only she would raise him up and be his inspiration. "Turn around," he urged her. He wanted to disappear into her light and her beauty. Stella joined her lace-gloved hands in prayer. Around her, the villagers turned their heads and glanced enviously at the two handsome gentlemen walking alongside her in their Florentine suits. How refined these city folk were, with their graceful airs. Do you see how fine the cloth of their suits is? Nina rested a hand on her son's shoulder. He jumped, woken from a dream he was not yet ready to depart from and made suddenly aware of the distance that separated him from the splendour of those Florentines. His aftershave now smelled sickly to him; his moccasins were outdated and his suit badly fitted. What an idiot he was! Why did he hope she would look at him? He was ugly with poverty. But, although he was no longer expecting it, she turned and flashed her blue eyes at him. To Giovanni, this was worth more than any divine visitation. He eked out a clumsy smile in response and frantically squeezed the harmonica in his pocket. He wished he could play entire symphonies and sing like a wild bird. Behind him, Valentina had noticed what was on the young fisherman's mind:

"Nina! Do you see that girl dressed in black?"

"No! Which girl? I don't see her. Who are you talking about?"

"The one holding a bouquet of roses."

"Oh yes, I see her."

"She's the Palomis' daughter, those rich folks from Florence."

"*Ouffa*! I don't think my son would get far with her. She looks so...distinguished."

"She's no prettier than my son's fiancée."

"But she's richer," Nina added wryly.

"For now, anyway," muttered Valentina.

The crowd crossed over the portico to gather around the pyre. Giovanni went in too, hoping he could still observe Stella unnoticed during the homily. The priest stood proudly in front of the crowd, his prayer book in hand as an altar boy draped the stole reverently over his shoulders. The man of God commanded silence. In the suffocating heat, the men loosened their ties, and the women fanned themselves. The bambinos scuttled between their legs to get a spot near the pyre, under the priest's watchful eye. In the middle of the pile of flowers brought by the villagers, the Palomi family laid their imposing bouquet of red roses. The altar boys lit the flames, and the priest began his homily: *"Brothers and sisters in Christ, the Assumption is, of course, one of the most celebrated feasts of the Virgin Mary, as we and so many others gather in her sanctuaries to pray. In Italy, our pilgrimages remind us of how much our ancestors trusted Mary to watch over the destiny of our country, praying for her protection during times of war and asking her to wash away their uncertainties about their future..."* The widows from the last war cried for their dead husbands. Through the black veils that covered their faces and ran down to their feet, they watched the divine flames flicker up towards heaven. They were shadows of people, lost souls waiting patiently for death to take them. They left their homes only to visit the cemetery or attend mass and spoke only when they had to, spending the rest of their time shrouded in the silence of their pity and grief. The two old philosophers from the Aragosta couldn't help but comment on the sight of them:

"Women always seem to find a reason to cry!"

"Are you telling me that men make women cry?"

"I never said that! I'm saying that women always find a reason to cry about men."

"So you didn't cry when you lost your wife?"

"Not that I remember. Anyway, I'll be joining her in heaven soon."

The firewood blazed, its twigs crackling and throwing out tiny sparks. Parents hurried to pull their children away as the flames grew hotter. The crowd drew back in wonder. The priest finished his homily: *"...grace and forgiveness. It is the most extreme faith that God requires; may he bless this feast as we give unto Mary the glory and fullness of hope she is due.*

Amen." The people of Livorno were united in their faith, repeating "Amen" in a solemn echo. The resistance fighters thanked their divine protector for keeping them alive, though they no longer understood the reason for their existence. The crowd prayed for an end to their poverty, and for the protection of the Almighty in the years to come. Tired of staying still, the children began to wriggle and wail. The villagers' vivid emotion worried them. Giovanni, ever the dreamer, was admiring the facades of this imposing fortress, whose arrowslits were illuminated by the blazing sun behind them. He'd glimpsed hope; perhaps even a sign or an oracle. One day, he mused, they'd say that he'd succeeded. People would speak in admiration of that fisherboy. He'd play the blues, and crowds would applaud. Standing alone, on the small stage of a speakeasy in a rough neighbourhood of New York, he'd feel the wooden boards creak under his feet, with a blinding stage light illuminating his face, and the acrid odour of cigarettes mingling with the scent of hard liquor. There was more honour in being praised by men than in praising God. It was getting late, and the crowd dispersed. The Florentines shook the priest's hand before returning to their cars. The *vecchio* headed for the Aragosta in high spirits. The children chased each other around the port. A handful of pious folk remained around the pyre. The fire had grown huge; by morning only ashes would remain. Giovanni climbed into his *gozzo* to dream about Stella. He remembered the day when he'd introduced himself at the Palomi villa and waited timidly in the garden while Stella finished her piano lesson. Delighted to have been invited, Giovanni walked along the rows of bushes and flowerbeds with their dazzling colours. Then, sitting on the ledge of the fountain, he was entranced by a melody — one of Chopin's, he later found out — that caused his fisherboy's soul to tremble. The symphony would awaken his imagination. The flowers seemed to dance and bloom before his very eyes. The shimmering of the trees and the crystal droplets of the fountain seemed to enhance the harmony of the music. He would have loved to be able to bring forth enchanting melodies from that grand piano, like Stella did. She spied him through the bay window, and her little fingers moved more and more rapidly, as she was eager to go out and see him. She finally came out and gave him a mischievous grin that clashed with her child-like manners and flowery dress. She skipped over to him giddily. She leaned her face towards his, and Giovanni, enraptured, hoped she would kiss him. She pushed him into the fountain instead. Seeing the Florentine from afar as she walked along the harbour, he played that same Chopin tune on his harmonica, with the flapping of sails as his orchestra. Stella waved to him, no doubt recognising the music of her childhood.

4.

Luca arrived outside the big auto garage on the north side of town, its back wall covered with sets of pincers, screwdrivers, socket wrenches, drill bits and flat-head hammers. Three mechanics were working on two Fiats, one positioned behind the other. The first man removed a tyre and rolled it away with practised ease. Another loudly wrestled an oil-stained engine onto a broad iron-top table serving as a workbench, next to a toolbox and a set of feeler gauges splayed open like a rich lady's fan. The third was welding a metal pipe, sending sparks flying amidst plumes of blackish smoke. Nobody paid any notice to the young man observing their work, waiting to be called upon. It would be some job, trying to stay on top of all this. "I need the big pincers," called one of them as he pulled a canister of oil off the shelf. Luca was getting impatient; he did have an appointment, after all. Beside him, a customer was waiting to get his car back. Finally, a mechanic spoke to the man: "Can you come back tomorrow? We still need to change the oil and de-grease the engine." The customer acquiesced and left. Luca took the opportunity to buttonhole the mechanic:

"Hello there! I have a meeting with the boss."

"Are you Luca?"

"That's me," he answered confidently.

"You won't get far around here with your leather jacket and all that hair oil," observed the mechanic as he slid his hands into his pockets.

"Give me a chance, I'm strong and I learn quick!"

"You know anything about cars?"

"I drove a Jeep once."

"I'm not asking if you can drive. Spark plugs, alternator, water pump, tailpipe...any of that mean anything to you?"

"No sir, not a thing. But I'm good with my hands."

The boss eyed Luca suspiciously. He wasn't worth the trouble. He wasn't getting the job. Disappointed, Luca left the garage and strolled through the streets of Livorno. The aroma of melting mozzarella wafting from a pizza oven made him hungry, but he hadn't a penny on him. Damnit! If there'd been a rally in Livorno today at least he could have lifted a few wallets. Those were the kind of trades he was trained for; an accidental bump, a hand slipped into the lapel of a jacket, and the job was done. He had no qualms about stealing. Would the man he stole from ever have given him a chance? Besides, money was made to change hands. Everyone had to eat. That should be a universal rule. Irritated at not being able to feed his groaning stomach, he headed for the market. Maybe the cheesemonger would have some work for him. He couldn't go on hanging around outside the employment office forever. But with this damned reputation that followed him everywhere...still, there was nothing stopping him from enjoying himself for the next little while. He'd seen the Palomis' black sedan rolling through town, which meant Stella must have come back for the Assumption. He had to see her again. He'd take Giovanni as his wingman; not much of a rival, and a loyal companion. And Stella wasn't suspicious of Giovanni; he'd even gone to her house to play the piano, and nobody even kept an eye on them. That meant he was harmless. How could Gio ever hope to get his lips on Stella? He'd have to go on waiting. Luca was manlier and more self-assured. Stella would never go for Giovanni. He was too attached to his dear old mama. When he looked at Stella he was saucer-eyed; you got the feeling he might start drooling at any moment. Best he stay close to his mother's bosom and leave this sort of thing to the men. Luca knew how to get what he wanted. Even if he didn't know Latin or good manners, he had a charm that couldn't be taught. So why not use it to seduce her? He'd arrived at the market. With a cigarette between his lips, he cast flirtatious looks at all the young girls he passed. He paid no attention to the movements of the crowd. He entered the cheese shop, shoving past the *mammas* who were queueing along the counter.

"Ciao Luca! Haven't seen you in a while," said the cheesemonger as he sliced up a wedge of parmesan.

"I'm still getting into trouble!"

"I have nothing for you. No work, anyway, but I can give you a piece of parmesan."

"Thanks. I'll pay you back someday."

The *mammas* were getting impatient and irritated. What a rude man! They'd been waiting their turn for ages. They fixed him with disapproving looks, and Luca insulted them merrily as he left. The market was at its busiest, and he didn't know where to look. On one side, the baker was tirelessly kneading a ball of soft white dough, sending puffs of flour flying in all directions. The smell of his sourdough was biting and acidic. The *mammas* were waiting, baskets in hand, for the latest batch of loaves browning in the wood oven. Next to him, the butcher was chopping up the bloody carcass of a gutted pig, its big round eyes fixed wide open. His apprentice sharpened knives on the mill, sending out sparks and causing the blades to hiss. On the other side of the street, cloth sacks overflowed with polenta, lentils and beans, like bottomless cornucopias. A little farther on, the fishmonger poured a bucket of ice over trays laid out with silvery-blue cod, shimmering mullets, slimy carp and ghoulish-looking seabass, whose gaping mouths unveiled rows of jagged teeth. "Two mullets, four hundred lira; two mullets, four hundred lira!" he called to the passers-by. On his right, the greengrocer was adjusting his bunches of herbs, arranging sprigs of dried thyme that crumbled in his hands; near the front of his table, he placed bunches of fragrant mint and parsley to attract the keenest noses. "Bunches of mint, fifty lira!" Prices had gone up since the war. The marketwomen were disgorging broad slices of oil-fried aubergine and courgette on white dishtowels, allowing the hot sun to tenderise their browned flesh. A horse-drawn cart loaded with barrels of Chianti pressed through the crowd. "Out of the way, move it!" the driver yelled at the pedestrians. The fruit seller was cutting apples in two; they were sold by the half to those who wanted some variety in their meals but hadn't much to pay for it. A young man in overalls was sweeping the street, throwing peelings and fish heads into the gutter. Enterprising young boys were helping marketgoers with their bags in exchange for a few dozen lira. Lower down the street, the *mammas* were serving Tuscan dishes like hare pasta and *ribolitta*, the traditional soup made with cabbage, beans and bread. "Fifty lira for a scoop! Why cook at home when you can buy it ready-made?" An old lady with ruined eyesight was asking: "What vegetables did you use to make the *pinzimonio*?" - "Red pepper, yellow pepper, cauliflower, cucumber and celery," the market women told her. "And olive oil from Florence, of course," she added with pride. The old woman was satisfied: "I'll take a portion." Further on, a small dog sat in front of the rotisserie, fascinated by the hypnotic movement of the chickens rotating on their spits. The roaster threw out a potato soaked in chicken fat to get rid of him.

Amidst the market's incessant hum, Nina and Valentina chatted as they worked, eager to cover all the latest news and gossip. Nina had tied a scarf around her head, but the sweat from her forehead still ran into her eyes. She splashed some water on her face and sprinkled some on the fish she had laid out on a white cloth. She sometimes lamented not having a moment to look at herself in the mirror in the morning, and having to don the garb of a fishmonger without a thought for the voluptuous beauty that had once served her so well. An old man came to drop his clothes in her laundry basket. In these difficult times, she did a couple of hours' ironing every day for those who needed it. A customer stopped in front of her stand: "How much for a can of San Marzano?" She collected a two-hundred lira note, which she would give to her husband at the end of the day. Wearing trousers and a white shirt, as she had when she worked in the factory, Valentina served out portions of *cacciucco* to her loyal customers. After serving one, she turned to Nina with a broad smile:

"We saw the mayor's wife walking along the harbour with a stranger!"

"That can't be true!" exclaimed Nina.

"Come on, marriage couldn't keep that girl down. She was always making eyes at other people's husbands."

"You know what, the mayor hasn't organised a summer ball since the end of the war."

"I think he's scared that his wife won't dance with him," said Valentina with a smirk.

"You may be right!"

"I saw some preparations going on at the main square. Surely we can have a ball this year. It would be a chance for Giovanni to dance with some girls."

"*Ouffa*! In our day, he'd already have been married a while ago."

"That's true, marriage was easier when we were young. The ball was the best place to meet someone."

Nina remembered herself as a young woman wearing her best dress, with piercing eyes, her hair done up in a bun, and thick dark curls tumbling over her forehead. Sitting timidly on the side of the dancefloor, a wooden structure built the night before by the men from the village. She liked music and swayed to the rhythm of the pitiful little orchestra made up of the few fishermen who'd volunteered. A Neapolitan *tarentella* began, and a young man came and took her by the hand, inviting her to dance for the first time. No matter how much he tried to focus, he was a clumsy dancer and almost crushed her feet on several occasions. Still, Nina was charmed by the awkward fisherman, whose expression had a certain poetry to it. Nina smiled; the memories of her youth were unchanging. She jumped suddenly when a man placed two hands on her shoulders. She turned around to see that it was Luca.

"What are you doing here at this time of day? Don't you have anything better to do than hit on market girls?" Valentina asked him with a grin.

"Well, I don't know about girls...but what about two market women who know me too well? I like them fine and slender like you, Valentina!"

"Quit joking around!" Nina cut him off. "Be serious for once. Aren't you hungry?"

"I have San Marzano tomatoes coming out of my ears," complained Luca as he cast a furtive look at Nina's stand." I'd love some seafood pasta."

"Come here and I'll give you a portion of *cacciucco*. At least then you can go home to your mother on a full stomach," suggested Valentina.

"How's your mother doing?" asked Nina.

"Since my father died, she's been getting worse and worse."

"Tell her to come and have some *cacciucco*. We'll always have something to offer her here."

"Nina, you're an angel sent from heaven! Do you know that, gorgeous?"

"Enough of your smooth talking! That might work with these young girls, but I've been around too long. You won't catch me falling for that nonsense."

"What nonsense? Nina, you know you're the light of my life."

"You're a little rascal, you know that! Go and find your Giogio and let me work. Tell him I'll be back late, I'm doing laundry tonight."

Nina watched her two men eating their *cacciucco*. Her son was hungry, but her husband looked at his plate sadly. There was nothing he wanted. His days of fishing exhausted him, and afterwards he couldn't recover his strength. He turned his spoon in the soup. The metallic scraping echoed in Nina's temples, its repetitions sounding to her like an ominous overture. Giovanni gave her a surprised look and smiled at her. Giovanni was her comfort. He looked like his father. He had the wide forehead of a dreamer, a daring jaw, and that slightly boorish and clumsy way about him. They were both as stubborn as could be, in their own way. They never listened, both sure they were right, always wanting to have the last word.

"You look like you're miles away. That procession the other day was just wonderful; very moving," said Nina to her husband to break the silence at the table.

"Yes, there are wonderful things that come out of the ordinary. Not divine things, just what's real. I pity those men who've never tried to tame the sea. They don't know what it is to pit their patience against death. They've never learnt humility. So yes, perhaps I haven't achieved much here during my time on earth, but what is it they say? 'It's harder for a rich man to enter the kingdom of heaven than for a camel to pass through the eye of a needle?' Well, I've always been poor and I've never complained. I dug my grave in the sea and didn't hesitate. So I'm sure I deserve a place in heaven. I'm a simple man. Do you understand that, Giovanni? That there's pride in dying a simple man?"

Giovanni looked at him, speechless. What could he say to that? He understood his father's sense of honour, of course, but just because he understood it didn't mean he wanted it for himself.

"Well yeah, I never said that you haven't lived with dignity."

"What are you saying? You're talking as if—" Nina stopped herself, overcome with emotion.

"Nina, there's no reason to cry," her husband reassured her.

"That's right, there isn't, because you're still here!" she snapped.

Valci senior placed his hand on her back. This tenderness seemed to calm Nina. Silence descended around the table once again. Valci ate his soup to appease his wife rather than his appetite. Giovanni retreated into his thoughts. He'd give everything he had to be anywhere else. His father's ramblings and his mother's tears affected him more than he would ever admit. He thought of Stella and her appearance during the procession. Once the meal was over, Valci senior started coughing again. Giovanni patted him on the back and led him to his bed. Nina mimed at her son that he should play a tune. The young fisherman took out his harmonica and brought it to his lips. The blues reverberated around their little house as Nina put her husband to bed. She carefully drew back the covers for him, knowing that this kindness would hurt his pride. She knew he could not bear to be vulnerable with her; to need her. She moved in silence, without looking at her husband. She was afraid to meet the sadness in his eyes. "Good-night," she whispered as she pressed herself against him. He felt a tear trickle onto his shoulder. He tightened his arms around her. Her scent would stay with him, he knew, even when he was far below. "Goodnight, my darling wife."

5.

In the gardens of the Palomi villa, Stella and her two brothers were sipping lemonade in the shade of a linden tree. Stella watched the white butterflies fluttering like a flight of angels among the lavender bushes, her bare feet savouring the feel of the fresh grass. She wafted the air with a fan made from Burano lace. She wished this summer would never end; she was enjoying life in the sunshine and the carefree serenity of the countryside. Florence and the constant hum of city life now felt far away, and vaguely ridiculous. In Livorno, she could relax and be idle without remorse. In Florence, there was always something to see, someone to meet, some fleeting emergency to fill her days. In a city, doing nothing was against the rules; to be idle was sacrilege. But Stella liked being bored sometimes. She observed her two brothers playing cards. Unlike her, they were unable to appreciate their surroundings. They missed the city; it was part of them now, and for these city folk their villa in Livorno was just another high-society luxury. She'd have liked to be in better company, with people who enjoyed the simple things. Her brothers stuck to their Florentine styles even when they were on holiday: they picked out their hats, their gloves and their jackets with the same care. They needed to maintain the air of superiority that separated them from these simple country folk. Appearances were everything to them, even here in the intimate solitude of their own garden. Stella was jolted from her reverie by her youngest brother, who spouted one of his trademark witticisms:

"Mrs Montini, perhaps some more lemonade to loosen your tongue? Oh that's right, I forgot that once you're married you won't be allowed to talk anyway."

"Idiot. If I'm unlucky enough to be married to that Montini boy, do you think I'm just going to be a silent wife? Besides, with that stutter of his there'll be plenty of time for me to speak."

"Hardly matters...what would you have to say anyway to all those businessmen who'll be calling round? They might have nice manners, but all they think about is money, which makes them profoundly uncouth and uninteresting."

"Well, why don't you invite me into one of your little private circles then? They like to make out like they're artsy and intellectual, but I'd be curious to know what any of that bunch of moustachioed fops really have to say for themselves."

"Enough, both of you. What if father heard you talking like that?" snapped the eldest brother, who'd been following their conversation with a disapproving expression. "Shame on you both. Business is bad right now, and we don't need discord within the family. You're a woman now, Stella. You should have learned to hold your tongue by now."

Stella got out of her chair, a thin smile on her face. Her younger brother held her back. "Don't leave me alone with him," he pleaded mockingly, but the young lady had had enough and wished to be free of their oppressive company. She went inside and sat down at the piano. She raised the keylid and ran her fingers over the keys. The velvety feel of the ivory sent shivers through her fingers, and she began playing a sonata that had stayed with her since childhood. Her holiday piano lessons felt very different to the ones she had in Florence. She thought of Giovanni, who would come to join her in the afternoons. There was a tenderness in his eyes she found comforting; she wished she could feel that comfort now. She didn't know anyone in Florence who could have looked at her that way. Was it the effect of the music? Was it love?

Giovanni and Luca climbed the stairs of the Livorno lighthouse, which had battled against the elements for over half a millennium. Its powerful beam had been shut off during the air raids; it no longer turned, and was now just a run-down tower. At dawn, when the *gozzo Nina* sailed away from the jetty, Giovanni watched it get further and further away until its yellow pinprick disappeared over the horizon. The two boys stepped over stones, beams and metal bars before climbing up the rickety scaffolding around the tower. The steps were cluttered, and the two friends struggled to get to the top. Luca was out of breath and tried to hide it by whistling bawdy songs. Giovanni laughed merrily. When they finally reached the top floor, Luca sat down against the stone wall, and Giovanni looked out over the vast horizon, where the cargo ships were disappearing towards their unknown destinations. The briny wind whipped against his face. He saw the flocks of seabirds billowing between sea and sky. He spread his arms out wide and took a deep breath of sea air, far above the waves that crashed over the rocks around the base of the lighthouse. Luca took out his wallet and lamented:

"I haven't a note to my name! Just these damn coins that wouldn't even buy me a ciabatta!"

"Well, if you throw all your money after women that's what happens. What would you do if you had a two-hundred lira note on you right now? Probably gamble it away."

"Calm down, pal! If I had that much on me, I'd be a rich man," said Luca sarcastically." I'd smoke a cigar instead of buying cigarettes."

"You think all you need is a cigar to pass as a bourgeois?"

"Doesn't hurt! I know those bourgeois better than you think."

"Go on then, show me your best bourgeois!"

Luca stood up and stuffed his shirt into his trousers, buttoned it up to his neck and unrolled the sleeves. He raised his knee and pretended to polish his shoes. Giovanni watched him. Luca was a dreamer, just like him. It wasn't just a game; he was in character. He turned his cap round the right way. His face changed. He affected a foppish air and turned towards the horizon:

"Mr Di Valci, don't you find this panorama simply exhilarating? However, it must be said that this view of my lands would be even better from my hot air balloon. I'll take you on a ride someday soon, dear friend, so you can see what I mean."

He appeared pensive, then turned as if he'd been called upon. He removed his cap like a top hat and flung it away. Giovanni caught it and placed it on his head:

"I would be simply delighted, Signore Di Luca, to accept your invitation. Shall we organise a banquet with some pretty ladies?"

"It will be raining dames, my man! There'll be ladies to satisfy every taste, especially mine."

"Will you invite Stella?"

"Gah, will you stop harping on about Stella!" Luca said irritably, suddenly serious again. "You've no chance with her. She's not the girl for you."

"How would you know?"

"How would I know? It's bloody obvious! Look at you in that cap, you look like a little boy trying on his dad's clothes."

"Take your gangster hat back then! So what if she's richer than me; I'm not just some deadbeat."

"No, but you're a kid who's under the spell of some rich girl. You think you love her, but it's really just that you can't accept your lot in life," said Luca, in a gentler tone.

"I know her better than you think."

"I'm telling you this for your own good, pal. Do you really know her? A couple of hours playing the piano in her mansion isn't enough to get to know a girl."

"You don't know anything about music. You don't know what it can do!"

"Gio, of course I understand. You were sitting there in a fine house with a pretty girl, all fine lace and fancy manners. You were a fish out of water."

They'd never agree on the topic of Stella. What was the use in talking about it? Luca lit up a cigarette and gave Giovanni a friendly smile. Giovanni took out his harmonica and played some blues into the rising wind. It was starting to get cold. Luca closed his eyes and began to doze off. Giovanni watched him and noted how his face softened when he slept, drained of its anger and defiance. When had Luca changed? Giovanni struggled to remember. Perhaps it had happened gradually. Life hadn't been kind to his friend. He'd been slowly consumed by bitterness and hatred, and built walls all around himself. Still, he'd kept a clever and playful side about him. He liked to live on the wild side. He'd developed a silver tongue and a gift for verbal sparring even before he could grow a moustache. Giovanni was barely off his mother's teat back then and was full of boundless admiration for him. He'd been proud to be a part of his friend's misadventures. He remembered the time Luca had asked him to keep a lookout while he was fooling around with the butcher's daughter in the *gozzo*. Giovanni took the job seriously. He patrolled like a sentinel, pacing up and down the quays with a watchful eye. He heard the groans and whispers from beneath the tarpaulin without fully understanding what was going on. He still had his innocence; he was barely ten years old. And yet, those noises were enough to give him his first tremors of arousal. His body was still a mystery and he didn't understand what was happening to him. Suddenly, he spied the girl's father making his way towards the *gozzo.* "Luca! Luca! Watch out!" cried Giovanni, who had strayed too far from the boat. Luca didn't hear him and was caught in the act. He ran for his life, with his trousers around his ankles. Despite this handicap, he still outran the butcher, the fear of a beating spurring his pace. The kids who were hanging around the jetty found the whole thing hilarious. "*Culo nudo, culo nudo!"* they cried. Giovanni smiled at Luca, who opened his eyes: "Remember the butcher's daughter?" Luca replied with a wink, and Giovanni began playing another blues tune. The two friends waited patiently for the sun to go down. On the horizon, the island of Gorgona fell into darkness. Sometimes it didn't take much to pass the time.

Night had fallen, and the two friends had left the lighthouse. Wandering aimlessly, they found themselves approaching the port, and Luca watched the navy officers guarding the entrance gate to the docks. With rifles on their shoulders, the watchmen inspected each vehicle that entered and exited the zone reserved for loading and unloading the cargo ships. Luca signalled Giovanni to stop before they were seen. Giovanni gave his friend a boost so he could see what was over the wall.

"There's a cargo ship in the dock," he said with his eyes alight.

"A cargo ship? So what? What are you up to?" hissed Giovanni, smelling trouble.

"Where there's a cargo ship, there's cargo! We'll have to climb this wall. Give me a boost again, and when I'm up I'll pull you up. Ready?"

"OK!"

The two friends kept their eyes peeled on the gate. A vehicle rolled up with its headlights on, honking to be let in. It was a Jeep. "Wait for the Jeep to go in, then we go over the wall," said Luca as if they were planning a walk in the park. They clambered over the wall and fell to their stomachs on the other side. A pair of German Shepherds started barking. The guards turned their heads but didn't seem to notice the two youngsters.

"Take off your shoes! We'll have to run to the containers," whispered Luca as he slipped off his moccasins.

"We're going to get caught," worried Giovanni.

Luca counted to three with his fingers, then took off like a greyhound. Giovanni did his best to keep up. The two hid between two containers as they got their breath back. "What do we do now?" demanded Giovanni, rubbing a stitch. Luca took out his pocket knife to pick the lock of the container. He almost broke his blade in the huge padlock, but finally it came loose. "After you, good sir," smiled Luca as he proudly opened the door for his friend. They were now safely hidden, and their eyes adjusted slowly to the darkness. They began to make out piles of canvas sacks and crates.

"Let's open this crate," whispered Luca, impatient for loot.

"It's wine! whispered the young fisherman as he took off the lid. Do you think it's red or white?"

"Who cares? Let's grab a bottle and share it between us."

"Luca, you're a genius!"

"It's Tuscan Chianti being shipped from Livorno. The Americans go mad for this stuff! We can get drunk in style."

The two friends prepared to leave; there was no time to hang around. Suddenly, Giovanni heard barking. Luca hurriedly stashed the bottle down his shirt. He heard boot steps coming towards them. "Quick, let's get out of here!" urged Luca. The young fisherman was gripped by fear as he slipped on his moccasins. The officers were still a ways off. The two friends made a dash for the other side of the docks and scaled the wall again undetected as if they were never there.

Giovanni and Luca sat with their backs to the harbour wall. The younger lad watched the passers-by admiring the charcoal sketches, and the lamplighter extinguishing the flames that had burned through the evening. His companion sat with his feet dangling in the water and stared into the void of the horizon. The moon shone a halo over the ocean. Luca had never known the life of a fisherman; maybe he'd have liked it. They listened to the sound of the waves and the fizz of the surf. The two friends passed their pilfered wine between them, taking turns to swig from the bottle.

"What are you dreaming about?" asked Giovanni to break the silence.

"I'm walking down a street surrounded by tall buildings...I mean really tall, like skyscrapers."

"Chicago or New York?"

"That's it! I think I'm in New York. I'm walking with heavy steps so I can leave my mark on the place," Luca went on, taking a slug of red wine.

"Are you wearing a three-piece suit?"

"Oh yeah. A three-piece suit, a Jaxon & James hat, gold cuff links and a pocket-watch."

"Are you some kind of big boss?"

"I own a bunch of factories all over America. A real business magnate."

"So what are you doing walking along Fifth Avenue?"

"I've just left my office on the top floor of the Empire State Building and I'm heading towards the Wall Street Stock Exchange to invest in some railways."

"So you're like Rockefeller?"

"Maybe, but I can't be sure. I've invested in Standard Oil in Pennsylvania and in Pittsburgh—"

"Do you have your own aeroplane?"

"I'm not finished, dear Gio! And to answer your question, I went to see the head of Boeing in person to buy the newest plane he had."

"The head of Boeing?"

"Not just him, I know all the big-wigs. When I touch down in Los Angeles to socialise I stay in my house in Hollywood. The weather's nice there and the water's warm."

Giovanni closed his eyes; his head was swimming but he felt good. He was caught up in the ride, lost in the foreign landscape of this dream. How was it possible to imagine all these places they'd never set foot in? He didn't even know the names of half the places in the world, he only spoke one language, only knew one culture – and even that went no further than the familiar surroundings of Livorno. His thoughts took him to the court of an oriental king, a feast at a grand castle, the lush nature of a vast forest or the heat of a scorching desert. He wished he could lie down in the sand dunes under rust-red mountains. There, he'd have time to think and find himself. The thought of a city appealed to him, the culture and the constant motion of life there, but he felt drawn to quieter places, too. Falling asleep there would be a mere instant in the passing of time, and his presence or absence would matter to no-one – a luxury he'd never been able to afford.

6.

Luca and Giovanni were excited; they had a free day ahead of them and were determined to enjoy it. Using the excuse that he wanted to hear Gasperi's speech, which was being broadcast at the Piazza della Republica that afternoon, Giovanni had obtained a reprieve from his family duties. Luca was already in fine form:

"When I got up this morning, I read that my shares in Standard Oil had tanked! Giovanni, business is bad in North Carolina – whatever shall we do?"

"You've really come along since last time. Where are you learning all this about American geography, the workhouse?"

"During the war, before the marines left, I got to study the map of America. I don't know why I wanted to, but here we are — now I know all the States."

"You want to get out of here someday?"

"Why leave? I already can't make a life for myself here...you need money to go other places. Anyway, I'm going to rifle through a few pockets if you're up for it — you got my back?"

"Always! But be careful, I can't have my mother hearing about this right now."

"Always with your mother — grow up, will you!"

The citizens were thronging into the Piazza della Republica which overlooked the town's main canal. The fishermen arrived in their *gozzo,* while others hurried up the Via Grande. Beside the imposing statue of Ferdinand III, the technicians were positioning a huge radio speaker, through which Prime Minister Gasperi would address the nation from the Paris Peace Conference. The subject was the defence of the country's interests against the four members of the UN during this post-war period, a major political and economic turning point. Alcide de Gasperi had long fought for an free and independent Italy, before joining the fight against fascism and being imprisoned on several occasions. Some people now saw him as a symbol of hope; a saviour. Perhaps even a hero. *Il fotografo* was threading his way through the heaving, excited mass of people occupying the square, taking portraits of families who'd come into town for the event, fishermen from up and down the coast, the farmers who worked the land around Livorno, and the shopkeepers and artisans from the town itself. The photographs would serve as a precious reminder for future generations, and this hodgepodge of people had gathered full of hope for that future. Men from the working-class suburbs had come with bags full of wine. They swigged from the bottles and passed them around in solidarity. Luca and Giovanni didn't need asking twice and held on to the bottles as long as they could. Giovanni's head was already spinning. The sailors from the navy school were singing military songs, whose stirring airs electrified the crowd. People sang along with them, and the children admired their smart blue and white uniforms. Giovanni and Luca went to mingle with the crowd of navy men. Luca hugged them and sang their patriotic choruses at the top of his lungs. They looked at him with surprise and disdain; they were soldiers, not revellers. They knew this lout wasn't from the navy school, so what was his game? Giovanni tried to call his friend away, but Luca wasn't listening. Giovanni was embarrassed for him.

"Come on Gio, sing a song for the homeland!"

"I have other things to do!"

"Like wuss out of things?"

"Did you not see the way they were looking at you? Making fun of you?"

Luca burst out laughing and grabbed his friend by the sleeve:

"Shame is for the weak, my friend. Remember that!"

The technicians were making their final adjustments; the crowd fell silent and listened to the voice that crackled over the speakers: *"In starting to speak before this world assembly, I feel that everything—except your personal courtesy—is against me. My indictment as a former enemy places me "in the dock" here, as it were. The most prominent among you have, after laborious debate, already drawn up their conclusions. Italy has faced sanctions for its fascist past, but today I come to ask for equality of judgement and new international cooperation. Our losses in the resistance against the Germans amounted to over 100,000 men between fallen and missing, without counting the soldiers and civilians who lost their lives in German concentration camps; and the tens of thousands of partisans and civilians who died by German hand. For 18 months this second Italian war was carried on while the*

Germans slowly withdrew north, looting and destroying what the air raids had not already laid waste ..." The memory of fascism still weighed heavily in the hearts of the people of Livorno, but they knew they would have to cast off their shame if the country was to be rebuilt. In 1944 there was not a home, not a wall, not a pair of bricks left standing. It was a ghost town. Dilapidated. The Occupation and the Liberation each fuelled bitterness in their own way. If the Americans hadn't come, would the city have been destroyed? But if they hadn't come, the Livornians would still be living under the yoke of fascism. Giovanni would never have learned to play the blues. Luca didn't mind the war period so much – it was easier for him to run his scams undetected back then. Livorno was itching to roll up its sleeves and wipe away its memories of the war: the shooting, the mines, the bombs, the evacuations of tens of thousands of residents to neighbouring villages. Some people had been shell-shocked; they wandered the roads, unable to remember where they came from or who they were going to. They slept under the stars and conversed with the ghosts of their dead companions. They'd seen their loved ones die in Allied bombing raids or leave to seek refuge on the other side of the country, never to return. Families were shattered. This could not happen again. Efforts at resistance were hampered by the treeless landscape and a lack of drivable roads; any scattered uprisings were quickly snuffed out. The fifth US Army entered Livorno to free the battleground city, but before fleeing north the Third Reich's saboteurs set off huge numbers of mines in the port. The resistance, a mere handful of barely armed men, was unable to prevent these acts of spiteful vandalism. In the crowd, one fisherman was looking to settle a score.

"My brother died for Italy, and he still has no memorial!"

"What did he do, your brother?" Luca turned to him and asked.

"He resisted fascism, fought against the blackshirts. He gave everything to save us!"

"Can you prove that? Is it written on his gravestone?" asked Giovanni to needle the man even further.

"You little good-for-nothings, you think this is funny? You've no idea what it's like to lose a loved one!" bellowed the irate fisherman.

"My friend Luca here lost his father," Giovanni corrected him.

"From fighting in the war?" the man asked.

"No, from drinking. Actually, from a puddle of water," Luca answered with a grin.

"Is this some kind of joke?" cried the fisherman.

"Of course not. His father fell in the gutter and drowned on his way home from the bar," replied Giovanni in a sombre tone.

The two lads continued provoking the fisherman, until Giovanni gave him a tap on the shoulder while Luca picked his pocket. They felt no guilt about robbing a liar. "See you later pal, say hi to your brother from us," laughed Luca as he pulled Giovanni into the crowd. He was ready to add a few more notes to his day's haul. Giovanni smiled as he watched Luca work. Finding himself just beside the radio speaker, Giovanni was briefly spellbound by Gasperi's booming voice: *"the problem is an economic one and not a political one! What you need then is an international administration, not a state; an enterprise built on sound financial foundations, not a juridical structure standing on the quicksands of politics! With regard to reparations, Italy, though prepared for all necessary sacrifices, must make it clear that she cannot underwrite undefined burdens for an indefinite period. Moreover, with reference to ceded or liberated territories, the enormous Italian outlay invested in public works must be properly taken into account. Gentlemen, it is with the idea of lasting peace in mind that I ask for your patience and careful consideration."* A hum began to brew among the crowd, who did not seem well-disposed to making further sacrifices. The more serious listeners were getting angry. What investments was he talking about? They certainly hadn't seen any here in Livorno, and they were impatient to get things moving again. Luca and Giovanni had had too much to drink. The older lad snatched a bottle from the hand of some country bumpkin, drank down six mouthfuls in one go and passed the bottle to Giovanni. The electricians were rolling up the long electric cables. The radio receiver was shut off, and discontent continued to brew among the crowd. Two women had come to hear the speech; they took pride in staying informed. They reacted with conviction:

"I'll still be voting for the Christian Democratic Party."

"Gasperi doesn't do things by halves: he'll look out for us."

"That's true! Not like Mussolini; he's not just in it for himself."

"I'm so happy. My husband and I have been working so hard, but we still barely have enough to feed the children. It's time for change."

"I hope these UN accords aren't going to squeeze us. We're already hard up, all we need now is people taking revenge on village folk like us."

"United we stand!" the crowd chanted in unison. Banners flapped in the wind, bottles were passed from hand to hand, and scuffles started to get rougher and rougher. Workers gathered around cooperative reps, who raised their poster boards as high as they could to attract new members.

"Livorno needs supplies! These fuel and transport shortages can't go on!" declared one in a solemn, booming voice. The people applauded, crying out: "We need to take action! We need to feed our families!" The *Tirreno* is back in print, the postal service is up and running, the Florence-Pisa station is open again: we're on the right track, my friends. Now we must keep up the fight and keep working hard. Livorno will rise again!" the co-op chief went on, earning hoots of approval from his colleagues.

"If Livorno doesn't rise again, I'll kick it up the arse!" cried Luca, waving his fist.

As all this was happening, the Crecis were hosting Valci senior and his wife Nina. Valentina liked to have her friend over; it lifted her spirits. She needed it these days.

"It's all so beautiful!"

Nina was busy going through Valentina's velvet-covered jewellery boxes, makeup cases and huge leather trunks. She explored the wardrobes, rifled through drawers and even lifted the mattress to unearth the dozens of handbags stored under the bed. She unfolded scarves, examined the lace, took dresses from their packets and inspected the hats as she turned them over in her rough washerwoman's hands. She unearthed a beautiful muslin dress. "What kind of material is this? It's so light and delicate. It's like a baby's skin." She just had to try it on. Valentina smiled at her friend's excitement. Nina struggled to get herself into the dress sent from New York. "It's amazing what those Americans can do! Imagine if I went to the laundry dressed like this, the other women would have a fit!" Valentina gave a little smile and helped her friend button it up. Every time they had dinner together they went through this little ritual. Once Nina had dressed, she sought out some jewellery.

"What could I wear to go with this dress, Valentina?"

Nina was like a magpie drawn to anything that chimed or sparkled, her eyes lighting up at the mere mention of a gemstone.

"Well, I have a few knick-knacks but they're all fake."

"I don't care if they're real or fake, as long as they're pretty!"

"Try this necklace. It's from a store called Neiman Marcus. My son told me about it in one of his letters; apparently they're the height of fashion in America."

"Perfect! I want to be the height of fashion too. I deserve it as much as they do. I make a mean *cacciucco*."

"You'd better not be doing any cooking in that dress!"

"You're right, the peeled tomatoes would clash terribly!"

Valentina fastened a necklace set with imitation diamonds around her friend's neck. Nina looked at herself in the mirror, satisfied. She was buxom in her middle age, and the necklace sat perfectly over her voluptuous bust.

"You're not going to leave those big boots on, are you Nina? I have a lovely pair of pumps from Bergdorf Goodman."

"Goodman? Isn't that a Jewish name?"

"Probably, but they make nice shoes. Don't forget to put some stockings on first."

"Silk stockings? I've always wanted to try those on!"

"Do you want a fascinator?"

"What's a fascinator? Jewellery?"

"No, it's like a hat but with pearls on it."

"Pearls! You're spoiling me. I'm going to look like a princess. No, a duchess. No, a queen!"

In the living room, Valci shifted awkwardly in a padded armchair. How did people ever sit comfortably in these things? His fishing clothes squeaked against the fine leather. Marcello was wealthy, and his sons certainly seemed to be helping him out. Valci had never accepted any of Marcello's offers of support. Finally, Valci got up and went over to the fireplace to look at the family photos. There was one of Marcello and Valentina's wedding day; she was very young, but she'd changed little and still had the same strength of character. The next photo was of her sons, their arms around each other's shoulders. It had been taken in Pontini park, where they spent their days playing football before the war. Valci remembered the last photo: Marcello had had it taken of himself, holding up a prize fish that weighed over ten kilos. All the fishermen came from around the harbour to admire the beast as it gasped its final breaths. Valci senior then sat down next to Marcello and broke the silence:

"I don't see any investment going on around here!"

"Be patient, Valci. Don't worry; Italy has strength enough to get back on its feet. We'll leave the shame of fascism behind. We'll move forward."

"You sure about that?"

"Ah, Valci! Are you telling me you haven't noticed the streets getting cleaner? They're starting to move the rubble away. You must be patient."

"*Ma daaaai*, I've had enough of waiting!"

The women were preparing the pasta, God's bounty, with tuna and wild mushrooms. In Tuscany, wherever possible, there was something from both sea and soil in every meal. As they sat down at the table, the wives felt another argument brewing between their husbands. When they talked politics things rarely ended well.

"Marcello, your sons didn't experience the war first-hand! We suffered here."

"Valci, what are you talking about? The war? If you knew what my two boys have been through in America..."

"Yes, but it's not the same thing."

Valentina tried to calm the two men as their voices grew louder.

"Valci, you should have seen your wife trying on one of my dresses; she looked wonderful."

Marcello ignored her tactic and answered cannily:

"The American government *interned* Italians. My boys were interrogated like fascists, like villains, like criminals!"

"Well, that's not the same as being bombed."

"It was worse!"

"But..."

"Here we collaborated quietly with the fascists; we had to, but we didn't suffer that much."

"Collaborated?! Collaborated? I never collaborated! You think I was afraid of those Germans? And that Mussolini, I knew from the start that he'd make slaves of us all!"

The citizens were dispersing through the side streets that led off Piazza della Republica; they were disappointed by Alcide de Gasperi's words. "So many promises and so little action," some thought. The navy officers monitored the residents making their way home. They remained calm, avoiding any altercation. In the past, these types of gatherings had often descended into riots. After the war, Mussolini's blackshirts had scattered along the peninsula, never to be seen gathering in numbers again. Some of them shaved their heads as a sign of remorse, while others kept themselves locked away until the shame of their treason seeped from memory. The *squadristi*, as they were known, were afraid of being reported and beaten by anti-fascists. Giovanni and Luca were heading home. Further down the street, two men were holding a former *squadistri* roughly by the collar. Luca quickened his pace to stop what looked like the start of a brawl.

"I wonder what's inside that bald head of yours! Let's open it and find out!" growled one of the men as he pinned his quarry against the wall.

"Once a fascist, always a fascist!" snorted the second man, slapping him across the face.

Luca called out to them. The two men turned to the young lad, who lifted his shirt to show them the blade of his knife. Seeing this, the two men let go of their victim and backed away, cursing him.

"Off you go now, boys!" said Luca.

His blood was up, but he kept an amused, superior look on his face as he lit a cigarette. He liked to lay down the law, and for people to be afraid of him. What a bunch of saps that couldn't even take on a whippet like him! He whistled to Giovanni to come and join him. "It's OK *ragazza*, show's over." Giovanni smouldered and didn't answer. He was ashamed. He'd behaved like a coward, lagging behind and doing nothing. He didn't know what had held him back. Maybe he was just too much of a dreamer, too distracted to notice the things that Luca did. He hadn't even realised what was going on, while his friend was ready to whip out his knife. And anyway, *squadristi* weren't worth getting beat up over. Luca was just looking for a thrill.

"Just because he has a shaved head doesn't mean he's a *squadristi*," said Luca, as if reading his mind.

"Still though! I don't want to defend their sort. They burnt our houses down. They hassled us every chance they got."

"Listen, the war's in the past. It's time for the future now."

7.

Valci senior looked out the window as the dawn unfolded in dazzling pinkish hues. He called Giovanni from his bed, who joined him at the window to see what the day's weather would bring. The boy gave his father a gentle pat on the back. He seemed to be doing better. Nina prepared two big bowls of coffee for her men. Later she would go to the laundry to rinse her husband's bedclothes. He'd been very sweaty again last night. Giovanni slipped on his moccasins while his father put on his yellow rubber boots, and with that the pair were ready for a day's fishing. "Take care of yourself," whispered Nina into her husband's ear as he embraced her. She'd see them again in the late afternoon. She went back to bed until the summer sunlight woke her. On the way to the harbour, Giovanni and his father ran into some other fishermen heading for the jetty.

"Valci, I heard we should head eastwards today," one fisherman suggested.

"You 'heard', did you? Last time I headed where you sent me, we came home with nothing but seaweed in our nets."

"I heard there's promise over east."

"It's a one in four chance lads," said another fisherman as he joined them. "East, north, south or west."

"Sometimes you just have to trust your intuition," insisted Valci senior.

In hopes of earning the sea's favour, he wiped clean the watchful eye painted on his *gozzo* while Giovanni untied the nets. The jetty shuddered as the little boats left the quayside one by one. Giovanni untied the rope from the mooring bollard and grabbed the oars. "Alright son, let's head east!" urged Valci eagerly. The boat moved slowly away from the coast; the lighthouse disappeared, and the calm of the sea surrounded them.

The café on Serristori street always had a set menu that included pasta and a coffee for a decent price, and locals often gathered there to eat lunch together. It was a simple, easy-going place. A lad leaning against the bar was joking: "I heard the mayor's wife slept with one of the Germans. I guess she couldn't resist that military charm!" "She can't resist anything in trousers!" another patron laughed, blowing smoke through his nostrils. Giovanni and Luca walked into the café. The chatter stopped, and a man wearing a white vest and suspenders greeted the two friends:

"Comrade Luca! Found any work?"

"Don't call me that, I'm not a communist!" Luca answered indignantly. "I voted for Alcide de Gasperi!"

"Looks like we're in for one of history's great debates," commented the barman. "No fighting, boys. No arguments."

"Come and join us, you won't regret it. We communists are all about solidarity with the little man," the farmer insisted with a paternal tone.

"Leave him be!" Giovanni insisted.

"What's it got to do with you? We know your father wants nothing to do with us, he's set in his ways."

"Watch out, you're poking the bear," joked Luca.

"What do you know about my father? He has values. He works to feed his family!" Giovanni was losing his temper.

"His family? The people are his family. We all have to help one another. We have to join forces instead of slaving away on our own. That's how you get trampled on. You stay weak, and no-one listens to you."

"If you find me some work, maybe I'll switch sides," Luca jibed with a broad grin.

"It's a deal. We'll think about it."

Further inside, two navy men were sipping milky coffees. They were tired; loading and unloading cargo ships all day was arduous work. The poster on the wall took their minds elsewhere.

"Could that Fiat 500 take me to the Dolomites?"

"What's in the Dolomites?"

"Fresh air!" exclaimed the other sailor dreamily, his moustache frothed with milk.

The table next to them chuckled at their ambition and probed them for amusement:

"Where exactly?"

"A town like Bolzano! With a little garden, a pretty house, and even, my friends, a chicken that would lay fresh eggs for me. I'd be a happy man."

"Why not add in a cow and a donkey for good measure? Bolzano! You've lost it. There's nothing there, and you couldn't even raise a cat, let alone a cow!"

"It'd be an adventure! I'd be far away in my Fiat 500 while you lot were still slaving away in the factory."

"Climbing the Dolomites in a Fiat 500; you'd be lucky to get as far as Florence!"

"Don't worry, friend. With an Italian car I can go wherever I want."

Giovanni and Luca grinned. In the end, everyone thought the grass was greener somewhere. But in Livorno, after the bombardment, there wasn't much to do except clear up debris. Giovanni and Luca needed something to break their own routine. Luca turned to Giovanni:

"Speaking of the rich, have you seen Stella yet?"

"I caught a glimpse of her at the procession."

"Pah! You're not going to get her into bed by catching glimpses. Come on, let's go see her!"

"But how?"

"Well, I just found us a couple of bicycles..." said Luca, pointing at the couple outside the window.

"There's no way I'm taking the woman's bike!"

"I'm the oldest, I get to pick! Get a move on!"

The husband and wife had parked their bikes outside the fishmonger across the street; Luca and Giovanni hopped on them and sped off. The woman ran out, fuming:

"My bike! Get back here, you scoundrels!"

She started to give chase, but the two bandits pedalled away furiously. "We'll bring them back!" Luca called over his shoulder, earnestly. They turned onto a narrow street to avoid the crowds on the main avenue, taking them out of the town and onto the winding country roads. Giovanni was getting tired. He hadn't paid attention and had ended up with the woman's bike, which he wasn't thrilled about. "Slow down, Luca!" But Luca was glad to be on an escapade and paid no attention to him, pedalling faster. Eventually he looked behind: "Keep pedalling, we're not far! The villa's just up here." Somewhere on the road behind them, the sound of an engine rang out. Shit! They quickly threw their bikes into the ditch and crouched down beside them. The beautiful car stopped in front of the villa's gate, and the driver stepped out to open it. They'd hidden just in time. The gate closed as the car disappeared up the path, and the two boys crept out of the ditch. Luca started whistling, but Giovanni stopped him. They were too close now to get caught. The two prowlers followed the wall that encircled the villa looking for a spot where they wouldn't be seen. Luca was stronger; he climbed up first then pulled his friend up on to the wall. They scanned the garden, before squatting down behind a bush like rabbits. They heard dogs barking. Where were they? At the edge of the villa, they spotted the cage with the two guard dogs in it, throwing themselves furiously against the bars. "Dumb animals!" Luca threw a stone at them, and they barked even louder. The governess strode out onto the porch to investigate this sudden commotion, casting a suspicious gaze around the garden. Hiding behind a tree, Luca cast a mocking smile at his friend who was kneeling behind the fountain. The old woman lingered for a moment then went inside and closed the door. The two boys crept over to the villa with stifled laughter: "Did you see the look on that old bat's face?" They'd crossed the garden and now stood beneath Stella's window. Luca grabbed the gardener's ladder and leaned it against the wall. "Hold that, Gio, and keep a lookout." He grabbed the ladder, which swayed dangerously, and almost fell when he put his weight on a cracked rung. "*Ouffa*! I could have broken my neck!" He knocked on the window. Nobody answered. He knocked louder. Giovanni was getting nervous; he could hear voices in the garden. At the window, the curtain moved. Stella's face appeared; Luca pulled a face and signalled for her to open the window.

"What are you doing here?"

"*Bella, Stella, Mortadella*! Come join us!"

8.

Giovanni prepared the *gozzo* for its unexpected guests while Stella examined the drawings on the flagstones, whose chalk and charcoal markings were being gradually carried off by the wind. There was a Madonna with her head bowed, whose hair trickled away in delicate wisps. Stella wished she knew how to paint; she remembered the day her parents took her to the Uffizi Gallery in Florence, where she'd stood admiring Botticelli's Venus. She wished she could convey that kind of grace, with the vision of an artist and the technique of the great Florentine masters. She hadn't been back to the Uffizi since the war. Many of its artworks had been shipped off by the Nazis, and not all of them had been repatriated yet. How could those boorish Germans ever appreciate Italian art anyway, with their souls corrupted by the violence of fascism? Could they ever cry as she had at the delicate *sfumato* on a cheekbone or the subtle highlighting of an expression? Luca interrupted the Florentine in her reflections, shaking her excitedly:

"Time to board! We're heading to a place that's perfect for a refined young lady such as yourself!"

"And where might that be?" inquired Stella, playing along.

"It's a secret, but it will definitely make you forget all about Livorno," said Giovanni from his *gozzo*.

"How romantic! I feel like I'm in Venice here on the Livorno jetty. A ride in a real *gozzo*? I can hardly believe my luck."

"Let's go, the *gozzo* is ready!" Giovanni said giddily.

He finished stowing away the nets and held out a courteous hand to Stella. The trio settled down in the skiff, and the *Nina* headed out to sea. They were heading for the island of Gorgona. Stella was leaning against the boat's eye, watching the dome of San Francesco cathedral getting smaller and smaller. She thought of the dome in Florence, the symbol of the city's wealth and expertise. And yet, she did not miss the city. She felt Giovanni's furtive glances falling upon her and pretended not to notice. Luca rowed with all his might and pulled one of the paddles out of the water to splash her. She furrowed her brow and told him off:

"Quit that, Luca!"

"Are you afraid of the water? Are you seasick? We're not there yet," Giovanni laughed.

"But where are we going? We're too far from the shore, we should head back."

"Don't worry *Bella, Stella, Mortadella*," Luca chuckled.

She pouted like a moody child who knows just how adored she is. After all, wasn't she being carried off like Helen was to Troy? Stella cast a shadow over the water, and Giovanni dipped his hand in it, trying to grasp something intangible. They were approaching the rugged island covered in thick, tenacious vegetation; locals called it the "green hedgehog". They could already see the ramshackle houses scattered along the coastline. The *gozzo Nina* came ashore along the pebbled bank of a small creek, and a group of sea terns took flight as Giovanni and Luca jumped out and pulled the boat up onto the shore, tying the mooring rope around a rock. Luca entertained Stella with his excessive gallantry, delicately lifting her from the boat and pressing her body against his. He carried her up the shore like that, showing off his strength and skill.

"Fair princess of Pisa, may you find shelter here."

"You two are too much! How chivalrous you are. But I hope I get a chance to dip my feet in the water before we head back," Stella admitted.

She was enjoying the attention. The young rascal's clumsy affections were getting to her. He had no idea what he was doing, of course, but wasn't it better that way? If she could see these two boys more often, she could look forward to forgetting about the humdrum of life in Florence. Her stays in Livorno would become forbidden escapades.

"I hope we're not going to be walking through any bushes," Stella worried.

"Don't worry, it's just wolves in there," teased Luca.

"Out of the question! We're staying on the shore."

"Don't worry, Giovanni will protect you!"

Giovanni was quiet. His love was innocent, and he talked to her about his childhood memories and the times they spent sitting at the piano. Stella answered him fondly, until she caught a glimpse of the Pisana tower in the distance. "If only we could climb up into that fortress. I'd love to be able to see the island from above." Of course, the two boys would have done anything to make her happy: Luca led the way, taking out his knife to impress the lady by clearing branches from the path. Behind him, Stella admired the huge chestnut trees and black alders. She was feeling revitalised, far away from Florence or their gilded apartment in Rome. She was careful not to tear her dress as she walked, Giovanni noticed. He was taking up the rear of their convoy, and her dainty, uncertain steps melted the young fisherman's heart as he revelled in being able to watch her to his heart's content. As they snaked through the mountains, the musky odour of the dense, wild vegetation seeped into his thoughts, and he eyed the citadel with a hunter's determination. Stella turned around and flashed a knowing smile at her friend. "Enjoying the stroll?" She liked to watch his expression when she spoke to him, his eyes dark as the depths of the sea. Luca, meanwhile, was playing at Robin Hood as he continued clearing the path. Finally, they arrived at the fortress.

"What would please our queen?" Giovanni asked with a grin.

"I want to climb to the top of the tower. And on my own!" Stella insisted.

"Does our queen need time to collect herself?" Luca teased.

"No, I don't need time to collect myself! And I'm not a queen! I'm not a precious stone, or a perfect woman, or a rare bird. I just want a moment to myself."

"We're just kidding around, Florentina, don't be getting all uppity on us now," Luca said apologetically.

"I'm not a Florentina, or a bourgeois. I'm just a woman. Stop looking at me like a trophy or a piece of cake."

"It's only because we like you!" Giovanni protested.

"Oh, boy!" she blushed.

Stella had climbed to the top of the fortress while the boys gathered wood for a fire. From the top of Pisana, Stella looked out over the sea, shimmering in the wind. She felt free for the first time in her life. She observed the shades of green unfurling across the hills and valleys. She wished she could share this feeling with someone close to her. She wished someone could accompany her in her contemplations, share her solitude and love the world in the same way she did. But apparently that was not to be her destiny; she was condemned to a life of being desired and misunderstood. She'd be a prisoner on a pedestal. She didn't know what she'd really hoped for from those two boys. Were they really any different from the others? She'd never know real love. Stella wiped a tear from her cheek. She might as well resign herself to her fate. After all, she had less to complain about than most people. She had money and a comfortable future ahead of her. She was pretty and educated. But what about her wedding night? She couldn't bear to think about it, spending her entire life sharing her bed with a man who disgusted her...she saw Luca down below, in a clearing at the foot of the fortress, examining chestnuts he'd gathered along the way. "What the hell's that?" he exclaimed as a little seed shell landed miraculously on his head. Stella's aim was better than she'd thought. "If I catch you I'm throwing you in the water!" he threatened, waving his fist at her.

They whiled away their afternoon on the island, with Stella looking enviously at the sea. If only she could swim. The little pile of firewood was taking shape on the riverside. Luca took out his fancy metal lighter and set fire to the dried grass, which crackled under the flames. "Would you look at that? I'm the god of fire!" The three friends sat around the rising flames, and Giovanni took out his harmonica. Stella watched him as he played; his eyes were closed and he seemed almost possessed. He must have found the same comfort in music that she did, but what he was playing wasn't very harmonious. It had to be said, the harmonica wasn't a fine instrument, and to Stella the notes seemed nasal and rough compared to the crystal tones of a piano or a violin.

"What are you playing? I don't know it."

"That's Chicago blues!" Luca said eagerly.

"It's nice; different."

"You like it? Different from all that mushy stuff you play in Florence! The blues comes from American slaves. They used to sing it in the cotton fields. They sang for life and liberty," Luca explained.

"I know about slavery. Who do you take me for?"

"A young lady who's too well brought up, and who can't break out of her shell, even though she wants to."

"Are you calling me a liar?" she asked, offended.

"I'd never dare," he answered with a cheeky grin.

They ate the grapes that Luca had generously picked for them. Gorgona grapes were sweet and tender; people said they were once given to Michelangelo in exchange for a few of his sketches. Together, the three of them passed the time easily, finding entertainment in the slightest thing. The time slipped by, unnoticed. The fire's flames shone against the waves that crept up the shore. Stella daydreamed as she drew in the sand, scattering pebbles and shells around. Suddenly she had an idea, and her face lit up:

"Luca, how far can you skim a stone?"

"Depends on the stone," he answered nonchalantly, knowing full well how good he was. "I have the strength of a catapult, the mathematical ability of Leonardo da Vinci, and the vision of—"

"Enough boasting, mister mathematician, philosopher, whatever! Come on, show me then!"

"I need a good fanfare to get started. Giovanni, play me a tune!" he said as he clicked his fingers.

"How many skips can you get out of this?" Stella asked him, holding up a pebble.

"I reckon six or seven, with a little bonus at the end."

Luca grabbed the pebble from her hand. In time with his fanfare, the young Olympian ran and flung his stone against the surface of the water. Stella counted: "One, two, three, four, five, six, and the final dip!" She clapped. The fire crackled, and the tide began to rise. Giovanni's shyness was receding, and Luca's desire rising. The bigger lad sat on a rock and took out a cigar he'd rolled carefully the night before. Like a regal gentleman, he lit it with his gas lighter. Stella approached him with a sardonic look about her:

"Mr Luca, are your business affairs going swimmingly?"

"Oh, my affairs? Business is booming! I was just discussing it the other day with my associate and *consigliere* Mr Giovanni. Perched in my office in the Empire State Building on Fifth Avenue, I decided to invest in my home country: Tuscany. Red wine! My future wife will be delighted! Perhaps she'd like to smoke this fine cigar with me?"

"A lady never smokes. Didn't anyone ever tell you that?" Stella responded, enjoying Luca's game.

"Those ladies are just putting on airs. Women drink, they smoke, and they make love just like men do."

"Which women? Are you talking about prostitutes?"

"Never! I only like ladies with class."

"Aha! So do I have class?" asked Stella, grabbing Luca's cap and placing it on her head.

"You look like one of the artists from the harbour in that outfit!"

"I don't know how to paint."

"But you could play the piano on the quayside!"

"Hmm, and how much would you give me if I played Chopin on the quays?"

"How about a kiss?"

"Give me that cigar, quit playing the fool."

Stella sat down beside Luca and took a drag on the cigar. She raised her head and tried to blow rings with the dark smoke. Giovanni sat apart from them, watching the fire rage. He listened in silence as Luca whispered and Stella muffled her laughter. There seemed to be some private joke between them. What could they be murmuring about? The atmosphere was calm. Sparks flew around the fire, which cast their three shadows over the sea. This wasn't a moment for the harmonica. The tide was rising. The fisherboy prepared his *gozzo* for the journey home. Their day was coming to an end.

9.

At the Aragosta, the *vecchio* were sipping *limoncello* in the late afternoon. They awaited the arrival of their sons and grandsons, who'd soon be mooring their fishing boats and coming to take them home. All the regulars knew the man sitting at the back; he was one of the oldest men in Livorno, and a loner who went fishing at night. He took no interest in others and never spoke to any of them. He'd once been an opera singer, but his tenor had suffered the ravages of time and alcohol, and now he seemed eternally ensconced in silence and solitude. On this afternoon, the man decided to raise himself from his chair and roll up his sleeves. The other patrons looked at his sunken face and his eyes creased with sadness. They'd almost forgotten he was there and wondered what had gotten into him all of a sudden. The old drunkard grabbed a stool and climbed onto the bar. The chatter stopped as the surprised patrons fixed their gaze on him. The old man clapped his leathery hands together: "Your attention please!" Was he going to make a speech? If so, what could he have to say? They watched him intently. The old fisherman cleared his throat and began singing the *Tarentelle del Gargano* in his worn-out voice. Startled laughter rippled around the cafe. He must be out of it. But the oldest among them were instantly moved by the melody, which dated back as far as the Kingdom of the two Sicilies. They tapped their feet to its rhythm, their youth flooding back to them. The old song breathed an energy into them they believed was long-departed. One man said to his neighbour: "Kind sir, may I have this dance?" The other man hesitated for a split second; it wasn't often that folks around here let their guard down. The two men started a waltz, and others joined them. A frivolous joie de vivre swept over the *vecchio*, laughing as they twirled like ballerinas. Passers-by peered at them through the window, wondering what in hell those old boys were drinking. They looked ridiculous, of course, but none of them seemed to mind; dying of embarrassment was the least of their worries. A bald grandfather shimmied alone in a corner: "Is that your natural rhythm or are you having a stroke?" they teased him. A blind man sitting on a chair smiled up towards heaven; seeing these old men dancing was as good as any flight of angels, by God. A bearded man missing half his teeth whistled and cried out: "These days the young folk of Livorno can't dance unless someone throws them a ball. They should see how we do it at the Aragosta!"

At the villa Palomi, the housemaid opened the windows wide. The breeze flowed in and carried off the smell of tobacco; the two sons had been smoking Cubans again last night. She adored the two boys she'd watched grow up, even though they looked down at her these days. She spied a wisp of dust on the clock and wiped it away with the corner of her white apron. She glanced up at the portrait of the boys' father, hung on a satin-papered wall. He'd had his portrait painted as if he were an aristocrat; modesty was one currency he did not deal in. His pose was vaguely ridiculous: leaning on a knob-handled cane in his study in Florence, his prized poodle by his side, he seemed to be sizing up the whole world from behind his horn-rimmed spectacles. He didn't often come to Livorno, but when he came he had all the furniture rearranged and wanted the menu planned out a week in advance. He was a strict employer and a stricter father. The clock struck six; it was time to wake Stella from her siesta. She went upstairs and knocked on the young lady's door:

"Miss, would you like some help getting ready for the ball?"

"No, give me a moment please."

What would she wear to the dance? The men and women from the village would all be looking at her. To them, she was the embodiment of Florentine wealth and elegance; an ideal to be imitated and observed. She wanted her look to appear natural, like a lady of the Renaissance. She laid out a few dresses on her bed, unsure which would be best suited to this pastoral affair. She held up a dress that glittered with amethyst stones and eyed it for a moment. Too stiff, and not fitted enough. Plus it covered her legs too austerely. It didn't suit her. Would this one be better? No, too *candore*. Its virginal whiteness reminded her of her schooldays with the nuns. She was a woman now. She tried on a blue dress scattered with sequins and pearls. Why not? It was very *sprezzatura*. Not too stuffy; discreetly elegant. Should she wear a hat? Some hair jewellery would be better. She arranged her curled locks over her forehead and sprayed perfume on her neck. No necklace, no bracelet. Light makeup. She smiled: she was perfect.

Built during the heyday of the Medici family, the Villa Fabbricotti was being prepared to host the Livorno ball. Inside, the volunteers were busy trying to ensure that everything was clean and ready. Working by the light of the great windows, the men were polishing the busts in the main hall, wiping their stone faces with warm cloths: the six grand-dukes of Tuscany who adorned the villa's facade had been moved indoors to give the evening's event a more prestigious feel. "This fellow doesn't look like much fun; why's he so stern? He reigned for fifty years and all he did was line his pockets!" joked the maid, before covering the statue until the start of the ball. The man in charge of the preparations walked up to the two monumental staircases overlooking the entrance and inspected the work of the women who were on their knees cleaning the marble. Elsewhere, two maid-servants standing on huge stepladders were carefully polishing the glass chandeliers. On the porch, a young lad was beating the rugs and spewing clouds of dust. His strong arms worked furiously on their floral patterns, subtly woven in the Sardinian style. He was eager to go and lend a hand in the kitchen: the chefs were busy cooking for the reception, preparing a medley of festive canapés for the evening. They topped *biscottino* with tomato sauce, anchovies and little balls of buffalo mozzarella. Meanwhile, the apprentices were preparing ricotta and pecorino shortbreads, aubergine croquettes with cheese and rosemary, and *conchicles* stuffed with tomatoes, courgettes and basil. The pastry chef was making dark chocolate tiramisus. The aromas from the kitchen wafted into the garden, making the gardeners hungry. They were almost finished pruning the ficus and cypress trees along the Via Roma.

Torches were burning on V*ia Roma*; night had fallen. Lace fluttered on corsages, necklaces glistened on chests, and bracelets glimmered on bare arms. The rich ladies who'd come to summer in their villas around Livorno were chatting gaily under the bright lights of the main street. The taffetas, mousseline and silk of their dresses swayed and rustled like will-o'-the wisps.

"Look at those young things, Madame Tirroni," sighed an old bourgeois whose white hair was done up like a fan of peacock feathers.

"Aren't they sweet, so shy and clumsy," answered Madame Tirroni, adjusting her satin dress affectedly.

"So proud of their paltry elegance."

"Soon they'll be toe to toe, falling head over heels and stealing secret kisses."

"They are not brought up with values. I fear we are about to witness a pitiful spectacle."

"Yes, in these villages they cavort like rabbits to forget about their misery," answered the other lady with a scornful pout.

"It's an act of kindness to attend their ball. Look how they admire us!"

"It's as close as any of them will get to seeing the rest of the world."

"Look at those women, they've got half a salad in their hair!"

"How could you go out looking like that?"

The village women had spent all afternoon doing their hair for the event. Some had set their braids with jasmine flowers, others wore tiaras fashioned from forget-me-nots and branches of pomegranate flowers. They had used whatever they could to dress up for the occasion. They moved in small herds under the shadows of the wealthy ladies, murmuring excitedly. They were giddy with excitement and the sweet, pink smell of the magnolias. They cast quick, envious glances at the rich ladies, who walked with confidence and gestured like birds showing off their plumage. Behind them, the young men made their way into the villa with affected nonchalance. They were elated, and simmering with excitement. They were being observed and coveted. Who would they dance with tonight? Many of the town's married couples had met each other at one of these balls. Tonight's attendees were eager to start their own families. People here married young and had many children: their fairy tales held no surprises or grand deeds. These pairings kept the young people in their home towns. Nobody was going off to seek their fortunes far away when there were mouths to feed at home. Most fates were sealed by the age of fifteen; twenty at the most. A group of fishermen and business owners made up the tail of the procession. Things had changed a great deal since their first dances. They still remembered the glory of the inter-war years when they worried about nothing, their misery forever behind them, or so they'd thought. Now they could only believe, could only hope, that two wars were enough for one lifetime. Of course, some of them had gotten rich. The fishermen looked scornfully at the portly men in suits who seemed to have suffered so little. The war had worked out well for some of them.

Stella was standing on the balcony with her back to the balustrade, gabbing like a magpie with the other rich girls. To them, she said the most unexpected, astounding things; she enjoyed throwing out contradictions and wild ideas to see who would peck at them. She liked to shock the other rich girls and chip away at their little certainties. She wanted to rattle their self-importance and self-love, to shatter something that she'd never felt herself: that hard, glossy sheen that frosted over them. She turned her dark, wide eyes upon Luca, who was so full of life and unbearable insouciance. He hadn't noticed her; he was too busy flirting with a fresh, naive young girl from Livorno. Stella felt a pang of jealousy. This was too much – she couldn't be jealous of some stupid farm girl! She reverted to her strategy: "Being rich is a chore; you're imprisoned like a jewel in a glass case. Everything's stilted, imitated, imposed." A debutante wrapped up like an Easter egg in a fine, pink, muslin dress was offended by Stella's provocations. Who did she take herself for? Her porcelain face contorted into a scornful pout. Her blonde-doll-faced expression annoyed Stella, who was desperately trying to meet the gaze of someone interesting she could talk to. Her eyes found Giovanni's; he was standing alone, his hands in his pockets, intimidated by the beauty around him. "Why did I even come?" he wondered to himself. Would he be able to dance with Stella? That damned Luca certainly wasn't going to help; the selfish bugger had left him standing there like an idiot. Still, he wasn't going to go over to his mother, who was chatting to Valentina – that would make him look like a lost child. He did his best to look preoccupied, gazing into the distance as if thinking deep thoughts. The girls from Livorno observed him with curiosity, this handsome young man with a poetic air about him. Giovanni felt their eyes on him, admiring and questioning. He cast a wry smile, which shifted suddenly to a sad, serious expression. Why wasn't Stella looking at him like that? She wasn't falling for his act. The Florentine was far too clever to be taken in so easily. A young lady came up to him as her friends looked on. Had they dared her to come and talk to him?

"Giovanni, why don't you come talk to us?"

"I'd have nothing to say to you," he grumbled without taking his gaze off Stella.

"And why's that? You think you're better than us? You act all high and mighty, but your father's a fisherman."

"I didn't ask you to come over," he said, annoyed.

"Don't give me that look, I'm trying to be friendly," she smiled as she ran her hand through her blonde curls.

"Sorry, I'm being rude," he answered vaguely, charmed by her warmth and pretty little face.

"I accept your apology, just promise me you'll stop acting all rough and tough."

"I won't make promises I can't keep," he laughed.

"What are you doing hanging out with the most beautiful blonde in Livorno?" interrupted Luca, who'd sprung up behind him.

"You don't have a monopoly on meeting women," joked Giovanni, somewhat irked by the intrusion.

"Wait till you see me on the dance floor! I dance like an Argentine!"

"And how does an Argentine dance?" asked the young girl mockingly.

"Watch out for me later and you'll see!"

"Don't you think I have better things to do? Giovanni, your friend is far too arrogant," she concluded before returning to her friends.

"What's that little chatterbox's problem?" demanded Luca.

"You scared her off!"

"Don't worry, there are plenty more to go round."

The sound of violins rose up in the main hall; this was the moment the guests had been waiting for. Giovanni and Luca joined the crowd forming around the huge doors that opened onto the dance floor. In the midst of all the hats and hairdos, they spied the pitiful orchestra made up of six *vecchio*, who'd forsaken their drinks at the Aragosta tonight and volunteered to play for the young people of the town. Giovanni found them laughable. All they knew was classical and *tarantellas*, and even those they didn't do particularly well. They could barely stand, hunched over like old goats, their wheezy breathing reminding him of his sick father. Valci senior couldn't leave his bed tonight. He'd have liked to come to the dance, to twirl his wife around and see her laugh with her head thrown back. He'd have liked to relive the happy memories of their youth, the ones he never talked about but that had once made him a happy man. Giovanni would play him a tune on the harmonica tonight; something bluesy, not like these flat, dismal old tunes that sounded like the bottom of an empty bottle. Luca had slipped away; when Giovanni turned around to share his thoughts, he was already gone. "This should be fun," he was about to say with a smirk. Oh well, he'd have to keep his cynicism to himself. Out of boredom, he walked over to the busts that lined the wall, among the chairs that were gradually filling up with tired or shy attendees. He observed the poor folk mixing with the bourgeois. Did they think they were seen as equals? They were subordinates at best, idiots at worst. Where was Luca? He was laughing with a girl: the butcher's daughter. She was sixteen now, with a curvy body and plump red cheeks. She guffawed idiotically at his jokes. Luca took her arm and invited her to dance. Giovanni watched them with amusement, wishing he had the courage to ask Stella to dance. He wandered alone, distant from the crowd that now filled the dance floor. The boards of the hardwood floor shone under the light of the crystal chandelier, reminding him of the polished hull of his *gozzo*. Would he always be a fisherman? Couldn't he think of anything else to do? And yet, he found himself missing the quiet, peaceful endlessness of the sea. Here there was no haven for his thoughts. He watched a young man wearing a well-fitted black suit approach a young lady, full of elegant confidence: "Excuse me, miss: may I have this dance?" She smiled at him, flattered. She cast an amused glance at her friends and accepted. Why should she refuse? He seemed rich and polite. Giovanni watched them as they waltzed. They were in their element; they probably got lessons from a private tutor. They were also as stiff as boards, devoid of emotion or passion: these people were too rich to feel anything of substance. Theirs were lives lived at ease. Their insouciance was nothing like Luca's; this wasn't passion or survival, it was the embrace of comfort, and sedation of the body and mind. Part of Giovanni would have liked to have his life laid out before him, but such was not his luck; he'd have to scrape for whatever he got. The young fisherman's expression softened as he watched a husband taking off his shoes before asking his wife to dance. They must have been hurting his feet. Of course, neither of them knew how to dance, but they were enjoying themselves too much to care. They watched a younger couple and tried desperately to follow them. The rest of the Livorno women vegetated in their chairs; couldn't their husbands ask them to dance instead of talking to each other? More couples formed. They looked one another in the eye wordlessly; these couples rarely had time for moments of intimacy, and they were enjoying this one. They looked into their partners' faces as if for the first time. One husband was in a poetic mood: he'd been fortunate enough to travel all over the country in his time, and whispered in his wife's ear with wine on his breath, telling her they were dancing at the foot of Vesuvius, or in the Colosseum under the moonlight.

Giovanni stopped observing and let his thoughts wander. He would kiss Stella in this immense villa. They'd be alone in the main hall: she full of grace and elegance, he somewhat clumsy but steadied by passion. His sensitive soul was beginning to cut the ties that bound him to his mother. He could not ask Stella to dance with Nina watching. His thoughts took him further. The comfort of his mother's love could no longer sustain him. That life was over. A life of being respectful, keeping his nose clean and mindless devotion to his parents. The life of a child. The orchestra shifted the tempo to an upbeat *tarantella*, as expected. Giovanni broke into a wide grin. The women rose from their chairs, excited for the chance to let loose and dance to something more fun than a waltz. While the rich ladies removed themselves from the dance floor with barely disguised disapproval, the rest broke into joyous movement. Stella broke ranks by staying on the floor. Why shouldn't she get to laugh and jig around with the others? Luca approached the young bourgeois and bowed to her: "*Bella, Stella, Mortadella*. May I have this dance?" She took his hand. Luca showed not a moment's hesitation; timidity was not a currency he dealt in. The pair began to dance, Luca twirling his partner indefatigably. Stella was flawless. Giovanni's throat swelled. He shoved his hands in his pockets and stood rooted to the floor. His dark eyes simmered with anger; not at Luca but himself. He was too soft, too sensitive for Stella. He cared too much. He wasn't sharp enough to make her laugh. He was a good boy. How stupid and boring she must find him! Giovanni's jealousy reached new heights as Stella seemed to hold her hand out to Luca, who kissed the back of it. Giovanni's pained expression did not escape Luca's attention. He enjoyed himself all the more when it made others jealous. What was the sense of conquest if no-one saw you do it? Galvanised by this pride, he played his two friends off one another; he fawned over Stella and paraded her like a peacock in front of the young fisherman, enjoying his moment of thuggish glory. The rich young ladies were green with envy; left to wither in boredom on their chairs — they'd love to have a dance partner like me, Luca thought to himself with satisfaction. Maybe they'd get the chance; he'd reserve that pleasure for later. When the orchestra switched back to the soft, strict rhythm of a waltz, Luca retained his poise and managed to put together a few of the steps he'd observed earlier. Stella was happy to play along with the provocation, delighted to overhear her friends' indignant whispering. Luca acted the gentleman, unaware of Stella's motivations. She was seduced not by her partner's moves or manners, but by the sense of courage she now felt in herself.

Giovanni walked out into the garden, far from the light of the party and the oompah of the orchestra. He breathed in the smell of the freshly cut grass, its aroma enhanced by the evening dew. He looked up towards the treetops extending into the sky, those ancient observers who had watched so many lives come and go, and seen the history of men being built up and washed away. What would they think of all this, in their infinite wisdom? His sadness must seem trifling to them. He listened to the rustling of their branches in the wind, as if they would whisper him consolation. In the distance he spotted his mother on the porch, staring up at the starry sky. She too had been unable to find her place at the ball. How could she enjoy herself when her husband needed her? Giovanni joined her. She greeted him with a sad smile: "My boy, you should be enjoying your youth. Why aren't you off dancing with the others?" He answered with a sigh and took her hand, leading her around the porch in a gentle waltz. Mother and son looked at one another lovingly, needing no words. Nina felt her son's disappointment; she'd seen what happened on the dance floor. She knew she should say something to comfort him but didn't know what. She was clumsy when it came to feelings; such things were difficult to express. Instead, she tried to comfort him with the warmth of her hands and the tenderness in her expression. All these things would pass; no sorrow lasts forever. It was a simple lesson, but one her son had not yet learned.

10.

In Roman times graveyards were kept far away from the cities, but in Livorno's English cemetery the dead sat close to the living. There in the heart of the town, new graves were dug among the old; white marble tombstones sat alongside simple stone slabs and wooden crosses. Moss crept over rich and poor alike; all were dust, unto dust returned. A figure wearing a black cap trudged slowly along the Via Grande, dragging his umbrella on the ground and clutching rosary beads in his left hand. The fisherman was the first to arrive this morning before the battered, rusted gates of the little graveyard by the harbour. There was no-one at the gate. The undertaker was busy preparing a grave for the day's deceased. The fisherman rattled the gate until the aged figure finally shuffled over, draped in a grey raincoat.

"Who are you here for?"

"For Valci's burial. There was a sign at the harbour to say he'd died."

"Come in, but don't make too much noise," said the undertaker, his voice hollow.

The loud gate opened, scraping over the gravel of the central alley that intersected the cemetery. The fisherman walked beneath the weeping willows, whose long, mournful arms draped over the marble gravestones and sculpted angels. The wind murmured through their branches like a voice from the next world. Here and there, green statues of weeping women were draped over the graves. He passed funeral vaults erected for the great families swept away by the century's wars. The fisherman cast a pious eye over the ancient epitaphs of his ancestors and tried to make them out. The wind had worn away their names and the record of their years on this earth. Finally he came to the new graves; Valci's was just ahead. He removed his cap out of respect for the recently fallen. Those men must be cold lying beneath the ground, he thought. They would never again feel the joy of existence; their bodies were bound to the earth, their souls risen to heaven, if there was such a place. He gazed into the hole freshly dug for his friend. Absorbed by his macabre thoughts, he did not see the couple who had joined him. The husband held his wife by the arm: her eyes were hidden under a black veil, and she refused to look up from the ground. More and more people gathered around, waiting in silence for the procession to arrive from the Church of Saint Peter and Saint Paul. They all felt the weight of Nina's pain; some of them knew what it was like to lose a loved one. The widows came here every Sunday to lay a bouquet and speak softly to those they had lost. They did not celebrate with the rest of the town on feast days, whose distractions could not begin to ease their pain. A fisherman turned his head; the coffin had stopped in front of the gate. Giovanni carried it with Marcello and the boat maker. The boy's shoulder was bent under his father's weight. Nina was on the verge of collapse, her legs buckling and the world around her seeming to unravel. Valentina held her by the arm. She murmured tender words of consolation to the widow, who did not respond, deafened by her sorrow. The poor woman's dazed expression was lost in the memory of the gruesome morning that had taken her husband from her. His lungs hacked, he coughed up blood; his very soul seemed to be clawing its way out of him. She had tried to soothe him with a cool towel on his forehead and a cloth soaked in *limoncello* under his nose. What else could she do? Could she have saved him? He had writhed like a lion in a cage, suffering like a being tormented in hell. His pitiful cries and wails still rang out in Nina's head. She stumbled to the ground. Before her eyes, she saw her husband's ashen face, the unmistakeable image of death. The final image, her final memories of him. Was she going mad? Was it a dream? Her hallucinating eyes kept bringing him back to life, but each time she saw him die again. The coffin was lowered into the grave. The priest made the sign of the cross: "*In the name of the Father, the Son, and the Holy Spirit. Death is a concept. Death is an event both awaited and unexpected, but an event we must all face. I see people here today whose age brings them closer to death; some fear its arrival, while others await it calmly. Valci left us peacefully, in his sleep. Having suffered with his health for several years, he fought until the last for the sake of his family. You all know who Valci was. Family was everything to him...*" The homily echoed in Giovanni's thoughts. It was true, his father had fought until his final breath. He'd battled bravely, with a look of unflinching determination in his eyes. He hadn't grown old like others did, their bodies sagging and folding under the weight of age. He'd kept his head high. He was unshakeable; a man of principles. A man resolved. A tear came to the boy's eye. Why hadn't he shown his father more respect?

He was too proud and conceited. He'd behaved like a scornful ingrate. Of course, it wasn't easy to stand alongside so proud a man and earn his praise. Giovanni had been afraid of disappointing him. He needed encouragement. He wished he'd spoken openly to his father. Did he really know who his father was? Valci had spoken little and never showed his emotions. His son felt duty-bound to be strong and silent too. As a boy, he'd idolised his father. He was a colossus; an invincible hero. A rock the sea could never erode. Giovanni felt completely safe at his side. Nothing could harm them on the *gozzo*; his father could handle anything. And yet, one day, something had changed. Giovanni did not know why. Something had shattered, and his father fell from that pedestal. Giovanni suddenly saw his weaknesses and faults. They were unbearable to behold, and he began to hate Valci senior for being imperfect. Life was too hard and too frightening to go through without a father who was invulnerable. *"O Lord, grant eternal rest unto our brother and all those who have died in Christ, by God's mercy, may they rest in peace. Amen."*

The priest shook his olive branch and sprinkled the coffin with holy water. Nina lifted her veil. Some of the onlookers made a sign of the cross and genuflected. Others formed a queue to pay their final respects to Valci. The women lingered to murmur what words of consolation they could into Nina's ear. The men placed their hands on Giovanni's shoulder as a sign of comfort. "You're the man of the house now; look after your mamma." Later on, Nina would host them at her home for the funeral reception. It was now the priest's turn to address the two family members. "May he rest in peace."

Giovanni lifted the shovel and began filling the grave with dirt. He would never see his father again. It was unbearable. The man of the sea now lay beneath the dirt, whose weight would stifle him. Giovanni could barely lift the shovel. Devoid of his senses, he heard only the sound of the stones as they rattled between the coffin and the walls of the grave. His eyes filled with tears. He looked for his mother. She seemed lost or absent. She managed a dull, lifeless smile. Giovanni drove the cross into the earth. He observed the villagers as they left the English cemetery one by one. He wanted desperately to speak to Luca, to share his pain with him. Maybe he was just late. Surely he couldn't have left him to do this all alone?

Nina was lying on her bed. In her head, the funeral procession played over and over, and the priest's words echoed in her mind. The memory of parting with her husband was ever-present, nor could she forget the image of her son planting the cross over his father's body. Valentina tried to soothe him; she hadn't left his side since the funeral. Fury was building in Giovanni's heart. He would hear no more tender words. Valentina's attempts fell on deaf ears. Where the hell was Luca? He needed his friend. He stormed out of the house and slammed the door, half-crazed with fury. Where would he find consolation? He ran to the market on Via Grande. Maybe the baker had seen Luca today. He yanked open the bakery door and interrupted the baker as he was serving a customer. How dare these people continue to live as normal? To them this day held nothing unique, and they queued to receive their daily loaves as always.

"Have you seen Luca?"

"Gio, my condolences."

"Have you seen Luca?!" the boy cried.

They looked at him aghast and shook their heads before returning to their conversations. He'd shattered their peace for only an instant. They would not let themselves linger on death or worry. They looked at him with pity; the poor boy who'd lost his father. Then they turned away. Giovanni cursed their entire selfish brood. He barged past a jolly woman with rouge on her cheeks, jabbering louder than the others, and left the bakery fuming. He passed by the stalls where the women sold meals ready to eat, asking them all: "Have you seen Luca?" One of them answered: "Who?" He wanted to shout and spit in her stupid, wrinkled face: "Luca!" One of them recognised the boy darting from one storefront to the next. Why wasn't he with his mother? The old woman caught his arm to ask him about Nina; the poor mamma would need her son. Giovanni pulled away irritably. To hell with these women and their lecturing. He had only one thing on his mind, and this goal gave him desperate energy despite his exhaustion. Giovanni wasn't even angry anymore but shell-shocked with desperation. He could not understand it: there were notices all over town announcing the death of his father. Everyone knew he was in pain. Had Luca been called up to work at a factory? Had he been in an accident? Giovanni did not believe it. It was getting late, and the moon was coming out. He'd spent the whole afternoon looking for his friend, but there was one more place to check. Giovanni headed for the café on Serristori, his final ounce of strength driving him onwards. Out of breath, exhausted from scouring the length and breadth of the town, Giovanni pushed the heavy door open. He asked his question; repetition had rendered it almost meaningless.

"Have you seen Luca today?"

"He was in here with a girl. They had two *cannoncini* and they left," the barista told him.

"Where did they go?"

"No idea, but they can't have gone far."

Luca must have taken her to his favourite hideaway: the lighthouse. Giovanni ran with renewed energy and hurried up the lighthouse's seemingly endless stairs. He heard moaning; it sounded like Luca was getting lucky. The door was ajar, swaying in the sea breeze. He poked his head around the doorframe. He could see clothes strewn on the floor, and further off two figures in the dark. Gradually his eyes adjusted to the dim light. He could make out the two figures wrapped around one another. Something captivating was happening; the fisherboy stood frozen, fascinated. A face was pressed into the girl's chest. Sleek, strong muscles were wrapped around her tender, supple body. She was on top of him, then he was on top of her. The girl's cries spiralled upward, louder and wilder. Giovanni's wits suddenly came back to him. He was shaken from his torpor. It was Luca. It was Stella. His betrayal was complete.

11.

Nina awoke with the first light. She reached out her arm; the bed was empty, cold and deserted. His absence — the absolute lack of him — flooded over her. She got up alone for the first time, as she would now do for the rest of her life. She dutifully prepared coffee for her son. Life had to go on. These little habits would sustain her. She held fast to them, and the hot steam and aroma of the coffee consoled her. She turned her weary gaze to her son's bed. He wasn't there.

Giovanni listened to the silence around him. It had enveloped him so completely that he no longer struggled against it, and had dulled the pain that seemed so unshakeable just hours before. His anger had evaporated during the night. The bitterness, the resentment and the acid taste of betrayal had ebbed away into the sea. He hadn't slept. His consciousness was adrift in an undefined plane between dreams and reality. He spent long hours looking back at his past with fresh eyes. What was friendship? What was love? The salty sea wind rose up and wafted against the face of the fisherman lying in his *gozzo.* Time had stopped. His wounds had scarred over as he contemplated the waves that rolled back and forth. Everything left and came back again.

Where was Giovanni? Was he fishing? Then Nina saw the note left conspicuously on the table; a carefully folded sheet of white paper. Her legs trembled and her heart pounded. She was afraid to read the words, but having them read to her would be worse. She hesitated for a second. Did she really want to know what could only cause her pain? She gently unfolded the paper and sat down.

Giovanni observed the entrance to the docks. A small army of people were unloading the trucks that were parked outside the gates: navy officers, porters and some of the men from Livorno who'd been given a morning's work. Inside the docks, cranes lifted containers onto the cargo ship as it prepared to depart. Without thinking, driven by courage he didn't know he had in him, Giovanni went up to a truck and grabbed a sack, hoisting it onto his back. He mingled with the porters and walked through the gates, watched over by armed guards who didn't look twice at him. Like a worker ant, he followed the dockers over to the cargo bay. He saw the travellers on the dockside, waiting to board, their bundles of belongings piled alongside the huge ship. Grouped at the foot of the gangways, the emigrants milled about as their papers were checked by the customs agents. Giovanni had never seen so many Italians leaving the country. He walked up the gangway and set down the sack, spying his chance to slip out of sight behind the crates. Now all he had to do was wait. A man dropped off the last of the cargo; Giovanni watched him from the corner of his eye. The porter went out, and the young fisherman heard him yell: "Loading finished for Marseille!" The cargo bay closed. Giovanni was left in the darkness. He was overcome with excitement: he was going to France. Livorno would be a distant memory. He'd never see it again.

Nina sat still, her son's letter in her hands. Something was crumbling around her. He was gone. Could she ever have stopped him? Should she have watched over him every night to ensure he wouldn't steal away? She'd felt it coming, and still she was in shock. A wife with no husband and a mother with no son. She knew that her life would now be spent waiting for him to return or send news; her son Giovanni, her son who had had her name painted on his *gozzo*, who used to be unable to sleep until she whispered "goodnight" in his ear. The sole reason she had left to live. Why would she get out of bed in the morning? Why continue to live alone? She felt paralysed, sitting alone in her kitchen. She cried. She heard the town coming to life around her but couldn't move a muscle.

On the quayside, a man was busy painting the cargo ship's departure. He painted scenes that inspired him. His canvas was set on an easel, and with brush in hand the artist sketched out his landscape, arranging the colours and shades of the sea and sky. He traced the line of the horizon. He knew more or less what he wanted the final painting to look like. The sun came up. He spotted a few shadows cast by the old fortress, and those of the few *gozzo* that were fanning out over the sea. He mulled over it for some time, wrestling his inspiration into place. In the foreground, he'd sketch a child diving into the water, or a mamma waiting for him with a white towel. On his wooden palette, he mixed the dense, oily shades with his paintbrush. In the sky, he'd form some seagulls with a few light touches of his brush. He'd add some *impasto* blue clouds. He turned his attention to the ship leaving the dockside. He concentrated; the movement had to look natural. The cargo ship sounded its departure; he had almost finished his painting by the time it had disappeared over the horizon towards Marseille.

Part II

Thou shalt not steal!

1.

Early in the morning, two men were walking through the third *arrondissement* of Marseille, heading for the port. They strode along with a casual gait and their hands in their pockets, looking on with disdain at the construction sites they passed, where their fellow Italians laboured under the watchful eye of their French foremen. Those workers were hardly more than slaves; their masters called them *babis* or *macaronis*, and they lived piled on top of one another in filthy households in the Belle de Mai neighbourhood. How could their people live like that? Had they forgotten what it meant to be Italian? The two men watched them carry heavy sacks, creaking under their weight like the dead toiling in hell. Graziano and Paolo would never lower themselves to such a task; to do so would amount to submission. They would always be able to find a few who refused to lie down and obey these witless French. The newspaper sellers were arriving with the day's news and began their hollering: "*Italian Echo*, *Italian Echo*, latest news, hot off the presses! Latest news!" Paolo stopped and bought a copy. He pushed his *montecristi* panama hat back on his head and read the headlines to Graziano:

"Violent clashes between French and Italian workers." "Italian emigrant workers: Say no to fascism! Long live socialism!" The politics section didn't seem to interest Paolo this morning, and he continued to riffle the pages with impatience.

"Maybe it's on the back page," Graziano suggested.

"Here it is! This is more like it. The cargo ship from Livorno arrived in Marseille this morning."

"That's what the boss told us."

"The boss is always right."

Paolo never doubted his boss and put all his considerable guile and skill to work for him. He was a practised diplomat and had an effective style of negotiation when it came to procuring the 'rent' his boss was due: this had earned him the sobriquet "Paolo the Fixer." Everyone in Belle de Mai knew him; he was the one who came to collect their protection money. He'd slip the money into his pocket, saying: "Mr Capuani will look after you." He took a commission, of course – a fair day's work earns a fair day's pay, and Paolo took great pride in his work. He knew how to settle altercations between pimps, reassure prostitutes and defend the interests of Italian traders and merchants. Wearing his striped dungarees and *montcristi* hat, the Italians of Marseille noticed him wherever he went. A crab seller on her way to the port said to her colleague:

"Look, there's Paolo the Fixer with Graziano!"

"Their boss must be after something in that boat from Italy."

"Sshh, don't say a thing. They must be on a job."

These types of jobs were never spoken about. That was the golden rule if you wanted to avoid getting on the boss's bad side: "Don't break the rules, and keep your mouth shut." Not knowing France's laws was forgivable, but the laws of the mafia were a different story. Paolo and Graziano waited for the Italian workers to gather in front of the cargo ship, so they could weave their way unseen into section two. The entrance to the dock was not yet open. Paolo was getting impatient; he had a restless disposition and hated being idle. Graziano looked around him with a dull, thuggish expression. A man pushing a cart called out to the queue of people waiting to unload the boat: "*Chichi figi,* fried donuts, five francs apiece." Graziano didn't need telling twice and made a beeline for the *chichi* cart.

"Grasso, one of these days you and your stomach are going to blow our cover," Paolo ribbed him.

"Ah! Leave me alone, I'm hungry."

Graziano, or "Grasso" for short, had always done the dirty work. He was as thick as pig shit and just as dirty. His value lay in his unfailing ability to obey without thinking: it was he who would be called on to strangle an old man, shake down pimps and set fires, among a litany of other offences. Everyone knew Grasso's broad shoulders. He was a monster of a man and always wore a three-piece suit. Nobody in the Belle de Mai ever wanted to have to deal with Grasso. Rumour had it that he'd strangled one of Mr Capuani's rival bosses with his shoelace. As Grasso was fond of saying: "If you live you live; if you die you die." The quayside was overflowing with workers, ready to unload the cargo ship in exchange for a twenty-franc note. The Italians jostled, and a controller hollered at them: "One at a time, one at a time!" The entrance to the dock had been opened. The men shoved forwards, eager to start unloading. The *porteïris*, as they were called here, waited with their wicker baskets to unload the fresh food they would take to the market.

In the back of the hold, Giovanni breathed in the bitter odour of the cargo hold. He breathed slowly. His stomach no longer ached, but he still felt the acid sting of hunger on his tongue. He'd gritted his teeth so hard that his jaw ached. Rocked by the movement of the boat, he thought about his father's death and Luca's betrayal. He did not hear the commotion arising from the docks. He was buried alive, six below just like poor Valci. He wanted to cry out, "But I'm not dead!" His senses came back to him slowly as the sound of the ship's engines ground to a halt. Had they arrived somewhere? He missed the daylight. He didn't know how many days and nights he'd spent there. Locked up like a madman, he'd be at the mercy of anyone who found him. Fear gripped him; the fear of being beaten, thrown in a cell, questioned by the authorities or even shot for being a criminal. Whatever happened, though, he was in a new country, far from Livorno. Only God knew what awaited him there. He was weak; he longed for a glass of water and a crust of bread. Just a drop, just a mouthful would be enough.

Graziano and Paolo entered the second hold of the cargo ship. Giovanni eyed the two men with suspicion. One of them kept a lookout while the other inspected the hold with furtive care. The young fisherman hid himself as best he could between the crates, losing sight of them in the process. He focused on the sound of their footsteps, crates being opened and moved around. The two men did not speak, which seemed to confirm his suspicions. Most people chattered while they were doing a job, unless they were hoping nobody caught them doing it. They must be traffickers. Giovanni would have to wait it out until they found what they were looking for, and hope that it wasn't in one of the crates hiding him from their view. They were coming closer. A shadow crept towards his hiding place, and then a dark figure stood over him. He'd been found. The figure was blocking the light, and Giovanni could not make out the face of the man in front of him. He was powerless. He was frozen. He had neither the strength nor the courage to get up. The black shadow dominated him completely, staring at him for what seemed like an age. Then the man grabbed him by the collar and examined him with his big, dark eyes, perplexed. Giovanni was taken aback by the young, almost child-like face in front of him. Was this to be his executioner? He didn't look like the sort.

"Grasso, get over here! Look what I found!"

Graziano hurried through the hold. Giovanni was terrified and raised his arms in a gesture of surrender. Graziano removed a pistol hidden in the folds of his jacket and pointed it at the boy's head. Paolo spoke calmly and with amusement:

"Wait a second, let him say his piece before you clip him."

Giovanni closed his eyes and begged the two crooks: "Please, don't hurt me." They pretended not to understand him. They spoke a few words to each other in French, but Giovanni could hear enough in their accent to know they were Italian. It might be his only chance.

"Please, I'm from Livorno! I'm an Italian!"

Graziano hesitated. Italy was Italy, after all: he couldn't shoot one of his own without a good reason.

"What shall we do with him?" Paolo wondered.

"Do we have to kill him?" Graziano asked with the conscience of a patriot.

"What if we take him to see the boss?"

"That's an idea."

Grasso removed the gun from the boy's temple. Giovanni exhaled. The two goons were going to let him live, through what sheer whim he could only guess. Graziano shoved him roughly towards the door of the hold. They transferred him into the back of a lorry. Sitting in the darkness, Giovanni saw the doors opening often, letting the bright sunlight in. A dozen or so crates were loaded into the truck. A few moments later, the engine started. Giovanni found himself locked up once more, this time like a rabbit in a hutch. The truck took sharp turns and banked hard; he tried to avoid getting crushed by the crates as they slid around. He heard the muffled sounds of the streets of Marseille. His heart soared: he was starting his day in France, far from the quaysides of Livorno.

The sounds of the city died down. The young fisherman wondered where they were headed. The humming of the engine came to a halt as Graziano jumped out and bellowed:

"Franz! Come and see what we found in the boat."

Franz the German opened the back doors.

"Ausgezeichnet!"

Franz liked to speak German in delicate situations; this was how he signalled the superior status he held as a former Nazi. Nobody understood what he was saying, but his glib, cruel smile was full of cold violence. He was a methodical man, one who never lost sight of his goals. A man of terrifying steadfastness. He observed the young fisherman carefully. His piercing, transparent blue eyes gazed, unflinching, upon his prey's defeated face. Giovanni felt his heart crumble in the face of this stony examination. The German's stern features, and the thin lips that cut like a knife through his pale, clean-shaven face, sent shivers through the young man. Part god and part monster, he was not of this world. Franz moved towards him with deliberate slowness. He cracked his knuckles one by one, pacing around his victim. He knew every method of intimidation, along with some basic torture and interrogation styles. He carefully removed a thin cord from his pocket and slid it around the fisherman's neck. Graziano wasn't fooled and laughed heartily at Giovanni's baffled expression: "Let him unload the truck; he can be useful for now." Franz signalled Giovanni to move the crates to the back of the warehouse. Giovanni began moving the merchandise, stumbling often under the weight of his hunger and fatigue. He crossed the warehouse, which seemed to go on forever, and observed the mountains of goods piled neatly in towers of wooden crates, their contents remaining mysteriously hidden. Were they weapons? Drugs? Luxury items? The old warehouse seemed to belong to the crooks, who ambled back and forth at their leisure, seemingly unafraid of the French authorities. They must have been powerful because nobody bothered them. What kind of deal had they struck with the French? Giovanni's mind raced with questions about how these thugs could live among the locals. They must all be in on it, he was sure. Absorbed by his thoughts, Giovanni failed to notice the long cables running along the floor and tripped head-first, dropping the crate he was carrying. Paolo was chatting quietly to Franz about his plans for their upcoming rackets and turned with a grin: "Watch out! If you fall like that again Graziano will take care of you." He spoke to the young man in Italian simply to get his point across more effectively, rather than out of any kinship. Giovanni looked at the one who seemed the most dangerous and the most hostile: Franz did not bother to look at him; he was busy monitoring the entrance to the warehouse. The boss would be here soon. The three goons were getting nervy and impatient. Graziano paced back and forth, nibbling at peanuts as he went. Paolo dusted off the big man's trousers, batting them anxiously with his hand. Franz ran his finger along the huge maritime map pinned to the back wall.

A black sedan rolled into the warehouse. The driver got out of the car and walked around it at a smart pace, a serious and occupied look on his face. He opened the rear door. A black loafer followed by a creased trouser leg emerged from the dark sedan with its tinted windows. Franz, Paolo and Graziano went up to the vehicle to welcome the man getting out. Giovanni turned to catch a glimpse of the man everyone seemed to have been waiting so nervously for. He was a man of refined elegance, his perfectly starched collar framing a handsome, manly face with a neatly trimmed moustache. He exited the car like a dagger emerging from a silver sheath. His thick eyebrows suggested authority and mistrust, and he raised them in curiosity at the boy moving his crates. Paolo was attuned to his boss's every thought and prepared to explain. Franz signalled him to keep quiet and welcomed Mr Capuani as usual. He kissed the boss' hand, dropping his knee to the floor as he did so. The former prisoner of war was careful to show his absolute devotion to the underworld boss, who had shown him generosity and given him a second chance. He was now his right-hand man: him, a German and a former fascist. Giovanni set down the last crate at the back of the warehouse. The boss addressed his two dogsbodies, Paolo and Graziano:

"Did you unload the cargo from Livorno?"

"Yes boss, it's all stored away here in the warehouse," Graziano answered with respect.

"Who's the youngster?" asked the boss, eyeing Giovanni.

"We found him in the cargo hold with the stuff from Livorno," Paolo answered nervously.

"Bring him here," Mr Capuani ordered.

Graziano signalled Giovanni to come over. The young man crossed the warehouse with trepidation. The mobsters observed him in silence. His entire body stiffened with fear. He took each step carefully, desperate not to fall in front of the boss, whose gaze seemed to pierce him to the bone.

"What are you doing here?" Mr Capuani's tone was dry.

"I left Livorno because—"

"Answer my question," the boss cut him off.

"What did you do there?"

"I was a fisherman's son."

"Who sent you here?"

The boss signalled to Franz, who produced his cord. Graziano held Giovanni by the arm. The boss asked him once more who had sent him to Marseille.

"Nobody sent me, Sir. I came alone."

He turned to Paolo, whose nerves were reaching a fever pitch:

"How many days in the cargo hold?"

"Nine," Paolo confirmed.

Mr Capuani paused to think. The long silences his authority imposed left his employees frozen. He was unreadable; this was his strength and his upper hand. They waited. Finally, a thin smile appeared on his lips.

"Keep him and give him something to drink."

For a man who was feared and respected, family was sacred and inviolable, as it had always been and would forever be. Family was not just blood, but those who had spilled blood in the name of his power and authority. Mr. Capuani's family was not limited to his inner circle, but to all the Italian community who relied upon his power. United we stand, and alone we are defeated. Giovanni approached Mr Capuani and bowed carefully as he had seen Franz do.

2.

They say Marseille is blue like the sea. It is pink too, like the rooftops that carve out its peaks and valleys. It is bordered by the *calanques*, the rocky inlets whose jagged teeth keep the sea at bay. Marseille is the namesake of France's national anthem, and like the song, it is boisterous and violent. When the sun was rising over the Old Port, Giovanni was still in a deep sleep. The day before, he'd left the warehouse with a twenty-franc note in his pocket. Paolo had slipped it into his hand with a complicit smile, his way of saying: "You're one of us now." It was also his way of buying Giovanni's loyalty — and his silence. Giovanni wasn't fooled. He now found himself in a new family. One whose company was far from comforting, but what did that matter? It was better than being on his own. His mind raced as he wandered rudderless through the streets, peering down each one with his curious and worried expression. The vast city still slept, and he was free to explore its harbour and its tenements. Would this be the city he'd someday call home? Would he know these streets, these cafés by heart? Would he call the shop owners by their first names? He cut back and forth through the city like a man possessed. A furious thirst for exploration had washed over him. He needed to see everything. Being a foreigner, lost, not knowing even the language they spoke here, was too much. He stopped walking at the port. The boats bobbing up and down on the water reassured him. No matter where he went, this was something familiar in which he could take refuge. He fell asleep quickly, exhausted by his thoughts.

The first of the Neapolitan fishermen — *nabos*, the Marseillais called them — were preparing their nets to go fishing on the open water. One of them approached the pile of nets the young man was sleeping on and gave him a tap on the shoulder:

"Hey there! Wake up, these nets have to go in to be mended."

Giovanni blinked. He looked vaguely at the face of the man speaking to him, unable to understand a word. He'd lost his bearings with sleep. The man repeated: "Listen lad, these nets are going to the mender." Giovanni looked around him. Until today, he'd never woken up in another city. He was free of the cargo hold and free of Livorno. Like a prisoner with his chains removed, he sprang up, surprised by how light he felt. He ran off without a word. The air was different here in the 'Phocian city'. To Giovanni, Marseille was a city of eternal youth; the city of rebirth. Everything seemed to be in constant motion, changing and alive. The workers milled about among a cacophony of Mediterranean languages, tempered by the smell of fish and sweet fruit. The taste of adventure galvanised him. It was time to start living in this new world. To hell with worry. He was an explorer; a conqueror. Marseille was more majestic and imposing than Livorno; the city's ambition matched his own. It was time to break with his destiny. His future would be different from that of his father, his grandfather and their ancestors before them. He had set off in search of something and would let Providence guide him along the path. He observed the Marseillais like a child with a new picture book, eyeing with careful attention what he had not been able to make out in the dim light of the night before. Along the waterfront, the ropers were busy making rigging and nets. Alongside them, basket weavers were hard at work, making funnelled lobster pots and shopping baskets with sturdy double handles. Giovanni knew how difficult it was to make a net; he'd sometimes had to mend theirs back in Livorno. The market women were shaking the port into life; their shrill voices seemed to ricochet off the cobbles before evaporating into the sea breeze. They were dressed just like the *mammas* of Livorno in their long skirts, wide aprons and headscarves. Their baskets were overflowing with fresh fish. "A great catch today!" Nina would have exclaimed. Giovanni saw dreamfish, urchins, whelks and other sea creatures he did not recognise. A zesty aroma wafted into his nostrils, cutting a trail through the salty odour of the fish. He turned his head to see the orange seller, peeling each fruit in a single, unbroken movement. Giovanni watched, fascinated by the level of skill she had accrued at this most mundane of tasks. Anything could be learned. One by one she unclothed their juicy segments, disrobing them one after the other with almost musical regularity. The young man was jostled by a child running past; the dozens of bambinos come to gather up the peelings thrown into the water. They laughed and squabbled, proudly showing off the wire nets they'd made and scampering deftly in between the workers. Who was looking after them? A fishmonger called to her son, "Bring my knife to the grinder!" Giovanni followed the child with his gaze as he headed over to the crowd gathered around the knife man. "*Qui vau faire amoula*?" cried the man sitting at his wheel. The children were spellbound by the sparks that flew from his grindstone. The grinder wore a heavy leather apron, pedalling to turn his stone and sharpening knives and scissors in exchange for a few francs. Giovanni watched him for a moment. His stomach groaned with hunger. With the money he had in his pocket, he should be able to find something to eat. He spied a woman selling snails, crying out "*À l'aïgo-sau lei Limaçouns*!" He raised his hand to her, wanting to try a local speciality. She set down a bucket filled with tiny snails in white spiral shells, cooked in a bouillon with garlic and salt. She rolled up a cone of paper, filled it with snails and handed it to him with a warm smile. Giovanni popped a rubbery snail into his mouth and swallowed it whole. It wasn't bad; it would do the job. He continued nibbling from his cone as he admired the boats lined up neatly against the jetty. In Marseille, people said the boats were curved like women, so they could go wherever they wanted. The boats were leaving the harbour for the day's fishing. Shoremen were helping bigger vessels to navigate their way out of the port; Giovanni watched them waving their arms in this strange sign language. So many jobs to be done. The port of Marseille was much more organised than Livorno's, where the lighthouse served as the only landmark. "So organised," he thought to himself. The dockers were unloading the cargo ships like a line of ants, transporting their prize crumb by crumb. Everyone had their place, and everyone their task. The young man turned his gaze towards the fort of Saint Jean, whose tower watched over the entire city, jutting from the end of a long wall that glowed amber in the morning sun. He headed up the long avenue of the Canebière, where a man was hawking his wares: ""*Estrassaire*, ragpicker! *Estrassaire*, ragpicker!" The rambling salesman carried a pile of old rags on his shoulder and even a rabbit's hide. He must be on his way to sell them at the market. The young man walked up to a stall. What was it selling? They looked like figurines for children. Giovanni looked with amusement at the little sculpted, hand-painted figures. All the people from the port were there. He could see a fisherman in his slacks and striped blue sweater, the grocer woman with her floral blouse and cotton head scarf, the knife sharpener in his thick leather apron at his wheel, the snail seller and her cones, and the ragpicker with his cart piled high with rags and pulled by his donkey. Giovanni cast his eyes over this busy yet silent congregation, not quite understanding what the dolls were for. Who would want to keep effigies of working folk in their home? Tourists, maybe. But the only language being spoken around him was French. For now, he only knew a few words of that language, languorous like Italian, but he would make it a point of honour to learn it fast.

Giovanni left the Canebière and headed up Boulevard d'Athenes. He found himself at the foot of a grand staircase, and climbed to the church at the top like a pilgrim seeking to wash away his past. He stood triumphant at the summit, as if proclaiming his discovery of France. Others had walked there before him, but had it meant as much to any of them? He studied the delicate stonework of the church to preserve it in his memory, intact and imperishable. At the top of the hill, cars were dropping off commuters at the Saint-Charles train station. He felt entirely unlike those men, who seemed to travel like it was a chore: businessmen in constant movement who no longer looked at or spoke to each other. They pushed and shoved in their stiff suits, each following his path without paying attention to others, taking care to interact as little as possible. This was the sadness that came with city life, as Giovanni would discover. At the entrance to the station, the passengers stopped at the kiosk to buy newspapers, forming a seemingly infinite queue of men in grey and black hats. Giovanni wanted to buy a map that would show him more of the city, and perhaps a newspaper. His turn came and the kiosk agent greeted him with a broad smile; he didn't look like the usual customers. The young man attempted an unsteady "Bonjour" — it was one of the only words he knew and he was eager to get it right. He saw an Italian paper, the *Eco d'Italia*, slotted among the dozen or so papers hanging in the back of the stand. That must mean there were a lot of his kind here. He made his way down the street leafing through the paper, its broad pages flapping like sails on either side of his face. The warm ink stained his fingers as he scanned the lines with impatience. Finally, here was something: *Room to let in family home. 18, rue Belle de Mai. Ask for Gustavo. Second floor, on the right.*

The road was long, lined with pink houses that all looked alike. Giovanni recognised a type of flower growing along their walls that was supposed to represent the passion of Christ. A lizard darted into a crack. The little creatures sat basking in the sun like the *vecchio* at the Aragosta, Giovanni thought fondly. He kept on walking as he looked for number 18. He saw a shop whose sign read *Cioccolateria*, and his heart swelled at the comfort of being among his own. Three Italians were walking down the street, laughing loudly with confident smiles. Giovanni said hello to them. *Ciao*, they said as they passed. Hearing the word here in France soothed him more than he cared to admit. Finally, he arrived at number 18. He climbed the spiral staircase to the second floor and knocked on the door. A thought suddenly gripped him: what would he say if they spoke to him in French? A voice called out: "I'm coming, I'm coming!" in Italian; Giovanni was reassured. A few moments later, an old woman opened the door, leaving the chain on: "Can I help you?" she asked before letting him in. The young fisherman observed the old woman, her skin grainy like an old tree with few leaves left on it. Beneath her wrinkled, face she wore slippers and a nightgown. Her small, nervous hands moved constantly as she spoke: "I'm Domenica. This is Gustavo's house; he's my daughter's husband," she explained in her creaking voice. She bombarded the young man with questions as she showed him around the family home. Did he know the gospel of Saint Matthew? How often did he go to mass? What about confession? She sat him down in an armchair and offered him some coffee. There was always hot coffee ready in the afternoon, she said. Despite her age, Domenica drank it as often as she could. Giovanni scanned the apartment, sitting uncertainly in his armchair. The place was poor but clean. There were no ornaments or flourishes, except for the icon of the Virgin and the copper crucifix hanging above the chimney. He was eager to see his room and enjoy the simple pleasure of lying on a bed, where he could look up at the ceiling and let his mind wander. The old woman came back from the kitchen. Giovanni had already had enough of her and wished she would stop with her questions. Domenica began telling him about her family, sparing no detail; at least she wasn't asking him any more questions. Giovanni pretended to listen, though Domenica hardly seemed to care if he was or not. He noticed a family photo displayed on the commode. A woman's face called out to him. There was something distinguished about her; something that stood out against the rough clothes and postures of the other family members. She had an absent smile, which Giovanni liked. He saw himself in its absence. He had also felt different from his own family. Was it vanity, this feeling of being separate; that inexplicable impression of not having been born where you should be, and needing to spend your life seeking out that place and the fulfilment it would bring? Was it a betrayal of his parents? Domenica interrupted his thoughts by raising her voice and fixing her eyes on the young man: "My son-in-law will be home soon. You're waiting for him, aren't you?"

3.

Fiora clapped her hands together twice, with a contented smile on her face. Her day's labour was at an end, and in the Pacchiano household that meant it was time to gather around the table. Gustavo rose from his armchair with a slight stagger and pulled out his chair noisily. He smiled placidly and turned to his two children, Maria and Claudio: "Come on, let's eat!" The young lady set a basket of bread in the centre of the table, ignoring her brother who mimicked her stilted manners as he filled the wine glasses. He wore his hat low over his eyes just like his idol, Humphrey Bogart — it almost fell in the steaming pot of soup Giovanni was eyeing hungrily. Gustavo gestured to his son to fill his glass higher. Domenica, the grandmother, stood like a sentinel at the head of the table: she had taken to standing up in prayer during mealtimes, rosary beads in hand. This did not stop her from casting a disapproving look at her son-in-law, who was already drunk before the meal started. Fiora sat down among her family and invited Giovanni to join them. "We don't stand on ceremony here, my lad," added Gustavo affably. He was the first lodger the Pacchianos had taken in since their grandfather died, leaving a room available. They had decided to rent it out, despite Domenica's reticence. "It will bring in some extra money," Fiora had insisted. Her pragmatic nature meant she was the family's decision-maker, Gustavo being unable, or unwilling, to manage the household finances. Nevertheless, it was he who had met Giovanni and spoken with him earlier, Fiora having come home late from the factory. "You can stay ten days to start with, then we'll see," Gustavo had concluded with an offhand expression. The boy seemed pleasant enough and didn't look like a low-life. Domenica observed the intruder joining them at dinner. He showed little decorum; his eyes were fixed on the soup pot and he barely spoke. The old woman spoke curtly as she asked Maria to say grace before they ate. The young woman joined her hands: "Lord, bless this meal and those who prepared it, and give bread to those who have not." Gustavo raised his eyes to the heavens; he was too impatient for these sanctimonious rituals. He grabbed the ladle: "Some soup, Giovanni?" The young man held out his plate and began to slurp down his soup. Tongues began to wag; Giovanni remained silent. They observed him with curiosity. Was he shy, or just ill-reared? Gustavo addressed Giovanni in an attempt to pry him from his silence:

"So, you're from Livorno? What brings you to Marseille?"

"I'm looking for work. There are hardly any jobs anywhere in Italy."

"My husband works on two building sites. I have a job, and Claudio does too. So we have four incomes for the family. The only way to earn is to work," Fiora concluded.

"Education is important too," Maria interjected.

"You and your schooling! Your stenography classes don't put food on the table. And they cost us an arm and a leg," her mother reminded her.

"Fiora, leave Maria be," Gustavo sighed.

"Papa, don't call me Maria! In France it's 'Marie'," the young girl said irritably.

Giovanni gathered that Maria, who was studying to be a stenographer in a school in the city centre, was proud to live in France and speak French properly. Apparently her dream was to work in the French civil service. Her father applauded her devotion to her studies, and Domenica her devotion to God: Maria accompanied her grandmother to mass every Sunday. Maria seemed to be headstrong; she rebuffed their praise and hated speaking Italian in the home. Giovanni was astonished by her behaviour.

"How was your day on the site?" Fiora asked to ease the tension.

"The boss has promised us work for the next two years," Claudio replied.

"Two years, that's a lot of work!" blurted Giovanni, surprised.

"There's plenty to be had in Marseille," Gustavo assured him.

"I was able to leave school at thirteen and get a job as a stonemason on the building site just like my father," Claudio explained with pride.

"You don't need a diploma to get a good job," Fiora said, looking at her daughter.

"Our daughter's working hard so she can get a job in the civil service. We'll all be proud of her," her husband retorted, finishing his glass.

Fiora returned to the kitchen, not bothering to respond. She took a whole sea bass, roasted in olive oil, from the oven. Gustavo placed his hand on Maria's shoulder, showing her that she had his approval and support. Giovanni was filled with pity for the young girl, who finished her bowl of soup without another word. He smiled at her; she paid as little attention to him as she did to her mother's comments. She was eager for dinner to be over. Fiora set down her platter on the table with authority, grumbling:

"Claudio, would you take off that hat?"

"It brings evil into the house," Domenica added.

Claudio removed his hat with a casual air. In this house, they still treated him like a little boy, even though he had a job and a fiancé. What more would it take for them to treat him like a man?

"That fish was expensive. I hope you appreciate that, Giovanni. We get the best fish in the world here, but nothing this good comes cheap!" Fiora told their guest with a satisfied smile.

Domenica looked up from her rosary:

"I was the one who prepared it this afternoon. I didn't even have the time to play tarot, but my daughter has no skill in the kitchen. Somebody has to do it."

After saying her piece, Domenica closed her eyes and resumed murmuring in Latin. Giovanni found the old zealot comical. There was nothing glorious in her obstinacy, pretending to be praying but listening to everything around her. Standing back from the table was just a better position from which to pronounce her judgements. Giovanni quickly saw how much influence she held in the family, and that he would have to earn her respect, if not her adoration. Nobody seemed to pay any attention to her comment, and Fiora continued:

"The boss gave me six metres of blue fabric 'for your dedication and overtime, *Madame Pacchiano*', as he calls me."

"I'll use it to make a tablecloth," Domenica decided.

"Speaking of overtime, the workers' union is gathering to demand a pay increase," Claudio told them.

"We're Italian; the pay increase probably won't apply to us," his father sighed, disheartened.

"If we vote for the socialists, we might get something."

"I doubt that would be the case. Just last week the French workers went on strike to protest cheap Italian labour," his father replied sceptically.

"A strike!" Giovanni said with disbelief.

"Indeed. You shouldn't be afraid, but in some parts of Marseille you'll see signs saying 'No to Italian workers'," he added with a tone of despair.

"My husband and my son are both proud supporters of the socialist party, even though we're not French yet," Fiora said, exasperated.

"The day we become French," Claudio interrupted, "we'll get the same pay, the same benefits and all the perks of being citizens."

"For now, we only have immigrant status," Gustavo explained.

"We really can't complain. We all have jobs now!" said Fiora.

Maria furrowed her brow, not missing the veiled attack. They resented her lack of solidarity, the way she denied her origins, and the fact that she didn't have a job above all.

"God be praised," Domenica offered.

"What's important is work and money; God has nothing to do with it," Fiora stated with conviction.

"God has something to do with everything. And you'd be better off if you went to church to pray!" her grandmother replied haughtily.

"I don't have time to spend all day praying; I go for the important feasts, and that's plenty."

"All you think about is work; you can't take that money to the grave."

"We Italians are good workers, and we're proud of it."

"Mama, please. We're French now," Maria sighed.

"We don't get the same benefits or pay that they do, and they call us *macaronis*," Claudio shot back.

"What about you, Giovanni? Have you found work?" Gustavo asked, not liking to see his children arguing.

"I have a meeting tomorrow about a job, but I'm not sure."

"You should become a stonemason," Claudio interrupted.

"Well, if you can't find something you can come to the site with us!" Gustavo assured him in a paternal tone.

"Here in Marseille you can always find something," Fiora insisted.

"That's true. You'll see, there's plenty of work here in France."

The meal was over, and they left the table to take their coffee in the living room. Sitting in his armchair, Gustavo stroked his belly and said lazily to his son: "Talk to Giovanni some; I'm going to doze off for a bit." The two boys began chatting, and Fiora made for the kitchen, where she would serve the coffee in the fine porcelain service she'd received as a wedding present. Music rang out through the house: Maria had gone back to her bedroom to listen to records. Fiora sighed as she thought how her daughter did not appreciate the value of things. She could have found work long before now, making soap or in a factory. Instead, she wasted her time shut up in her room, studying her days away. Maria was finally free to daydream and she listened with glee to her latest Charles Trenet album.

Nobody understood her, but that didn't matter as long as she could enjoy these precious moments of solitude when they came. She opened her wardrobe to pick out a dress for her next stenography class. Her wardrobe was home to all her indulgences; this was thanks to her father, who never tired of spoiling her. To work for the French government you had to dress prim and proper. It was a status, a privilege. This skirt was too long; too austere. This dress was too form-fitting, and perhaps a bit racy. She needed to be discreet yet elegant, like a model civil servant. She already imagined what her job would be like. She'd have her own typewriter, a technological marvel that would enable her to write poetry, stories and even novels. She could write out all the thoughts that came into her head. Learning to be a stenographer was not a chore to Maria, but a ticket out. She had promised herself that she would complete every task given to her and even work extra hours. "Maria, can you turn down that music? We can't hear ourselves in here!" Gustavo yelled from the living room. Claudio grinned at Giovanni:

"It's been the same serenade every night since Charles Trenet released his last song. Maria loves French music."

"And my son loves Humphrey Bogart," Gustavo added.

"He's a legend!" Claudio beamed. "Have you seen *Casablanca*?"

"No, I don't get to the cinema much," Giovanni replied honestly.

"Ah! You should; it's a great story about a love affair between Bogart and Bergman," Fiora added. "Now Claudio's trying to get his fiancé to agree to go to Casablanca for their honeymoon! The fool wants to go all the way to Morocco!"

"Your fiancé?" Giovanni asked, surprised.

"Two years now. She's Italian, but she works in Marseille."

"What about you, Giovanni? What do you do for fun?" asked Gustavo, taking a draw on his cigar.

"I like to play the harmonica. I play *tarantellas* and some blues."

"Did you say blues?" Claudio jumped at anything American.

"Can you play us a tune?" asked Fiora, who was slouched on the end of the couch.

Before Giovanni could respond, Gustavo called his daughter to join them: "Maria, come and listen!" The young man was to entertain them. Giovanni stood up shyly and faced his audience. Maria joined them begrudgingly and rolled her eyes, wondering what the fisherboy could possibly have learned to play in whatever sea-salted backwater he came from. The Pacchianos were sitting comfortably. Maria remained standing and smiled as she watched the young man quiver and fumble to remove the instrument from his pocket. Giovanni felt intimidated. He put his lips to the harmonica and took a deep breath. Domenica took on an air of blissful innocence as if she were at mass. The fisherman began playing a Sonny Boy tune. He closed his eyes and let Livorno return to him. Emotion washed through his heart. The swelling of his soul poured into the harmonica, as it had once done when he played on his *gozzo*: the infinite freedom of music within the prison of routine. He'd dreamed of a life elsewhere, and the sadness in his desire was something only music could express. The blues took both courage and regret, and he had both in full supply. As he played, Giovanni allowed his desire for life to possess him. His blues were deep and powerful. Maria watched him with fascination. She'd been blindsided and sat down alongside her family. There was something deep about him after all. His eyes were open but glazed over. Maria tried to decipher the man who suddenly seemed beyond her reach. Her eyes wandered over his face; he was handsome. It was impossible to know who he was in this moment, or tell where his mind was. She suddenly understood what it meant to be a fisherman, and the innate poetry of a life spent battling the sea.

"I haven't seen one of those in years," Gustavo said when Giovanni put the harmonica back in his pocket.

"They're pretty rare these days. My father gave it to me."

"I think it's wonderful to be able to play an instrument," Fiora insisted.

"Maria, you should try the piano," Gustavo suggested.

"Marie, please, not Maria."

"He could play at the church," Domenica suggested.

"He's not going to play that at the church!" Maria scoffed.

"And why not?" Fiora grinned.

Giovanni sought Maria's eye; he hadn't spoken to her since he arrived.

"Maria, are you learning French?"

"It's Marie, not Maria. And to answer your question, I'm learning to write fluently in French."

"I'd love to learn French."

"It's a Latin language, like Italian. You'll pick it up quickly," she assured him with a smile. "How did you learn to play the blues?"

"It's a long story, but the short version is that I learned from a US Marine."

"An *American* taught you?" Claudio gasped.

The grandmother's snoring kept Giovanni awake; it seemed to shake the whole house. A feeling of satisfaction and contentedness had settled over him. Happy to be sleeping in a real bed, he let his eyes blur against the ceiling. The Pacchianos had enjoyed his performance. He knew that he'd never played with such intensity before, and no wonder – it was the first time he'd felt the blues since he arrived in Marseille. Pride had awoken in him now that he'd followed his dream. He remembered how that feeling started: after the day's fishing, he'd wash the *gozzo* quickly so he could go and see Benjamin at the US Navy barracks. When Giovanni arrived at the camp, he'd say "Benjamin" timidly to the security guards. They escorted him to the soldiers' dormitory. Giovanni was proud when he entered the smoky room where those American heroes slept. He felt privileged, the kid from Livorno they welcomed into their pack. He got on with everyone despite his age. They all said *hello* or waved to him, and offered him cigarettes and even chewing gum. He looked at them with admiration, those big fellows who played at cards and threw darts at pin-up pictures. Some of them sat in the corner to write to their sweethearts or their families. They proudly swapped pictures of the girls waiting for them at home. It gave them courage and lifted their boredom. Others did push-ups and sit-ups. They counted their reps and sometimes high-fived each other when they finished. Some of them read comic books. Benjamin, meanwhile, was the group's musician. He took Giovanni aside to teach him the blues. The young boy idolised him. Ben had given him a book of songs by Sonny Boy, and the young fisherman buckled down to learn the notes and riffs so he could play his first song. He blew clearly into the holes as Ben corrected him patiently. Purse your lips like you're about to kiss a girl, and use your tongue to pick the note you want, Ben mimed by kissing his own hand. What a way to learn the blues! Giovanni had never even kissed a girl, but he made sure never to mention that. The young fisherman fell asleep with a smile on his face.

4.

What would they want him to do? Giovanni waited on the steps of the church of Saint-Antoine, tying and re-tying his laces and fixing his hair in a constant cycle. He paced back and forth in front of the church. Paolo the Fixer was late. He wished he hadn't got himself into this mess as he sized up the people coming in and out of the church. He stared at the man reading his paper, then another who was wandering back and forth, and looked out the corner of his eye at a young woman who hurried into her building, her basket of shopping in her hand. An old woman emerged from the church after her morning prayers and looked at the fisherman with curiosity. Did she know what he was doing there? Giovanni looked away, ashamed, but the old woman walked down the steps and mingled with the passers-by without giving him another thought. Impatience had made him suspicious; she was just a churchgoer. An old believer with nowhere else to go. How would she have known Mr Capuani? Still nothing. He was definitely at the right meeting point; he'd checked a hundred times, retracing his steps, doubting himself, and coming back. He wanted to flee and seek refuge in the thick nest of the city. But his legs would not carry him from the steps. He'd already been warned not to run, and assured that his new employers would find him and skin him like a hare should he try. It was not worth the risk, Giovanni reminded himself. And he'd get paid for his labour. The work they gave him might not be so bad. But what the hell did they want him to do? The question pounded over and over in his head. He had no skills to offer them. He knew nothing about Marseille. Finally, Giovanni spied the figure in the *montecristi* hat, striding across the square while chewing on a cigarette. Giovanni felt a surge of relief; at least he was in the right place. Paolo the Fixer removed his hat and twirled it around his finger, calling out:

"Come on, let's get going — we have a lot to do!"

"Right," Giovanni replied obediently.

"I'll say that you're a friend of mine, OK?"

"OK. What should I say?"

"You don't say anything. Just watch and learn."

With that, the pair headed into the labyrinthine streets of old Marseille. Giovanni followed Paolo, obeying the instruction to stay silent. In return, Paolo occasionally gave him a look to reassure the boy that they were on the same team. Eventually, they came to a corner where a few streetwalkers were plying their trade. A red light hung above the entrance to an old building; Giovanni did not yet know what this meant. A man was sitting with his back to the door, waiting with contented indolence while his brown face baked in the sun. Giovanni wondered if he was there to meet them, or just a doorman. The man saw Paolo the Fixer coming, rose lazily to his feet and gave a friendly wave to the mobster, who said with steely neutrality: "I'm here to see the owner" and shoved past him impatiently. Inside, a heavy, bald man was slumped over the counter, sliding a glass of whisky around on the bar. He was tucking his shirt back into his trousers when he noticed Giovanni. "Who's this?" he asked. "He's a friend of mine," Paolo assured him with a cold smile. The man acquiesced, nodding to the shy-looking young lad. After this brief introduction, the young fisherman tried to examine his surroundings; 'watch and learn', Paolo had told him. The atmosphere was dank and heavy with the smell of stale alcohol. Sitting at the bar, three women were chatting about the dip in customers that month.

"I hope the skinny one comes back today."

"I'm looking forward to the big one with the blue eyes."

"Ah! I don't like him. He's a bit of a nutcase."

"Only 'cause you don't know how to handle him."

"Listen to this one! If you keep that up we're going to have to settle this outside!"

They burst out laughing. The girls here teased each other with affection; they hugged and kissed each other often. Inside these walls, there was no privacy. They looked out for each other and faced everything together. They shared the same men and gossiped about their sexual habits. The johns were reduced to their physical characteristics; the fat one, the big one, and so on. The girls didn't need to know their names: their job was to get them hard, get them off and get them coming back. A satisfied customer was a source of regular income for the owner, who paid the prostitutes based on their level of experience. Not having to work in the street was a benefit they worked to protect; their graces and their tricks of the trade set them apart from the other girls. Sometimes they got clients who were neurotic or twisted; this never worried them, as long as they had the owner's protection. They recognised Paolo the Fixer, who was busy negotiating the 'rent.' After a moment, they noticed the odd-looking kid observing them, and their chatter petered out. They stifled laughs and winked at each other. Embarrassed, the young fisherman looked away. The place was a dive; the ground was carpeted with cigarette ends and lifeless cockroaches, likely dying of suffocation. The prostitutes lit cigarette after cigarette as they chatted. The place must bring in a ton of money, thought Giovanni as he noted the crates of whisky and pastis that had just been set down on what seemed to be a dance floor.

"How can I help you today?" the owner asked Paolo.

"I'm here to collect Mr Capuani's *pizzo*."

"*Pizzo, pizzo*...let's see. This month we managed to scrape up a hundred and sixty francs."

"Is that all?" Paolo the Fixer eyed him with an unconvinced expression.

"I only have twenty girls here."

"What about the booze?" Paolo demanded, nodding at the crates.

"Alright, alright, let's cut to the chase. Two hundred and fifty francs."

"That's more like it," Paolo the Fixer responded. "We'll ensure your business stays protected."

The fat man handed him two hundred-franc notes and a fifty, as Giovanni looked on with fascination. He'd never seen so much money in one pair of hands. Who the hell were these people? The door to the joint opened, and a customer walked in.

"Who's in charge here?" he mumbled as he staggered inside.

"I am, good sir," the big man answered politely. "Pick a girl. Twenty-five with bedsheets, twenty without."

The clamour began; as Giovanni and Paolo left they heard the hookers croaking at one another: "He's mine, he's mine!"

Paolo and Giovanni went looking for a taxi. They found themselves on a busy street, where Paolo flagged down a car that was trundling slowly along.

"Where are we going?" the fisherman asked.

"Get in!" Paolo the Fixer told him with a snide grin. "To the dump, if you please," he told the driver.

Sitting in the back, Giovanni observed the streets gliding past the window as they passed through the outskirts of the city. The roads were lined with shantytowns built from bits of scrap, and liable to collapse at the mere sight of a storm. The thick quilts intended to seal up the windows could barely withstand the rising wind. The war had left its mark, and people – most of them immigrant workers – had built these haphazard encampments while they waited to integrate into the local population. The young fisherman noticed the smoke that billowed from the canvas roofs. The residents piled up rubbish and burned it to heat their water. A boy was playing with a tyre, rolling it along the verge of the road. People entertained themselves however they could, with whatever they had to hand. Children jumped around in puddles of mud streaked with white suds, which trickled down from where their mothers had thrown the washing water into the gutter. Clothes hung on strings of cord tied between posts. The young man was deep in thought. He was now Paolo the Fixer's partner. What would his mother think about that? He had abandoned the values she'd tried to teach him. She'd be furious. Had her son really left everything behind just to become a petty crook? The vehicle slowed down and turned on to the dirt road that led to the dump. The young man continued looking out the window. The shantytowns had disappeared. There was no-one around; they must be getting close. He thought suddenly of the Pacchianos. Would he have to betray them too? His worried stare turned to Paolo the Fixer:

"What do I have to do?"

"For now, just stay calm and keep quiet."

"How many days do you need me for?"

"It won't be every day. For now, you're doing fine," Paolo the Fixer reassured him.

"We're here," the driver said.

The two men got out of the car, and Paolo the Fixer led the way through the mounds of filth. Gulls hovered cautiously overhead. The mountains of garbage gave off an incredible stench, made worse by the heat. Giovanni felt the air might choke him and covered his nose with his arm.

"How do you breathe in this?" he asked Paolo.

"I'm used to it," the gangster replied.

Alongside the path, workers waded ankle-deep into the rubbish, their plastic boots torn to shreds by the rubble and scrap metal. They pulled out whatever could be used as fertiliser or sold to farmers, and wiped the sweat from their beaded foreheads before plunging their hands back into the shapeless mass of coagulated filth. Giovanni felt sick. He was about to vomit when they finally arrived in front of a large brick building. One of the workers called his manager, who emerged dressed in a three-piece suit that clashed with the fetid, apocalyptic landscape around them. He shook Paolo the Fixer's hand, who gestured nonchalantly to Giovanni:

"He's a friend of ours."

"Pleased to meet you."

"Mr Capuani must have told you we were coming?" Paolo the Fixer asked him in a friendly tone.

"Of course; I've been waiting for you."

The manager took out a wad of notes from his desk drawer and began to count them out. He was proud and detached, unfurling the dirty money like cards at a poker table. "There you go," he said as he handed the notes to Paolo, who quickly slid the wad into his pocket. "Many thanks. You can count on our friendship and our support."

People recognised Paolo the Fixer by his *montecristi.* In the Belle de Mai neighbourhood, residents looked at him with respect. Two women on their way home noticed the mobster:

"Look, it's Paolo the Fixer!"

"And Graziano!"

"I don't think that's Graziano, but he's wearing a nice pair of loafers."

"Maybe he's the new recruit."

"Let's hope this one's a bit more understanding about the *pizzo*."

Paolo the Fixer and Giovanni climbed the stairs of one of the buildings, the mobster whistling gaily. They reached the third floor, and Paolo the Fixer knocked on the door. There was no answer and not a sound to be heard. Paolo the Fixer turned the doorknob violently, but it did not open. "Open this damn door or I'll knock it down!" he roared. An old man opened it; Paolo the Fixer shoved him aside and dragged the young fisherman into the room. Seeing the two gangsters, the old man bowed his head in fear and respect, and said in a plaintive tone:

"Don't worry, we'll give it to you! Metodio! Metodio! The *picciotto* are here! Bring the *pizzo*!"

A baby could be heard crying in its makeshift crib. An old woman trembled in her armchair, knitting in hand. She stared blankly at the crook and his associate. She knew why they were there. Metodio had failed to pay his *pizzo* to Mr Capuani on several occasions. Metodio's wife soothed the baby while he looked for the money he owed the boss. Giovanni looked around him. Cooking pots hung from the kitchen wall, and an Italian flag had been pinned to the ceiling. The emblem of a nation; of a community. The Italian families had rallied to the strength of a powerful leader. Seeing the work boots on the threshold, memories of Livorno flashed in Giovanni's mind. He saw the fishing boots he would toss on their doorstep when he came home. Here was a simple, devout family like his own. There were icons and little statues dotted around. What life could they be hoping for? Their child had just been born, and the family was already being harassed by Capuani's men to pay their taxes. Paolo the Fixer was getting impatient: they knew that he would come at the end of every month, on the same day and at the same time, so why weren't the fools ready? Metodio finally emerged from his bedroom with a scared look on his face and a handful of crumpled notes in his hand. He handed them gingerly to Paolo the Fixer, who counted them with mechanical detachment. This done, he put the notes in his pocket and slapped the son in front of his father.

"If you have money for statues, you have money for me. The next time I knock on your door, be ready."

Giovanni felt a swell of pity for the old man, who'd just watched his son scramble desperately to gather the *pizzo*. He kept his eyes to the floor and followed his colleague out.

Sitting in his wood-panelled office, Mr Capuani waited impatiently for Paolo the Fixer and Giovanni to return. Behind him, a painting of the Virgin and Child brought a feeling of calm to the room. Mr Capuani was tired of dealing with administrative documents and letters of intent and threw his pen down on the table. He spun his globe around and thundered: "Where are they?" His men did everything in their power to collect the taxes, and he made every effort to ensure the protection of the Italian community. His recent request for a wage increase for workers had failed. Franz the German jumped up from his chair to try and calm his master's impatience. He gently returned the pen to its holder with a swift, precise movement that spoke to his excessive perfectionism. The former prisoner of war did not like to see his boss angry. Things would work out, whatever the situation was now. These were passing concerns. The two men would be along soon, but the boss was irascible:

"Get tonight's pay ready."

Graziano emerged from the accountant's office, eager to show his devotion to the boss. The accountant, whom they called 'the Brain', was responsible for keeping Mr Capuani's books. Everything was recorded to the last detail, and every penny accounted for. Everything was written down. His office was overflowing; he arranged his binders on shelves and filed papers in a pile that he kept among the binders. They avoided talking to him at the end of the day; he was to be left alone. Grasso's chewing annoyed the Brain, who was too flustered to arrange his papers.

"I could glue them to one another with that nougat you're chewing," he snickered at Grasso.

"Have you finished?" Graziano asked, eager to get his pay.

"A few more minutes and you can go and buy your donuts," he said with another snicker.

Graziano gave him an aggressive look. The Brain always sniggered at whatever he said, toothpick between his teeth. He was disgusting. Where had the boss dug him up, anyway? The accountant had been working for Mr Capuani for over 15 years. He was meticulous and always on time – except on payday. Someone knocked at the door. Franz laid a hand on his gun. That must be them. Grasso opened the door, and Paolo the Fixer entered the office, followed by Giovanni. Paolo the Fixer set down the pile of money on Mr Capuani's table, which the Brain scooped up to count.

"Any problems?" the boss asked with suspicion.

"No trouble. Everyone paid up," Paolo the Fixer replied.

"What about the kid?"

Paolo the Fixer raised his right hand to signal that Giovanni's initiation into the organisation had gone smoothly. The boss gave a slight smile and handed his leather briefcase to Franz. The Brain handed twenty-five francs to Giovanni. Their day was coming to an end.

5.

At the textile mill, the machines were running at full tilt, their deafening noise preventing the workers from talking to one another. The hum of the spinners reverberated throughout the vast hall, shaking the windows of the manager's office on the first floor. From the gangway, he oversaw the women working in their neatly spaced rows, like a regiment from the last war. The women on the floor knew that they, like soldiers, were replaceable. They took pride in their work, and the arrival of the new English machines would mean there was less of it to go around. Some were getting ready to look for jobs elsewhere, although they would miss the friends with whom they exchanged knowing looks when the supervisor turned his back on them. He was always there to keep an eye on them, never giving even a hint of a smile. Wearing their white or blue blouses, the *midinettes* were divided up to undertake a series of highly specific – and repetitive – tasks. At the entrance, a dozen or so women were washing and preparing swathes of cotton, linen, hemp, raw wool and silk with meticulous care. Their practised hands worked expertly to separate the short fibres from the long. With their pairs of combing cards in hand, a second group of employees would comb out the textile fibres. Next, everything would be wound onto spools. The last group, which included Fiora, watched over the spools that had been loaded onto the racks, letting the thread out through a porcelain hoop. This was what they called warping in the trade. Fiora loved her work; she arrived at the factory on time every morning, and like all the *midinettes,* she kept her uniform neat and clean. After the laundry, she dunked her blouse in hot water laced with starch before she ironed it. Once the mixture had fully soaked into the material, its light weave looked almost as good as high-end fabric. She was proud to wear it and an exemplary employee. She never hesitated to work overtime and hoped her devotion would help her climb the ladder. The more she worked, the more she earned, although a kilo of linen was worth one worker's salary. She was responsible; she was essential. She would make herself seen and made a point of staying at the factory when the others were eager to get home. No job was entirely secure, and she wanted to be a model employee. "Stay focused, Madame Pacchiano, you're doing an excellent job," the boss shouted down to her. She smiled in response; there was no point in trying to respond amidst the din. Fiora kept a trained eye on the thread feeding constantly through the loop. Her mind worked like the machine, her thoughts and worries pouring through in a constant feed. She fretted about her daughter. Maria was a woman now, and it was time for her to find a match, but she was a complicated girl. She hardly seemed to think about family and future, only of her career in the civil service. At least she had dreams; at her age, Fiora had not had the option of continuing her studies and had joined the workforce as soon as she could, with her husband's permission of course. Times had changed, but still: Maria should start working and try to meet someone. Her friends had tried to introduce her to charming young men on many occasions, but all their efforts were in vain. What was the point? Maria would not listen. She was blinkered, either busy typing away on her blasted machine or planning her next visit to the cinema. The thread passing through the loop snapped. Fiora emerged from her thoughts and shut off the machines.

"What's going on?" the boss shouted from the gangway.

"One of the threads was bad, it snapped!"

"Fine, get it fixed and start the machines up again."

Giovanni wasn't so bad, and he was Italian. Could he court Maria? It was too soon for Fiora to tell. She needed to have the young man under her roof for a while longer to get the measure of him. Time would tell if he could get Maria to settle. For now, Fiora liked him because he seemed ambitious. He'd left his whole family behind to find work; a noble motivation indeed. He seemed loyal and hard-working. But her daughter was obsessed with the idea of finding someone French: someone who wouldn't understand them, and who would look down on their traditions and their values.

"On your marks, set, type!" barked the teacher, perched like a sentinel behind the dais. Every week, just before their lunch break, the forty young women in the stenography class were challenged to type out a letter as fast as they could. Ten minutes ticked by to the sound of their furious typing. Two supervisors walked back and forth through the classroom, looking to see which of the girls might make it as civil servants. They took notes in their little pads; these notes would be used at the end of the year to select the few students who had shown excellence in concentration, behaviour and appearance. Only two candidates would be selected to work in the prestigious French civil service. Mentalities had changed since the First World War. Lots of people were taking typing classes; women sought emancipation through work. The teacher knew all her students well, but she focused her attention on those in the front row. There was Françoise, who was probably the most eager, curious and energetic among them. Her energy sometimes worked against her; though she was fast, she made too many typos and left things out. Beside her was Monique, who had a good head on her shoulders. Her behaviour left something to be desired, though; her every gesture suggested nonchalance. They wouldn't like that in the service. Third was Chantal; she had potential, but she was too easily discouraged: the teacher looked with concern at the young woman as she ripped the page from her typewriter and crumpled it in her hands, before putting in a new one and starting everything from scratch. Finally, there was Maria, a young Italian who had merit in spades. It was hard to deny that Maria was her favourite. The girl was fully focused on her task; there were only a few minutes left. She typed faster and faster, still taking care to avoid the slightest error. She continued typing even as some of the girls gave up, discouraged by seeing how far ahead the more competitive students were. Others sighed and ploughed on. Maria kept going, focused on her goal. She wanted so desperately to be a civil servant. She was not obliged to join the workforce, but she knew that being a housewife was not for her. Marriage could wait; that was a goal for the future. She loved being part of a group: her classmates stuck together, and she felt like one of them. She had her place in this group, and it was an important one. The teacher readied her whistle as the girls who had given up looked on. Maria typed faster and faster. The teacher blew three times. Everyone stopped; it was time for lunch.

Students chattered loudly in the school yard; boys were waiting at the gate, and the girls hurried to join them. They shared teenage kisses, eager to show off in front of their friends. The more chaste girls gathered in the inner courtyard to talk about the latest film they'd been to see. Maria and her friends met under the linden tree, as usual.

"I figured out a way to not wear tights when it's hot like this," announced Monique with a crafty smile, leaning casually against the wall.

"Hah, that doesn't surprise me coming from you," Maria laughed.

"All you do is draw a line down your calf," Monique went on, proud of her innovation.

"What if the teacher saw that? Is it worth the risk? You'll get kicked out, and you can wave goodbye to the civil service," said Françoise, scandalised.

"Don't be such a killjoy! Do you have to take everything so seriously?" Monique sighed, lighting up a cigarette.

"I do laugh, I just like to be responsible too. If I find a good husband, he'll be happy to have a wife in the civil service. I'm hoping I have plenty of mouths to feed!"

"I wish I could just go walking along the coves with my boyfriend," said Chantal, jumping on any opportunity to talk about her beau.

"I thought it was over between you two?" Maria exclaimed.

"No way! He's so nice and so handsome, I can never stay mad at him for long."

"But will he marry you?" Françoise asked.

"Our dear Françoise thinks only of marriage," Monique teased, blowing smoke in her face.

"What's wrong with that? You don't want to go ruining your reputation for some good-for-nothing skirt chaser. Who'd want to marry you after that?"

"I know what you're really looking forward to: the wedding night!" Françoise went red and clenched her fists; Monique always knew how to get under her skin.

"Calm down now, ladies," said Maria.

"What about you, Maria? I heard a handsome young man has moved in with you," Chantal probed, always curious about matters of the heart.

"Tell us about him!" Monica said excitedly.

"He's Italian," Maria answered curtly.

On the construction site, a crane was pivoting above the two six-storey buildings. Building was due to be completed in six months, and the workers were hard at it, trying to get finished on time. The Algerians were tasked with lugging the heavy bags of cement to the upper floors. They had no protective clothing and were often heard complaining about the dust that got into their nostrils and gave them a hellish cough. They were hired by the day and were the lowest-paid workers on the site. "Strong lads, those Algerians," exclaimed one of the Spaniards who was working on the rebars that would reinforce the structure. He and his compatriots were cutting the huge steel bars, held up by breezeblocks, which they would then bend into shape by hand. Their fingers and knuckles were streaked with blood; the gloves wore out fast. At the entrance to the site, a container served as an office to the site manager, who was drinking his coffee and muttering to himself. They needed to pick up the pace; the site was behind schedule. He scanned the blueprints in front of him: if they started the third floor today, they'd be able to make up for yesterday's delays. A foreman entered:

"Sir, the masons have finished plastering on the first floor."

"Already?"

"Yes sir, all the teams are done."

"Even Gustavo's? Bring him in here, I want to talk to him."

The foreman left the container and hollered Gustavo's name. Finally, the Italian made his way over to the office. The site manager gave him a pat on the shoulder.

"Gustavo, you and your team are going to start the third floor for me today."

"Ouffa!" Gustavo exclaimed. "We've been hard at it since this morning—"

"Gustavo," the manager interrupted. "I promise you'll get extra pay at the end of the day. Don't let me down."

Gustavo hadn't been given much of a choice; he left the office and wiped his brow with the back of his hand. Now wasn't the time to feel discouraged, but by God he was tired! His back was killing him. He took a quick swig of brandy to restore his strength and went off to find his son, who was busy preparing the mortar: "We're heading up to third!" Claudio whistled to his Italian colleagues and motioned for them to follow him. Of the five men who came with him, Giovanni was the least experienced. He panted, not used to working in the heat and dust of the site. Black droplets trickled over his face like a leaking oil tank. He tried to focus on the money he'd get at the end of the day. "Come on lad, keep up," one of the masons called out to him with an encouraging grin.

Giovanni upped his pace; he was running late. The stenography class was almost over. He ran through the streets of Marseille at a clip. On his way through the Old Port, he bought a cone of snails from a *porteïris*. What would Maria think of this surprise? He felt clumsy. He hurried through the centre of town. He stopped at a fountain and splashed some water over his face. He combed his hair using a bakery window as a mirror.

He wiped the dust from his trousers. He was almost presentable. He finally finished his sprint to the school. He was in such a hurry that he'd forgotten how nervous he was. He paced up and down the street in front of the school, until he saw Maria and Monique chatting gaily on their way home. He slowed his pace and feigned nonchalance as he walked up to the two students. "Maria, Maria!" he called to her. She turned around, surprised, and smiled awkwardly at him.

"I wasn't expecting to see you here."

"It's a surprise," Giovanni explained as he held out the cone of snails.

"I'm sure it is...and it's Marie, not Maria."

"Snails! How romantic," said Monique, rolling her eyes.

Giovanni bowed his head timidly. Maria didn't know what to say. She didn't want to hurt the boy's feelings. It was Monique who broke the awkward silence: "Shall we go for a walk along the *calanques*?"

The sun was setting along the coast as the waves rustled against the sand. Giovanni had taken his shoes off; his footsteps were silent. He did not dare look at the girl walking beside him. He could tell she was lost in thought, absorbed by the landscape. Her shadow fell over the grey pebbles. He felt clumsy again. He was a neophyte when it came to love. Wasn't he too poor to have a chance with this girl? Her candour and grace unsettled and intimidated him. She was singing one of her Charles Trenet songs, her gentle voice wafting into the sea air. Giovanni wished this moment would last forever. Why was life not made up solely of moments when he felt like this, walking alongside a pretty girl? The sun was hot on his neck. His eyes finally met hers; she smiled at him. She stopped singing without realising it; her voice had trailed off as her great brown eyes saw something new. She'd never seen such a look of tenderness as she now observed in the young man's eyes. He blushed. He wanted so badly to kiss her but was petrified. He mumbled a few unintelligible words. She laughed. She took him by the hand to reassure him. They kept walking in perfect silence. It was getting late.

In the Pacchiano household, Domenica was playing tarot with some of her friends. This was how the old women spent their days when the men were working and the house was empty. Domenica served the coffee in their fine porcelain cups. She was attached to her traditions and took pride in being a good hostess. Hospitality was the most important virtue for good Catholics. Ernestina shuffled the cards in her long fingers, her many rings clinking together as she did so. Snug in her pale pink suit, she was the most elegant and refined of the ladies gathered here. She spoke little, fully absorbed in the game. She was the wiliest opponent, never falling for Domenica's tricks. Domenica was holding the money today though, as she was the hostess. Ernestina would have to keep an eye on her. She finished doling out the cards, and Marta made her play with a trembling hand. They pretended not to notice; the poor woman wasn't well. She forgot things often.

"Where did this beautiful porcelain come from?" she asked Domenica.

"It was one of Fiora's wedding gifts. You know that."

"Oh yes, I'd completely forgotten."

Leopoldina smiled at Domenica. This wasn't the first time their friend had expressed her enthusiasm for the tea service. Leopoldina never forgot anything. Her memory was a curse; she repeated everything told to her and everything she saw. She omitted not a single detail and had a knack for making the most banal anecdotes sound like juicy gossip. Her friends enjoyed being entertained by her stories from Belle de Mai, though they couldn't help but wonder if one day they would end up on the wrong end of one of her jibes. "She's such a gossip, you have to watch what you say all the time!" they whispered when she went to use the lavatory.

"I hear the butcher got married!" Leopoldina announced, throwing her trump on the table.

"Is she Italian?" Marta asked, curious.

"Nobody knows!"

"If she were Italian we'd all know her," Domenica said with suspicion.

"Domenica's right! Italian or French, what does it matter to you lot?" Ernestina scoffed.

"If she's French, the butcher will be earning more money."

"So?" Domenica sighed.

"I hear that some Italians in Belle de Mai are going to be given French nationality," Leopoldina agreed.

"Who said that? I'd take these 'I hears' with a pinch of salt," Domenica said.

"I'll always be Italian," Marta replied. "I don't like to pretend otherwise."

"It's not just pretending," Ernestina insisted, "it means more money."

"Between money and loyalty, I side with the nation," Domenica stated confidently. "Not like my daughter, who would have taken French nationality if she could."

"*Ouffa*! Isn't that a fine thing!" said Marta.

"That goes double for my granddaughter Maria," Domenica sighed. The hours ticked by, and the old women finished their game. They left the Pacchiano household one after the other, saying that Domenica's family would be home soon. Domenica would be offended if they all left at once. They'd see each other at Sunday mass. Domenica was on her own again; it was time to prepare dinner before the family got home.

6.

"Dear Mama,

As you can see, I haven't forgotten you. I've been in Marseille for four months now; the time has flown by. I've had so much to do and learn and explore. It's a huge city. I found it overwhelming at first, but there's a magic about it as well. I feel so free here; not knowing anyone is a wonderful feeling. Livorno is just a village compared to Marseille. I think it would be impossible for me to live there again, I'd feel like I was shut up in a cell. There's work to be had here; you can try to make something of yourself. There are lots of Italians in Marseille, so it hasn't been too hard to fit in. We all live as a community in the Belle de Mai neighbourhood. The French call us the 'babi'. You often see posters up in the street saying: "Italians out — French jobs for French people!" A few scammers have even offered me a false ID card if I vote for the socialist party. But with my accent and my limited vocabulary, it will be a while before they stop calling me a macaroni. I guess those idiots haven't tried our food if they think it's an insult to call me that! I miss your cacciucco and our long talks.

Here I live with the Pacchianos, a family from Piedmont who've been in France for a long while now. It's funny to see the two cultures colliding. We start our sentences in French, then finish in Italian. We eat spaghetti and we mop up the sauce with French baguettes. The French and the Italians are like cousins, I think. It hasn't been too difficult for me to learn the language, especially since Maria, the Pacchianos' daughter, gives me lessons at night. She's very patient with me, and makes me repeat things like a parrot so I can try to hold a conversation. My conversations in French are still quite basic, but I can go to the market or introduce myself without sounding like an idiot. Her brother Claudio has introduced me to some of his friends; we play pétanque together. It's a game of skill where you have to throw metal balls as close as possible to a little wooden ball called the 'cochonnet.' Claudio said it means 'little pig', but didn't know why they call it that. Even though I'm usually quite good with games, my first try was fairly embarrassing. I only scored one point, and even that was because I hit someone else's ball with mine. Because I lost, they made me do this old tradition called "faire Fanny." I had to kiss the behind of this fat lady painted on a wooden board. Everyone laughed, and even though I was embarrassed I ended up laughing with them. After all, it wasn't too big a price to pay to make some new friends. We drank pastis all night and sang in the street like happy fools. Pastis is a bit like the limoncello of Marseille. If you'd seen your Giogio drunk as a lord, you'd have dragged me back home by the ear! But here, Fiora and Gustavo aren't looking to teach me any lessons. Gustavo is the head of the family, and he spends all his free time drinking in the cafés. When his wife can convince him to stay at home, he gets bored and finishes all the bottles of wine or pastis. Fiora goes a bit too easy on him; she loves her husband, but the way her mother Domenica looks at him would turn you to stone. I can't stand the old witch. Every night, she begs Claudio and me to play tarot with her, and when we're too nice to say, no we always regret it. She's a snake, always cheating. It's like an obsession with her. Luckily Claudio is a good friend, and we have a few tricks up our sleeves to get back at her. She's deaf in one ear and she can't see that well, so we use that to our advantage. Last night was our crowning victory; I can't remember the last time I laughed so hard! The poor woman thought she was winning, with a chicane in her hand and lots of trump cards, but she didn't realise that Claudio and I had perfected a secret language: we pretended to be singing so we could tell each other what cards we were holding. She thought we were just humming tarantellas, and we took her to the cleaners! She cursed us up and down and couldn't understand how she lost! She was so humiliated she pretended to have a headache so she wouldn't have to finish the game. Claudio and I celebrated by opening up a bottle of French wine and talking all night. It wasn't easy getting out of bed the next morning! I work on a construction site with him and his father, and the days are long. We work with Armenians, Turks and Moroccans. You hear all sorts of languages, it's like working on the tower of Babel! But we manage to understand each other; we share our meals and sometimes our wine. It's very different from the lonely days on a fishing boat. Papa would have enjoyed the feeling of solidarity.

I can feel my eyes closing; it's almost midnight. I have so many things to tell you; I'll continue this letter tomorrow.

Me again Mama. Let me tell you about Marseille. There are so many types of jobs here; people find ways to make a living out of every little thing. Imagine that a pot fixer (they call them 'ferblantiers' here) can work night and day and still have more customers than they can handle, from housewives to chefs. Then there's the hardware man who sells nails from a bucket. When I arrived at the Old Port, I saw the grinder who sharpens knives for all the local merchants. And believe it or not, on Saturday mornings in Belle de Mai we get woken up by the ice cream man, Papa Polo, who honks his horn to announce his arrival. Last Saturday, Maria made me try the pistachio flavour - it's her favourite. Papa Polo cut us a big block of it with his ice pick. We had to hurry home because it was melting so fast on our fingers. We devoured it like little children — we didn't even leave any for Claudio! She was right - it was delicious! Maria made fun of me, I had ice cream all over my face. I got my own back by giving her a 'pistachio moustachio'. It almost suited her! The next day I went to see the shellfish divers at the port. We got on great; they're all Italian, so I enjoyed speaking my own language to them. They couldn't believe I was once a fisherman. I wonder if you'd recognise me now. On Sundays, I wear a suit like a real gentleman. If it weren't for this damn accent, people would take me for a local, a real Marseillais. Maria would like that; she looks at me more and more fondly these days. We went walking along the calanques with her friends last week. It's even more impressive than Gorgona. We went down to the beach and walked along the water in our bare feet. I like to feel the sand between my toes, and I make sure I do it as often as I can. I sometimes go walking alone, to daydream or play the harmonica, and I think of you. That day, though, there was too much chatter. Monique, one of Maria's friends, is always trying to provoke me. "He's handsome, for an Italian! So manly," and stuff like that. It makes me blush, especially in front of Maria. But what could I say to her? I don't want to be impolite and embarrass Maria. I was uncomfortable, but luckily I had a good excuse to get out of there — I'd promised Claudio I'd go to the cinema with him. We went to see 'Dark Passage'. Claudio already knows it off by heart, he's seen it three times this week. Humphrey Bogart is his idol. He's a really stylish American actor who always wears a hat and smokes cigarettes. I love going to the cinema in Marseille; it's where all the young people hang out, especially to court each other. Who knows, maybe one day I'll be there in the arms of some pretty girl. Can you imagine that, Mama?

I hope that you are doing well. It will be Christmas soon; I wish I could be by your side. Life can't be easy without Papa there. I hope that you're managing to live without him. Please say hello to Valentina for me.

With love,
Your Giogio.

7.

The taxi was headed deep into the sinuous back streets of old Marseille on a rain-soaked night; Giovanni watched the droplets trickle down the window as they drove. The city was invisible in the darkness. Paolo the Fixer counted the money he'd taken in that evening. “We're going to have a good night,” he said to his accomplice. Giovanni gave him a tired smile. The day had been hard. He felt heavy and sticky with sweat and was eager to clear his head with an artificial thrill. The car finally came to a stop, and the two men got out and went into the club.

Giovanni crossed the floor, avoiding the noisy groups and the blinding lights of the chandeliers. He stole into a red-carpeted corridor lined with alcoves, where oriental lamps cast a dim red light over the men smoking opium. Giovanni was hypnotised by the gurgling of the fountain that towered over the corridor on its marble base. He dipped his hand into the basin and watched the water run through his fingers. A memory came back to him of Stella pushing him into the fountain at her villa. That was a long time ago when he was just a kid. He went into the last alcove, which was unoccupied. On the floor were two mattresses with red silk covers, topped with tasselled cushions. Everything here was decadent, laid out like an oriental feast. He lay down and stretched out his tired legs. His eyes glazed over as he looked at the subtle pattern of the scarlet wallpaper. A painting caught his eye as he crumbled the opium powder into the pipe. It showed camels crossing the desert, surrounded by a sandstorm. In front of them, two Bedouins were inching forward, trying to cut through the air that whipped about their faces. These old-fashioned images set him dreaming; he felt like those men, battling against whatever unknown fate the Almighty had laid out before them. Life was a long road. He thought of the legend his mother had told him when he was a child, about the family of poor fishermen who invented *cacciucco*. Struggle was part of progress. But today, he needed to restore his strength and relax a little. He took his harmonica from his pocket and turned it over in his fingers. Its silvery surface glowed red in the alcove. The instrument went everywhere with him; it had shone under the Livorno sun, and now it filled with the white smoke that curled from the pipe. He heard the sailors in the opposite alcove smoking what they called the 'drug of the poets.' Long stints at sea were hard on the mind; the sailors needed to clear their heads. One of them greeted him warmly: "Ciao Giovanni! Haven't seen you here in a long while!" The young man smiled briefly at him, then turned away and inhaled another puff. He was not in the mood to chat; he was in melancholy form. His eyelids were heavy, and his thoughts erratic; they came to him one instant and flickered away the next. He liked being in this limbo, between dreams and reality. Everything seemed clear; a soggy heat came over him. It cradled and consoled him. When he was about to pass out, he heard jeering laughter ring out. The two sailors looked at him. They were mocking him. They were in stitches. Giovanni got up to show them that nobody made fun of him and got away with it. But once he was up, he saw that the two sailors were passed out too. His mind was playing tricks on him. He was in a cold sweat. His thoughts ran away with themselves. The trickling of the fountain grew louder as if the water was flowing around him. The gurgling was hypnotic. He saw the alcove fill with dark water. He heard the lapping of waves and the wind of the sea whistling in his ears. His hands gripped the silk bedclothes. He passed out.

He found himself on the open sea, the *gozzo* cutting cleanly through the waves. The horizon was far off, and the lighthouse on the coast disappeared from view. A vulture was perched above the eye painted on the boat. Giovanni observed the huge bird of prey, sitting statue-like before him. The creature's yellow gaze dazzled him. The young fisherman lifted an oar to chase it away. It flew off, beating its great wings, before landing on a bloated body floating in the water. Blood flowed from the throat in a foamy trickle. Giovanni recognised the corpse; it was the prostitute Paolo the Fixer had beaten when she refused to pay the *pizzo*. The vulture cawed as it ate her eyes out. Giovanni was overcome with fear. The boat would not move. He did not know where the coast was; the horizon was all around him. Red clouds gathered in the sky. A hand gripped the side of the boat, and Giovanni jumped. A head rose up. It was his father. The face creased into a smile. A line of blood ran along his forehead, and he cried with laughter as he slid back into the boiling sea. Lightning shook the *gozzo*. He found himself tied up in the warehouse from his first day in Marseille. His mouth was taped shut. Franz the German was pointing his revolver at him.

"Ausgezeichnet!" he said, emphasising every syllable.

Franz the German got up from his chair and walked towards the young fisherman. He ripped the tape off his mouth. He removed a cord from his pocket and slid it around Giovanni's neck. He slapped him.

"Talk. What is the girl's name?"

"Maria. Maria Pacchiano."

"What is the girl's name?"

"The French call her Marie."

Franz the German burst out laughing, his blue eyes colder than ever. He pointed his *beretta* at Giovanni's temple. He looked him right in the eyes as he pulled the trigger. The shot rang out.

Giovanni awoke with a start, wrapped up in the silk bedcover. The walls of the alcove seemed to be shifting amidst the opium fumes. A hand was on his arm; a gesture from the beyond. His eyes blinked open to the face of a stranger. The oddly reassuring face spoke to him: "You seemed like you were having a nightmare." Giovanni was surprised by the apparition, whose wide, almost violet eyes were fixed on him. The man was sitting on a cushion and smoking a pipe. Giovanni suspected he was still dreaming; he couldn't be sure if this man was real. "That's a lovely harmonica you have there," the stranger continued in a pleasant tone. Giovanni liked the suave way he spoke; he seemed very refined. Giovanni observed the signet ring that wound around his finger. "It's a lion; my family's emblem. I can see you're not in the mood to chat, young man." Giovanni smiled at him. He didn't know how to respond; he didn't want to disappoint him. He picked up his harmonica to play some blues. Intoxicated by the scent of jasmine emanating from the handsome stranger, Giovanni improvised a languid melody. Time seemed to stop. Each note resonated around the alcove, seeming like it would hang in the air for eternity. The two men looked at each other, and their eyes locked. Giovanni felt the weight on his shoulders dissipate with the opium smoke. His mind was focused on the man smiling at him. Paolo the Fixer came into the alcove and shook him from his waking dream: "Let's go play cards."

Paolo the Fixer and Giovanni sat around the card table and began a game of *scopa*. The croupier's stony, unreadable face stood out in the darkness as he shuffled the cards in his white-gloved hands. A man took a seat at the table; he was a regular. He had a reputation for keeping his cool at the table and losing a lot of money with a level of dignity that commanded respect. He stroked his long moustache nervously. The croupier dealt out four cards onto the red tablecloth on which all eyes were fixed. The players lifted the corners of the three cards they'd been dealt. The bet was twenty francs. The croupier observed them as they attempted to hide their nerves, but they each had a tell. Paolo ground his teeth, Giovanni scratched his ear impatiently, and the third man kept stroking his moustache between his thumb and index finger. The time ticked away; the cards came and went, and the ante went up and up. The candle wax melted and trickled down the candlestick. Giovanni watched the small flame flickering. Paolo the Fixer had lost all his money. He left the game in a huff and stalked away without a word. Their opponent was tenacious and had decided to stick around. The croupier kept on dealing cards, as static and stiff as his red uniform. Giovanni watched him working like a thing inhuman; a machine unfazed by the lateness of the hour. He held men's fate in his gloved hands, and his composure was his greatest asset. The young man had been sitting there for hours, gambling away his pay and waiting for his luck to turn, but he'd been bored since Paolo the Fixer left. He folded his hand and quit the table, leaving the gentlemen's games behind and heading for the basement.

A doorman kept an eye on the patrons coming up and down the stairs. Giovanni slipped some cash into his inner pocket. "Good luck," the doorman said discreetly. Giovanni walked down the metal staircase that led to the basement. Below, men gathered around a red carpet whistled and shrieked as if they were at a cockfight. Down here, the atmosphere was muggy; men milled about in their shirtsleeves and vests, they spat on the ground, whistled through their fingers, booed and shoved one another. A skinny little Spaniard rolled up his sleeves and shouted: "Give me those dice, it's my turn to throw!" He put on a show; the half-pint knew how to entertain a crowd. Another man sat slumped in a chair, monitoring the games like a grouchy old elephant. In truth, he was a dangerous man, and no-one dared defy him. He counted the points, divided up the players and got rid of troublemakers. A man named Ratto, who got his name from being the stingiest player there, entered the game. He confronted the little

Spaniard by throwing a one-franc coin onto the red carpet. The crowd guffawed; it wasn't much of a bet. Giovanni joined Paolo the Fixer and Graziano as they watched the spectacle, Grasso plunging his meaty hands into a bag of nuts. He chewed them loudly in his flabby jowls, as Giovanni looked on with disgust before throwing a note onto the carpet. He wanted to play. Ratto saw his bet with a few coins and spat loudly on the ground to intimidate his opponents. The Spaniard continued gesticulating to raise cheers from his friends. Giovanni remained aloof with a disapproving smile on his face. Paolo gave him a slap on the back: "Go on boy, I'm betting on you!" Grasso did not protest, observing the scene with a placid air. He never bet but found the show entertaining. The judge gave the signal for the game to commence. The Spaniard threw his dice; it wasn't a great score. Ratto wound up his arm and tossed the dice onto the mat. A four-three. They jeered at him. Was the miser about to lose his money? It was Giovanni's turn.

"Go on, show us what you've got!" sneered the Spaniard.

"Don't burst a blood vessel, it's just a game," Giovanni replied.

"Go on then, throw! I hope you're ready to lose!" Ratto shouted in his face.

"I can't throw with your stinking breath in my face!"

"Ah, every time you play it's the same thing!"

"And get your money out of my line of sight, it's bad luck!"

The other men guffawed; Giovanni knew how to amuse them and bring a little humour to the game. They chortled and waited for the young hoodlum to throw. Giovanni stretched the moment out. He tossed the dice in his hand, then backed up, took a step and threw. He landed a pair of sixes. The crowd howled with joy or disappointment, depending on how they'd bet. They pushed and shoved, notes were snatched from hands, fights started. Giovanni pocketed his winnings. Amidst the din, the Spaniard raised his head and cried out in a rage: "*hijo de puta*!" He believed the dice were loaded, and Giovanni had cheated. Silence fell over the crowd; nobody dared say a word. They looked at him with cruel expressions. "Who said *hijo de puta*?" the judge demanded. The crowd dispersed, but the potbellied judge diffused the situation. The players threw the Spaniard to the ground and rained kicks on him. Then they threw him out of the joint, his mouth bloodied. "Don't come in here again!" the gamblers warned him. Giovanni left Paolo the Fixer and Graziano to watch the dice game, stealing off quietly.

He entered a small salon padded with silk and furnished with couches, divans and loveseats. The scent of white lilies filled the air. Among the flowers and the light of the chandeliers, a few of the club's prostitutes were chatting. They told each other sob stories, their imagined misery rivalling their material woes. They stopped talking when they saw Giovanni and switched to gliding their legs together and adjusting their busts. Their dresses had side slits to show off their pretty, fishnet-clad thighs. They were elegant, as prostitutes go — their makeup was tasteful and their perfume not too strong. Giovanni approached them as a regular, meeting eyes with his favourite.

"My goodness Giovanni, where have you been?" Zézette cried, adjusting the corset that showed off her ample bosom.

"Maybe he wasn't interested in your droopy tits!" her jealous colleague with the bleached hair interjected from behind her.

"What's it got to do with you? Have you seen what you look like? You haven't bagged a customer all night!"

Giovanni grinned at the quarrel he'd sparked. They were fighting over his money as much as his handsome face and good manners. The richest clients weren't always the most graceful lovers. The favourite joined Giovanni and blushed as she took him by the hand. This signal of modesty and shyness pleased him, even if it might have been the symptom of some venereal disease. "Come with me, my fine Italian," said Zézette, removing his hat. "We'll take our usual spot." She pulled back the heavy red curtain and they entered her room. Giovanni sat down on the four-poster bed. He unbuttoned his shirt and let it slip from his shoulders. Zézette lit a candle over the headboard. The young man liked to make love in the light of a burning flame. She straddled her lover, who was lying on his stomach. She rubbed his back and kissed him. He enjoyed the softness of her expert hands and caresses. Her fingers tickled him, sending shivers along his spine. She knew how to pique his desire and make herself seem irresistible. She dug her fingernails into his flesh like a cat. Giovanni closed his eyes, lost in her embrace. His thoughts were blank. He felt his skin tightening, heating up, electrifying. He breathed in her perfume as she leaned over to lick his ear and nibble the lobe with her teeth. The innocent aromas of violet and rose petals contrasted with her mature, lascivious ways. She grabbed the candle and let a drop of wax fall on Giovanni; he tensed up and clenched his fists. She let another drop fall; the drops piled on his skin. He stopped himself from crying out. A face appeared in his mind; that of the mysterious man who'd woken him in the alcove. Startled, Giovanni turned over violently. Zézette lost her balance and fell off him. She got up, stunned. "Is everything OK, my lovely?" The young man said nothing and unbuttoned her corset. Her milk-white breasts slid between his hands. He bit the end of her pink nipple. She wanted to dance for him. She wiggled her hips and sensually removed her skirt, revealing her fleshy legs. She untied her skirt at the back. The young man undressed quickly and motioned for her to join him. Zézette found his expression gloomy tonight. What was up with him? He was usually more eager. Was he fed up with her? She could see that his mind was elsewhere, whatever the reason. "Is something wrong?" she murmured into his ear. His mind was wandering; he thought about the dark-haired man in the alcove. She got on all fours. He caressed her cheeks. He allowed his hands to wander over her body. Zézette's flesh ebbed back and forth in the light of the little flame, and her chestnut hair rustled between his fingers. She breathed hard and clenched her fists. A moment passed. He withdrew and lay down on the bed. "What's wrong?" Zézette whispered. The thought would not leave him and kept his orgasm at bay. He did not want to let his pleasure fizzle out, so he waited on the bed a few moments as Zézette lay down beside him. Eager to finish the session, she asked him if he wanted to continue. He got up and pulled on his trousers.

"Where are you going?"

"I can't," he said as he left her bedroom.

"Where's my money, you little bastard?"

He hurried back to the alcove. The dark-haired man wasn't there, but his cologne lingered in the air. Giovanni had to find him. This meeting was part of his destiny, he somehow knew. Providence had brought them together. He needed to find out why, and solve the mystery. Giovanni retraced his steps, searching for the unknown stranger. Where could he have gone? Surely there was no way their meeting could lead nowhere! He couldn't let him get away so easily.

"What's up, friend? You look lost," a sailor said to him.

"I'm looking for someone; a tall, thin fellow with long hair who looked like some kind of aristocrat."

"He was here, in one of the alcoves. He just left."

Giovanni ran to the exit, still buckling his belt. He galloped down the little street like a madman. A little ways ahead, under the light of a lamp, he made out the dandyish figure walking down the street.

"Hey, Mister!" cried Giovanni, breathless.

"Yes?" the man replied with surprise and satisfaction. "Did I forget something?"

"Yes. No. It's me, Giovanni. I was in the alcove, you woke me up."

"I thought you looked familiar."

"I need to talk to you."

"Meet me at the Fonfon on Sunday at noon, we'll have a bouillabaisse."

"What's your name?"

"Spielman. Aleksander Spielman."

Giovanni walked through the streets of Marseille. He wanted only to breathe the fresh morning air. He had no idea where he was going and strolled at a gentle pace. The morning mist was refreshing after his night in the club. He thought about Aleksander Spielman, whose blue-eyed gaze was stuck in his mind. His dark hair gave off an aroma he'd never smelled before. He was probably from Paris. It must have been five in the morning. Giovanni was tired and dragged his feet over the cobbles of Belle de Mai. The shops would be open soon. The sky was clearing. That man had had such graceful manners. He must come from some great family for it to have its own emblem. Their brief encounter in the alcove had confused him, to the point where he had been unable to indulge himself with Zézette. Marseille was awakening; he returned to the Pacchiano household and went to bed. A feeling of comfort washed over him: the feeling of having met Aleksander Spielman.

8.

At six in the morning, Graziano slid back the heavy door to the warehouse. Franz fidgeted impatiently with the keys. Paolo lit a cigarette, casting furtive glances about him. There was no-one else around. Giovanni was cold and tired; he'd spent the previous day on the site. They went inside as the day's first rays of sunlight spilled over the dusty floor. A musty odour greeted them; there'd been heavy rain the night before. A fresh pile of boxes was stacked at the back of the warehouse. Giovanni knew better than to ask what was in them; curiosity was not kindly received in this workplace. His job was blind obedience, so the boss could be sure that no-one ever saw all the cards he was holding. The four men climbed the stairs to the office. Franz unfolded a map of Marseille on the table. He ran his finger along the map with a studious gaze and stopped at the La Loubière district. It would happen here. Franz looked up at his cohort to choose the right person for the job. Giovanni observed that Graziano was looking away; the slob would always weasel out whenever he could. Giovanni wanted the task to be his. He put his hands behind his back and stood up straight, signalling his readiness to undertake the responsibility. Franz got the message but paused for effect before giving the order:

"You're going to drop off a package."

"Which car?"

"You'll find out when the time comes."

Sitting in the office, Giovanni shaved the blocks of soap into thin slivers, whose purpose was to mask the smell of the drugs that were being moved tonight. His thoughts were heavy. He hadn't had a choice when he arrived in Marseille; Capuani had picked him up, and he'd had to win over this bunch of shameless crooks to survive. They showed not a trace of doubt or remorse about their work; they were animals who hunted easy prey. But was he not one of them now? He completed every task without complaint and even asked for more. He'd developed a taste for money. Like a rat that's tasted blood, there was no going back. He'd become dangerous and greedy. The soap crumbled in his hands; the smell of the lavender cloyed in his nostrils. If Capuani knew...in the end, he wasn't scared of him. It would take more than a little bit of *pizzo* to get him in trouble. The knife slipped in his moist palms; he wiped the greasy blade on his sleeve. Five more bars to go. His everyday life was a lie. He'd never tell his mother about this darker side of Marseille, just his rosy existence with the Pacchianos. What about Maria? Wasn't he lying to her as well? He was a shadow of the fisherman's son from Livorno. Maria didn't know about the work he did for the boss. As far as she knew, all he did was slave away on the building sites. He was lying to the woman he claimed to love. Had he lost his respect for everyone and everything? He was a liar and a traitor to boot. Down below, he watched Capuani's men unpacking bags of heroin from the boxes. They came upstairs, and Grasso opened the door with a leering grin. Behind him, Paolo was smiling as well. What did they have in store for him? Under Franz's watchful eye, the two henchmen dropped the drugs in front of Giovanni, giving each other a knowing look. Grasso unpacked the merchandise. Franz would be the one to taste it; he was the expert. He could not be fooled — he'd used enough heroine to know when it was pure. He cut a line with the blade of his knife and rolled up a hundred-franc note. He snorted the line in one go. They awaited his verdict. He shuddered, and his face contorted. His eyes flickered like an epileptic's. A low wheeze escaped his pinched lips. He seemed possessed for a moment. "*Ausgezeichnet*! The shit is pure." Franz sat down. The drug seemed to tickle the nerves in his face, which juddered with uncontrolled tics and spasms. His jaw was clenched, and his pupils dilated. His eyes seemed to be in orbit. Paolo the Fixer waited patiently for him to come down. Graziano squirmed in his chair and winked at Paolo the Fixer. Giovanni noticed they were in cahoots; something was going on he didn't know about. The buzz of the heroin plateaued, and Franz was back in the room. His face was once again glacial and impenetrable. His brow furrowed, and he licked his lips. "There's something for you. Come on, follow us," he announced to Giovanni in an oddly charming tone. Giovanni was dubious about this pleasantness but had no choice. He followed the three gangsters, who led him to the padlocked door to the basement. Franz spun the key on his finger, then held it out to the younger man, who wondered desperately what they had in store for him as the German inserted the key. The padlock gave way, and the door scraped open to reveal a small, dark space. In the middle sat a tall cage, and an animal lying in the darkness rose to its feet. The creature threw itself against the bars, its raging eyes burning in the dim light. The monster barked and grunted so loudly the walls seemed to shake. Franz flipped the switch, and a weak light bulb hanging from the middle of the ceiling revealed a furious dog. "It's a gift for the boss," Franz sneered, "so don't forget to feed him some meat!"

Giovanni stole through the narrow streets of La Loubière, his package in hand. His steps were hesitant. He was afraid of being caught in possession of the mysterious parcel. The young man doubted that this package contained drugs; it seemed too heavy. His mission was to find the car; Franz had given him a detailed description, but just once. He'd be in trouble if he missed it. He repeated Franz's instructions in his head. He repeated them so often they lost all meaning. He lost his way. The directions hung in his consciousness like a song fading in and out. He cursed his dozy brain. As he tried to remember, he noticed a group of policemen on their beat at the end of the road. The sight brought him crashing back to reality. He was vigilant; his senses on edge. He could almost hear the blood pumping through his temples. He had to act, to find a solution. If they found him he'd be done for. He didn't know La Loubière. He crossed onto the opposite pavement, then decided to retrace his steps. He'd try another route on the cross-streets. It was better to take a detour than to get caught before he'd even started. He went into a narrow passage that opened onto a parallel street. There were people there; he felt like they were looking at him with suspicion. He pulled himself together. Nobody knew him here; why would they be looking at him? For once, he was on his own. Paolo the Fixer wasn't with him this time. It was time to prove his mettle. His expression shifted to one of determination. He was up to the task. Finally, he spied the car parked on a perpendicular street. He looked around; the street was calm, with only a few scattered pedestrians. It was a residential neighbourhood. The vehicle seemed to be locked; he'd have to go the extra mile. But he'd have to do it fast. He took the strip of string steel from his pocket. Paolo the Fixer had shown him how to break into a car a hundred times. He slid the slim blade down the window towards the lock. The time ticked away; he looked for the lock, groping around even though he'd done it before. You had to do these things right. He looked around him. He didn't want to get caught red-handed, and his posture was a giveaway. Suddenly, there was a click; the door was open. A resident walked out onto the street; Giovanni opened the glove box and took out some papers, pretending to examine them with interest. The resident passed and smiled at the young man, who seemed to be thinking hard. He was gone. Giovanni waited a few minutes and read the car owner's license. The moustachioed face rang a bell. *Jules Chapus.* Wasn't he a politician? He looked French, anyway. It was strange, but he had no time to lose. Whoever the moustached man was, he was nobody to Giovanni. He put the package out of sight under the seat and closed the door gently. His task was complete, and he walked back up the little street thinking only of his date with Maria that evening.

Giovanni was waiting for Maria at the Piccolo Fiore. He swept the breadcrumbs from the table with the back of his hand, trying to make the scene as neat as possible before his date arrived. The restaurant was lit by candles stuffed into old Chianti bottles; it was a popular place for Italians to come and enjoy a romantic dinner. He wiped the table once again. He'd combed his hair in the Italian style, with a line down the middle and a light layer of *gomina* oil, in an attempt to impress Maria. He patted his hand around the edges, feeling for errant strands. He hoped that Maria would like this place. It was quiet and intimate, so they could talk as long as they wanted without having to worry about their privacy. Among the seven tables scattered throughout the dining room, a couple were holding hands while staring longingly into one another's eyes. The waiter emerged from the kitchen and served them two dishes: "*Frittura* of courgette for *la signora* and *lasagna* for *il signore. Buon appetito*." The waiter approached his table:

"Would sir like something to drink?"

"I'm waiting for a friend."

"Will you be dining?"

"Yes, of course," Giovanni smiled warmly at him, hoping to curry favour. Everything had to please Maria, even the waiter's demeanour. The said waiter brought two sets of cutlery, wrapped in napkins, to the young man in the stylish three-piece suit. He was in his Sunday best but dressed for something holier than church, the waiter chuckled to himself as he observed Giovanni's fidgeting. The young man asked him what was good on the menu. The waiter replied that everything was good; Giovanni did not seem satisfied with this response. The waiter gave an amused smile and told him: "You should try the *lasagna*. Our chef makes the pasta himself, from scratch." The young man acquiesced: "Perhaps I'll try it. Thank you."

The door opened; it wasn't Maria. Probably someone who worked in the kitchen. He worried that he'd overdone it. The door opened again, and this time Maria walked in. Giovanni rose and pulled out her chair as gallantly as he could, feeling embarrassed and overdressed. Maria walked over to him with timid steps. She was wearing a long skirt and a white blouse, and removed her jacket with small, careful movements as she adjusted to the space. She took her hair out of its bun and let it fall through her fingers, leaving the classroom behind her. The sweet scent of her perfume filled him with vivid emotion. She sat down.

"So why this place?"

"They serve iced melon with *prosciutto*."

"Do they now? I see that *monsieur* hasn't lost his Italian ways after all this time in Marseille."

They talked in the candlelight, Giovanni staring at Maria, whose dark curls bobbed up and down when she was excited. Her eyes dulled when she was remembering something, and her face cast over with sadness. She had a seriousness uncommon for someone her age; he knew she was diligent about her studies, but there was something more to it than that. She carried a weight from another life. Like him, she saw the world as a puzzle to be decoded and understood. Like him, she was determined to conquer it, despite her deceptively gentle nature. She passed her hand over her lips and paused.

"I don't think I really had a childhood, in the sense that I was never carefree. I've never felt...light. I've always had goals, and been working towards something. I've always wanted to get out. I knew I was worth more than this life. When I saw my mother coming home from the factory, dead on her feet, I told myself that I had to study extra hard at school. School was my only ticket out. The only chance I had. I saw my destiny. You know I believe in God, Giovanni. This destiny was to succeed and to free myself. Liberty, independence — they're not just words to me. They're my creed, my psalms, and I'll keep repeating them until I succeed. I work hard at school, ten times harder than the rest. I started at a disadvantage because I'm Italian. I didn't want them to see someone whose future was to be a maid, a worker or a slave. Luckily, when I was a young student I had a teacher called Madame Béranger. She was so nice to me, the most kindly and attentive teacher you've ever met. She was about to retire, and she'd had so many students over the years, but she took a special interest in me. She believed in me and helped me along. If you only knew how much she changed my life. I was so proud that she'd noticed me! I was just a poor

Italian girl from Belle de Mai. She gave me extra homework, and she made sure I did it all. She expected a lot from me. I'd sooner have gone blind than disappoint her."

"You must have really admired her."

"I was very fond of her. They made fun of me at school. The other girls were jealous of the attention I got from Madame Béranger. One day, they put spaghetti in my schoolbag. I put my hand in to get my book, and they all laughed at me. I never found out who it was, but I had my suspicions. Claudine was always giving me dirty looks; I got better marks than her, even though her father paid a tutor to give her lessons three times a week. She was dying of jealousy."

"Did you tell on her?"

"No, I had no proof. And you know, it sort of taught me that I was on my own, so I'd have to be tough. The world isn't fair, but so what? People are nasty and jealous, but what does it matter? They can't stop me. Little Marie doesn't go down that easily!"

"But you have friends now; you're not alone anymore."

"Yes, since I started the stenography class things have changed. I met Monique; she was a bit cold at first, but she has a heart of gold. And then I met the others: Chantal, your typical romantic, and Françoise – she's the wise one. We laugh together, we go out, we feel free. And we help each other too. You know, there aren't a lot of government jobs up for grabs. Sometimes I get really worried. It gets so bad I can't sleep at night. And then I tell myself that I've been successful so far, so there's no reason it shouldn't continue. I pull myself together, and I work twice as hard."

"What about your father? I can tell that he encouraged you, and believed in you."

"Yes, at home he's the only one who thinks school is important. He's a bit too fond of the bottle, but he knows what's going on. He knows that if you don't want to live a life of servitude you have to study. He pinned his hopes on Claudio at first. He's the oldest, and he's a boy. But Claudio has no ambition. His grades were average, and he just wanted to get out and start working. Papa didn't force him; he took him to the building site, and you know the rest. Mama was happy about that because it meant more money coming in. I suppose he's happy. I don't think he's ever realised that Papa is a mason because he didn't have a choice. When he came here, he didn't speak a word of French, so he was counting on his children to succeed. He drinks because he's unhappy; he'd have liked to do something better with his life. Sometimes, when he's had too much, he'll tell me 'Maria, my daughter, I've wasted my life. I'm just someone's minion here. Don't make the same mistakes I have.' "

It was four in the morning; the blue hour, when sun and moon shone side by side over the silent streets. Through the windows, halos of embers could be seen in the fireplaces. A few lost souls wandered the streets with the stray dogs. The streetlamps were coming on; the sky was clearing. The stars faded away. Suddenly, a blast rang out. Shards of glass were sent flying, and the body of a car was torn to pieces. A scream of violence shattered the night. A bomb had gone off in La Loubière. The residents hurried out into the street, the men armed with their hunting rifles and the women in their nightgowns with their children clutching at their legs. A few of them approached the wreckage; there was hardly anything left. They gathered around, their shock turning to anger. Who could have done this to them, here in La Loubière? It could only be those accursed Italians and their mafia; after all, those animals had no respect for civilised society.

9.

"There is money missing from the count. One of you is stealing from me!" Mr Capuani thundered. The Brain opened his binder and presented it to the boss. The numbers could not lie, meaning there was a traitor in their midst. Mr Capuani's bushy eyebrows leapt as he erupted with rage, his thick lips trembling. His fists clenched. He smacked his palm against the globe, sending it into a furious spin as his underlings looked on nervously. Franz remained still; he had nothing to hide. He looked the other three goons up and down. They were pale. "There's *pizzo* unaccounted for. Who is stealing from me?!" Capuani was building into a fit of theatrical fury. Giovanni did not appear to be overflowing with confidence. Paolo suspected him but said nothing; they'd talk about it later. Grasso looked like he was ready to soil himself, but that could be due to any number of reasons. Paolo the Fixer stared at Giovanni. He wanted to shake an admission out of him, find something in his eyes that would give him away. Franz cracked his knuckles one by one, warming up his killing tools. Giovanni watched him do it; each stiff crack sent a chill up his spine. If he got caught, there would be no mercy from Franz. Capuani's eyes picked over them, ablaze with rage. He stopped shouting and let cold steel silence descend upon them. Silence brought confessions; it was far more of a torture than people realised. For the guilty, it felt like endless suffering: the truth was in there, a prisoner clambering to escape, and it took all the body's strength to stop it. Capuani did not move a muscle. He waited, but nothing came forth. One of them had the answer. Not knowing made him powerless, a feeling he could not abide. Nothing could stay hidden from the boss; he had a gift for uncovering the truth. He turned to the painting of the Virgin and Child, as he always did in times of need. He closed his eyes in thought, allowing his faith to calm him. Mother Mary had never let him down. One day or another, he would find the traitor and make an example of him, so this never happened again. He turned to Franz, his faithful right hand who would serve as his eyes and ears. "I have guns coming in from Italy. Franz, you stay with me. You three, go and fetch my weapons and bring them to the warehouse."

The immigrants from Italy had disembarked the boat and been waiting on the docks since the day's first light. Penned in behind the railings they were on dry land, but they weren't in Marseille yet. The customs agents would soon be there to check their papers. The people waited, impatient and apprehensive. One man lay with his head resting on his bundle, reading the gospel of Saint Matthew. He flicked through the pages in search of some life lessons. It had been a long journey. He thanked Jesus over and over for having guided him to this promised land. His wife sat on their only suitcase and unhooked the strap of her dress to breast-feed their baby. "*Amore, amore*", she cooed, wondering where they would be sleeping tonight. It seemed impossible that the customs agents would be able to check the papers of all these people; it would take weeks. Her husband put away his bible and promised her that brighter days lay ahead of them here in Marseille. God would always help honest, hard-working folk. His wife acquiesced but did not seem convinced. "Time will tell." She handed a handkerchief to an old woman who was sobbing, her head between her legs. She wiped her nose and let her head fall between her knees again. The border agents were finally here. They hesitated, unsure where to start. Was there really room in Marseille for all these wops? They were already coming down with *macaronis*. An agent stopped and looked down at the old woman as he passed by. He felt a swell of pity. She wouldn't last long at her age and in her state, unless she knew someone here. Her baggage consisted of a sack of clothes and a few bags of rice. As he checked her papers, he tried to encourage her to turn back, but she insisted: "*Francia, Francia per favore, povera Italia, nessun lavoro*." She tugged on his sleeve to help herself up and begged him, clasping his cheeks. He did not understand what she was saying and eventually lost patience. The crazy old woman could do as she liked. The agent approached a man playing the guitar, with his daughter beside him playing with a yoyo in her bare feet. The other bambinos looked on in amazement as the disc slid up and down along the string. *"Brava, brava,"* her father smiled at her. A young man carrying a knapsack was lying in wait for the agents. "I'm Italian, and I'm a socialist!" he called out at the top of his voice. "I have papers!" Nobody answered him. The agents circulated among the crowd and eyed each immigrant with curiosity. So many mouths to be fed and watered.

"Look at this bunch of bumpkins! They don't half stink; it's ruining my appetite!" grumbled Graziano as he stuffed dried figs into his mouth.

"Yes, yes they do. It's the same every time there's a boat to unload," added Paolo as he cast a disapproving stare over the mass of people.

"Do you see that woman with her tits out? They're swinging all over the place."

"There's not much in them, barely a trickle. She's too scrawny to be a dairy cow. I know you prefer them with a bit of meat on their bones, you dirty oaf."

"Well, I don't want to squash them, do I?" retorted Grasso with a grin. "Besides, I like it when there's something to hold on to."

Giovanni was moved with pity for these wretched souls. He did not join in with his colleagues' jokes. He saw his fellow countrymen in the crowd. They looked like his own, the people he'd grown up with, and those he'd loved with his childlike heart. He smiled as he listened to them speak. It broke his heart to see them caged like starving animals. The agents shoved their way through them, unmoved. What did Paolo and Grasso have against these people? Those good-for-nothings had turned their backs on their own without hesitation. Money had corrupted them; they'd sold their souls. But what could you say to them? They wouldn't even understand. The concept of taking pity on those who had left everything behind in the hopes of a better future, even forsaking the land of their ancestors, was lost on them. He just wanted to find these damn guns and get it over with, so he could stop listening to their jokes that sickened his heart.

The van rolled into the warehouse. Graziano opened the back doors. "*Ouffa*, the guns are all here. Now you boys can put them away. I'm heading up to the office; let me know what's in the crates." The two others had already started going through the cargo. Graziano climbed the staircase to the upper level so he could observe and take note of everything that had arrived for Mr Capuani. "Fifteen *Berettas*," yelled Paolo the Fixer. Grasso noted everything down for the Brain's ledger. The boss hadn't been in a good mood lately, meaning they needed to be extra diligent in their work. Paolo the Fixer took the opportunity to pull Giovanni over to him.

"Listen, you little bastard! I hope it wasn't you that took that *pizzo.* I warned you, Capuani won't just kill you. He'll make you suffer. Slowly but surely. The truth will come out. You can't hide anything from the boss."

"What are you talking about?"

"Don't act coy. You're not the first idiot to think he can keep a little *pizzo* for himself, and everyone who did suffered for it. They all ended up broken men. We know where you live. We know everything about you. Don't be a fool, Giovanni."

"What's next?" Graziano called impatiently.

"Twelve more Berettas," Paolo replied.

Giovanni lowered his eyes and gripped his harmonica in his pocket. He'd been a careless fool. If Paolo suspected him, it wouldn't take the others long to catch up. He shouldn't have underestimated them. All of this for what? A handful of francs that would be no use to him in the grave. What would he do now? If he confessed to Capuani, would the boss be merciful? Out of the question. He was happy to be a traitor, but he would not be a coward. He had to find a solution. He'd lie, he'd make it out. He'd find a way. He was meeting Aleksander Spielman on Sunday.

Gustavo was sprawled over the counter, his expression blank, his jaw slack and a pint of beer in front of him. He ran his tongue over his moustache. The foam had a salty taste. He began laughing to himself. The barman looked at him and shook his head with pity. It was time for him to go home. "I'm thirsted! And my beer is empty," the drunkard suddenly belched. He felt a hand on his shoulder and turned: "Ah, Giovanni! What are you doing here, my friend?" He suggested they drink a last beer together; the young man refused politely. There was never one last one with Gustavo. He needed to get him out of there. "Already? Even the hens aren't in bed yet!" His friends from the site chuckled. Their leering, ruddy faces annoyed Giovanni as he struggled to get his landlord out the door. Gustavo descended from his bar stool with some difficulty. Giovanni took him by the arms and led him through the streets. The older man whispered:

"You know, Giovanni, I know I drink too much. Once I start, I can't stop myself. I can't even count how many I've had. At first it calms me. We have a good laugh, and then I think about my good wife waiting for me at home. I know I'm a loser. So I drink even more, to help me forget. But by then it doesn't calm me anymore. It gets worse and worse. I think about my life, about everything I could have done over there, in Italy. I was smart enough. But there was no work. You know, Fiora's very patient. She complains out of habit and to keep me on my toes, but in the end she understands me. When a woman loves you, it's unbelievable how tender she can be. She still thinks about our first date. She never stops talking about it. I was young and handsome then, with an athlete's physique. I was even romantic. You have to sweep a woman off her feet, and not just with flowers! You have to talk about the future, whisper sweet nothings, and treat them like princesses all day and all night. And I was good at it! I've known a lot of women, of every kind, the kind who'd make your heart shudder. Each one more beautiful than the last! But Fiora had something else. Something I couldn't explain. I was so in love with her. By God, what happened to me Giovanni?

"Come on, you're drunk. You'll feel better tomorrow."

"I know I'm drunk. It's about the only thing I know for sure, my lad. You're a good boy. You have your whole life ahead of you."

Gustavo began to weep in Giovanni's arms.

"Let's go home, Gustavo. Your family's waiting for you. It'll be OK. You'll have something to eat, and you can see your wife and children."

"My wife and children. The lights of my life. I know how disappointed they are in me. Sometimes I can't even look them in the eye. And Maria! My precious daughter. She'll go far, that girl. She's good at everything she tries. She takes after her father."

Gustavo suddenly felt ill; he stopped to vomit, and all the beers he'd drunk came back up. He leaned against a well, barely able to stand. He cursed when he saw there was vomit on his shoes; Fiora would be furious. Giovanni patted him on the back. "It'll be OK, you'll feel better." Gustavo stood up straight and wiped his mouth with the back of his hand. "I feel better already. How about a little smoke to get the taste out of my mouth?" Giovanni handed him a cigarette. Gustavo struggled to light it, breaking several matches and throwing them to the ground in a fury.

"Giovanni, you know Maria? She's not what you think. She loves it here in France. I love it here too. I don't know what she's told you, but she's at the top of her class. My daughter excels. She has a God-given gift. She's special. And I love her as much as I did on the day she was born. Now, Giovanni, don't make me say it...I love them both, Maria and Claudio, of course I do, by God. But Maria has something else. I'm especially fond of her. But Giovanni! She's complicated. She blames everyone and no-one at the same time. She refuses to be called Maria because she thinks of herself as French. She's torn between her roots and her adopted country.

It's not easy for her. If you want me to explain Maria, it would take a while. I'm being serious now. I'm sober."

"I can tell," the young man replied with a smile.

"My daughter, Giovanni! Maria is a flower fallen from heaven. She must not wilt."

Gustavo held up his trousers; God only knew how he'd lost his belt. He warbled a song from Piedmont through the wisps of his beard. It was off-key. The passers-by smiled at him, amused at his drunkenness. Gustavo accosted two women who were eating lemon sorbet outside a café. "That looks delicious!" he marvelled. The women laughed with him. "Would you like a taste?" one of them asked him. "No thanks, I'll stick to beer!" Gustavo replied. He was about to topple over, but Giovanni held him by the arm. He asked the young man to let him sit down on the pavement. He spat on the ground and took a deep breath of the night air. He felt better.

"You want to know about Maria? She has a kind heart, like a nanny goat. She knows what she wants: to work for the French government. And she's smart enough to do it. You know that, Giovanni? She can do it. My daughter, Maria! She can do it. She's not scared of anything, and she puts her heart and soul into her work."

Gustavo pushed the door open with his foot. His feet caught in the doormat and he fell flat on his face. It wasn't the first time he'd made such an entrance.

"Damn doormat! Who put that there? It could break an honest man's back!"

"Come sit down, Papa," Claudio took his father by the hand and grinned at Giovanni.

"Bring me a chair, son. That one's too far away."

"Are you sure you wouldn't like us to bring you a throne?" Fiora retorted, watching the scene with irritation and amusement.

"Oh yes, the gentlest women always have the cruellest words!"

Gustavo sat down in his armchair, finally safe from the inherent danger in standing up. He needed a smoke. He turned his jacket inside out, unable to find his cigarettes. He took off one shoe, then the other, and looked inside. Still nothing.

"Claudio! What did you do with my smokes? They were here a minute ago."

"In your shoes?"

"How do I know? Maybe."

Giovanni gave him a cigarette.

"Thank you my lad, you're a gent. Not like some people I know," he added, eyeing his mother-in-law.

The old woman did not take the bait, wondering instead how her daughter could ever have fallen for such a deadbeat. She set the table, murmuring her prayers just loud enough for everyone else to hear her, intoning the names of Mary and Joseph with a dramatic flourish.

"What about Jesus? Did you forget the poor lad?" Gustavo laughed, stretching his toes.

"Heaven forbid! I will tolerate all manner of foolish talk, better to hear it than to be deaf, but there is to be no blasphemy under this roof!" Domenica fumed.

Maria emerged from her bedroom and looked around. It seemed that dinner wasn't ready yet; she made to retreat, but her father called to her.

"Maria, my daughter, light of my life. Bring me a drink, there's a good girl. It's hot enough to parch a camel in here!"

The young woman poured a glass of water for her father.

"Water? Are you trying to kill me? Isn't there any wine for your dear old papa?"

"Gustavo, you've had enough!" Fiora grumbled.

"Enough? I've hardly touched the stuff today, and I'm as hungry as a wolf."

"Oh yes, 'the stuff' – when you call it that I know you've been at it all day long."

"What are we eating tonight, my darling wife?" asked Gustavo, rubbing his belly.

"You have some nerve on you! Sitting there resting your feet and expecting to be waited on hand and foot!" Domenica grumbled.

"I still don't know what's on the table for tonight."

"Neapolitan pizza, with plenty of anchovies – just the way you like it," Maria interjected with affection.

"Maria, my darling. You're my favourite!"

"For God's sake Papa, it's Marie!"

10.

"*Let us be thankful, and may God preserve us. The advent has come, all that is good has come, through God's grace we have seen another year. We are no greater, may we be no less,*" Domenica intoned as she took out three saucers from the cupboard. These would be perfect: they were slightly chipped, but they'd been in the family since her late husband's day. He'd loved the traditions of Marseille; he'd loved traditions in general. When she thought of him, it was without sadness. Rituals had a way of transcending time, unlike their frail bodies. It was the fourth of December, Saint Barbara's Day, when she would bless the harvest and the men who sewed wheat seeds to cultivate the land. She was from a farming family. She wondered what had become of them, back in Italy. All dead, no doubt. She would no longer know a single face in her village, and none of them would know hers. She remembered their Christmases in Italy; when December came, she was always busy tending to her crib. Maria had always loved the little figurines when she was a child; they made her eyes light up. She'd been an adorable child and was now a strong young woman. Domenica was proud of her granddaughter; she was upstanding and honest, like her grandmother. She certainly preferred her to Claudio. Life was made up of these little favourites. Claudio wasn't a bad egg, but he wasn't the sharpest tool in the box either — he'd taken after his father. She thought about what she would make for Christmas Day; not everything she wanted to, unfortunately. There'd be the traditional nougat *mendiants*, of course, which stuck to her teeth and pulled her dentures out of place but were her favourite treat. Domenica opened the bag of soil that Claudio had brought her the night before. She poured some into the saucers and set the lentils and wheat seeds into the soil. They would have to wait and see what this year's harvest had in store. For Christmas Eve she would cook a turkey stuffed with dried fruit. Dessert would be the *Cachofué* log, which they would light according to tradition. She turned on the radio, and a voice crackled out: "*Yesterday, the Mayor of Marseille issued a communiqué to announce that he would be holding a rally in response to the explosion in La Loubière. French citizens are invited to attend in protest against the violence. Mayor Gaston Deferre will address all those Marseillais and Frenchmen...*" Domenica switched it off. She'd seen anti-Italian protests come and go since she arrived in Marseille. Holding a rally during advent was a scandal! Christmas was a time of peace when they should be celebrating the birth of their Redeemer. It was a time of happiness and good cheer. She would hear no more of it.

At break time, Maria and her friends gathered in the schoolyard. Stenography was Monique's favourite class, but today's lesson had been hard. Maria was not very talkative. It was almost the end of the year, and they'd be getting their results soon. She needed to show her mother that all this schooling wasn't just a waste of time. Maria listened to her girlfriends chatting, her mind elsewhere. Giovanni was charming and seemed to be making plenty of money here in Marseille. But apart from when he worked at the site with Claudio, they never saw him. She didn't know what he did on the side. Where did he go? The young Italian was certainly a mystery; since he'd arrived from Livorno, everything had gone his way. His French was excellent, but his ambition frightened her.

"Maria, you seem a bit out of sorts today," Chantal said tenderly.

"Leave her be, she's probably just in love," said Françoise coyly.

"Me, in love?" Maria was peeved. "That will never happen, so dream on."

"Oh yes, I know what's eating you. That Italian who's staying with them! She's hung up on him!" Monique was convinced.

"What are you talking about? That's not true!" Maria insisted. "It was just a hard class; I couldn't follow what the teacher was dictating."

"Lay off! Is there something I don't know about? Who's this Italian?" Chantal asked, curious.

"Let it go," Maria snapped. "There's no Italian to speak of, and no Frenchman either."

"Shall we change the subject? Did you hear about the car that exploded in La Loubière the other night?" said Françoise.

Maria wished they could have picked a different topic. She suspected that Italians were probably behind the explosion; maybe it was payback for something. It certainly wasn't good news for the community, in any case.

There'd be repercussions when it came to giving out French nationality and even work permits for new immigrants.

"Probably the Italian mafia again," sighed Chantal, not pointedly enough to nettle Maria.

"Who else?" Françoise murmured in agreement.

"Italians aren't the only crooks in Marseille," said Maria, eager to shift suspicion from her community.

"Maria's right. It could have been the Armenians!" Monique agreed. Maria left the conversation, saying goodbye to her friends and heading home to help her grandmother prepare dinner.

Fiora clapped her hands together twice. The meal was ready, and they were all hungry. Nobody knew where Giovanni was, so they'd have to start without him.

"Where is that scamp? I bet he's off with some girl. At his age there's only one thing on his mind!" said Gustavo with a cackle.

"He's very secretive about his affairs," Fiora mused. "I wonder if he's hiding something from us."

"We don't know much about him. You took a complete stranger into your home. You're too soft-hearted," said Domenica, looking up from her rosary.

"He told me he was working on other sites."

"Don't be naïve, Claudio. Nobody works on the building site at this hour!" Fiora rolled her eyes.

Maria had been silent until now but felt her anger rising:

"What does it have to do with you? 'Where is he?' 'What's he doing?' Mind your own business!"

The rest of the family looked at her with slightly stunned expressions, taken aback by her ardent defence of the young fellow from Livorno. A seed of suspicion began to take root in Fiora's mind. Could Maria really be in love with Giovanni? She did look at him rather tenderly, and then there were those French lessons every night...who knew what had sprung up between them? The young man was polite and respectful. He had nice manners. Maria probably liked that about him, but what should Fiora think? The lad seemed to have a good head on his shoulders. He paid his rent on time. As long as he didn't get her daughter pregnant, what was the harm?

"We didn't mean anything by it, dear. We were just wondering. The lad does live with us, after all," Gustavo replied softly, placing his hand over Maria's.

His daughter smiled at him. She'd better lay low for a while; her emotions had betrayed her. She was meeting Giovanni later; for now she could suffer in silence. What did their talk and gossip matter? After all, they didn't know him like she did.

Maria was running; she was late. The meal had seemed to go on forever. She'd struggled to get away, but now she was finally free. The cool evening air refreshed her, and she felt her cheeks flush. It would make her look even more beautiful. She hoped that Giovanni hadn't given up and was still waiting for her. She decided she was pretty enough to wait for. She'd also decided that she would kiss him tonight, after turning the thought over in her head all through their dinner. It would be her first kiss; she wanted it to be tender and to remember it forever. She applied her lipstick with no mirror as she walked; it would have to do like this. She approached the Saint-Charles station, where her love awaited her. He was lighting a cigarette and looked up, standing with his mouth agape for a moment before he collected himself. He held out a bouquet of flowers to the young woman with the glittering eyes. She was relieved to see that he was as nervous as she was.

"So you got away from your mother?"

"Looks like it!"

Giovanni was thrilled at the risk she was willing to take for their secret rendezvous.

"Where are we going tonight?" she asked with a beaming smile.

"To the train station. It's a surprise!"

"Well it's not a surprise now that you've told me!" she teased.

Giovanni did not answer. He was a decidedly puzzling young man, thought Maria. She hoped that one day she'd be able to grasp that intangible part of him, although some part of her also hoped it would always remain out of reach. The mystery was part of what attracted her to him. Giovanni warmed his hands in hers and kissed her politely on the cheek. She blushed. She had an adorable way about her; he squeezed her cold little fingers and felt a swell of tenderness towards her. The two lovers walked up the steps of the station, Maria eager to uncover the surprise.

"Do you prefer first or second class?" the young man asked, holding the door open courteously.

"Why do you ask? It's a bit early for a honeymoon..."

"We have to earn the money for our tickets first!"

Maria looked at him, wide-eyed. He grinned at her, giving nothing more away. They walked across the station, whose glass roof unveiled a curtain of stars. Giovanni seemed in a romantic mood, and Maria was enjoying it. The tired and weary travellers around them did not seem to notice the beauty of this place, semi-coated in darkness. The lamps seemed to float in the air, painting the nooks and corners of the station with a soft yet vibrant light. Maria had been through the station before but was suddenly seeing it with fresh, child-like eyes. Giovanni was focused on his surprise: he'd been working on his plan for several days. He hoped that Maria would play along. He dreaded to think what would happen if she didn't: he had little experience when it came to seducing women, and the fiasco of his love for Stella was scant reassurance. Today, though, he was not paralysed by fear, but galvanised by it. He felt courage he'd never felt before and was ready to go all in.

"Can you dance?"

"Dance? Here?"

"Why not? I'll play the harmonica on one knee, and you can dance, and all these people can throw us their coins."

"Are you sure? But what kind of dance should I do?" Maria asked in a very hesitant tone.

"Don't overthink it, just dance! Take off your shoes!"

Giovanni dropped to his knee and took his harmonica from his pocket. He threw his cap at her bare feet. The young man was stock still as he played his harmonica. The sound of the blues rose up in the station, to the surprise and delight of the other passengers. They approached the buskers with curiosity, gathering round to observe the show. It helped that their train was late and they had nothing better to do. Maria watched them gather and began to dance reluctantly. The fibres in her muscles stiffened, and she felt clumsy. She was off-tempo. She looked at Giovanni worriedly. What was she doing? This was uncharted territory. Giovanni's eyes told her to keep dancing. They filled her with confidence and serenity, and she felt reassured. Those kind eyes stayed fixed upon her, supporting and freeing her. She looked back at him and felt a sort of osmosis happening between them. She let it take her over. Her body relaxed, and her limbs unhinged themselves. A lightness came over her; the music and the movement flowed through her willowy limbs. She'd been carried off to somewhere safe and warm, and she danced without a care for the world. She was blinded, absent from the stage and present only in her mind. She felt herself being guided by a voice from a distant place. Giovanni watched her; she'd been possessed by the music, moving with a sensuality and grace he'd never seen in her before. She was going faster than his melody, and he scrambled to catch up. The station's clock had not yet struck midnight. His heart beat to the rhythm of the second hand that ticked around its face. Time seemed to stop and expand. He wanted to kiss her, to embrace her and feel her flesh against his, to become one with this sublime creature whose gaze pierced his own. The onlookers were amazed; the two young lovers had made something beautiful together. "They must be artists," one woman said. "Maybe they're just having fun." A child came up and threw a coin in Giovanni's cap; others followed, and it was soon full of coins. Giovanni watched them with amusement, but Maria was still swept up in her dance. Slowly, the music died down. Maria opened her eyes. The passengers applauded. She saw them for the first time, her heart beating fast. She struggled to believe what she had done, that it was she they were applauding. She turned to Giovanni and thanked him.

Giovanni and Maria sat on the steps of the station. Maria was collecting her thoughts, and Giovanni his emotions. The full moon cast a silvery halo over the misty Marseille night, illuminating the domes of the Saint-Jean cathedral. Maria looked up at the sky and pointed to a shooting star: "Did you see that?" she exclaimed. The young man smiled at her; he hadn't seen anything. He thought only of kissing her. The day's last passengers descended the steps. It was getting late. Maria rested her head on Giovanni's shoulder. She listened to the man playing the guitar further down the steps. Giovanni took her hand and looked at the group of youths smoking under a street lamp. Maria's heart was beating fast. Giovanni was overcome with joy. The memory of their performance in Saint-Charles station would be etched in his mind forever. He'd won Maria over. She felt complete. "I love you," she whispered into his ear. Giovanni summoned his courage and turned his face towards hers. She closed her eyes and let it happen. Her lips brushed against his. They kissed.

11.

By the small harbour of Les Auffes, in Marseille's seventh *arrondissement*, Aleksander Spielman waited patiently for the charming young man he was to dine with. He turned his signet ring around on his finger. Would he be nervous? The young man's features had faded in his memory; he now retained only a vague outline of the face. The harbour walls were white as winter, reminding him of his childhood in Krakow. In his mind's eye, Krakow existed only in winter, bright and shimmering in its coat of ice and snow. He used to play in the park in Kazimierz with the other Jewish children. He watched the musicians, who would sometimes distract them from their games. He liked the Yiddish songs and the sound of the violin. He liked the indefinable glow in the eyes of the musicians. This light had been a mystery to him; something as inviolable and mysterious as the ways of the Lord. The black-bearded rabbi at the synagogue disapproved of Aleksander. He did not understand the boy's interest in music and would have liked to see him paying closer attention to his study of the Torah. Aleksander's family wanted him to become a rabbi. He smiled at the thought; music had carried him far away from that destiny. His gaze returned to the sloping streets around Les Auffes. Giovanni had still not arrived; the young lad seemed to know how to keep a man interested. Aleksander Spielman felt a brief instant of boredom. Then he took in the landscape around him and lost himself in its detail. He tried to feel its soul. The cold that nipped at his face, and the wind that batted his eyes, were swept up in one of Chopin's nocturnes. Around him everything changed, and all became music. There was the percussion of crunching ice as the rowboats nudged against the harbour walls. He heard the creaking of wood and stone, scratching and jostling one another *vivace*. Bigger boats bobbed up and down *moderato,* as if trying to shake free from the ropes that moored them to the jetty. Ice melted on the rooftops, each drop sounding a note, each note flowing together as the nocturne swelled, lapping into every corner of his bleak, glacial memory. Then the music stopped. Aleksander Spielman opened his eyes. Giovanni was standing in front of him. They turned and went into the restaurant.

Spielman's cheerful gaze was fixed on Giovanni, who felt more than a little intimidated and struggled to grasp the finer points of his dining partner's badinage. He felt clumsy and ill-mannered. He ate his *bouillabaisse* carefully, but still found strings of cheese clinging to his chin. He should have ordered the shrimp, like Aleksander. The musician smiled.

"You have quite an appetite, young man! At your age, that's hardly surprising. How old are you, or did you tell me that already?"

"I turned twenty-one this autumn," Giovanni replied innocently, gulping down his mouthful of soup.

"Well then, your life's ahead of you. May it be both intoxicating and intoxicated," grinned the older man as he signalled the waiter to bring him more white wine.

The distinguished waiter also made Giovanni feel ill-at-ease and was careful to serve Spielman first, his left hand on the napkin shrouding the bottle and his right hand on the neck, as was the proper form in these sorts of places. Couldn't he have poured it himself? Giovanni would have preferred a more intimate setting, where he could talk freely with this mysterious man who drank his wine with dainty little sips. In fact, Aleksander Spielman sniffed the wine more often than he drank and seemed to enjoy swirling the glass underneath his large, aquiline nose. He hesitated for a moment, then gave Giovanni a wry smile and asked him:

"Tell me, do you have a special love in your life?"

"Yes, her name's Maria."

A hint of disapproval, perhaps even disgust passed over the pianist's face. Giovanni did not know why, but he felt he should defend his beloved.

"She's the most beautiful Italian in Belle de Mai, and she speaks French perfectly."

"I suppose she's an artist, like yourself."

"Not at all! She's learning to be a typist at a school in the centre of town. She's very studious. She wants to work in the civil service," he added with pride.

"It's good to be studious...but it can be boring too, can't it? I thought you were more of a wayfarer, having found you as I did, convulsing in an opium haze with your harmonica by your side."

Giovanni did not know what to say. Aleksander Spielman had honed in on the contradiction that was eating away at Giovanni, the lie and the impossibility of knowing who he was and what he would become.

"Have you finished eating? Or have my impolitic inquiries affected your appetite?"

"No, it's not that..."

The young man's sad expression gave Aleksander Spielman pause, in spite of himself. Despite all the artifices he might effortlessly deploy in a game of seduction, he would always have a soft spot for vulnerable and handsome young men.

"What about this harmonica? What can you play on it?" he added softly.

"The blues."

"Blues, eh? You really are a soulful type. But then, what musician isn't? When I play, whether it's in my living room or at the Opera, it's always with *spleen*, as they say. But I love that feeling. It's what inspires great men. Without the sadness that comes of love, they could never have done what they did."

"What do you play?"

"Piano, of course. Did I not tell you that? I attended the Warsaw Conservatory, back when I was young and beautiful like you."

"Warsaw? Where's that?"

"It's in Poland."

"Why did you leave?"

"Well, really I left twice. The first time was when I left Kazimierz, the Jewish neighbourhood in Krakow. That's where I grew up and had my first love. No other city can inspire me like Krakow. She was born for music, and music was born for her. I grew up loving her, and since then, I've cherished her in my playing. But I left to attend the Warsaw Conservatory. I stayed with my aunt for a few years, then left the country when things started to get bad for the Jews. Can you imagine the anger and the sadness you'd feel at seeing your own people persecuted? I thought things would get better when Pilsudski was in power. We all hoped so, back when we still had the strength to hope and hold our heads high."

"And what happened?"

"In 1935, the Nuremberg laws made our situation untenable. Antisemitism became legal, legitimate and omnipresent. Lots of Jews went to Palestine, but I wanted to stay in Europe. I could have fled further from the violence of the Germans, the invasion of Poland stunned us all, even though I was in Paris at the time. Then came dear Maréchal Pétain;

that was a frightening time, but I couldn't bring myself to stray too far from the music of the West and its artistic circles, the bohemia, and the power of its history. I had a few friends in Paris who were able to protect me."

"Will you go back?"

"Never. Poland has lost its innocence. She's the only woman who ever broke my heart."

"Did your family stay there?"

"You might say they did."

Aleksander Spielman finished his wine, his eyes dulled. He sighed. Giovanni kept talking, oblivious:

"I'm from Livorno."

"Is that on the Italian coast?" said Spielman, rising from the table.

"Yes! I used to fish there with my father."

"You were a fisherman in Livorno. I see. I'm afraid I must go. Come visit me in Paris, I'll take you to all the best places."

12.

"Italians out of Marseille!" spat one protester.

"*Macaronis* out! Bunch of low-lifes! Bunch of crooks bringing your shit to France!" cried another.

"They're good for nothing!" replied the first protester.

"This time we should go to Belle de Mai and set fire to their shops!"

"Not just there, let's burn their fishing nets! Why should those *nabos* get to fish in our waters anyway?"

At Jean Jaurès square, anger was rising among the protesters, who waved their patriotic flags with furious energy. Their protest had been spurred by the explosion in La Loubière earlier that week. They raged against all Italian immigrants, who were poisoning their city like parasites, preventing them from living and working in peace. Among the dense crowd that was preparing to march along Belle de Mai, two dock workers cried bitterly:

"Out with the mafia! Out with the crooks!"

"Let's drown them in their fish barrels! We'll fill them with oil!"

Behind them, men had begun picking up cobblestones, saying that the shopkeepers in Belle de Mai would get what was coming to them. Their livelihoods had to suffer; they'd come back to find their windows smashed and their shelves broken. The old folks shuffled behind, leaning on their canes. "Looks like it's going to get ugly. Stay to the back; we're too old for this kind of thing."

The Pacchianos had locked themselves in their home and turned off all the lights. Like most of the Italian families in Belle de Mai, they feared that the protest would descend into a riot. They'd barricaded the door and closed the shutters and would wait for it to blow over. They whispered to one another as if the protesters could hear them. Gustavo turned on the radio. The mayor, Gaston Deferre, was addressing his fellow citizens: "*My Dear Marseillais, I understand your frustration. France cannot stand idle when acts of violence are committed. The explosion in La Loubière affects us all. It is hardly a sign of reconciliation between Frenchmen and Italians. Citizens of France, I implore you to calm your anger on this day of protest...*" Giovanni was beside himself, his guilt gnawing at him from the inside. Bile rose in his throat. It was all his fault. It was he who had brought the bomb to La Loubière, and he would never tell anyone what he had done. The burden of guilt was for him to bear alone. He looked at the wholesome family whose daughter he was courting, the family who had taken him in off the cargo boat when he was no-one, with nothing, and spoke barely a word of French. They trusted him, and he'd betrayed them. Now they were imprisoned in their own home, unaware that he had caused these protests and they were all victims of his stupidity. He fixed his gaze on Maria's face. She smiled at him, and it broke his heart to smile back at her. He was a criminal, the lowest of the low. He almost wanted to scream the truth, so he would be beaten and banished from Belle de Mai forever. He almost wished they would put him on trial. How could he atone for what he'd done? Would he ever be able to extricate himself from his lies? Domenica grabbed her granddaughter's hand, terrified. "Don't worry, the Lord will protect us!" she murmured in Maria's ear. Gustavo and Claudio were listening carefully to the Mayor's radio announcement. "Who even says that it was Italians that did it? We're always first to be accused," snorted Gustavo, draining his glass of wine. He got up and checked one last time that the iron bar was firmly in place over the door. Fiora felt suffocated: today was a work day. Money was being lost, and time wasted.

"Gustavo, it's not the first time that they've protested against us," said Fiora with exasperation.

"I hope it's the last!" Gustavo railed, turning up the volume.

"We should pray to the Mother of God," sighed Domenica, slipping her pearl rosary beads through her fingertips one by one.

"I heard they're going to be throwing stones through windows," Maria added.

"It doesn't look good," said Gustavo.

"Have there ever been fights between Italians and the French?" Giovanni asked.

"If you have to ask, I'll tell you, you've never seen hatred like it!"

"Real fights?"

"Fights, he says! People injured, killed even! And most of the time us *macaronis* didn't do a thing to provoke them!"

"...Let us cherish peace in our country and in our city. We all know how difficult that peace was to obtain; we all saw our men and children die for their country. Let us honour them by preserving the peace they gave us and remaining united and dignified in the face of the violence that has reared its ugly head once more. I know that you, my fellow citizens, cherish your city as much as I do. Marseille has for centuries been a place of hospitality, a cosmopolitan city where cultures are mingled and shared." The Marseillais were seething with rage, bellowing the hateful slogans they improvised as they marched. The rally began to unravel; the first cobblestones were thrown, and the first windows smashed. The men were on the lookout for an Italian – any Italian – to set upon. Where were they all? Did they not have the stomach to show themselves? They pounded on doors, passing around wine and beer. Inhibitions were lost, and a few of the more drunken louts spurred the crowd on. They pulled a cart piled high with wood into the heart of the Italian quarter.

The roaring hum of hostility rang out through Belle de Mai. The Pacchianos were like rabbits in a trap, powerless. All they could do was wait and fume. Domenica lit a holy candle. She trembled as she recited her prayers. Despite her faith, tears filled her eyes. Fiora hugged her mother to console her. Giovanni was filled with pity for the grandmother; it was the first time she had shown such naked vulnerability. Hatred was a feeling she could not comprehend. Her world was being turned upside down. Gustavo paced back and forth, muttering to himself. He clenched his fists. In his head, he let his violent desires play out. If it weren't for his adopted family, he'd go out and show these racists what he was made of. His mutterings worried Maria. Her eyes met Giovanni's. She knew that something wasn't right. Did he have something to say? The young man rolled up his sleeves. He needed to atone for his sins. He would take responsibility for his actions.

A rioter was pulling along a canvas sack filled with cobblestones. The rumbling of the loose stones resonated through the street, dirtied by the protesters. He stopped in front of a restaurant window, eager to find out how much noise a cobblestone would make when it went through that lovely vitrine. His expression bore a smile of gleeful violence. He threw the first stone. The window smashed, and the shards of glass cascaded to the floor. He threw a second stone, which hit the countertop inside. He threw a third. He was in a violent frenzy and could not stop. He wanted to destroy it all. A woman approached, looking to find a suitable place to set down her wicker basket filled with old rags. Broken windows were not enough to satisfy her vengeful smile; she'd been carrying her pile of tinder since Jean Jaurès square. It was worth the wait. She shoved the basket inside the door of the restaurant and struck a match. The bitter smell of the oil caught the attention of the rioters, who hooted and yelled their approval. Further up on the corner of the street, a rioter was breaking car windows with an iron bar. He took his time, breaking each one with delight. Hearing the noise, others joined him and slashed the tyres with their knives. This done, another poured lighter fluid over the seats and threw his *zippo* inside. The French stood back and watched the fire rise. Like children at a winter bonfire, they looked on with wondrous approval as the engine exploded. La Loubière had been avenged.

Giovanni was outside, the fresh air lapping at his face. Maria had begged him not to go. He couldn't sit there any longer; he could no longer pretend. He had to do something about all this anger, all this rage. Being shut up with the Pacchianos any longer would have driven him mad. At first, he was blinded by the daylight, but gradually his eyes adjusted. There were wild men running in all directions, cudgels in hand, trampling throughout the pillaged streets. It was a battleground. The storefronts were in ruins. He stepped over shards of glass, piles of rocks and scattered objects from the ransacked shops. Cars and restaurants were being consumed by flames. They shoved past him without noticing who he was, almost causing him to fall once or twice. He did not know where to look or how to act. How did you defend an entire neighbourhood? How could you repair the irreparable? He cried out. A roar escaped him. A lout who was gathering debris turned and looked at him. He approached Giovanni with the look of a cat who's found a cornered mouse. Had one of these Italians really dared to come out? Giovanni smiled coldly at him, his dark eyes provoking the rioter. He grabbed the Frenchman by the collar and spat in his face. The dye was cast; the Frenchman was stunned. He could not decide how to react. Giovanni watched him without moving. He waited. The first punch landed on his jaw, and pain seared through his teeth.

"Is that all?" he demanded.

The Frenchman hesitated. The Italian wasn't even defending himself. Giovanni insisted:

"Are you a man or not? This is what you wanted, isn't it? To beat up a wop?" He took a punch in the stomach. He folded over but felt a surge of elation. More Marseillais had gathered around, encouraging their man to continue the fight. Now he had to show them he knew how to handle an Italian. He let loose on Giovanni, who did not react, taking every punch. His assailant worked hard to wipe the smile off his face. He landed blow after blow, exasperated that the boy would not hit him back. It wasn't a fair fight. There was no fun if it was too easy. "Aren't you going to defend yourself, for God's sake? Are you mad or what?" Giovanni said nothing, looking at the protesters with hatred in his eyes. He recognised a few men from the port. They were shopkeepers, fishermen, workers. It was everyone and no-one. Just a blur of angry men. A punch shook him from his observations. He no longer felt any pain. He was on the ground, semi-conscious. He saw his mother looking at him in sadness. He saw Luca jeering at him, and Maria crying. He got up, tottering. He wiped the blood from his face. "Come on then!" The Frenchman was fed up. Couldn't this fool stay down? Did he want to die? Luckily a friend came to help him, raining down kicks on the young Italian, who stumbled and fell. They laughed and poured beer over him. He was no longer a threat, but a source of amusement. He ran off amidst their taunting jeers and headed for the port. He needed to find the sea and reconcile with his pain.

Sitting on the jetty, Giovanni let his thoughts drift out to the horizon. The cargo ships were shrinking in the distance. He dreamed of being somewhere else, as he had always done. But now, a weight hung over him. He had left home to become a better man but was miserable. His body was wounded, and his face horribly misshapen. He smiled; it was a face that suited the contradiction within him. Did all ports look alike? His heart yearned for Livorno. Should he flee once more? Should he go back? What had he done with all they'd taught him? His mother would be ashamed; the thought tightened his throat. An albatross landed at his feet, and there was something calming in its yellowish eyes. "You don't worry about anything, do you? You fly over the sea, catch your fish, rise into the clouds, then sometimes you come and sit yourself down here, happy as you like. It's a good life to have." The bird looked at him. The moment hung in the air, vacuous yet potent. It was not his destiny to stay in one place. He wasn't ready to drop anchor yet. He had not yet found the place that fit him, somewhere that could entertain and console him. Could he really leave Maria behind? He began playing the blues. The music calmed him and brought him closer to himself. He knew he loved her. Their love was real and meaningful. He remembered Stella and his boyhood dreams of winning her affections. It all seemed unreal now. He was unable to recall what her face might have looked like, or the sound of her voice. Stella was a mirage; an illusion. She'd left his mind so quickly. He kept playing, and the albatross flew off. He no longer blamed Luca. After all, he'd been a friend for a time, and that was all that had mattered then. Would he even take the time to notice a man like Luca now? What use would he have for a deadbeat like that?

The protesters had deserted the streets. They left a devastated neighbourhood in their wake. There was nothing to be heard but the crackling of the flames, and not a soul to be seen – only the spectre of violence that hung over the streets. Time had frozen, and yet the bells of Saint-Antoine pealed six o'clock. A door opened, and an Italian came out to survey the damage. The carnage seemed endless. He called his neighbours to come and help; he banged on the doors and whistled to his friends. A small band of helpers gathered, soon followed by another. They came out and called the rest of their families to join them. Belle de Mai must be saved. They'd get back on their feet together. They organised themselves: one person went to get water, another looked for sheets to smother the fire, another gathered debris, and the last group scoured the neighbourhood for the injured. Maria was out like a shot; she ran through the streets in search of Giovanni. She asked everyone she came across if they'd seen a young Italian. They all shook their heads and said they were sorry. People were busy putting out fires and gathering up their belongings. Maybe she was talking about the young fellow who was fighting with the French. Fighting? Maria was more and more worried. Why did he need to play the hero? She hoped he wasn't injured. Why did he go out so early? She kept up her desperate search. He couldn't have disappeared. He must be here somewhere, but in what kind of state? She called out to him, the sound of his name consoling her. When she was beginning to lose hope, an idea came to her: he might be at the port. He liked to go and look at the boats and play the blues when he was feeling down. She ran to the water. When she saw her lover sitting on the docks, her heart leapt with joy, but her mind was dark with anger. How could he have done that? How could he have disappeared in the middle of a riot? She hurried over to him, her fury wilting the closer she got to him. She took him in her arms. "Oh Giovanni, I was so scared."

13.

It was Christmas night, and the steps of the church of Saint-Antoine were thronged with residents of Belle de Mai. This was their gathering place, the forum for the events that gave shape to their lives, where they met their old friends to catch up on all the goings-on from the neighbourhood. Tonight they were here for midnight mass. White snowflakes fell and faded amidst the cheerful crowd. The churchgoers chatted gaily, decked out in their best clothes: the women wore dresses, hats, heels and perfume, while the men were in suits and polished dress shoes, their hair and moustaches oiled and combed and their dickie bows tied snugly under their chins. The choirboys proudly sported their white robes and the gold crosses around their necks. Their angelic voices would soon resound under the nave; they would wear serious, solemn expressions as their *mamma* looked on with misty-eyed pride. They'd been practising every Sunday with the priest and the organ player, but for now they were relaxing pre-performance and building a snowman together. Angelo had even brought a carrot for the nose. He produced it proudly from underneath his robes, and the other bambinos wished they'd thought to do the same. The younger children looked up in wonder at the huge gold star perched on top of the Christmas tree. "Do you know about the star that the shepherds followed?" Domenica asked them. She'd once taught catechism and still enjoyed giving instruction to young souls and guiding them along God's path. She softened her voice to tell them the story of the wise kings and the birth of Jesus. She was a good storyteller, and the children listened with delight. Domenica's friends were getting impatient; they were eager to fill up on news and gossip from around the community. Ernestina showed off her new satin dress, which she was wearing for the first time. She unwrapped her fur coat so they could see the fit, the fine fabric and the dark shimmer. "It's so lovely!" Marta gasped, touching it lightly. Leopoldina observed them from on high; still showing off their glad rags at their age! She cast her cynical, inquisitive gaze over the assembled crowd. Her eye stopped at the young man who lived with the Pacchianos. They didn't know much about the boy; there was something deceitful about him, and he was far too handsome to be living under the same roof as a young lady. Domenica would not say much about him. Was there a secret being hidden? She could already picture sweet young Maria falling pregnant, and Fiora trying to conceal the affair. The Pacchianos did not seem to realise how much interest there was in them; instead, they were chatting with the Lombardis, the family to which Claudio's fiancée belonged.

"When will this wedding of ours be happening then?" asked Mr. Lombardi, hovering over the 'ours' to signal his involvement. It was his daughter being given away, after all.

"We'll arrange a date very soon, but these aren't the kinds of things you want to rush," Gustavo answered in a serious tone.

"Couldn't agree more. After all, it's not just a wedding day – it's the beginning of an eternal union between these two, and the date of all the anniversaries they'll share."

"We wish them a diamond anniversary at the very least!" Fiora smiled.

"The wedding should not take place during Lent," announced Mrs Lombardi, who was a stickler for traditions and superstition.

"And certainly not in the month of May, which is dedicated to the Virgin Mary!" Domenica retorted.

"Of course not, we must respect the Virgin and all virginity," Gustavo said, winking at his son.

"Valentina can use my wedding dress; it's still pure white and made from fine lace. I'm sure it would be a perfect fit," Fiora said with pride, cutting short her husband's bawdy jokes.

"You still had your figure back then," he joked.

"As did you, my dear," she replied, patting his belly.

"We'll see about the dress. But what about the date?" asked Mr Lombardi, who was not in the mood for frivolity.

"Let's be done with this date! What did you have in mind?" Gustavo asked irritably.

"A spring wedding is always a happy marriage."

"Spring? What did you just say about Lent and the Virgin Mary?"

Giovanni stepped away, eager not to get too involved in what seemed like an overly complicated affair. He looked around, observing how every family had its ways. Close friends greeted each other with ciao, but if you didn't know someone, or they were fresh off the boat, they'd get a *salve*. Amongst them, Giovanni recognised the butcher with his thick arms, bushy moustache and friendly smile. Giovanni sometimes went to him to pick up their Sunday chicken. There was always a big crowd in front of his shop. He was good at his work, always keeping a slice of ham for the children and a friendly word for the parents, and his big dog that kept guard over the street was appreciated by the neighbours. The cheesemonger standing at his side was a different breed. The skinny little man looked out at the world from behind his glasses with a cold expression. You always felt that he either disliked you or thought you were an idiot. His wife was a heavy-set milkmaid with reddened arms, who reminded Giovanni of the laundry women in Livorno. They were an odd couple and struggled to find their place amidst the conversations on the steps. The rest of their group slipped away, and they stood awkwardly in front of the door. Giovanni had had enough; he was cold and bored. Where was Maria? Like him, she was detached from these conversations, futile in their pragmatism, in which she took no interest. Giovanni watched her wandering dreamily through the crowd, wondering what could be going through her head. Did she think about him as much as he did about her? She had become an obsession, the only thing he saw when he closed his eyes. He was madly in love and consumed by work and worry, in that order. He smiled as he watched her walk; there was something unique about the spring and sway in her step, even when she was walking slowly. She stopped and leaned over to talk to one of the children. The child smiled; what could she have said to him? Giovanni liked watching her without her knowing. Wasn't that the best way to get to know someone? He wanted to know everything about her, to understand everything, and to find the key that would unlock the great mystery of Maria. One day, he'd be able to foresee her every move, play her laugh on his harmonica and see her face engraved over his, her body printed on the palm of his hands, her smell around him always, and she would lie down beside him every night. Maria took off her leather glove and adjusted her hair bun. Giovanni went over to her and took her by the hand. She jumped and turned around, smiling at him: "You again!"

In Belle de Mai, the only cars people owned were the kinds whose engines backfired and sputtered black smoke when ignited. But the sedan that was driving up to the church cut through the night air with a gentle purr. One of the children saw it first; even at his age, he knew what it meant and who it belonged to. He pointed to the car; the other children turned to look, followed by their mothers, then by everyone. The chatter stopped, and the crowd stood frozen. The car slowed to a halt, and its two yellow eyes dimmed. A man got out and opened an umbrella with a firm click. The Italians on the steps observed his every movement, recognising the figure even in his dark suit. It was Paolo the Fixer. He opened the back door, and the crowd held their breath to see if *he* had really come in person. One fine leather brogue stepped into the snow, followed by a second. Giovanni shuddered. The crunching of the snow sent shivers up his spine. Wrapped in a thick black overcoat, Capuani made his entrance. His eye took in each face around him; he held himself above them all, superior and omniscient. Surprised whispers rippled through the silence; the crowd were fascinated, if uneasy. Why had he come? He was known to be a devout Catholic but did not worship in public. Capuani had ways of making himself known, even as he remained invisible. The families made way for him. A market woman stared at him, saucer-eyed. It was the first time she'd ever seen him in the flesh. He passed so close she could almost have reached out and touched him. Her husband doffed his cap respectfully. Capuani was in their corner. He was powerful and infallible; they must stay in his good graces. Giovanni feared that Paolo the Fixer would give away his secret and hid himself behind Gustavo to avoid meeting his eye. Capuani was first to enter the church, genuflecting as a true believer does, his head bowed and his eyes closed. "Father, thy kingdom come." The crowd waited for a moment on the steps until the clock struck midnight. The choirboys took their places in front of the altar as the families filed into the church.

Giovanni walked in, arm-in-arm with Maria. Every time he entered a church, a memory came back to him of his dear *mamma* kneeling in front of the altar, praying to the holy saviour. He had looked wide-eyed at the figure on the cross with his crown of thorns and asked her:

"Who is that man?"

"That is Jesus, my boy."

He pretended to understand, but it remained a mystery to him why the woman who had brought him into the world knelt with such reverence before this powerful figure. He had felt a twinge of jealousy towards this other son, inanimate, absent and mute. He looked up into the stone alcoves that towered over them and thought about how many souls they had seen come to pray, how many Christmases they had endured. He was overcome by a surge of spirituality. The seraphim voices of the choir seemed to transcend time and space. The Italians were praying to the Holy Spirit, hoping to receive his fullest grace, and the priest began his reading from the book of Isaiah: *"The people walking in darkness have seen a great light; on those living in the land of deep darkness, a light has dawned. You have enlarged the nation and increased their joy; they rejoice before you as people rejoice at the harvest, as warriors rejoice when dividing the plunder..."* Domenica listened attentively to the mass. She would not have missed the liturgy of the birth of Christ for anything in the world. Her wheat seeds had sprouted, meaning next year's harvest would surely be bountiful. She looked tenderly at Maria and hoped good things would come to her soon. Maria discreetly held her lover's hand. She listened seriously to the lessons being explained by God's representative at the altar. She wanted to marry the young Italian in a church. The Lord works in mysterious ways; she who had always wanted to end up with a Frenchman would probably spend the rest of her days with Giovanni. Peace filled her heart. She was expecting something in the days to come; like the shooting star she had seen outside the station, she would watch over Giovanni without his knowing. She would pray for him. She would love him. Her gaze fell upon the cheesemonger who sold her the *provolone*. He too was praying for a year of prosperity among the community united by faith. He raised the palms of his hands towards the ceiling when saying the "Lord's prayer" and stole a glance at Capuani. During the universal prayer, the boss knelt in humble reverence. He prayed that justice would be visited upon the person who had stolen the *pizzo* paid by these Italian families. Tonight, his mission was vengeance. The priest concluded: *"Go in peace to love and serve the Lord Jesus Christ."* The mass was ended, and the priest laid the Baby Jesus in the manger, as was tradition. The little girls gathered round to look at Mary, kneeling in her blue robe and white scarf. The men nodded in solidarity with Joseph the carpenter, sporting a beard and carrying his trusty staff. The donkey and the cow sat comfortably beside the holy child. "You see, the cow is warming Jesus with his hot breath," said a father to his son as the boy admired the figures in the crib. The Magi were there to welcome Christ. "Look, that's Gaspard! He brought gold to the son of Ave Maria!" said one mother to her two sons.

Maria and Giovanni sat on the rocks in silence, admiring the constant gurgling din of the Aygalades waterfall. Maria looked at Giovanni's shimmering reflection in the pool. The moon cast a halo around his face, and his thick hair was ringed with stars. He was beautiful, and the night air suited him. His piercing eyes took on their fullest glow. She breathed in his scent. She wished she could dive into the smell of the crook of his neck and warm herself in his arms. Her chastity and shyness held her back. What was he thinking about? He was silent, running his hand along the surface of the water gloomily. She could not have guessed at his inner turmoil. He seemed so calm, and yet he thought only of kissing her. He did not know where to start. He'd brought her this far, and now he was numb with fear. What if he was too rough or too clumsy? He'd only ever slept with prostitutes and feared that was no way to treat someone he loved. These situations were beyond the scope of his experience.

"What are you thinking about?" she asked softly.

"You," he smiled.

To his astonishment, she leaned over and kissed him. He was relieved. She had reassured him; she took the first steps with an ease he didn't know she had. She trusted him. Giovanni's pulse quickened. Did he really deserve that trust? He wanted to cry out and admit to being a traitor, and throw the weight from his shoulders. He took her in his arms, and felt like crying. She whispered tender words to him. She told him she loved him and how wonderful he was, and yet his heart was too heavy to be completely joyful. He pretended to be a wise guy, but here he was, clumsy with emotion. Maria drew him gradually away from his fears, as he had done for her in Saint-Charles station. She had the power to make him forget. Her caresses took away his pain. Her kisses wiped away his remorse. He was strong, worthy, loved. Nothing but this moment mattered. Their bodies burned like a fire in the winter cold. She pressed against him and clung to his body, electrifying his every nerve. Her eyes fixed on his. Their white light breathed desire. He was taken aback by her desire and reverted to modesty. He sat down.

"What can I play for you?"

"Now?"

"Yes, I want to play for you."

"Blues, then. Something like you."

He played, and she distracted him. She kissed his neck, tickled him and blew him kisses. He couldn't help laughing, hitting false notes and playing nonsense. He threw himself on her like a wild animal. She shrieked with laughter. There she lay, wrists pinned to the ground, laughing under the weight of the lover who held them. He looked at her. She stopped laughing.

"Go ahead," she whispered.

14.

Today was a big day for Giovanni. He needed to find the courage to be a good man, to keep his promises. Maria was counting on him. He imagined her at her stenography class, studious as always but her heart pounding with nerves and joy. He'd have liked his mother to be there; she'd always hoped to see this moment. The religion she had passed on to him was all about love. She prayed to the Virgin Mary, on her knees beside his bed, and left the oil lamp burning all night so that he would sleep peacefully, protected by her voice and the Madonna. It was not by chance that he had chosen this day to make his request. It was in homage to his mother. Today, the Statue of Notre Dame de Lorette was arriving in Paris after its journey from Rome.

Giovanni observed the Pacchiano family. Their eyes were riveted on the television. All the Italians in the city were awaiting the arrival of the statue, which had been blessed by Pope Pious XII. The Virgin Mary was a forgiving mother, a hearer of prayers and a consoler of injured souls, dispensing security and comfort. In Marseille's little Italy, the mother of Christ held a place of particular importance. She was their protector. Like them, Mary had been forced to flee her own country, taking refuge in Egypt to protect Jesus from persecution. Giovanni observed the Pacchianos' every movement. He ran his hand through his hair nervously. How would he go about asking for Maria's hand in marriage? Definitely not in front of their grandmother. Fiora and Claudio would be going back to work. Domenica stood in the way. The pearls of her rosary slipped between her fingers with repetitive clicks. The sanctimonious old dame was eagerly awaiting the statue's arrival. The aeroplane from Rome had not yet landed. On the screen they showed the Italian delegation, ready to accept the statue from their countrymen. The French authorities were holding back the crowds of Italian families who'd come to admire the statue of Jesus's

Mother. The plane touched down. Domenica clenched a fist around her rosary. Giovanni watched her from the corner of his eye. Would she stay there praying all day? He had to find a way to get around her so he could speak with Gustavo alone. Was she praying for her granddaughter? Maria might have told her something. Domenica had had a dream the night before. While she and her friends were playing cards, she was carrying the porcelain tea service that Fiora had received as a wedding gift. Everything fell to the ground and shattered into a thousand pieces as her friends looked on, aghast. She kept her vision to herself and spoke of it to no-one. She gave Gustavo an inquisitive look. Her son-in-law was not religious but had taken a whole day off for the occasion. Gustavo's heart was heavy. Maria had come back late last night. This morning, she got up far too early for her typing class. His daughter had held Giovanni's hand all through midnight mass. What was going on between those two? He'd find out soon enough. They'd soon loosen his tongue and tear a strip off the little bastard.

"What time are you going back to the factory?" he asked Fiora.

"The boss gave me two hours off. I can't believe I'm being paid even though I'm not working. Isn't that incredible?"

"It's a shame Maria can't be here for the ceremony!" Domenica sighed.

"They'll be getting their annual grades soon," Claudio reminded her, "so we'll find out if Maria's been chosen for the civil service."

"That's it, that's it! Our beautiful statue!" exclaimed Domenica, not taking her eyes off the screen for even a second.

"Look at that herd of sheep baahing over a lump of stone!" Gustavo snorted.

"What does it look like?" Domenica asked, barely able to see it.

"It has a crown of stars," Fiora said.

"She's crushing a snake with her foot," Claudio added.

"She's carrying a puppy," said Gustavo with a grin.

"Gustavo! That's the Baby Jesus!" Fiora fumed.

"She must be so beautiful. So beautiful," Domenica repeated, her voice trembling with emotion.

"She's lovely!" Giovanni confirmed.

"Well, that's that, I have to get back to the site," said Claudio, who'd only taken an hour off.

"Mama, don't forget to buy a fish for tonight," Fiora called as she closed the door behind her.

"Where are they all going? We have to finish this bottle of wine!" Gustavo laughed to himself.

Domenica left to go and buy the fish for dinner. Giovanni found himself alone with Gustavo, who was sipping his glass of wine. The moment had come; it was now or never. Gustavo lay down on the couch, preparing to catch the young man out. He closed his eyes and pretended to be falling asleep. The young Italian remembered Maria's advice. Early this morning, they had spoken before Maria went to her class:

"If he starts falling asleep, just sit down on the couch as if everything's normal. As soon as he opens his eyes, start talking."

"What if he's been drinking?"

"Don't worry, he can always muster a bit of clarity."

"Wish me luck."

Giovanni sat down. He was ready. Sure enough, Gustavo opened his eyes. The little fish had taken the bait, but it was he who broke the silence:

"Gustavo, I need to talk to you!" Giovanni blurted out.

"You need to talk to me or you want to talk to me?" asked Gustavo, blinking with a crafty smile.

"I want to confide in you, as a son would to his father—"

"Ouffa! Hold on, let's open some pastis! We can't have a serious talk without a drink. And don't tell Fiora."

Gustavo poured a pastis for Giovanni, who watched the clear liquid turn cloudy white. The father looked at the young man with suspicion. He wanted to know it all. The whole truth. He hoped that the drink would loosen the boy's tongue.

"You know, Gustavo, I'm very fond of your daughter—"

"Listen to me, young man! I'm disappointed. I took you in, I helped you find work. I trusted you. I'm not finished yet. And you think you can seduce my daughter?" he pointed his finger at the boy.

"Gustavo! I respect you—"

"Listen to me!" the father interrupted him again. "Maria is a serious young woman. She wants to go far in life. She has a dream, to work for the French government. And you're leading her down the wrong path. You're breaking her concentration. She comes home late at night. How is she supposed to work? Aren't you ashamed?"

"Gustavo, please! Let me speak. Since I arrived in Marseille, I've always respected your family. And I am grateful to you. I also want Maria to succeed; I want her to be happy. I've never wanted to harm her."

"So what are you playing at? We saw you, holding her hand in the church. That's a mark of disrespect to the Pacchianos."

"What do you mean?" the young man hesitated, feeling more and more uncomfortable.

"Maria, my daughter, has never been interested in boys. And then you show up and you besmirch her honour. Look at me, I'm being serious. What have you two been doing?"

"Just going for walks—"

"Don't toy with me! I wasn't born yesterday! Look me in the eye, young man. It's all riding on that girl. I never had a chance to get an education, because my parents were poor. But Maria can do whatever she wants; she'll make it happen. But if you get her pregnant...you hear me? If you get her pregnant, you little worm—"

Giovanni was lost at sea. He managed to stammer: "Gustavo!" He looked ready to beg.

"Don't get on your knees yet, boy," Gustavo told him. "It won't work. If your intentions were pure, would you need to humiliate yourself?"

"Gustavo, I'm crazy about Maria."

"Crazy? I don't need you to be crazy, just show some damn respect!"

"I want to marry her!" Giovanni had finally reached his last nerve.

The Pacchianos were gathered around the table. Fiora wondered what was going on. Since she'd returned from the factory, Gustavo was acting very out of sorts. He smiled constantly and wasn't joking around with anyone. He wasn't drinking. Something unusual must have happened while she was away. "What's going on?" she whispered to Domenica, who was removing the salt-baked fish from the oven. Domenica shifted her eyes to signal she was none the wiser than Fiora. She pretended not to know, but in her heart of hearts, she sensed that a happy event was coming. Her vision was anchored in her brain. They sat around the table; Giovanni felt a weight had been lifted. He hadn't had time to speak to Maria, but she understood from his contented smile that things had gone well. Gustavo went into his bedroom, leaving his family to wait and wonder.

"What's with him today?" asked Claudio innocently.

"No idea," replied Maria, giving nothing away.

She winked at Giovanni and held his hand under the table. His face gave nothing away; this wasn't the time to mess around. Gustavo came back, a bottle of wine in his hand. Fiora examined the bottle, recognising its importance. Pacchiano had bought it when his daughter was born. He'd promised to open it on the day a man asked for her hand. Fiora was moved. She said nothing, but a tear ran down her cheek.

"Mama, is everything OK?" Claudio asked, worried. She motioned to him to take off his hat.

"I have something to announce," Gustavo said with great solemnity, standing at the head of the table.

"What's this all about? Gustavo's making speeches now?" Domenica needled, irked that he was in her spot.

"Let him speak, he's the man of the house," Fiora retorted, eager to hear what her husband had to say.

Gustavo uncorked the bottle and poured wine for everyone. They remained silent and waited. Claudio raised his glass.

"Nobody drink! Can't you see I'm about to make a speech, you twit! What are you going to toast when I haven't announced anything yet?"

"And why is that hat still on? Show your father some respect!" Fiora added.

"But...this is how Bogart wears it."

"Are you a movie star? Are you from America?"

"No, but—"

"Then take it off!"

"For Christ's sake, let me speak!" Gustavo cried.

"Sorry, my dear. Go ahead."

"My son-in-law is so touchy," Domenica sighed.

"Put a sock in it, Gran."

Domenica was rattled and looked to her daughter for support. Gustavo cleared his throat and raised his glass:

"A man whose values I respect, an honest working man, a man I think of as my son, a man whom I love and respect, has asked for my daughter Maria's hand—"

"Papa, it's Marie."

"Oh yes. As I was saying, he has asked for Marie's hand in marriage. The wine you are about to drink should be savoured, for it is no ordinary wine. It is a symbol. It signifies that my daughter is about to leave the family that raised her and start her own. That she will leave her father's protection to be cherished by her husband."

"Isn't this a bit much?" Fiora laughed, having never seen Gustavo so serious.

"Too much? My daughter is to be married, and you think it's too much?"

"Is this speech going to go on much longer? We want to drink!"

"Alright, I'm almost finished. As I was saying: Giovanni, you are now a part of this family. Cheers!"

The Pacchianos raised their glasses to Maria and her fiancé. Fiora wept with joy. Her daughter had found a match; all her worry had been in vain. Domenica threw herself upon Giovanni and hugged him tight, laughing with surprise and delight. The old woman had been worried about this moment, but she'd always had a soft spot for the young man. "Take good care of her," she whispered in his ear. Giovanni felt intimidated but kissed her on the forehead. Pride filled his heart; he was part of the family. These were his loved ones; his in-laws. If only Nina could be there. But you can't have it all. Claudio put his Bogart hat back on. He motioned to Giovanni to kiss Maria. Giovanni crossed his glass with Maria's, looked at her tenderly and did just that.

15.

A worker was tied to a chair. The cord dug painfully into his skin. The rays of sunlight that fell through the warehouse's glass roof fell like a lead weight on his head. His glazed eyes were rooted to the floor, absorbed by the blackish dust that swirled and settled as his tormentors moved around him. Graziano's shadow stretched out before him. He looked at the man moving around his chair, imposing, massive and brutal. He ran his tongue over his lips; his moustache tasted like blood. He must be bleeding from the nose; his face was numbed by the pain. The salt in his sweat pricked at his wounds. The sensation reassured him; he was alive. Someone hit him in the back of the neck. The iron bar rattled his body, slack as a bag of flour. He cried out. He closed his eyes, and they hit him again, in the legs this time. The electric shock of pain shot up his spine. "Who did it? Talk!" Grasso barked at him, kicking over his chair. "Who was it?" The worker smiled up at him from the ground. His expression was coy. Did they really think he would talk now? He'd been in fights before. His daily life was suffering. He spat blood onto the great brute's shoes. "Now that's just disgusting. You're like a pig. Do you know what I do to pigs?" Grasso took the worker's arm and bit into it until it bled. The man screamed. Paolo the Fixer snickered as he lit his cigarette:

"Eat him up, big man!"

"He's too skinny, and he stinks!"

"You want some *ragu* to go on that?"

"Let's stuff his arse with olives, see if that helps."

"I'd have suggested anchovies up the nose, but you're the expert." Franz looked down on them menacingly. He cracked his knuckles one by one. He'd stayed back on purpose, marking the distance that separated him, the specialist, the pragmatist, from these brain-dead thugs whose skills extended only as far as smacking people around and cackling like hyenas. Giovanni heard the tell-tale grinding of teeth that meant Franz was losing patience. The German came down the stairs; Grasso and Paolo the Fixer stood back with respect. They stopped laughing, and observed him. What was the sadist about to do? They had to admit, he brought imagination to the game. Paolo the Fixer watched him remove a knife from his belt. The worker sensed that something had changed. The silence did not bode well for him. Two polished boots appeared before his eyes. He heard the clicking of a flick-knife opening up.

"Are you going to gut him like a fish?"

"You'll see."

"You'll have no problem dragging it out of this traitor."

"Shut up."

The stare of two blue eyes chilled the worker to the bone. Franz knelt down beside him and touched his knife against the worker's eyeball: "If you close that eye, you lose it."

Giovanni threw the body hastily into the trunk. The worker had bled out. He hadn't talked. The traitor would burn like a holy effigy. He'd had to clean up the blood and tie a rag around the eyes in order to avoid suspicion; any trace of blood on the floor was a sign of murder.

"Giovanni, start the car!"

The young man sat in the driver's seat, waiting for Paolo the Fixer and Graziano to get in. As he was about to put the car into first gear, he froze. He felt the cold metal barrel of Grasso's Beretta against his temple. Had his time finally come? He kept his eyes on the windshield. He didn't move or make a sound; this was not the time to feed their suspicions. He knew all too well that they would tolerate no excuses. He waited, like a rabbit in a trap. Paolo broke the silence:

"I warned you, Giovanni."

"What's going on?"

"You goddamn rat!"

"I've always followed the boss's orders!"

"Do you take us for fools?"

"What are you talking about?"

"Start the fucking car. We're going to the dump."

The car crawled along the winding path; Giovanni watched Graziano's face in the rear-view mirror. Grasso had his dull, cow-like eyes fixed on him and kept the gun pressed against Giovanni's head despite the jostling of the car. All he had to do was pull the trigger. It seemed impossible to think this oaf would be the one to take him out. "Stop in front of that heap," Paolo the Fixer ordered. Giovanni knew all too well what this place was for. Nobody heard gunshots out here, or at least nobody cared what happened in a dump outside the city limits. "Get out!" Graziano mooed. The young man did as he was told. They ordered him to open the trunk, take out the body and hide it among the rubbish. Giovanni moved like a man on his way to the gallows, seeing all his sins brought to life before his eyes. His movements were not his own; he was somewhere between life and death, convinced that his end was near. The worker's body sank into the detritus. Giovanni handed the shovel back to Paolo the Fixer with grave solemnity. "On your knees." This was it. Giovanni closed his eyes, clenched his fists and waited. He was shaken from his torpor by the sound of an engine; the car was speeding off. The two crooks had spared him. The mountain of rubbish was on fire. Butterflies of black ash fluttered from the worker's body. 'And unto dust we are returned', the young man thought as he made off, his heart pounding with fear.

"Merry Christmas Mama,

I wish I could have spent Christmas with you, but I'm sure that you didn't spend it alone and that Marcello and Valentina kept you company. I'm counting on them to watch over you, and on you to watch over them. I know how Valentina likes to treat you with the little gifts she gets from New York; I remember how you used to smile when she'd give you a scarf or a pair of gloves, always beautifully wrapped and slipped discreetly into your market basket. She liked to try and surprise you, even though you knew it was coming. She was discreet enough not to give you presents in front of us, knowing that we could never give you anything so luxurious, and she didn't want to embarrass you either when you had only flowers to offer her in return. Marseille has lots of Christmas traditions. On Christmas Eve they serve thirteen desserts. Italians in Marseille don't earn much, so most people don't buy all thirteen. At the Pacchiano house, we had nougat and candied almonds — Domenica, their grandmother, made them, but she has dentures so she couldn't even eat them! I felt bad for her, but Gustavo wasn't as concerned as I was and he ate a pile of nougat right in front of her. She didn't take the bait and even filled our Christmas stockings with all kinds of sweets. I think she misses eating them herself, so she likes to see us eating them for her. Maria's favourite sweets are Pierrot Gourmand lollipops. Claudio likes liquorice, and I like the 'roudoudous'. They're little sweets moulded into the shape of seashells; maybe they remind me of my days fishing in Livorno. We ate so many that when we got to the table we weren't even hungry anymore. Fiora told us off for eating our dessert before dinner, but another roast fish wasn't really that original of a Christmas meal anyway. Domenica was chuckling away to herself, happy that her gifts had been so successful. Gustavo opened a few bottles of wine for the occasion, and I have to admit we probably drank more than we ate. When it was time to get ready for midnight mass, we were in a bit of a state. I had to tie Gustavo's tie for him. Luckily the cold sobered us up fairly quickly, and after our walk to the church we felt better.

I have to tell you something important: I've been going out with Maria for over a month now. She's a brave and studious girl. I know you'd like her. I'd really like you to meet her one day. She's beautiful, and I admire her so much. It's difficult to explain what I feel for her. I'd never felt anything like this before. After midnight mass, I took her to the Aygalades waterfall. We talked a lot. She said "yes." It was spontaneous, I didn't even have a ring. Everything happened naturally. She whispered wonderful things to me that I'll never forget. On the day the statue of Notre Dame de Lorette arrived in France, I took my chance to ask her father for her hand. Believe me, Mama, he was no pushover. I confided in him like a son to a father. In the end, he unbuttoned the top two buttons of his shirt, looked me right in the eyes and put his hand on my shoulder. "You're one of us now. Take good care of her." Then he kissed me on the forehead.

Gustavo's already looking for a place for us to live in Belle de Mai. The rent isn't too high, but you have to look around to find something decent. That's why Gustavo has also got me a permanent job as a mason, not just an apprentice. My pay's going to go up soon. Maria's already thinking about how she'll decorate the house. Of course, I know that we could live happily in Marseille, but do I really want to spend my whole life in Belle de Mai? Did I really give up being a fisherman to become a stonemason? Of course, you'd tell me that finding love is reward enough. You'd tell me that you have to put down roots somewhere and that happiness isn't always to be found elsewhere. But you know your Giovanni; he's too ambitious to be satisfied by any one city. I wanted to explore the whole world, and for now, I've only known Livorno and Marseille. But if Maria is accepted into the French civil service, I'll have to support her career choices. It's her dream. Only four or five girls from her stenography class will be chosen to work in the government. We're all waiting for her end-of-year grades. I know that Maria can do it. She's a hard worker, and she's smart. I'd be so proud of her, my pretty wife working in the French government. But something makes me hope that she doesn't get selected for Marseille. I want to go to Paris. They say it's the most amazing city. Maybe Maria and I could take our chances up there. I recently met a concert pianist who lives in the capital. He was telling me how great it is — he called it the City of Light — and told me to look him up if I was ever in Paris. For now, I'm focusing on the wedding and working on the building sites. We'll see what happens. I'll write to you again soon.

All my love,
Your Giogio."

Belle de Mai had been swallowed up in a terrible snowstorm. Gusts of wind whistled between the buildings, and Italian families soothed their children as they struggled to fall asleep. The children wanted to look out their windows to see the storm, but it was getting late. Their parents put them back to bed and did their best to keep them warm, throwing logs on the fire or keeping the stove lit. The Pacchianos were beginning to worry: "She shouldn't be much longer, she should have finished her messages by now," Giovanni told Gustavo, who was pacing back and forth with his fists clenched. It was nearing midnight, and Maria hadn't come home from her class. She had left the school and started to hurry back, her notebook in hand. She'd never been so late. Gustavo would be furious. Giovanni would be annoyed. She went up an alley, trying to read the street name but unable to. The snowstorm prevented her from making out any of the signs to tell her where she was. She was lost. She finally arrived in front of what seemed to be a wide boulevard. The streets were deserted; there was not a soul to be seen. She hurried on. She'd be getting a serious talking-to when she got home. At the same time, a man in a long black coat was walking briskly along boulevard de la Madeleine. His blue eyes pierced through the snowy blur from underneath his cap. The snow crunched beneath his feet. A branch snapped under the weight of the snow and fell at Maria's feet. It had just missed her. The man undid the belt of his coat. He took a twenty-calibre round from his pocket and loaded it into his Mossberg shotgun. His prey was near. Maria looked to see if there were any shops she could recognise. The man raised his shotgun. He pointed it at her back. She turned around. "Is that you, my love?" He pulled the trigger, and the young woman fell. The shot rang out around Marseille.

16.

The lavender hue that came before the dawn cast a sad light over the city. The Neapolitan fishermen left their homes with shovels in their hands; the roads to the Old Port were all blocked with snow. Last night's blizzard promised a good catch for today, and the fishermen shovelled bravely, swinging their spades back and forth to cut a path to their day's labour. Arriving on Rue Toussaint, two fishermen spied a dark shape protruding from the snow, further on down the street.

"What's that?"

"Looks like clothes."

"You think?"

"I don't think anything, I said that's what it looks like."

"Let's take a look."

They crept towards the pile of snow, afraid of what they might find when they brushed away the uppermost layer. They walked in single file; the first man spotted something stiff poking out of the snow.

"I think it's a hand!" he hissed, frightened.

"You do it, I feel sick."

"You think I'm better at identifying bodies than you?"

"It's so small. It looks like a woman's hand."

"Poor lass must have got caught in the storm."

The two men leaned over the shape. They made out a face through the thin sheet of snow. It was a young woman, her dark hair spread about her. Frozen streams of blood trickled from her nose. The fishermen looked at her with trembling lips. The thought of this young woman being stalked by death moved them to tears.

"Her face is so peaceful."

"She's beautiful. She's dead but so beautiful."

"Let's move the snow from around her body."

"What was she doing around Belle de Mai?"

"Is she Italian?"
"Good God, I hope not!"

"Maria! Maria!" Fiora trembled, her throat swelling and her eyes straining to look at her daughter's body. She waved Gustavo away with her hand. He was frozen, unable to say a word. His mind would not accept it. His wife cried, wailing to the heavens. His face crumpled with pain and distress. "Maria, Maria!" she cried with all her might. What had she done to deserve this? Her child, her flesh and blood, was gone forever. She ran her hand through Maria's bloodied hair, pulling out her bun and closing her eyes. She kissed her forehead. She ran her hair through her fingertips one last time. A police officer grabbed Fiora by the shoulders and pulled her up. "I'm sorry Madame, but we must take the body to the coroner." Fiora's cries rose higher and higher. She broke down, her voice rasping: "My daughter! My daughter..." She shrugged the policeman off, and he let her cry over the body. The Italian families gathered around Fiora were shaken. They watched the mother trying to wake her daughter. The Pacchiano girl had been murdered. She was dead. The Italians were dumbstruck. They were all numb, all hurt. The girl was so mature and so kind. Who could have done this to her? She was to be married; she'd just gotten engaged. She was going to work for the French government and make the whole community proud. To come so close, only to be cut down. Fiora stroked her daughter's body one last time, before collapsing in her husband's arms. The crowd moved forward. "Get back, now!" shouted a policeman, raising his baton.

Part III

Aleksander Spielman

1.

In Paris, tall trees rustled in the gardens and the acacias were flowering on the avenues again as the Parisians took comfort in the bright colours of spring. On the balconies of the *Haussmannian* buildings, blackened with soot, violet bellflowers and red begonias were coming into bloom. It was late afternoon, and the square in front of the Opera was busy with traffic as bicycles chicaned through the lines of cars and carriages. The incessant sounding of *klaxons* signalled that it was rush hour. Nannies were taking children home from school, wrapped up in their duffle coats and giddily munching their afternoon treats under the watchful eye of the Opera's green dome. A little girl picked crumbs from her croissant and threw them to the pigeons, then shrieked when one of them landed on her schoolbag. An American tourist turned at the sound and was relieved to find it was nothing serious enough to break the spell of the city's charm. In front of him, a couple were looking at the posters displayed in a Morris column, trying to choose between the latest Jean Gabin film and a show at the Bobino theatre. The sound of an accordion wafted over the square, the same elderly musician singing the same Edith Piaf songs he did every day. His voice was unwelcome competition for the newspaper hawker, who was trying to flag down passers-by. A man bought a copy of *France Soir* and scanned the headlines as he walked: *"Fire in the city centre," "Charlie Chaplin meets Abbé Pierre," "Give your wife the gift of freedom with a Moulinex food processor!" "Housing Crisis: families living like sardines," "Clashes in front of the Citroën factory in Javel," "Watch out for counterfeit Menier Chocolate!"*

At the Nutcracker café beside the Opera, an old woman was arguing with the waiter: "Now Lucien, you listen to me. I've been coming to this café for over thirty years, and I've known you for six! And how many times have I told you that after my onion soup, I want my *croque-monsieur* cooked for twenty minutes. It should be golden. Look at this, it's as white as snow!" The young waiter gushed his apologies and took the dish back to the kitchen. It was the end of the day, and Lucien was up against it. He readjusted his tie under his waistcoat, shone his shoes with the corner of his serviette, re-tied his apron and took a deep breath before he pushed through the swing doors and re-entered the dining room. He swayed past the other waiters, tray in hand. Despite the swarms of tourists and the high-maintenance regulars, Lucien liked his job at the Nutcracker. It had retained the feel of the Belle Epoque, with its crystal chandeliers and copper bar top. He'd seen a few celebrities there, too. They were usually photographed when they came in, and guests could admire the picture of Michèle Morgan and Gérard Phillipe drinking Champagne together, given pride of place between the two grand mirrors. A customer signalled to him from the back of the room. Lucien went over to the card players, who'd finished their bottle of Côtes-du-Rhône.

"I'll have a *tomate*, please," one of them said to Lucien as he dealt the cards.

"Right away, sir," the waiter answered politely.

The waiter came back a few minutes later, his tray loaded with a glass of tomato juice, salt and pepper and a jug of water.

"For God's sake," the card player sighed, "don't you know what a *tomate* is? Pernod with a spoonful of grenadine."

"So sorry, I mistook you for a tourist," Lucien mumbled as he took back the glass.

"These tourists, they're a nightmare! They refuse to enjoy proper French cuisine. But it's the government's fault. All our tourism brochures talk about is châteaux and cathedrals. That's all well and good, but why not throw in a recipe for Normandy sole or something? Better they come for that, instead of asking for overcooked steak and cucumber!"

"Alas, you can say that again, sir! Do you know what I served three tourists for breakfast yesterday? Smoked kippers with plum jam! All washed down with a glass of milk!"

"Good grief!" the card player reacted, holding his hand over his mouth in disgust.

Lucien pedalled along the banks of the Seine, his beret pulled down to his ears. The green stalls of the riverside booksellers were overflowing with postcards and books of every genre. He stopped his bicycle between the Pont Neuf and the Pont Saint-Michel, sure he would find a book worthy of his bedside table. A book by Camus, *The Plague,* caught his eye. He handed over a few of the coins from his day's tips. A golden-brown *croque-monsieur* was worth its weight in literature. It was six o'clock by the time Lucien arrived in the Latin Quarter. He pushed his bike into the courtyard of the apartment building and ran into the caretaker; there was no mail for him today, and none for his roommate either. The Italian would be disappointed. Lucien climbed the stairs to the top floor. The bedroom door wasn't locked; it hadn't closed properly in ages.

"Hello, my friend! Are you done snoozing yet?"

"Any mail for me, Lucien?" Giovanni asked, stretching out lazily.

"Not today," Lucien shook his head.

"My mother hasn't written to me for a week."

"The letters take time to get here, don't worry."

Giovanni got out of bed, his sheets scattered across the mattress. He'd writhed about all night and all day, unaware of the hour. He felt no inclination to rise with the rest of the world, and no connection to them. He lit a cigarette; he liked the sound of the lighter as the cool metal snapped open under the pressure of his thumb. He watched the cigarette burn down, crackling yellow and red until it was dust. He held it firmly between his fingers. He smoked too much these days, and when he wasn't smoking, he was coughing up what he'd smoked the day before. It calmed him, he liked to think, or at least kept his mind occupied. He could not bear to remember. His waking hours were spent trying to erase every trace of memory, every word he'd heard and every face he'd seen. But forgetting was more difficult than he had anticipated, even when he devoted all his energy to it. To forget her was to betray her, to murder Maria a second time. A noise broke his train of thought; a pigeon was cooing at the window. Its eyes were perfectly round, composed of a black circle inside a white circle, and devoid of emotion. The bird lived in the moment, seeing everything through its simple, round eyes. "Listen, friend, you can't live in this mess forever!" He wished Lucien would leave him alone. His roommate's futile optimism bored him. Lucien could never understand. Maria Pacchiano was dead. He wanted to scream and smash all the furniture, and it took all his energy to contain that rage. He lay down on his bed again and stared at the ceiling, listening to his own breathing. He was alive. Despite all his sins, he was the one who'd survived. The world was profoundly unjust. Lucien tried another approach:

"Get dressed at least. You barely look like a person anymore. At this rate, I'll come home to find you've turned into a pillow or a slipper."

"Very funny. Leave me be. I need to reflect."

"*Reflect*? Are you having a laugh? Come on, we're going out tonight!"

"Where to? And with who?"

"What do you care? You've been hibernating in that pit for five months."

"Not this time."

"There won't be any other times. Today is the day you go out."

"I don't want to do anything, leave me in peace and let me die if I want to. I don't owe you anything. Last I checked my rent was paid."

"These tragic speeches of yours are getting old. Maria's not coming back; let her lie where she is, eating the flowers from the root up. The worms will look after her."

"Have you no respect?" Giovanni's anger flared.

"I respect the living, and that's plenty."

"You journalists are so busy chasing stories, you have no heart left for the people in them."

"Yeah well, this 'journalist' hasn't sold a story for a month now."

Tempers were rising. Jean-Pierre was shouting in Lucien's face: "Yes, I'm a communist and I'm not ashamed to admit it!" Lucien launched into a tirade on Marxists, Trotskyists and Stalinists, and how none of them could agree with one another. Jean-Pierre lost his temper, shouting about the travesty of the Communist Party being excluded from the government. Lucien stayed calm and finished the bottle of wine without batting an eyelid. Claudine tried to calm Jean-Pierre down, but the bespectacled student would not listen. Now he was talking about Jean-Paul Sartre. Lucien preferred Camus. Jean-Pierre liked Malraux even better. Camus supported colonisation, but Malraux was a hero: he'd gone to fight in Spain.

"What was your precious Sartre doing then, eh?" he asked Lucien with a sneer.

"He was theorising about universal responsibility. After Sartre, there is no more pretending, no more hiding away. We are defined by our actions. There can be no collusion without traitors, no idleness without the lazy, no ignorance that is not wilful."

Claudine liked Camus. She found Jean-Paul Sartre somewhat cold, and his philosophy esoteric. She preferred novels anyway. She'd seen a play by Jean-Paul Sartre; she couldn't remember the name, but it was too political anyway. "How can a thing be too political?" Jean-Pierre scoffed. Giovanni wasn't listening; he was tired of watching them debate and butt heads over mere ideas. They did not know that real life wasn't found in books; there was more to it than ideas. Life just happens to you, without rhyme or reason. It was true that he hadn't read much, and he felt worlds behind these three friends who could spend hours arguing over fictions that had nothing to do with them. He hadn't even read Dante, a revelation that had shocked Jean-Pierre. When he'd seen Rodin's sculpture of the gates of hell, he assumed that all Italians had read Dante. As if Italians had had nothing better to do these past few years, and as if there were copies of *The Divine Comedy* just lying around Livorno. He could read, and that was something. Claudine placed her hand on his and looked at him with her wide, compassionate eyes:

"Giovanni, you seem pensive. I'm sure all this must seem dull to you."

"We're not boring him, he just needs to brush up on his French literature," Jean-Pierre interjected with a triumphant air.

"You're drunk, and you're working our last nerves with your Sartre obsession," Lucien quipped. "I'm going to order another bottle."

"No, I just have other things on my mind," Giovanni replied to Claudine with a smile.

"I heard you play the harmonica. Lucien told me you play the blues. I'd love to hear you play sometime," the young lady told him.

"Lucien's not a fan of my music; he finds it uncouth and says I need to hear some real French music."

"Lucien's tastes are a bit old-fashioned. He likes protest songs. I've even seen him weep listening to Barbara."

"That's not true! What are you talking about?" Lucien protested, returning with a bottle of *Bourgogne*.

"Everyone knows, there's no point in denying it! We all saw you!" Jean-Pierre laughed. "Pour me a glass."

"Perhaps it did happen, once."

"Oh yes, the truth comes out! He admits it!" Jean-Pierre continued, holding up Giovanni's glass to be filled. "Let's get this Italian drunk so he at least laughs along with us."

"We should take him to the Opera as well. It's right by your work, Lucien. Paris has a fine orchestra and some of the world's best singers. Lucien, take him to hear Verdi, Puccini, Vivaldi and all the rest!" Claudine suggested.

"Enough of Italy and all those love stories!" Jean-Pierre exclaimed. "Aleksander Spielman is performing a magnificent concerto at the moment."

The name struck Giovanni like a blow. He repeated it to himself, trying to decipher the hieroglyphics of his memory. He knew the name was important, so why had he forgotten whose it was? Jean-Pierre had launched into another endless monologue. Giovanni could not concentrate. It must have been in Marseille; he hadn't met anyone important in Paris. "What do you think, Giovanni?" Claudine asked him. He mumbled some vague reply. She looked at him with confusion but didn't press him further. Lucien's friends saw Giovanni as a sort of simple dreamer. He dredged the depths of his memory; he'd tried so hard to forget Marseille that it now seemed impossible to focus on any one thing, and his thoughts were interrupted by the conversation. "Sartre's just finished *The Respectful Prostitute*; the first performance will be in November. I wouldn't miss it for the world," Jean-Pierre continued. '*Respectful Prostitute*'...Aleksander Spielman...there was something that connected them, but Giovanni could not put his finger on it. Then all of a sudden, it came back to him. The card club, the opium, the nightmare interrupted by that impossibly refined gentleman. He'd been unable to climax with the prostitute afterwards and had chased the man down on the street. Then he remembered their conversation in the restaurant. Aleksander Spielman, the elegant pianist who'd graced Giovanni with his company all those months ago.

2.

The great lights of the Paris Opera dimmed and went out, and the conversations stopped. Sitting in the vast crowd, Giovanni basked in the silence before the performance began — a silence unlike any other, as two thousand people held their breath. All eyes were fixed on the stage, waiting for the slightest movement of the curtain, but the thick velvet remained an immutable wall of scarlet. All of Parisian high society was reduced to a vague mass, rendered mute and swathed in darkness. Their power, their money, their expensive tastes — none of it mattered now. Giovanni was one with the crowd, feeling close to other people for the first time in many months. The curtains parted, and the silence swelled with anticipation. In the middle of the stage sat the piano, wreathed by the circular beam of the spotlight. Around it there was nothing; it was well known that Monsieur Spielman had no patience for the superfluous. His music must fly like an arrow, reaching its target unimpeded by any distraction. The man himself appeared, walking towards the light with a steady, placid gait. Giovanni recognised him; sitting just meters away, he felt he could almost smell the cologne and hear whispers of the Polish accent. Aleksander Spielman sat down on the bench. He removed his white gloves and laid them beside him. He ran his hands just above the keys, gently reassuring them as was his ritual. Finally, he laid his fingers upon the ivory. The pianist began to play a Schubert sonata, *moderato*. Giovanni heard a child walking through the night, his feet sinking into the crisp snow. It is young Aleksander strolling through Kazimierz, the Jewish neighbourhood in Krakow. Aleksander likes to sneak out after dinner to look at the old synagogue, admiring the stonework of this sacred place even at the tender age of eight. He likes to seek refuge in the solitude of his faith. Giovanni remembered his mother praying, and the tears that would sometimes come to her eyes at the church in Livorno when she'd found the priest's sermon particularly moving. He wished now that he had faith, so he could be buoyed by hope and slake his thirst for forgiveness. He wanted so desperately to atone for his sins, but there was no absolution without faith. He believed in nothing; life was suffering, and death brought no resolution. Aleksander wonders if the synagogue is open. He jumps the gate and pushes against the building's heavy door. It does not resist. The sacred texts of the Torah resonate between the child's temples as he hears a distant voice in the midst of song; this voice he would seek for the rest of his life. The pianist began the second movement of the sonata, *andante poco moto*. His brown hair tumbled over his shoulders, with the spotlight casting a blue haze around his feathered locks as Giovanni looked on, transfixed. He wanted to run his hand through that hair as he had once done to Maria, when he would look at her with such solemnity, taking his happiness so seriously. Maria sometimes made fun of him. Aleksander had loved Sebastian; they were teenagers, and they met secretly at night after dinner, behind the synagogue. Their love was forbidden; criminal, even. These moments were of innocent intensity, full of romance. They met perhaps a dozen times. They didn't talk much, and Aleksander knew little about Sebastian's life. Speaking would have made their sacrilege too real and shattered the magic of those ethereal moments. Aleksander never told his parents about his love for Sebastian. Spielman began the third movement of sonata number sixteen, *scherzo*. The pianist's body tensed. One day, his mother had found a letter from Sebastian in her son's desk, announcing he was getting married and explaining that the two could never see each other again. Aleksander watched his mother wail and cry. He would go to hell; he had disgraced their family name and ruined their lives; what if his father found out; her life meant nothing to her now. A tear ran down the pianist's cheek. The entire hall was brimming with emotion. The next day he would leave for the Warsaw Conservatory. He would never see his parents again. Sebastian was gone. The pianist closed his eyes. He saw only freezing white; the white of winter and of loss. Aleksander Spielman began the final movement, *allegro vivace*. He was in France, far from Kazimierz, when one by one, family by family, everyone he'd known as a child was sent to their death. The pianist lifted his hands from the keys. The silence of the ending echoed that of the beginning. Aleksander Spielman took a bow, and the Opera lights came to life once again amidst deafening applause.

In the grand foyer, lined with mirrors and interspersed with chandeliers, the cream of Parisian high society discussed their thoughts on the performance, dainty coupes of Champagne in hand. Giovanni wandered through the gallery, admiring the statues and the paintings on the vaulted roof. It was all very grandiose; all this pomp and luxury impressed him. He eavesdropped on the conversations between the women in their evening dresses and the men in their tuxedoes. Aleksander Spielman was incomparable. They'd remember this concerto for the rest of their days. A historic performance, anyone with any taste would agree. A nice change from French records and their gushingly emotional lyrics. It was getting late, and time to go for oysters at the Coupole, or *escargots* at the Procope. Giovanni watched them file out in pairs, and his stomach writhed in knots. It was time to seek out Spielman. Would the pianist recognise him after their lunch in Les Auffes? He made his way towards the dressing rooms, but an usher blocked his path:

"Sorry sir, this area is off limits to the public. Only those on the list can come through."

"And who might you be?" Giovanni demanded, taking a serious tone. "Do you know who I am?"

"I'm very sorry to detain you, but Monsieur Spielman only sees guests who've been put on the list to come back here. It's my job to stop anyone who isn't—"

"I am the duke of Palarorski!" Giovanni insisted, rolling his Rs. "If you don't let me pass I shall have more to say to you."

"Please excuse me, your grace, I didn't recognise you."

Giovanni paused for a moment in front of the door, which was slightly ajar. He stole a glance into the dressing room. Aleksander Spielman was removing his makeup in front of the mirror. Two younger men were fawning over him. They examined the bouquets of roses while commenting on the performance:

"Aleksander, you had them in the palm of your hand. You were beautiful, you played like a god. You were, in a word, perfect. Perhaps a slight wobble in that third movement, but I doubt many in the audience had ears trained enough to notice."

"Of course, all the Delavallères have well-trained ears," Spielman smiled.

"Well, my father was a great opera director, after all."

"Indeed he was..."

Giovanni finally got a look at the pretentious young man's face. He was tall and blond, with a Roman nose and stilted manners. His suit was immaculate, and he wore a black satin bow tie under a starched collar. His pale, manicured hands shone under the diamond-studded lamps. He heard the sound of a Champagne cork popping. An effeminate young man had just served Spielman a glass.

"Thank you, Ambroise, I'm almost ready. Pour a glass for our friend Simon Delavallère. Let's toast and get out of here; the show's over."

At those words, Giovanni entered. He felt their eyes on him. He was unsure what to say, and so he gave a weak smile and mumbled a *bonsoir*.

"Who are you, young man? You do realise this area is off-limits to the public?" Aleksander said with polite contempt.

"The floor staff are woeful. You only have to look at this boy to know he doesn't belong here," added Simon Delavallère with a sneering smile.

"I like the way he looks," whispered Ambroise, raising his eyebrows at Giovanni.

"You're shy for an intruder. Go on and introduce yourself, since you're here!" Spielman ordered.

"My name is Giovanni Valci. I'm Italian, but I used to live in Marseille, which is where you and I met. I play the harmonica, and we talked about music—"

"The harmonica! Good heavens, we have a true artist in our midst!" mocked Simon Delavallère.

"Don't be such a boor, Simon. Let him finish. You were saying, young man?"

"When I arrived in Paris, I heard people talking about you and I wanted to see you again. I heard you play just now. It was...stupendous. I loved hearing your music. It made me feel the same as I did the first time I met you."

"Ah, it's a declaration of love!" Simon laughed.

"Who wouldn't want to hear such a thing?" added Ambroise, handing Giovanni a glass.

"My friend, you strike me as an honest lad. Come with us this evening."

"This should be a laugh..." Simon Delavallère rolled his eyes.

Giovanni was smoking a cigarette on the balcony of Aleksander Spielman's apartment. His gaze blurred over the streets of Paris, empty in the small hours of the morning. In Livorno, it would soon be time to head out in the boats. In Marseille, the shipyards would be filling with workers.

On the corner of one street, the lights of a bakery flickered on. He wanted to go down and get himself a croissant, and enjoy the serene charm of the deserted city. He could not stand the shrill voices of the other guests. He felt a hand on his shoulder. "Come and join us, my dear," Ambroise urged him with a friendly smile. Giovanni followed him obediently. After all, he should be making an effort now that he was here. A woman whose dress reminded him of a parrot's plumage fell upon him:

"I heard that you're Italian. *Roma, Venezia, Napoli*! You're from the most beautiful country in the world! I wept at the tower of Pisa, I prayed at the Vatican and I painted Rome from every angle! Did I tell you that I paint watercolours? Did I tell you I write poems? Italy is my muse, and you're Italian. Tell me all about it! Take me on a journey through your home country."

"I only really know Livorno and the coast around there."

"Livorno? Where's that?" she asked with disappointment.

"Livorno is a fishing town, and it has the Fortezza Vecchia, and the island of Gorgona. It's a small town near Florence. That's where I grew up."

"And what does one do in Livorno?"

"What does *one* do? You sleep, you eat and you fish..."

"That sounds deathly boring," sighed Simon Delavallère.

"You don't know the pleasures of a simple life, my dear Simon. Travelling expands the mind; you should take yourself to see how other people live, and you might return to your precious Saint-Germain-des-Prés with more humility," Spielman replied with disdain.

"I don't have the time to travel for pleasure. We businessmen aren't as free to roam as people think."

"You should take things easy, Simon! Enjoy your youth, as it will be over in a flash!" exclaimed the eccentric woman.

"Who's talking about enjoyment? The world does not exist to be your distraction," Aleksander cried.

"Do you miss your beloved Poland?" Ambroise enquired.

"That's not the point," the pianist replied coldly.

"Immigrants are like wild beasts whose appetites we cannot satisfy," Simon jibed, stung by Spielman's reproaches.

"We all know where extremist sentiments can lead us...it's dangerous to know nothing of other cultures, and criminal to feel superior to other peoples. But we're not here to talk about that tonight, we're here to celebrate Aleksander's success," Ambroise soothed.

"The French have a gift for quickly forgetting what they'd rather not remember," Giovanni commented, gaining confidence.

"How dare you? Italians are hardly any better, invading our shores to get away from your ridiculous politics," Simon cried.

"Gentlemen! We are here to discuss, not to argue," the woman insisted.

"She's right," said Ambroise. "Let's open another bottle of Champagne."

Aleksander withdrew to the other side of the room without a word. He had no need to excuse himself. All of his friends knew that there were certain issues he would never bend on. He could be sociable, casual and in good form, but certain topics would always reveal his intransigent temperament. He was not ashamed to be an immigrant, drawing strength and pride from this status instead of hiding it. He liked to recall his courage and obstinacy, and he had more than enough knowledge of European culture to embarrass any of the pretentious types who might look down on his Polish accent and eccentric manners. The pianist ceased paying attention to the content of the conversations, immersing himself instead in the music of their voices and the flickering light of the candelabra. The guests seemed to enjoy the soft ambiance, and he enjoyed observing them from a distance. Giovanni was sitting on the chaise longue with Ambroise, who was talking poetry and reciting verses by Lord Byron. The young Italian only had eyes for the pianist, whose melancholy inertia was somehow not without grace. Aleksander turned to him, feeling his gaze and the slight pressure of another soul being focused upon him. Giovanni got up, emotional from drinking, and went over to address his idol:

"I said this to you earlier, and I'll say it again: the way you play reminds me of our meeting in Marseille. The interest you sparked in me, like I was recognising something familiar in a foreign land."

"These are what our friend Goethe would call 'elective affinities': we are always fascinated by that which we resemble but remains beyond our reach. You have the soul of a musician, and like me, you've been uprooted. But between Poland and Italy, and between piano and harmonica, there is a particular chasm that we call life. Your life and mine each retain their own mystery."

"I'd like to know more about you. It sounds ridiculous, but I feel a certain connection between us, and I need to understand it."

"Let's take this moment to speak properly, then. I hope you know you're about to burst a dam."

"You seem quite modest, if I may say so."

"I have my secrets and my pains, of course — everyone does — and I'd go as far as to say they contribute to my fame. But talking is not painful to me; we can talk about anything and everything. Talking exposes less than music. When we play, we cannot cheat, and we cannot hide."

"I think that too. Sometimes people have asked me to play the harmonica just to hear something or break the silence, but playing music is never...harmless. But I know that I don't play a noble instrument, and I usually look more like an entertainer than a musician."

"It's astonishing that you would say that. When I was a boy, I was fascinated by the old accordion player in my neighbourhood. Nobody paid him any attention; people would sometimes throw him a coin, but they never looked him in the eye. But I can still see his face as clear as day, the light in his eyes when he played, and the deft movements of the thick, red fingertips that protruded from his gloves. What was it that made you take up the harmonica?"

"It was a gift. The only one my father ever gave me. I don't know the story behind it. I don't even know who it belonged to, or if someone else played it before I did. I'd like to think that one of my ancestors played it. If they did, my father never told me as much. You know, fishermen in Livorno aren't very talkative. They don't share much. I don't know anything about my family. When you're out there on the water, only the present counts for anything. You don't think about the dead. And still, people in Livorno are always praying. I couldn't tell you how young I was the first time I heard my mother in church. When she spoke to God, it was with her whole heart. Sometimes she cried. Tears of faith were the only kind allowed. With my parents, words were so difficult that I turned to music to express myself. I realise now that I never believed in God. But I'm still superstitious, and I think of this harmonica as a sign of providence. I don't know what it means...maybe it's what led me to you."

"I like hearing you talk," Aleksander smiled. "What do you play?"

"The blues, though I'm surprised that would interest you. You're surrounded by people who are so cultivated and well-spoken."

"Perhaps, but most of those folks have no poetry to them."

"Ambroise was reciting lots of Lord Byron to me earlier."

"You don't recite though, do you? You speak, and you think...it's refreshing. Blues, you say? That's surprising, for an Italian. Let's go get some air; it's stifling in here."

3.

Giovanni had fallen asleep on Aleksander Spielman's chaise longue. The other guests had left, leaving only a graveyard of empty bottles and bouquets of flowers as evidence of the previous night's festivities. Aleksander opened the windows, and the sounds of the bustling city wafted into the apartment. The young Italian was sound asleep. He was beautiful; a peaceful demeanour suited him. Aleksander felt an urge to play Debussy, thinking the melody would accompany the dreams of his young guest, but as the music started, Giovanni opened his eyes and looked about him, bewildered. After a moment he recognised the pianist's apartment and observed something that had eluded him the night before: a portrait of a young man hanging among the musical instruments on the wall. It was the only thing that seemed personal or hinted at Aleksander's true character. The young man in the painting had a sombre, worried expression. Behind him, snow was falling on a synagogue. Giovanni sensed immediately that the artist had commissioned the painting specially. He was surprised to feel a pang of jealousy at this unknown figure who meant so much to so great a man. To be loved by Aleksander Spielman must be an incredible thing. He rose and leaned against the grand piano. Aleksander smiled at him and kept on playing. Giovanni watched the deft movements of his fingers over the keyboard. He remembered the child-like fascination he'd felt watching Stella playing Chopin in her villa. He glanced at the sheet music. He recognised the notes, even though he hadn't read music for over ten years. The lessons came flooding back to him. He placed his hand on the page, waiting for the final note. The pianist did not object, and Giovanni turned the page for him.

It was late afternoon, and Aleksander Spielman and Giovanni were walking in the square in front of the *hôtel de ville*. They walked where the wind took them. The French flag fluttered in the breeze, the dust swirling over the cobblestones. Two girls were playing hopscotch, their skirts billowing as they hopped between the chalk-drawn squares, like small frogs playing on lily pads. Giovanni watched them with amusement, his heart feeling lighter in the presence of such distinguished company. He hadn't felt like this in a long while, walking with his eyes open and living in the moment. Spielman smiled, his eyes lost in the minutiae of the city, paying no attention to the locks of hair that fell over his face. An artist had set up his easel beside a lamppost and was beginning to sketch out the lines of the grand building. The pianist and the young Italian paused to observe the painter, who explained, "All the points must converge towards the line of the horizon. It's like a train travelling towards the infinite beyond, never to return." Giovanni watched the pianist out the corner of his eye and saw a dark cloud form in his gaze. But the Pole gathered himself and suggested they go and pick up some roast chestnuts, a popular delicacy in Paris. He chuckled at Giovanni's clumsy attempts to pry open the nuts with his fingernails. "Careful you don't burn your tongue! You'll rob me of your precious conversation." The young man swallowed the powdery chestnut flesh and almost choked. Spielman looked at him tenderly, as he would a child. They walked towards the vast market of Les Halles, as the pianist wanted to buy flowers for his apartment. Flowers were like love, he said: best enjoyed in short-lived arrangements.

"I've never had much luck with love," sighed Giovanni. "The only woman I've ever loved, and who loved me in return, was murdered. And it was my fault. I'm a curse."

"You mustn't say that; you're still young. Nobody brings bad luck; life is made up of such things so God can test us."

"If you knew what I think of God...Maria was here, she existed, and she had a bright future ahead of her. I refuse to believe her death had a purpose."

"She still lives in your heart, does she not? The dead only disappear when those who knew them are also gone."

"I suppose I don't have the mind of a philosopher, as you do."

"You still have to believe in something."

They turned onto Rue Saint-Eustache, which churned with activity. There was no space left in the main market building, so all the streets around it were filled with shops and stalls. The Parisians ate their meat soup standing up between the carts. Pallets were piled up in odd spaces, and stalls overflowed with fresh produce. Cabbages fell and rolled over the cobbles, with pedestrians almost slipping on salad leaves or bunches of radishes. The market traders called out to the passers-by in their friendly, booming voices, making a little song out of each price to catch their ears. The two friends entered under the glass roof, where the rays of sunshine mixed with the brouhaha of Les Halles. It was immense, with aisles as wide as city streets dividing the market into blocks. They passed stalls laden with fresh fish, cheese and meat, then flowers, leather, vegetables and bread. Aleksander Spielman stopped at the shoeshine stall:

"Would the pianist like his brogues shined?"

"Yes, please; my Richelieu Cordovans are in dire need".

"Up you go then!" the shoeshiner said, nodding to the chair with its specially designed platform.

"How are your grandchildren? Not here with you today?"

"They're running about over in the park. You can't keep them still, and they grow like weeds at this age. And how is your piano? That's all I can ask you in return! A handsome man like yourself with no children, it's a waste. Those women don't know what they're missing!"

"I fear I wouldn't be much use as a husband!" Spielman replied, winking at Giovanni.

"Would your friend like a lick of polish?"

"No thank you, Madame, I'm fine."

"You know that the first thing a woman looks at in a man is his shoes."

"Madame, these poor brogues have crossed the Mediterranean and the whole of France, and I polish them myself every day."

Aleksander took Giovanni to his favourite vendor among the flower stalls. He had a soft spot for the sublime disorder of the flowers, even though elsewhere in life he craved neatness and simplicity. He caressed the stems with his fingertips. The sugary scent of the peonies had a childhood familiarity to it, while the stamens of the lilies stood erect, silky and provocative. Giovanni observed the pianist's fingers, white and slender like a woman's. Spielman had an eternally gentle touch; he lived in the present and knew how to appreciate the world and embalm himself in its music without ever imposing himself or jolting its tempo. He had a certain delicate quality, one which Giovanni had never seen in a man.

"Flowers have their own language. Men have sought them out since Antiquity," Aleksander mused, looking up at Giovanni.

"The last time I saw bunches of flowers like these was at a procession for the Virgin Mary."

"A form of holy adoration...I just like them on my table."

"It's odd, but I never would have thought of a man liking flowers. I thought they were for giving to women."

"The greatest men are passionate about flowers."

He pinned a rose to Giovanni's buttonhole and looked at him with a satisfied air. "There you are, more handsome than ever." The young Italian blushed. "Help me pick out some flowers, I want you to like them since you're going to be my dinner guest for tonight." Giovanni didn't know any of their names and was unsure where to start. Aleksander reassured him: "Pick with your eyes, your hands and your nose. The rest doesn't matter." Giovanni took to his task like a determined schoolboy. He caressed the fragile petals and lifted the flowers to his nose. Spielman explained to Giovanni the language of flowers and their importance in French culture. Of course, they were a thing one saw every day, but they were also rooted in the collective subconscious. Every people has its superstitions, its rituals and its symbols. What interested him were the subtle ties of which we do not speak, but which bind us into communities. A daisy carried more meaning than a flag; it stood for friendship. And friendship never divided anyone, never sparked any war. "Offer me a bouquet of red roses and my passion will be unleashed upon you..." Aleksander continued in his dream-like cadence, philosophising at random. His impromptu discourse was more than enough to inspire Giovanni, who hung on his every word.

Aleksander was sitting on the chaise longue with the grace of a Roman nobleman, a glass of wine in his hand. Giovanni was ensconced in the armchair opposite him. The gramophone was crackling jazz; Aleksander had chosen something he hoped his guest would like. The two men looked at one another, and a silence fell over them, the silence of intimacy that can arise between two strangers: a clumsy, meaningful quiet, difficult to break without smothering its charm.

"Your rose is wilting. Do you know the poem? *Mignonne, allons voir si la rose...*," murmured Spielman.

"No, what's it about?"

"The passage of time, enjoying one's youth...come and sit next to me; we can't even clink glasses at this distance."

Giovanni obeyed, too in awe of the pianist to consider doing otherwise. He felt too clumsy to speak and took out his harmonica to show it to the musician. "You'll have to play it now...you can't take out an instrument without doing it that honour." A shudder went down the young Italian's spine. He was terrified of how he would sound; a fisherman from Livorno playing the blues for a world-renowned pianist. The young man lifted the needle off the record. He put his lips to the harmonica without thinking; after all, the blues was what he knew. The pianist put on a nonchalant air. Giovanni began playing a Sonny Boy tune. The blues crept through the apartment like a distant memory. Spielman closed his eyes; he was already transported. He was on the train that had taken him to Warsaw, to a better life, and the singing of the slaves blended with the sacred words of the Torah, the hope for the new, the power of a cry for help, of an uprising. Giovanni thought the pianist was asleep and played to accompany his dreams as Spielman had done for him that morning, with the music that was imbued with his story, the war, Italy, fishing, his childhood dreams and his ambitions for glory in his own New World. What would he achieve here in Paris? He'd searched for answers in Marseille and found none. And yet he'd seen the dark side of his heart, a side the guileless child from Livorno could never have imagined. The clubs, the prostitutes and the beatings he gave those poor folks in exchange for a few measly francs. But his cynicism and the disillusion he felt towards the human race had taken on a noble, tragic air now that he had lost Maria and was playing for someone he admired. He wanted to compose an ode to the memory of his Italian fiancée, whose life, so full of ambition, had been taken cruelly from her. During his first months in Paris, he'd stayed in bed day and night, turning that magical moment in the Saint-Charles station over in his mind. He'd felt the warmth of the life he might have had with Maria, his every fear breaking like waves upon the rocks as she gave herself up completely to the sound of his harmonica. Her body was more than flesh and bone; there was something of the divine beneath her skin. Making love to Maria had been like passing into another world of tender sensuality, in which their communication was almost spiritual: the world he had hoped to see in Livorno when he looked at Stella with his wide, innocent eyes. He'd known betrayal, but it hadn't made him mistrustful. On the contrary; he had lost Stella, but destiny had ferried him to greater horizons. Would he have had the strength to leave without that push? Spielman opened his eyes, his gaze dark and impenetrable, and yet fully present in the moment. Giovanni leaned into his playing without fear. Come and join me, Aleksander Spielman, I know you can see me. I am naked and defenceless before you, and your gaze does not shatter me. Timidity was for the weak, for those who could not come to terms with the dark, violent part of themselves.

They had met in an opium joint in Marseille, hadn't they? Like him, Aleksander had come to smoke so he could escape this flat, cloying life, and the banalities of the everyday that prevent one from creating and suspending moments in time, like sacrifices to eternal beauty. He wanted to absorb from his idol that inspiration that enabled him to survive the atrocity of his memory; that dignity that shone through in his every movement, and in every piece he played. Overcoming his pain, drowning it in his art, was what he prayed for. What had he found in Paris? Nothing worthy, nothing profound. Was he still a child to be protected? Was he still the naive young man, unprepared for what life might throw at him? Spielman embodied everything he wished to become. Would he be a mentor? Did he hold the key that would release Giovanni from the prison of his guilt? The music ended; his air was spent. He looked at the pianist, not moving. What was he expecting? Surely not applause or recognition, just something that suggested Spielman was aware of his existence. In this moment, he craved the stability of being able to lean on so great a man. Spielman had to repay the trust Giovanni had shown him by playing the blues. "Well, you could knock me over with a feather. Who could fail to succumb to this power that seems to inhabit you?"

4.

Giovanni had been talked into going to an underground club, where the bands played French pop music. Lucien loved the place: "You'll see, or rather you'll hear. This kind of music is the soul of France." They sat in the front row, and waited for the young guitarist to take the stage. The musician spent his days busking in the streets of Montmartre for passers-by and tourists; this audience was larger than he was used to. With one foot on his tambourine, he began strumming with his fingernails, and sang through his moustache in a bawdy voice, telling the story of a poor strumpet who'd fallen into ill health. "The soul of France is more upbeat than I'd have thought," Giovanni joked. Lucien furrowed his brow and motioned for him to keep quiet. Giovanni could not understand why his friend took it so seriously; it wasn't like they were at the Opera. People were here to forget their troubles, half-listening to the music while they ordered cheap beer in tall glasses. The young Italian struggled to understand all the lyrics; the slang and the wordplay were lost on him. The singer was now telling the story of a young immigrant who built houses and lived in a shantytown. Giovanni thought of Maria and her love of Charles Trenet. This guitarist would never have sung those songs; Trenet's lyrics painted France in rosy hues, all about love and the promise of tomorrow. He understood now that she'd needed the comfort of blind affection towards her adopted country. She'd avoided anything that might taint her perception of France; her own personal El Dorado. She'd been devoted to that dream, but fate was cynical. The guitarist took his bow and lit a cigarette before he was even off stage. Lucien clapped as hard as he could, like a boy at the circus. The MC told them there would be a pianist up next, as soon as the old stage hand had finished tuning the piano. There was no dressing room in this type of joint. The young woman climbed onto the stage, hitching up her skirt and unveiling her fishnet tights. She approached the piano, swaying her hips. Giovanni undressed her with his eyes. He was instantly drawn to women with curvaceous figures. He'd forgotten what it felt like. His body brought him back to reality; he was still young and alive. The young woman shook her head, and a few locks of hair fell down over her bosom. She placed her coral-varnished fingertips on the keys and began to make the strings hop. Her small fingers were deft yet fleshy, white like a cream pudding, awakening a hunger in the young Italian. Her deep, suave voice rang out the first couplet. It was a reassuring voice, even though it had an element of the forbidden to it. Giovanni noticed the engagement ring on her finger. She was taken. What was she doing here, then? Parisian customs surprised him every day. She finished her song to rapturous applause from the regulars. To Giovanni's great surprise, she came and sat beside them.

"It's so nice to see you again, Lucien! I didn't think you'd be here tonight," she said gently. "I hope you liked my song..."

"The pleasure is mine. Every time I come, you're even more enchanting."

"You're just flattering me. And who's this charming sort with you?"

"My friend Giovanni. Friend and roommate, I should say."

"I'm delighted to meet you," she whispered warmly.

"Me too..." the young man stuttered, embarrassed.

"So what are you doing tonight?" she asked, turning to Lucien.

"I'm editing a story; I can't say too much about it. It cost me too much to get hold of it."

"You should be enjoying the good times! You're shutting yourself off in your work. If you want a big scoop, you'll have to go to the Suez canal or Algeria. War always makes the news."

The woman caressed Lucien's arm with the back of her hand: "Sweetie." The young Italian felt a pang of jealousy. The singer's sensuality had gone to his head. Where was he in all this? A third wheel. "I can't!" Lucian murmured. Giovanni reflected on his situation. He was alive, and he needed nothing else, not even Capuani's *pizzo*. He wanted to live, to enjoy Paris and to breathe the air freely. And what was stopping him? In Paris, no-one knew him, and he could pass for a stranger. He'd spent months lying in bed, consumed by bitter remorse. He had no work, nothing to do. He slept. He smoked like a taxi driver. Being a stranger in Paris soothed him. It liberated him from his guilt. The Parisians were consumed in their daily routines. Nobody judged him; no-one looked twice at him. He'd wanted so badly to explore this city with Maria, but that dream was dead. Aleksander Spielman had given him back his taste for life, and his desire to explore Paris from every angle. He too had once been a stranger, and had managed to become a local. His circle made Giovanni feel ill-at-ease: their excessive politeness, their diplomacy, their well-bred accents, their mind games, high culture and well-bred accents. It made it impossible for a foreigner to become a part of their circle. Why not come to these underground venues instead? There was a good atmosphere, and people came as they were. They left happy. They came to have a good time. That was all he really needed if he was to shake himself free of this hopeless chagrin. Desire was returning to him, but it would take more than a blank slate and the body of a bar singer to make him forget Maria for even a second. The singer got up:

"Gentlemen, I shall leave you to your serious contemplations. I'm in the mood to party tonight, so it's going to have to be without you!"

She hurried up the narrow staircase that led to the street. Lucien's brow furrowed once again as he watched her go. Giovanni sipped his wine and asked with curiosity:

"Who was that?"

"It's a long story. We had an affair. We still see each other sometimes."

"But she's married!" Giovanni cried.

"She is. But you know, I don't really believe in the need for fidelity. Love is more than that. The bourgeois would have us believe that love can be reduced to a contract; just a scrap of paper you sign at the mayor's office and a few words from a priest, and that's supposed to matter more than all the desire and freedom of human feeling. I respect women too much to keep them as prisoners. And there are worse things than adultery. A woman having an affair is better off than a frustrated wife badgering her husband because he can't satisfy her, and secretly wishing she could get rid of him and start living her life again."

"So you don't believe in soul mates or the sacred bonds of marriage?"

"Of course not. I'm a different man every day; I'm a stranger to who I was last week. If I marry a woman now, how is she going to be able to keep me happy, understand me and still get me hard ten years down the line?"

"Yeah, but I think...or at least, I thought—"

"Yes yes, I know, you're a dreamer, full of sentiment."

"Maybe it's just how I was raised. My mother loved my father until the day he died. I wanted to do the same with Maria."

"That's exactly it; you've never considered that there could be another way. It niggles at me, it ticks over in my mind: I want to do things differently to how my ancestors did. I don't want to give up my life. My choices are mine, and I want to make them freely."

"I think my friend Spielman is like you—"

"Your friend now, is it?" Lucian interjected with a sardonic grin.

"He was a Polish immigrant, and he came to Paris before the war. We understand each other. We've had similar experiences and share the same feelings."

"Where does he live?"

"In one of the fancy neighbourhoods. His piano faces out the window. You can even see the Eiffel Tower from it. His friends aren't like you."

"What does that mean?" Lucien pounced.

"They're...strange. Most of them look you up and down like they're wondering what you're doing in France."

"You should be careful of Spielman. If I were you, I'd think twice about spending time with him. You don't get to where he is in life without getting your hands dirty somewhere along the line."

The next day, Giovanni walked into a music store just off Boulevard Saint-Michel, where Aleksander Spielman had asked him to go and pick up some sheet music. Brass saxophones and clarinets were lined high and low on the walls. A brand-new drum kit sat temptingly before him. There was no-one behind the counter. The young Italian took a drumstick and tapped the cymbal twice. "Coming!" yelled the clerk as he descended the spiral staircase from the floor above, where the pianos were kept.

"What can I do for you?" he asked politely.

"I'm here to pick up some sheet music for Monsieur Spielman," Giovanni replied.

"Just a moment, I'll go and fetch it."

The clerk disappeared into the back room. It seemed like this might take a while. Giovanni's mind was listless, and he let his eyes wander over the burnished wood of the guitars. From the upper floor, a mysterious melody was coming from a grand piano, snaking its way into the young Italian's ear. In an instant, he was transported: although his childhood was now far behind him, his father dead and he far away in France, the music carried him to where it had all begun. In the hills above Livorno, the Palomi villa seemed to wait for him, and he walked proudly through the great gate that had been left open for him. Little Giovanni was expected at exactly four in the afternoon. As he walked along the alley that led to the house, which seemed like a castle to him, one of the guard dogs began to bark. Fortunately, the governess had come out on the porch to welcome him, his legs shaking but his heart filled with courage. He was to attend a piano lesson with Stella. Giovanni did not understand the world he was about to enter. The symphony rang out around the store. He was far away, in his homeland. "Come in, young man," the lady had said with an amused smile. She knew he was poor and innocent. His mother Nina had dressed him simply in a white shirt, trousers and his only pair of loafers. He even wore a belt. He entered the magical villa and admired the fine chandeliers. He crept up the marble steps of the grand spiral staircase. He stopped in front of a Second-Empire-style mirror to check that his hair was neat. "Stylish, well-brought-up young men wear their hair parted down the middle," his mother had taught him. He had not yet reached the top of the stairs when Stella began playing the piano. His heart pounded. He was about to see her. No matter what she played, he loved her. It was an undying flame that flickered in his childhood memories, still burning despite all he'd been through in life. Above him, the melody struck at his heart like the voice of the divine. He felt oddly drawn to it. "Come sit down," Stella had said to him gently. The big window was open, and the white curtain wafted back and forth in the breeze. "Sit up straight and behave yourself," his mother had whispered to him as he walked out the door. He walked towards the bench, overwhelmed by her beauty and her grace. Giovanni wanted to speak to her, but sat quietly on the bench beside her. The young Italian decided to go up the spiral stairs. Who was playing, and why did it enchant him so? He came to the piano room, where at the back a woman was gliding her fingers over the keys. She did not notice he was there. Her hair was tied up in a bun. The magic petered out in the young man's heart as she finished her piece. He waited a few moments; it had been merely a reverie. He made to descend the stairs, looking back at her one last time. She turned to put the sheet music back in her bag. It was Stella. He froze. She stared at him. His face was familiar, but she did not recognise him. Where could she have met a young man with those stern features? His suit was too scruffy for him to be one of her husband's friends. Was he a musician? "Ciao, Stella," he murmured with an awkward smile. She saw more clearly the two dark eyes that were fixed upon her; their light was strangely familiar, and she felt like she had known them for a long time, in another life. Could it be Giovanni? But he had grown so old. Time had not spared him. She suddenly felt old too, and realised their childhoods were gone forever.

5.

It was Stella, the girl he had loved so much and for so many years. As a child who could barely look her in the eye, and never knew what to say for fear of disappointing her, he could never have imagined that one day he would find himself here, with her, on the edge of her bed and the precipice of his innermost desires. He moved towards her and took her strongly in his arms. She was his. Finally, he could hold her body against his; he could breathe the perfume on her neck, kiss her mouth and plunge his eyes into hers without fear. He slipped the strap of her dress down over her shoulder; she was naked, vulnerable, fallen from her pedestal. He marvelled at the perfect roundness of her breasts and the soft slope of her hips; he kissed her body all over as she stood still, smiling down at him. She let her hair down and unveiled herself, full of wild grace, a woman unbridled. He could hardly believe it was happening. His teenage nights of desire and worry came back to him. He threw her on the bed, ready to show her that his innocence was lost and he was no longer intimidated by her. She wasn't his first, however much he'd loved her, and this time would not be the last.

Stella was sleeping. Giovanni slipped from her arms, taking care not to wake her. She sighed and turned over. The young man got out of the bed and lit a cigarette by the window. He opened the curtain and looked out over the street. The streetlamps were coming on; it must be six. He recognised Stella's piano in her room; she'd taken it with her all this way. It made sense that she couldn't live without it; it was the only material object she truly cared for. "The jewellery, the furs, the dinner parties...it's all so dreadfully boring. Do you see, Giovanni? The things that should excite me exasperate me," she had confided in him, slightly tipsy, the night before. He hadn't understood her distress until now. The bedroom was luxuriant but sad. Nothing in it was personal; everything was a show of wealth. In this apartment, the white piano from the villa in Livorno shone like a smooth pebble on a riverbed. Giovanni walked over to it and ran his hands along the wood. He'd loved this instrument like he loved Stella. The two were inseparable in his mind. Stella was the music of his childhood; the first melody to have touched his heart. He looked at her. It was difficult to believe. How had he run into her in Paris, a city so full of strangers? Destiny was leading him to reconcile with his past, with Livorno. His birthplace now came to him only through his mother's letters. Had Livorno changed as much as he had? What was left of the port? Without his father, nothing could be the same. And yet, the town had seemed inert to him for so many years. Only his father's death had changed anything. If he'd only known that the boredom he felt when he was twenty would now seem so peaceful and charming...he suddenly felt nostalgic for the *gozzo*, the port, their home, and his dear mother. Would her face look different now? He noticed a picture of Stella's wedding day hanging above the bed. A man in his forties had his arm clasped around the shy young girl, squirming in her white dress. He recognised the smile; it was the smile Stella used when she was trapped. Not at all like how she'd smiled on Gorgona, or how she'd smiled last night. He wasn't even jealous. How could he be? The little moustachioed man was ridiculous; he could never satisfy her. Stella seemed to wake, finally. She stretched out:

"You're already up? Aren't you tired?"

"Nope...and I haven't finished with you, either."

"Come on then!" she laughed, opening her arms to him.

It must have been near midday, and they had not left the bedroom. Giovanni ran his hands through Stella's hair over and over, as if trying to leave his mark on her. She was pressed against him, her face mere centimetres from his. He liked seeing her close up. She was beautiful, even with her eyes puffy and tired, and her mouth that smiled and laughed constantly through those small, dancing lips that he wanted to kiss all the time. Suddenly, the Florentine got up and sat at her piano. She played something he didn't know; something melancholy. Stella closed her eyes, playing from memory. Her life had escaped her. Had she ever really been in control of it? She'd learned music, classics and modern languages, great literature and fine arts. What did any of it matter? She could do nothing with it, spending her days alone in her husband's apartments, wasting away in capitals where she knew nobody who understood her. She'd never had a friend she could open her heart to. The only people she knew were businessmen and their wives. She had nothing to say to them, but those were her people now. She was just like them, on paper at least. Why couldn't she conform to people's expectations of her? She dreamed of working and feeling useful. She'd have been an artist, an archaeologist, a translator, or perhaps even a mathematician. If only they'd given her a chance, she could have taken over her father's business. She'd have proven herself. So many lives, possible and impossible. She'd be a mother looking after her children; at least that would give her life meaning. Would she be a good mother? Was it important to love the father of your children? Perhaps her husband would not be the father...with any luck, her children would look like a man she respected, and whose line she was proud to carry on. She finished the piece and turned to Giovanni. She did not speak. The two lovers stared at one another. She could love him, she thought to herself. She needed his tenderness more than ever. He wished he could know what was going through the young woman's mind. Did she have regrets? Did she love her husband more than she let on? Stella joined Giovanni on the bed and hugged him tight, as tight as she could. He felt a tear trickle down his back to the bottom of his spine. He asked her no questions. A few hours went by, and the daylight faded from the window. They had lost all sense of time. Both had been trying desperately to fill their days with something, anything, all this time, and now found themselves happy to let the day pass them by.

"Tell me something. It's probably not the right time, but I've always wanted to know. Why did you choose Luca?" Giovanni asked with feigned nonchalance. Stella closed her eyes for a moment before replying:

"I knew I was going to be married. I wanted to live before becoming a prisoner; I wanted to feel something else. I didn't want to lose my virginity by contract. I wanted to choose when it happened, and with whom."

"But why him?"

"You mean, why not you?" she answered, kissing him.

"Well...yes, why not me?"

"I'm not as cruel as you think. I didn't want to give you false hope, knowing there could be no future between us. With Luca, it was simple; he never asked me to promise him anything. He never expected anything from me. With Luca, I knew I could just lose myself in the moment. I needed that freedom."

"Losing yourself in the lighthouse? Just another notch in the brickwork?" Giovanni grimaced.

"Exactly! Just like anyone else, for once. Like a woman, a free woman."

"How long did it go on between you two?"

"Not long. Luca felt guilty when you left."

"Now that I don't believe. He could have thought of that before he did anything. He didn't even take the time to come to my father's funeral. Think about that. I buried my father alone, without a friend by my side. I'll never forgive him for that."

"Calm down, it's all in the past now," she soothed him, stroking his forehead.

The moon shone through the white curtain as Giovanni dreamed. He saw his hands buried in the keys of a piano, as a cloud of smoke rose up. Blood trickled along his fingers; the blood of guilt. Frightened, he tried to pull his hands back, but could not. The instrument flopped and wiggled like a fish. He could not settle the animal as it gulped with deafening music. The beast reared its head, and its jaws opened. Giovanni saw Maria's hair, stretching out and winding around him like ropes. They tightened around him, choking him. Maria's face emerged from the watery keyboard. Her eyes were closed and her lips bruised. Giovanni shuddered, an electric shock running up the length of his spine. He wished he could console his murdered fiancé and whisper tender words to her. He could not speak. Her hair strangled him, creeping into his mouth and out his ears. The melody came louder from the piano. He wished the cacophony would stop. Maria's mouth came to kiss him. As their lips met, Maria's body shrank and disappeared. The racket died down. Giovanni turned and saw that a thousand spectators were watching him. The public stood in ovation and deafened him with their applause. Giovanni was confused; his legs trembled. "But it wasn't me! I didn't do it! It wasn't me playing!" he stammered innocently. The clapping grew louder and louder. He tried to make out their faces but was blinded by the lights. In the first row, an old woman shrieked, "Giogio, my Giogio!" It was his mother. Nina's hair had turned completely white, and her small dark eyes had sunk deep into their sockets. Her lips were as dry as coffin boards. She was so old. Giovanni walked to the edge of the stage and held out his hand, wanting to touch his mother. As he leaned towards her, her face changed. It was Stella. Her lips moved, but he could not hear her. She seemed terrified, trying to warn him of a danger. The audience was entranced, their applause booming like the crashing of waves on a stormy night. The crystal chandelier shattered, its shards falling on them like a sharp rain. In the dawn light, Stella got up to make coffee. She set a piece of brioche on the tray and served the coffee in a big bowl. She returned to the bedroom and sat down at the piano. The young Italian awoke with a start.

"Where is your husband?"

"Don't worry, there's no chance of him showing up here!" she answered, laughing. "He's at a board meeting in Florence."

"Doesn't he ever come to see you? Are you always alone like this?" he asked, his senses returning to him one by one.

"He comes and then goes off again. Sometimes he leaves a note on my night stand. He tells me that he'll be back soon, but that's it. Luckily I happen to know where he is today. He called me a few days ago. Our conversations are flat, uninhabited. There's no feeling between us. It's like a seed that never sprouted and can never bloom. My husband is in finance, and he works constantly so he can earn more. He manages the fortunes of the great Italian families. Where am I in all that? Am I not his family? Can't he show he cares for me with something other than money? I know it's not a bad life I have here, but I don't know how else to entertain myself. I'm sick of eating alone, sleeping alone, having nobody to talk to."

"How long have you lived in Paris?"

"My husband inherited this apartment last winter. His parents left it to him. I moved in about three months ago. But I haven't really had time to settle down and make friends. I'm trying to get into a routine and develop some habits. I find habits reassuring; they help you paper over your loneliness. You do things mechanically, without thinking, and you don't take the time to ask what life would be like if...well. I go to the museums a lot. To the Louvre, the Orsay, the Orangerie. I love the Tuileries gardens, but when I see all the families walking there, all the little boys with their hobby-horses and their mothers running after them, their boats in the fountains, all that life and that love make me wish I had a family too. I wonder if it will ever happen for me. Then I walk along the river and look at the Seine. At night I walk without looking at the time. I walk past the terraces of all those brightly lit cafés and restaurants, and I see the people eating together. Maybe I should have stayed in Florence...but then I'd have to put up with my family and their conversations. They don't understand why I'm unhappy in my marriage; it's a concept they struggle to grasp. I don't think they've ever asked themselves what it means to be happy. It's as if you can't be unhappy when you have money, and you shouldn't have the time anyway when you have high-society responsibilities and obligations. I tried to talk to my mother about it. It was over Christmas, when my husband wasn't there. Of course, he sent a courier with a gift: a beautiful Cartier bracelet. My mother saw how disappointed I was when I opened the package and read the telegram with it. He couldn't make it back; he was in Germany. I knew he was with one of his mistresses. My mother wouldn't hear of it; I don't know if she was trying to reassure me or just telling me to accept the convention. 'Smile, be pretty and don't worry about it.' "

"Are you sure he has mistresses?"

"Yes, I can smell it on him...literally!" she laughed. "His shirts sometimes smell like women's perfume. He doesn't care if I notice. I don't think it occurs to him that it might hurt me. It's normal for him. Marriage is a contract; love has nothing to do with it. I don't think there's much room in his heart for love. For him, women are distractions, and his wife...well. His wife is for taking to dinner. And even then he's not with me. The men talk to the men, and the women talk to the women. It's not really couples dining together, it's businessmen and their wives. They eat in a hurry so they can retire to the *fumoir* and play cards and smoke cigars. The women go home to put the children to bed, but I don't have any of those. My husband would need to show a little more conjugal initiative for that to happen."

"He's never touched you?"

"Of course he has. In the beginning, he seemed to enjoy my company. We laughed, we went out, but it didn't last long. Barely a month. We had to cut our honeymoon short because of his business engagements. I could have loved him; I wanted to, I wanted for it to be possible. You know, I didn't marry him willingly. I found him ugly and hollow. But I became attached to him quite quickly, and then he disappointed me just as quickly. Disappointed is the wrong word. He hurt me, he smothered my dignity."

"Do you have lovers of your own? I mean, apart from me?"

"I've had a few. Does that shock you?"

"No, it doesn't shock me. Nothing you do shocks me. I know you better than anyone, and I don't judge you. I want to understand, to know everything that's happened since the last time. I want to know the person you've become."

"My lovers aren't really important. Apart from you, I mean! I never loved them. It was out of spite and pride. I wanted payback. I didn't want to be imprisoned by the marriage if he wasn't going to be."

"You'll have to tell me about it. I want to know everything! But I have to go."

"Now, already? But I'm not finished enjoying you!"

"I'll be back," he laughed.

"You promise? What do you have to do?"

"I have work to do for Aleksander Spielman."

"Aleksander Spielman? You told me you worked for a pianist, but you never said it was *him*!"

6.

Giovanni opened his eyes. The room was dark. What time was it? Where was Stella? Lucien's snoring told him where he was. His roommate would soon be up to get ready for work at the Nutcracker. The young Italian used this moment of peace to smoke a cigarette out the window. He looked outside; the sun was rising, and the stars were fading away. The postman was at the end of the street. He cruised down the street on his bike, his bag full of letters and his cap pulled down over his forehead. Giovanni smiled at the thought of all the hope and expectation that little man carried on his bicycle, and the precious connections he maintained between the separated. Would he bring news from Stella? Giovanni missed her; she was in Florence with her husband. She seemed even more perfect now that she was far from him again. Every time he remembered her, his mind painted her in brighter colours. What was she doing in Florence? What could she be doing without him? He felt that she could not live apart from him, that she existed only for him. And yet, he had to accept that she was with her husband, in that great city where she'd been raised and he'd never been, amidst all those rich folks and the strict codes she'd been brought up with. Would she forget him? Didn't she prefer to be with her own kind? Would she dare to continue loving a fisherman's son when she returned? They would remind her of her true class and her sense of duty. Perhaps her husband would be gentler and more attentive to her, and she'd rediscover the qualities that had drawn her to him when they were first married. Everything can change so fast; in love, nothing was set in stone. You couldn't be certain of anything; the ground might be pulled from beneath your feet at any moment. What would he do if he found himself alone in love? He should have told her before she left. He'd tried, but the words would not come out. She'd been sitting between the columns in the Parc Monceau, swinging her legs under the bench. She was so beautiful. He'd wanted to scream that he loved her. But nothing materialised; it was too difficult to be vulnerable around her. He hadn't seen her for ten days and had no news. "I'll be back soon!" she'd promised before disappearing into the bowels of the Metro. The postman stopped in front of their building. Giovanni jumped, throwing his cigarette out the window, and leapt down the stairs. He ran into the caretaker, who was waiting for him in the courtyard with an inquisitive smile, holding an envelope addressed to Giovanni in his hand. She could see his eagerness to get the letter and did her best to find out who it was from. Giovanni wanted to get away from her as fast as possible, impatient to read it. Unfortunately, the caretaker was all too aware of his impatience, and if the young lovers might be meeting here, in her building, she was eager to get a head start on the gossip. Eventually, Giovanni managed to close the conversation and tore open the envelope on his way back up the stairs. It was indeed a letter from Stella:

"Giovanni,
If only you knew how much I enjoy writing your name. I feel silly, like a schoolgirl writing the name of the boy she likes all over her notebooks. You've made me into a dunce, I should be mad at you! I'm no better than all those scatter-brained girls I used to make fun of. Maybe I was jealous of them. Sometimes I wonder if loving you is my way of overcoming the boredom. And then I think of your smell, your voice, and your laughter when you tease me. I wander through the streets of Florence all day. Everything reminds me of you; all the streets look like you...well, as much as a street can look like a person. When I see a young man with brown hair, walking like you and rolling his shoulders, I always hope that it's you, that you've come to find me, even though that would be madness. But it's never you, it's always someone undesirable. How my husband bores me! My family are driving me mad. I get away as often as I can. I've been like a teenager since I met you again. Without you, I love only my solitude, where I can think about you in peace. Giovanni, it feels so wonderful to write down everything I've been feeling these past days.

With love,
Stella."

"She loves me! Stella loves me!" Giovanni cried, slamming the door. Lucien awoke with a start. He looked around him in a panic, mumbled a few curses and turned over, pulling his quilt over his head. Giovanni was happy and relieved. The past few days he'd been unable to concentrate or stay still. His every thought was of Stella. He didn't want to go out with Lucien, and he followed Aleksander's instructions half-heartedly, waiting for the time when he could lie alone in his bed and think only of her. He waited for that moment all day long. He sometimes cursed himself for letting himself fall asleep too soon, wishing he could keep thinking of her all night. His eyes turned to the nightstand, and his euphoria evaporated when he saw the photo of Maria. He was a traitor. How could he have done this? He'd forgotten her. How could he be happy in love after what he'd done? There was no way fate could be so kind to him. No doubt his punishment was on its way, if God existed, or if there was justice on this earth.

Someone knocked on the door. Giovanni jumped up from his chair; he'd fallen asleep with his cigarette between his lips. Lucien was gone; he hadn't even heard him leave. They knocked again. Giovanni hurried to the door. Could it be her? In a panic, he remembered the photo of Maria and threw it under his duvet. He opened the door. It was Stella; the reality of her suddenly superimposed over a ten-day dream. Giovanni had idolised her to such an extent that he was slightly disappointed. But he was happy; he squeezed her tight, having missed the feel of her body so badly. Stella buried her face in his neck. She hid her teary eyes from him, feeling shy and exposed. She did not want to seem won over: her lover must believe that she was strong and independent, capable of living without him, capable of holding back, and even of not loving him one day. She regretted sending him the letter. She should not have opened up that way. What if she'd given him too much power? What if he got bored of her now that she was conquered? She pulled herself from his arms and sat down on the bed.

"This is where you live?" she asked with a touch of disdain.

"It's where I've thought of you," he answered, slightly nettled. "I just read your letter; sounds like you missed me."

"I sent it six days ago; the post must have been late. I think that the trip went to my head. I'm so melodramatic in Italy!"

"So you didn't really feel what you wrote?"

"I wouldn't go that far, but I probably exaggerated a bit. I had nothing to do in Florence, and you know I can get a bit verbose. I'm a bit like Madame Bovary."

"I see...you need to love someone so you can feel alive, whether it's me or someone else. Do you want coffee?"

"Yes please, I'm tired. I came straight here," she said, lying back on the bed seductively.

Giovanni filled the moka pot. So, Stella had hurried over to see him. She must be fonder of him than she was letting on. Why was she holding back? Why couldn't she leave what she'd written as it was? What was she protecting herself from? She was probably disappointed; he hadn't had the time to wash and dress up, his apartment was a tip, and the reality was probably sobering to her. On top of that, he hadn't declared his love in the Parc Monceau, and he hadn't replied to her letter. His heart tightened; what he feared was already happening. He wasn't ready for it yet. He filled their cups and brought them to the nightstand. He lay beside her in the little bed, on top of the photo of Maria. They smiled at one another and kissed.

"What have you been doing these past few days?" she asked.

"I've been very busy. When you're Aleksander Spielman's right-hand man—"

"His right-hand man? I didn't know he played one-handed," she teased.

"He trusts me. He takes me everywhere with him," he replied in a serious tone.

"Do you know his inner circle?"

"Of course, although I don't really have much in common with any of them. They're all superficial, just hangers-on."

"Tell me more! Who are they? What about the parties?"

"They like to hang out in all the artistic circles, and they're always boasting about discovering new talent and helping bring people along with their taste and their critical eye. They're full of themselves, and yet they can't really do anything. They just have money, the right upbringing and some culture. They have no curiosity: they like what they know, and what they know they're meant to like...and these are the people who are supposed to be fostering art and creativity. They just feed off the art scene, like parasites. And yet people listen to them like the sun rises and sets to them. They have so much influence, and they're just caricatures. They're everything that's wrong with high society. I'll give you an example: there's Simon Delavallère, who's the son of one of the biggest theatre directors in Paris. He's only ever nice to people who can give him something: money, prestige, admiration. With everyone else, he's cold and aloof. He acts friendly to me now because he can see how close I am to Aleksander. Before that, he treated me like an underling, not worthy of the slightest courtesy."

"What about the others?" Stella was fascinated.

"They're all the same, really. There's one who stands out though; I just met him recently. They call him 'the beau of Saint-Germain.' He's just a kid, eighteen years old, and as perfectly formed as a porcelain doll. Nobody knows his story; he's very discreet. He spends more time drinking Champagne than talking. But he's always sober, and gentle as a lamb. He introduces himself as an artist, but we've never seen any of his work. Spielman tells me he studied at the greatest art school in Paris. Sometimes he'll do a little sketch on the corner of a napkin, then he gets nervous and crumples it up. I think he might be the one who did the painting in Aleksander's apartment. But they don't really speak to one another, as if there's some secret between them."

"What about the society parties? Where do they happen?"

"At people's apartments, in restaurants, at the Opera - it depends. They get bored easily, that lot, so they like to change things up. Last week we were at Simon Delavallère's. Everything there is expensive and horrible. Apparently, he redecorates every year. But he has paintings by some of the great masters, and a few Renoir sketches he must have bought in Switzerland."

"If you don't like them, why do you go?"

"I don't really have a choice; I have to go with Aleksander."

"I thought it made you happy. You make out like you can't stand them, but deep down you admire them. I know that scene all too well, and I can't stand it."

"You don't know it at all! You just know Florence; the Paris scene is different."

"Look at you defending them! I bet you've never even dared to play the blues around them. You can't be yourself with those types of people."

"I don't play for them, but that's not why. I'm learning the piano, and I don't want to mix myself up. Aleksander says it's best to focus on one thing at a time."

"You obey him like a child. I thought I was with a man now. So you haven't changed at all since Livorno?" she cried, springing out of the bed.

"Please don't go."

Aleksander Spielman had gone out, and Giovanni opened the windows wide. A strange wind blew through the apartment. Earlier on, Aleksander had been practising on the piano with Giovanni turning the pages for him. He tidied up the scattered pages on the table. Spielman liked things to be neat and orderly. He was a perfectionist. Schumann had to go between Schubert and Strauss. Giovanni finished filing the pages and sat down on the piano stool. He wanted to compose a symphony in memory of Maria Pacchiano. He listened to the rustling of the trees and the chirping of the birds. Voices carried up from the street below, audible for a fleeting moment before they were gone again. He put his hands to the keys, as if trying to reach out and touch the other side. The past came back to him. The wind whistled in his ears, and he heard a music that he played without thinking. What was Maria doing in the streets of Marseille at that time of night? She worked too hard. She'd stayed at school and hadn't seen the time going by. She must have been shocked at the storm raging outside when she left. She was so absorbed in her work that she hadn't heard the wind howling. She wasn't scared; Maria was afraid of nothing, and she knew the city like the back of her hand. Her hair was dotted with snowflakes. She batted them away from her eyes, she groped her way forward, singing softly to reassure herself and keep her courage about her. Giovanni remembered the way she sang when she was afraid, and sometimes when she was angry. He remembered her slight Italian accent, the false notes she camouflaged by lowering her voice. It was adorable when she sang off-key. The window banged shut, and the light swung back and forth. Giovanni no longer knew what he was playing; his hands moved along the keys seemingly of their own volition. All was white and impenetrable. No light shone through the blizzard. The streets were empty. Was she alone? She began to wonder if she'd ever get home. She wanted to stop, sit down and wait. She'd had enough. Giovanni wanted to console her, to take her hand and show her the way. Together, nothing could harm them. His hands moved quickly on the keys. His heart beat like a metronome gone haywire. He felt the heat between his ribs. Nothing could harm them when they were together, but he hadn't been with her. He'd been at home, waiting by the warm hearth. Had she called out to him? Had she thought of him? She continued to brave the storm, like a lonely soldier. As long as one foot went in front of the other, something had to happen. She heard steps coming towards her. Was it him? Had Giovanni found her? He must have been worried and scoured the city to find her. She spoke to him, but he did not answer. Had he heard? He came closer, blinding her with his torch. The light showed her wide eyes filled with terror. It wasn't him. A brief struggle and her life was over. It was Giovanni who sounded the death knell.

7.

The grand hall of the Paris Opera was empty. Facing out over the hundreds of plush red seats, Aleksander Spielman was practising, with Giovanni standing beside him to turn the pages. The young man's mind was wandering; the concierge had brought him a letter this morning. He'd recognised his mother's handwriting and stowed it carefully in his pocket. He could barely focus on the pianist's rhythm, wondering what she had to tell him. He hadn't heard from her in several weeks. She was probably dying of loneliness while he was living the high life, getting lessons from Aleksander Spielman, going to dinner parties, indulging in his romance with Stella and his nights at the cabarets with Lucien. He was flooded with guilt. He'd made sure to write to her every week: he wasn't always in the mood to do it, and had to carve out the time between all his other distractions, but it was his duty as a son. He had abandoned her in Livorno; now he owed it to her to stay in touch. Why hadn't she been writing back? He feared the letter contained bad news. He wanted to take the time to read his mother's words. "I think you have me confused with some greater pianist if you think I can play that fast," Spielman joked. He could see that Giovanni's mind was elsewhere. It was more than just his usual dreamy demeanour; he was troubled.

"I think that will be all for today," Aleksander said, taking his hands from the keys."

"Didn't we say until 6 o'clock?"

"It's best if you have some time to get ready for tonight's dinner."

Giovanni sat on the terrace of the Nutcracker café as Lucien was hailing down passers-by: "Oysters fresh from Cancale this morning! You sir, try our steak tartare with the chef's special sauce! All the stars have tried it! Michelle Morgan, Jean Gabin, sir! Our veal is as tender as a baby's bottom!" A pedestrian stopped and scrutinised the menu board. She did not sit down; it was far too expensive. Lucien raised his arms in exasperation; what did she expect in this neighbourhood? Had she somehow failed to notice the world-famous building their terrace overlooked? It's only the bloody Paris Opera, for god's sake. Lucien turned and noticed Giovanni. He didn't come here often. He walked over to his roommate with a broad smile and held himself erect with his hand behind his back:

"What can I get you, chum?"

"I'll have a coffee," Giovanni answered.

"My dear son,

Even though you are a man now, and you are far away from me and no longer need your dear mama, you will always be my child. This you cannot forget and cannot deny. You can't ever truly leave your family or your country behind. We all like to think we've outgrown our own, but to do so is a grave mistake, and what we do as adults always carries some measure of our childhood selves. And what a child you were! Such a dreamer, and gentle as a lamb. You liked my stories about far-off places. Oh, my son. I always knew you would have to leave one day. Is the world so different where you are? Have you found what you were looking for out there? Part of me hopes you have, because I wish you nothing but happiness, and yet I also hope you haven't, because your childhood dreams were too naive to bring you true happiness in life. I hope that sometimes you have failed and been disappointed, that you've suffered and managed to get back on your feet. It's the strength you find in yourself when you fail that makes you a man. But I have faith, because you weren't just a dreamer, you were also a hard worker like your father. But I'm not like either of you; I don't have your stubbornness. I have trouble living in my old body these days. And my mind is troubled, as you can tell; my mood is morose, and I keep talking about the good old days. But what else do I have left except those memories? My life is behind me, though yours is in front of you. I enjoy hearing about all your adventures. I don't get enough letters, but that's not a reproach. I never get tired of reading them. You don't talk about Maria anymore. You should send me a photo of her. I'm sure you chose a wonderful girl. I sometimes dream that the two of you will come to Livorno to visit me. And who knows? Maybe you'll bring a beautiful baby with big, dark eyes. How I long for that day. When the wind rattles the door, I sometimes think it's you kicking it open like you used to do. When I look down at my coffee in the morning, I sometimes hope that when I look up I'll see you and your father sitting across from me. What are you doing in Paris? They tell me it rains often in France. It's as sunny as ever here in Livorno. There's only the sun to see me getting old. You wouldn't believe how old I am now. Since your father died, age hasn't spared me. It's not easy to pass the time on your own. I'm lucky that Marcello and Valentina are still around. But friends only count for so much when you're sleeping alone, eating alone, and have no-one to hold in your arms. I miss your embrace, my son. I wouldn't have thought that you were the one I would miss the most. It's true that you and your father were both somewhat wild and independent, but you had your charm, your warmth, you loved me in your own ways. I'm sure Paris would make my head spin, with all those bright lights, the shows, the beautiful people. I wish I could see it all with you. I'd have liked to travel and see the world, like you're doing. But as you know, I've spent my whole life in Livorno, and it's all I know. I don't regret it; it was my destiny, and I've loved every day of my life here. I wasn't unhappy. And now, when I read your letters a part of me is there exploring Paris with you.

I want to tell you a story, like I did when you were a child. It's the story of your harmonica. I could have told you it sooner, but your father never wanted to hear me talking about the Great War. It was too painful for him. You see, when he came back from the war, he was a changed man. He wasn't always the gruff old man that you knew. I first met him thirty years ago, at the Livorno ball. He was like you, a smart young lad with wide, dreaming eyes. I loved him from the moment I saw him; he was so different to everyone I'd met before. We were seventeen, just children really. At that age, we were innocent. Your father wasn't involved in politics, even though there was a lot of it going around in Livorno. Europe was tearing itself apart. It was all anybody talked about in the cafés, at the harbour, in the market, everywhere in the village. Every day we'd read in the papers about the war that was raging in the countries around us. We feared for our homeland and wondered what would become of us. Italy was still young — it had been founded only 50 years before. We'd upheld the Triple Alliance, but we stayed neutral, and we were far from the fighting. But we knew that it would arrive at our door one day or another. We couldn't sit there not doing anything, but we didn't want to be cannon fodder either. The men argued and fought with one another in the street. They wanted to be involved and had big ideas. They wanted to show their mettle. But your father didn't want that; he just wanted to fish and live a simple life. In the papers, they said that everything started when the heir to the Austria-Hungarian throne was assassinated. In the village, they said it was about money, power, territory and politics, and that little people like us were being used as pawns. We didn't know much, but we knew that. Finally, Italy decided in May 1915 that it would side with France and Great Britain. We wanted to regain Dalmatia and Trieste. So that was it, and King Victor Emmanuel III started recruiting men from all over the country. One morning, men from Livorno were called to the front. It was official. We were knocked sideways. Our men would have to give themselves to the war effort in the name of honour and their homeland. They would sacrifice themselves for the values of their country, and to protect their families. Only children, the old and the infirm were spared. Like all the others, your father was sent to the northern front. You should have seen what it was like at the station. It was so sad. All those goodbyes were heartbreaking to watch. Mothers were inconsolable, wives felt like widows before their husbands had even left. I didn't want your father to see how worried I was; I wanted to be reassuring. But I was so scared. I stared at his face as long as I could, so I could keep it in my memory forever. He kissed me quickly, he didn't like to be overly sentimental, and then he got on the train with the others, his army pack slung over his shoulder. It was car number six. He waved to me from the window. We didn't cry for each other then; we didn't want to let it break us. He was so handsome. In just a few days he'd become a man. He was strong. He'd stopped dreaming. His face had changed. I looked at him, so proud and strong, and I admired him. I knew that man would come back to me. He was the love of my life. The stationmaster blew his whistle, and the train moved off in a cloud of black smoke. It moved slowly at first, and then it sped up and he was gone. All the women stood there on the platform, not knowing where to look or what to say to one another. All we could do was wait. We were powerless, rudderless. There was nothing more we could do. It was several weeks before I got a letter from him. I had no idea what was happening. It was unbearable, I didn't know what to think. Waiting without knowing is worse than knowing. He could be dead already. Should I mourn? I didn't dare; I wanted to continue to be strong for him, no matter how far away he was. That's what got me through those weeks; I couldn't betray his memory by believing he was dead, and I had to be here when he got back. The news from the front wasn't good. I saw women in mourning every day. They'd received the official letters, and they were waiting for the bodies of their sons or their husbands to be repatriated. The cemetery had to be expanded; the bodies were piling up. Families watched their relatives' bodies rotting away. We put clothes over them so we wouldn't see their sunken faces. And not everyone had been found. Like other volunteers, I helped care for some of the injured men who returned. They were in an awful state, some barely clinging to life. For us women, it was the only way we could feel useful. Time dragged on, but one day I got a letter.

I was so relieved. Your father told me about the horrors of the trenches. He said it was a bloodbath, and they were constantly running from bullets and shells. In the trenches, they waited around all day long for their orders, dying of hunger and thirst. They fought over jugs of stagnant water or bits of stale bread. They could not wash or even take their boots off. They sat in the muck, sometimes in puddles of their own urine, attacked by flies and vermin everywhere. Nothing grew there; just body parts and stumps of trees. It was a mass grave, and the smell of death was everywhere. Your father had one friend; a poor fellow from Turin no older than twenty. He'd brought his harmonica, and he played it to help soothe their souls. He played at night when nobody could sleep, and he played during the day when they dozed through their fear. It brought a little bit of light into their lives; a little piece of Italy in that music. He wasn't a hero, just a good mad with a big heart, who was generous without knowing it, whose faith made him strong. The kind of man your father would look up to. Your father never liked all those hotheads who wanted to fight, those big-talking men who were cruel and sometimes criminal. The men he admired were the ones who wanted to survive, and who wouldn't give up. In his second letter, he told me the young man from Turin was dead. He didn't say what happened. Just a short sentence, with no detail or emotion. It was too hard for him. And when he came back from the front, he didn't say any more about it. He just brought back the harmonica. And when you were born, he'd play you songs on the harmonica and set the instrument down by your bed. It would be yours once you were old enough to play. It was a way for your father to share the values that meant the most to him. And you, my son, you took to that instrument like a duck to water. For your father, it was like seeing his friend brought back to life. It moved him to hear your play; I saw him looking at you with his eyes open wide, his mind far away. He was probably having visions of soldiers being cut down and mines exploding at the front. When you learned the blues, you really made that harmonica your own. Your father didn't stop you; some things just have to happen in their own way. The first time he heard you playing the blues, I could see the disappointment in his eyes, but then he started laughing. You didn't understand why; you thought he was making fun of you. I remember, you refused to play for him for a week. He told me sometimes that he was proud of you, but he'd never dare say it to your face. I think that you reminded him of the young man from Turin, because only music could soothe you, and blowing into that harmonica was your way of facing the world.

It's getting late. The sky's dark and I can see the full moon. It's beautiful, that silvery light that watches over all of us. I hope you can see it too. I miss you. I wish I could hold you tight in my arms.

All my love,
Your dear mother,
Nina."

An old woman had sat down at the table next to Giovanni. The young man seemed emotional; his eyes had been fixed on that letter for over a quarter of an hour. His coffee had gone cold, untouched. Young people were sensitive types, all nerves and jitters. They didn't know that all things pass in time and that nothing really matters in the end. She sipped her grenadine, her little afternoon treat. She loved sweet things despite her doctor's remonstrations; at her age, why should she worry? Giovanni finally looked up from his letter. He looked around like a man freshly woken from a dream. If he'd known that story from the beginning...his father really didn't like to share. And yet, those were the stories on which the bonds of family were built. His father had always lived in the moment, never wanting to tell old stories. He didn't play the blues anymore, but suddenly felt the urge to take out his harmonica. His mother was right; you can't abandon the past. He began playing a tune. He turned to the rest of the terrace. Lucien watched him with a grin. Look at him go, finally smiling for once!

8.

Stella walked idly through her rival's apartment. She hadn't wanted to come tonight. It was Monsieur Spielman who kept Giovanni apart from her each day, and when he talked about the pianist he gushed compliments, full of enthusiasm, his eyes flashing and his hands gesticulating wildly. She was jealous, but how could she admit that to her lover when she was the married one? She walked over to the piano, framed in the centre of the living room. She imagined it was tuned to absolute perfection. She dreamed of owning such a beautiful instrument, or at least being able to play one from time to time. She pictured Aleksander carried off in his music, his delicate hands pattering over the keys, his dandyish figure stoic and straight. Giovanni was lying on the chaise longue, reading a book Lucien had lent him. It was a book of poems about the war, love, and the life of an artist. He didn't understand everything; the language was somewhat convoluted but had a certain grace. Stella sat beside him and read over his shoulder. "Tah-dah!" Aleksander Spielman broke the silence, emerging from the kitchen holding a pot of his famous *kneidler* in his gloved hands. He set it in the centre of the table. "Dinner is served, my honoured guests." The meal started awkwardly, but after some wine, they soon began to open up to one another. Stella found her host to be a sensitive and cultured man, nothing like the pretentious type she'd imagined. He spoke from the heart, spurred on by the eager attention of his two young guests.

"I remember it like it was yesterday. I felt like I was the most wanted man in Warsaw. I jumped every time I heard a noise and walked through the station with my back to the wall like the world's worst spy. I finally got on a train without being stopped and made my way to the bar so I could hide amongst the crowd; that way, if a ticket inspector came in I'd have time to hide. I didn't have a ticket. The journey seemed to last forever. I didn't sleep a wink the whole night and changed cars every half hour so I wouldn't get caught. I think that even if I'd had a ticket, the excitement of the adventure would have kept me awake. I had nothing with me but a few verses from the Torah. Even though I'd come from quite a well-off family, being penniless didn't scare me. On the contrary, it was a chance for me to prove that I was capable of facing the world alone. After a few hours I could barely stand. I finally found a free seat in third class and dozed beside a very nice family who said they'd wake me if there was any danger. At first light, I woke to see the sunlight over the beet fields. I hadn't realised it, but I'd left my home country. There was no hope left for me in Poland; the country seemed to me like a mother unfit to protect her children."

"So you just left your family behind without a care?" Stella queried, forgetting herself.

"I hadn't heard from my parents in years. They banished me from Krakow due to my...inclinations. I'd been living with my aunt. She was a loner, an old widow who lived modestly and spent all her days composing. Music was her only passion, and she rarely went out. She still had a few friends in high places in the Conservatory; in her day she was beautiful and talented, and some of them remembered her that way. It broke my heart to leave her, but she begged me to go. She wanted the best for me and said that she could see a great future ahead of me."

"Why did you come to Paris?"

"I'd always heard people talking about Paris, and one of my friends had studied here. He described it as the brightest, most plentiful city you could imagine. 'It's a place of music, of culture, a city on the rise,' he told me. You know, I was never even able to finish my studies at the Warsaw Conservatory, despite the help from my aunt's friends. One day, out of the blue, I got a letter hinting that I shouldn't come back. They didn't say why, but I knew the reason. I locked myself in my room for weeks and composed; I was in a fury. I had loved the Conservatory, but now I wanted to burn it to the ground. But back to the journey. I was on the train, dreaming of the future. I spoke Polish, Russian, Yiddish and a little English, but not a word of French. I had no idea how I would communicate, but I hardly cared. I was free. I'd let my music do the talking. When the train rolled into the Gare de l'Est, it was early morning. I sat looking at the great glass roof for hours. I wanted that moment to stay in my memory forever. I've always liked to frame those symbolic moments and keep the places safe in my mind. That's how I give my life meaning, and where I find my inspiration. Then I set out along the path of life and sat myself down at a café beside the station. I lit a cigarette – I still smoked then – and the waiter came over and started talking to me. He didn't stop, and I understood not a word. All of a sudden he stopped; he must have known that I wasn't French when he saw my pack of cigarettes. I smiled at him, not knowing what to say. He came back with a coffee and a croissant – he must have decided that's what everyone gets when they arrive!"

"What a story," Stella gasped. "You really left everything behind and just got on a train."

"I learn more about you every day," said Giovanni, impatient to hear more.

"You yourself have a rather unique story; we seem to both be adventurers!" Aleksander smiled.

"But your story isn't finished, Monsieur Spielman – please continue. I'm eager to hear how you came to be as we find you today," said Stella eagerly, squeezing Giovanni's hand.

"I'd told one of my old friends from the Conservatory that I was coming; he was playing for the orchestra at the Paris Opera," Aleksander Spielman went on. "He was a pianist like myself, and we both had an eye for handsome young men, so those were two things we had in common. He welcomed me with open arms. I was broke, but he was nice enough not to make me feel like it. I never wanted to live on charity, so I went out looking for work straight away. I played in the cafés, in the stations and in the cinemas where they still played silent films. I didn't earn much, but it was enough to buy myself Polish pickles at a shop I found in the Latin Quarter, and to give my friend flowers on the nights he performed. It was a bohemian existence. Andrei, my host, would sometimes take me to the Dome to meet other artists; people would drink all night there. The painters came to show their latest works, and sometimes a few charitable souls would buy them if they could. I also met several poets and writers who never made it big, despite their talent. I can't even remember their names now; fallen into obscurity, and no doubt the lives of low repute they were already on the verge of. I had some fleeting love affairs; nothing serious of course, but they all helped me improve my French. There's no better way to learn a language than through love."

"You must have met a lot of men – your French is perfect!" laughed Stella.

"I met enough to never really know most of them."

"You're very funny, Monsieur Spielman," she decided as she finished her glass of Champagne. "I had no idea. But you still haven't finished. Do go on."

"I was telling you about the Dome, the best café in Montparnasse. But the Dome isn't what it used to be...back in those days you could get a plate of Toulouse sausage and mash for less than three francs. It was a bargain for impoverished artists like myself. Andrei came to add to his collection of nudes."

"But how did you become so famous?" Giovanni asked. "I still don't know."

"It was a stroke of luck for me, and a stroke of ill fortune for Andrei. They made me his understudy for the Opera orchestra. His predilection for young artists eventually meant he fell victim to what they call the 'lovers' disease': syphilis. He was in hospital for a few weeks, and I took his place in the orchestra. I was ready to prove my worth, and, I must admit, show that I was more talented than my friend. It worked, and someone noticed me. His name was Simon Delavallère. He was the son of one of the biggest theatre directors in Paris. He came to find me in the Procope café when the other musicians and I were celebrating our latest performance. He was cold and scornful and acted like it was a great kindness for him to come to me since I had no fame and no graces, but he was in dire need of a pianist to accompany a French singer at a show the next day. I accepted immediately; it was an incredible opportunity. I spent several weeks working with that singer, and we toured all over France. I even composed a few pieces for her. She became a true friend, and she was the one who really helped my career to take off, even though she needed me. She introduced me to that hermetic inner circle of classical musicians, and one thing led to another..."

"Was it hard during the Occupation?" Stella inquired.

"Certainly. We all had to do things we would sooner forget."

Aleksander couldn't sleep. The conversation at dinner had dredged up too much of the past, and he now found himself alone with his thoughts. He would play the piano, his best means of escape. He was in the mood to play Schubert's Unfinished Symphony. It was gentle yet violent, full of suspense and hesitation, and it would guide him along the path to forgiveness. He pulled the pages from his library, and a pile of unbound pages fell out at his feet. He gathered them up and found a title page: "The Death of the Innocent." Giovanni must have composed something.

Curiosity overcame him, and he decided he must play it. He laid his hands on the keys and followed the music, listening to the melody his fingers brought forth. Slowly, he found himself relaxing into the young Italian's imagination. He absorbed his delicate sensibilities, clumsy and sometimes abrupt, but soft and gentle as well. As he thought of his friend while turning the pages, swathes of memory unfolded behind his eyes. He was in Warsaw, on his way home from the Conservatory. His head swimming in music, at first he did not see who was in front of him. But when he saw him, his legs turned to jelly. His love had not changed; the expression on his face was somewhat harder, his beard thicker, his hair neatly combed. But behind all those manly designs, he saw the candour and tenderness of the man he had always loved. He took him in his arms without thinking. He found comfort in the scent of his skin. Aleksander Spielman looked at the painting in front of him: it was of Sebastian at the age of fifteen, the Sebastian who'd never yet betrayed him. He sighed; there had been no tears over it for a long time now. He turned a new page and began the second movement. His long silk gown clung to his skin. It was the beginning of their reunion; they met secretly whenever they could, his aunt allowing them to use her spare room when she went out for groceries. What they were doing was wrong; they were sinners, flouting the laws of marriage and religion. It lasted a few seasons. One day, while he was walking with his aunt, they passed Sebastian with his two children. His hands clenched into fists. That image of Sebastian in the park, running around with his family, living a blissful life he could never be a part of, would always haunt him. Aleksander Spielman's heart was broken. He'd been nothing but a third wheel. "Happiness is never eternal," his aunt told him. Even she was worried about him. Nationalism was spreading across Poland; a few weeks later, he was expelled from the Conservatory. He knew the reason why and was enraged. He decided to leave Poland. Aleksander's fingers slowed to a crawl. What he'd just played was wonderful. He'd have to get to work. He needed to practise before his next concert.

9.

Giovanni and Stella were walking in the Tuileries gardens, one of the loveliest spaces in Paris and the oldest French-style gardens in the capital. Some three centuries earlier, the Sun King himself had ordered his gardens to be redesigned and enlarged, stretching from Place de la Concorde to the Louvre palace along Rue de Rivoli. In the king's gardens they talked of business, marriages, and all things more suited to discussion in a garden than in a church. It was said that the gardens were so grand and spacious that all the children of the city could walk there at the same time. Giovanni and Stella smiled at the labours of the children there today: there were buckets to be filled with sand, balls to be chased, and hoops to be rolled around. Stella remembered her childhood. In Livorno, all the children played with spinning tops. She liked to watch them moving, sometimes in a regular pattern and sometimes in sketches and scrawls. As light as a goose feather, the top seemed like it was writing her messages in the dust. The wind rustled the sand in the Tuileries gardens, and the old folks shook it from their papers. It was Sunday afternoon; the central alley of the gardens was drenched in sunlight and thronged with Parisians. Stella wanted to steal away into one of the side alleys, away from prying eyes, where peaceful souls and lovers could while away their days. She and Giovanni turned onto Castiglione alley. The tumult of voices died down, and calm resided. Stella grabbed Giovanni's hand:

"We should leave," she said with determination.

"And go where?" he asked, taken aback.

"Wherever, just far away from here. What's keeping us here? I'm suffocating in Paris and in my marriage. I want to not care, I want to feel free. Don't you want to have me all to yourself? Let's stop living in hiding and go back to Italy. There's nothing keeping us here; we're foreigners, I'm homesick, and I want my life to have meaning," she cried.

"Let's be reasonable—"

"I can't be reasonable anymore. I've been reasonable all my life, and look where it's gotten me."

"You don't know what it's like to be poor. I don't know if you'd manage. If we both left now, what would we live on?"

"On love and fresh water!" she laughed.

"You say that now, but you don't know...and anyway, I'm happy with what I have going with Aleksander. I like the life I've built for myself here in Paris."

"So that's all the love you have for me?"

"Don't be childish. We'll see in good time what the future holds for us...why do you want to rush things?"

Stella stepped away from him. She didn't speak until they'd reached Place de la Concorde. She walked without looking where she was going, absorbed in her thoughts. Giovanni let her be; he felt clumsy, not knowing what to say to reassure her. He understood her pain; it was real but fleeting. It would arrive from time to time out of the blue, sparked by her ill-conceived notions of romance. Stella looked at Giovanni from the corner of her eye, trying to find a trace of the adventurer who'd opened up a world of possibility to her. But all she saw was a man resigned, dimmed by disillusion. She hadn't been lucky enough to know him in Marseille. Maria had doused Giovanni's fire. Was he really any more passionate than her husband? He was too sensible for a lover. What was the point of an affair that offered no sense of escape? The young man put his arm around her shoulder, and Stella felt his familiar comfort once again.

Aleksander was practising at the Opera. His work demanded rigorous perfection. Humility was an essential quality in the world of music: every performance must be exceptional. There was no room for error; it was a herculean struggle. Giovanni hated feeling idle; he was in the artist's apartment and was bored. He would return to his composition. It was time to finish it, so he could mourn properly. What use was a homage if it were not perfect? Stella was rushing him; no doubt she could sense the turmoil within him. He was not completely whole, still burdened by memory. He needed to return to the past and tame it into submission. But in the Schubert section, between The Unfinished Symphony and *La jeune fille et la mort*, he found nothing. It couldn't be. It had to be there. Had he made a mistake, blinded by his emotion? He searched frantically through all the files. He tossed them out onto the floor, shuffled through them, paced back and forth and came back to the shelf. Could he really have lost it? Sickened at the thought, he laid his head down on the shelf, and his eye was drawn to something unusual. Aleksander's desk drawer was ajar. It was usually always locked. Giovanni was curious; he looked over his shoulder and pulled the drawer open. There was nothing much of interest, just a few press clippings and some family photos. He picked up a photo of Aleksander as a child, standing proudly beside a new bicycle. Giovanni smiled; the boy already had a daring look in his eyes. He closed the drawer and heard a dull noise. Something had fallen out of the back and was lying under the desk. He picked it up; a leather notebook engraved with the pianist's initials. He sat down on the chaise longue and opened it over his knee. It was Spielman's diary.

21 June 1940
Pétain is now president. Paris is occupied. Will General de Gaulle's call to arms change anything? Andrei and his network are more active than ever. They've been plastering posters of the General over the Chimay hotel in Vendome square. Can the Resistance gain enough strength to oust the occupiers? The Krauts are everywhere, and the Nazi flag is flying over the Arc de Triomphe. What a symbol. France's dignity has been besmirched; there can be no beauty here any longer. Tonight was the most humiliating experience of my life. I had to play; I had no choice. When the concert was over, and I stood in front of the audience, I bowed before a hundred German officers. They'd invaded the Opera. I was in front of the enemy. For three hours, I played without raising my eyes from the music: I was outside myself. I could not be there; like a puppet, I obeyed without thinking. But in the midst of the applause, I saw the terrified faces of Sebastian, of my aunt, my mother, my father, and everyone I knew, faces being smothered by the same hands that were applauding me. I killed Kazimierz, I killed the synagogue, I killed my childhood, and I cannot bring myself to cry. How am I not angrier? I'm waiting for Andrei to help me escape this hell. I cannot continue to betray my honour like this, and soon my identity will be discovered. The story begins again...music is no sanctuary for a Jew. You must earn it, beg for it and even hate it sometimes. When I was banished from the Warsaw Conservatory, I thought naively that I would never feel such rancour and injustice again. I needed to believe it then; I wouldn't have been able to go on otherwise.

24 June 1940

Andrei got me an appointment at the Paul Dupont print shop on Rue de la Victoire, so I could get the false papers I need to travel south. I went there today and was surprised to discover everything was brand new. I thought they might be using somewhere less sophisticated as cover. Two machines were running at full tilt, watched over by a little man in a grey suit. He turned and looked me up and down, stroking his moustache. He didn't really look the part; there was nothing strong or rebellious about him. He looked like butter wouldn't melt in his mouth. He was so very French, so very Parisian. Was I even in the right place? But he put my doubts to rest, that little man, by asking me: "Are you here for the party invitations?" I nodded, but he insisted. "I'm picking them up for my aunt," was the response I had to give. He smiled at my discomfort and waved me into the back office. He had an ingenious system: he pushed on one of the bookshelves to reveal a secret door. We went through a cubby hole and down a staircase that seemed to go on forever. The smell of the sewers rose in my nostrils, getting stronger the closer we got to the light of the hideout. I heard the crackling of a radio, and a few words in English made me think that they must be communicating with London and the General. Two men were listening and taking notes. I looked around me. A huge, faded map of Paris was pinned to the wall, showing hiding places and safe routes to take. There were a few photos with notes scribbled on them attached to the map. There was a printing press, a desk, a radio transmitter, thick paper and black ink. That was their whole set up. The little man with the moustache hurried back up to the print shop, and the two men got to work without a word. Two hours later, I left with my fake ID. I am now Bernard Pichet, and I was born in Boulogne on May 28, 1914.

27 June 1940
I have a rehearsal tonight. I have to go in order to avoid suspicion. A week from now I'll be in Marseille. Andrei knows someone who can put me up for a few nights. I can't sleep; I just play the piano all night. Practising non-stop is my only relief.

29 June 1940
I've opened my Torah; it is still dear to my heart. I read, or rather I listen: I hear the gruff, monotone voice of the rabbi in Kazimierz. I see my mother beside me, and I see my little brother. What has become of them? The Torah shrouds me in its reassuring words. Rules are calming in times of chaos. The future illuminates the past; time does not exist in the Torah. Its

words take me on a journey through the phases of my life, filling me with its teachings. I repeat "he who strikes another man and kills him shall be put to death," and it brings me peace.

1st July 1940
The clock in the Gare de Lyon train station was set to German time, and Nazi officers were everywhere. I walked in front of them, my eyes fixed on the clock hands to keep my head raised and my mind occupied. I had to pass through a security checkpoint manned by two guards and their dogs. The animals frightened me the most; I had an irrational fear that they would betray me. Can a dog be trained to sniff out Jews? I joined the queue as calmly as I could and set down my case on the cobbles. There was no turning back now. I'd played my hand. I played Wagner in my head to steel myself. It made me feel like a war general, but the guard's stern voice shook me back to consciousness. I was powerless, like prey. He ordered me to show my papers, and I handed them to him with all the confidence I could muster. His colleague grabbed my case and emptied it onto the floor. I'd been careful to leave my Torah at Andrei's, and there was nothing suspicious in there. My sheet music blew away in the wind. I didn't flinch; my life's work no longer mattered. The first guard studied my papers carefully; he must have been able to smell my fear. He looked me up and down for a few long moments. It took all my strength to smile at him. I could barely stand. "Bernard Pichet, *Es ist gut"*, he concluded, handing me back my card. I gathered up my clothes; despite the humiliation, I'd never felt so free. Now I find myself on the shores of the Mediterranean, sitting at a café by the port, waiting to meet Andrei's contact.

A key turned in the lock, and the door opened. Giovanni jumped and instinctively hid the journal in his jacket pocket. He'd had no time to tidy up, and could think of no explanation. Sheets of music were scattered over the rug, and the desk drawer was still open. There he stood like a frightened rabbit, incapable of moving. Aleksander looked at him with amusement. What was the boy afraid of? The living room was a mess; he must have been looking for his composition. The pianist had kept it in his satchel, but the young man didn't seem to suspect him. What was he hiding? Giovanni mumbled an excuse and moved towards the desk. Spielman understood; the boy had found his journal. Fair was fair; one invasion of privacy deserved another. "I'm going to Les Halles for some flowers; be a dear and tidy that up before I get back," he said crisply.

Giovanni had escaped by the skin of his teeth. He got to work, relieved. But all of a sudden, Aleksander's reaction seemed suspicious. The man was a perfectionist and abhorred disorder. And yet he had offered no reproach. Why hadn't he flown off the handle? Why hadn't he asked Giovanni to explain the mess? Surely there was no way...and yet, it was the only explanation. Aleksander Spielman had stolen his composition.

10.

Giovanni climbed the spiral staircase of his apartment building. He was supposed to be meeting Stella tonight, but there was only one thing on his mind: reading more of Aleksander Spielman's journal. When he opened the door, he barely recognised the place. Lucien had tidied up; even the beds were made. This worried Giovanni, as he had hidden the diary under his pillow. It was no longer there; Lucien had stowed it in the drawer of his bedside table. Had he opened it? Had he read it? Giovanni decided he would trust his friend. He lay down on the bed and began reading again.

03 December 1940

Sleep is my worst enemy. I sleep with one eye open, haunted by the fear that they'll come for me in the night, as the Vichy soldiers are known to do. Neighbours inform on one another, and the soldiers come and pillage their apartments without a care. Everyone's out to gain what they can from the situation; it's a regime built for opportunists. The only thing most people are guilty of is having things their neighbours want. But I'm Bernard Pichet. I mouth the name to myself silently all through the night. It's become my mournful prayer of betrayal. I'm Bernard Pichet, and nobody could find fault in a man who's always polite and smiling, discreet and upstanding as one should be. I feel like a coward when so many Jews have been reported and deported. I struggle to play this game and look at myself in the mirror. Today, I had to attend a march for Marshal Pétain on the Canebière. I had to play the part; Bernard Pichet is a good French patriot and a Catholic who would want to honour that hero of the Great War. How can I describe the spectacle I saw today? All of Marseille was in a jubilant mood. Thousands of banners honouring the great Marshal Pétain fluttered over the streets. We welcomed the hero who'd saved France from German invasion. Pétain waved to the crowd, and they went wild. His kindly face and military dress fascinated the people. Flanked by a group of women in traditional dress, Pétain reviewed the troops. There was a military parade along Quai des Belges that lasted several hours. We admired the proud patriots in their fine uniforms, with children on their parents' shoulders throwing flowers at the soldiers. Their jubilation pained me more than I had imagined it would. I feel so alone tonight; mine is the solitude of an outcast living among those who do not yet know they hate him.

08 July 1942

Before the war, I was very disciplined when it came to cigarettes. I smoked no more than three per day: one in the morning, one at lunch and one in the evening. Each one marked the passage of the day. It was my ritual, and I stuck to it. Now though, I smoke impulsively every time I get my hands on a pack. I have no self-control. I go through my stock as fast as possible. I went through a whole packet this morning between eight and ten. Sitting on the terrace of a café by the port, I indulged this guilty pleasure with a glass of pastis. Today I received a very interesting ration: in addition to the pack of smokes I'd already finished, there were five eggs and some milk. I was able to get some thyme and some chives. It's been a long time since I ate an omelette. I plan to savour every mouthful as if it were my last.

While Giovanni was falling asleep reading the diary, Aleksander Spielman was perfecting the young man's symphony. It needed to be streamlined, the clumsier passages scraped away without tarnishing its sense of spontaneity. The piece's intensity was made even more charming by the fact that it started off unsteadily, before finding its feet and eventually overpowering the listener. Aleksander edited furiously, correcting himself and then starting over. Something was holding him back. He would smoke his evening cigarette on the balcony. He needed to take a step back from it. He must get to the bottom of Giovanni's esoteric ways. He must inhabit the boy's sensitive soul, otherwise nothing great would ever come from this symphony. Giovanni awoke, the diary open on his chest. He yawned and began reading again.

14 July 1942

I am not alone; France is resisting the Occupation. That is what today has shown me. I had heard rumblings of something going on, and that Radio London had given instructions to the Resistance. My curiosity brought me outside. The streets were busy for the public holiday, but the atmosphere was morose. It was painful to see. I remember 14 July celebrations in Paris before the war, with people dancing on the banks of the Seine, and children running gaily through the streets. But now, how can one celebrate the birth of a Republic when half of the country is occupied? I was walking along Quai des Belges with those memories when I felt something taking shape. All of a sudden, I saw a dozen or so men hurrying towards the Canebière. Others joined them, and the crowd grew quickly. I followed, keeping my distance. They gathered in front of the Grand Café Glacier, beside the headquarters of the *Parti Populaire Français*, where the collaborators were keeping guard. The crowd had swollen, and the police were struggling to keep it contained. The protestors broke through their lines and made it to the doors of the Parti Populaire's offices, and the two sides squared off. It was like watching a Greek tragedy. The chaos ended when shots were fired; two protesters were dead, and the crowd fled. I went home feeling stunned and shaken. I wished I had thrown stones at the offices of the Parti Populaire. I wanted to scream my hatred for the Occupation. But I'm too afraid of having my identity uncovered.

05 September 1944

My apartment in Paris is intact, and I have reunited with my dear friend Andrei. The metro is still not up and running. Gas rations are in short supply. The black market is still running, and every day the papers publish new lists of collaborators. This morning, I burned my false papers. Bernard Pichet's name was consumed by the fire. With some difficulty, I have begun to play the piano again.

10 September 1944

"Paris outraged, but Paris liberated!" Those are the words of General de Gaulle himself. But the Liberation brings its own outrages, which this time are the doing of the Parisians themselves. They are punishing the women, a facile and hypocritical vengeance. Any woman suspected of sleeping with a German has her head shaved in the street. My fellow citizens repulse me. Yesterday I witnessed the hideous spectacle of the shaven women being paraded through the city. The people jeered and spat on them, their anger dishonourable and dirty. But men are made this way; they need scapegoats. If it's not the Jews, it's the women. What does sleeping with a German matter when there are others walking among us who ferried men, women and children to their deaths?

Those were the journal's last words. Aleksander had never spoken of this period in his life. He'd lived through the pain and shame of hiding, even giving up his own name and identity. What could a man aspire to when he had abandoned the very thing that defined him? It explained, no doubt, the pianist's manifest desire to stand apart. Aleksander Spielman was no longer ashamed; he was proud of everything that distinguished him from the everyday. Giovanni had not known this occupied France, but it was not the first time he'd tried to imagine it. The Pacchianos had sometimes talked about it. Maria did not like to remember it; she held France in too high esteem to admit that it had been conquered. He imagined the friend he now admired so much, running for his life in a city that was now such a symbol of resistance and struggle. Had Aleksander wandered as far as Belle de Mai? Had he been to the same places Giovanni would later frequent? In his mind, they were still two separate worlds. In Marseille he had seen only the cruelty of the Italian mafia and its twisted rackets. He could not imagine neighbours informing on one another, or the sense of betrayal and collusion. It was difficult to think of Pétain being greeted with such joy by the people. The children who'd once admired the Marshal now spoke only of the General. The flowers they threw for their heroes had been trampled by history. Celebrated in one stroke, and decried in another. The wheel of time spins without purpose. To the victors, the spoils. Whatever they said, history was always rewritten. The same people who were so warm and caring in the post-war years might well have ratted out their neighbours not long before. How could you know? There was no way to recognise them. Had he ever shaken the hand of a monster, thinking it was an angel? At least the mafia did not hide their evil ways. You knew what to expect from them. Aleksander Spielman lifted his hands from the piano. The symphony would be perfect for his next concerto. He cracked his fingers and closed the key lid, giving it one final caress to signal his satisfaction.

The next morning Giovanni went to Aleksander Spielman's apartment. When he emerged from the elevator, he heard the sound of the piano resonating throughout the floor. The artist was never usually awake at this time. He'd been hoping to stow the diary safely back in its drawer without being seen. He was eager to rid himself of the weight, not liking the thought of a secret separating him from his friend. He kept the diary in his inside pocket and entered without ringing the bell; Aleksander trusted him enough to give him his own key. The young man's throat tightened at the thought. In the living room, Giovanni found Aleksander in his robe, playing furiously with a cigarette between his lips. He wore none of his usual sublime elegance; his hair was dishevelled like he'd been trying to pull it out all night. Had he had a bout of insomnia? Giovanni tiptoed through the room so as not to startle him. The artist did not raise his reddened eyes, and his taut hands continued to stab at the keys as if trying to dislodge them. "No! No! And no!" he cried with jitters, before closing the lid. Giovanni was worried. What was going on? Spielman turned to him and repeated three times, lowering his voice *diminuendo*:

"No practice today!"

"What's wrong?"

"Have a read of this. You didn't know? It seems that everyone does," Spielman wailed, handing him a copy of *Le Parisien*.

"What does that mean?"

Aleksander left the room in a fury. The young man sat down in an armchair, shaken, and began leafing through the pages. He read the headlines: the market sellers were on strike, and the French were worried about a third world war. Finding no answers, he continued to look through the pages. *"Communists oppose colonisation", "Aleksander Spielman lends his talents to collaboration!"* Giovanni went pale. His hands trembled. The first lines were enough for him to recognise the writing as belonging to his friend, Lucien. That traitor!

"Who would have thought it? The list of collaborators runs long, and we are still uncovering new names every day. It now appears that the great Aleksander Spielman played piano for German soldiers after their invasion of Paris was complete. In the audience, officers from the highest ranks of the German army had a chance to preview the talents of the man who would become one of our greatest musical heroes. What does he have to say? We await the great pianist's explanation with baited breath. Will the composer, a Polish Jew, be able to explain his actions? Aleksander Spielman fled to Marseille under a false name during the Occupation — was he afraid that his deeds would be uncovered? Had he taken an opportunity we do not yet know about? The artist has always been secretive about his activities during the war, and the circumstances of his rapid rise to fame in the years after the Liberation. Indeed, in those early days of freedom, Spielman was lauded on the biggest

stages in Paris. His success continues to this day, and he is due to perform his next concerto at the Opera Garnier in a matter of months. All the Parisian elite will be in attendance, and tickets are selling like hot cakes. But how will the public react to this shocking revelation?"

Lucien, that cheating bastard! All this for a fistful of francs. Judas! Giovanni could not believe it. How could he trample on the man's honour like this? He hadn't wasted any time: he'd written the article during the night, and here it was, printed the next day. Had there been even a moment's hesitation? Giovanni remembered his thoughts from the night before: nobody deserved to be trusted blindly. The most dishonest people were those with a gift for being liked. Aleksander emerged from the kitchen holding a cup of tea. He saw the desolation on the young man's face.

"Are you feeling guilty?"

"Yes. I took your diary. This is all my fault. I was curious; I found it by accident and I couldn't help myself. I kept it with me in my pocket almost the whole time. Just once I left it hidden in the apartment. That damned Lucien read it and decided to share your secrets with the world. What could I ever do to make you forgive me?"

"Nothing. It's not your fault; you were betrayed by a friend. Those journalists! I am outraged. What do they know of what it was like? What would they have done in my place? I did what I had to, but I couldn't stay in Paris. I had to flee. Once again, I had no choice. And to a journalist that is collaboration! My life was in danger; I had to act and I had to submit to my fate. They could never understand. This story is a knife in the back. It's an easy scoop, of course. When you're famous, the slightest faux pas has the press baying for your blood like starving hounds."

Giovanni walked aimlessly on the quays, his hands in his pockets along with a few scant coins, a bus ticket and his ever-present harmonica. The sunshine was oppressive, and he looked around for shade. He'd become a night owl; the midday heat was too much for him. He stopped under a tree, where an old bookseller spotted him and called him over. The old man recognised the handsome young fellow with the foreign accent who'd often walked that way in the evenings. He offered the boy a beautiful leather-bound volume, put aside for him specially, he insisted. It was a book for a connoisseur of fine tastes. Giovanni politely refused; he no longer had the means to indulge in such pleasures. "Next time, then! Don't worry, things will be looking up soon!" the old man reassured him with a pat on the back. Giovanni laughed sadly. He might be right; he'd certainly lived long enough to know what he was talking about. But Giovanni was in low spirits and did not believe that any stroke of luck could turn his fortunes around. He wandered through the streets of Paris, turning down new roads and exploring new neighbourhoods, observing the Parisians in their routines. He had nothing else to do; it had been a month since he last saw Aleksander. His memory was haunted by the furious look on the pianist's face when he'd handed him the article. On that day, Spielman had remained polite and reserved. Every word was spoken neutrally, even the vague pardon he had issued without conviction, simply because he was not the kind of man given to anger and remonstration. The reality was worse: ill-feeling had set in between the two men. Giovanni had come back that night to see how he was doing, but Spielman had sent him away as diplomatically as possible. Aleksander's excessive politeness was the most obvious sign of his disapproval and disappointment. Giovanni had seen this before. He had understood that it was a farewell. Since then, time passed in a blur. Giovanni continued walking towards Notre Dame cathedral. He clasped his harmonica in his pocket. It was his ever-present talisman, but his luck had run out. More than anything, he wanted to beg his friend's forgiveness. But his lamentations would seem ridiculous; he was not the one who'd been betrayed. He imagined Aleksander reassuring him with pity, and the thought was unbearable. How could he make a case for his being accepted once again? Nothing he could say would heal this wound. In any case, Aleksander had in all likelihood already forgiven him; he was not the type to wallow in rancour. No, he simply wanted nothing more to do with him. As Giovanni arrived in front of the cathedral, he knew he had probably been replaced already. The building was as majestic as ever. His gaze settled on a beggar feeding pigeons on the square in front of the church. Throwing crumbs to them was his whole existence; he seemed happy with his simple life. Giovanni was miserable; he'd known too much happiness to be content with what he had left. Stella was still pushing him to leave with her, but he found himself incapable. All because of that idiot Lucien. They'd fought and parted ways with a black eye apiece. It had changed nothing and brought him no comfort. He was still the crook from Marseille who'd thought he was refining himself in Paris. He hadn't changed. He now lived in a rat's nest on the northern side of the city. He was ashamed of his poverty. Stella said nothing; she tried to spare his feelings. He had to believe she still loved him. Should he go with her? For the moment, it was a decision he was still not ready to make. Only reconciliation with Spielman would ease his troubled mind.

11.

Giovanni walked up Boulevard Raspail towards the famously bohemian neighbourhood of Montparnasse. He liked its busy, narrow streets littered with creperies, cheap theatres and cafés. It was vivid with culture and nightlife, imbued with the sweet scent of those thin buckwheat crepes. But Giovanni's mood was clouded with apprehension, for tonight he was attending Aleksander Spielman's birthday party at the La Coupole brasserie. He'd been surprised to receive the invitation, but knew it could be no mistake: every year the pianist cultivated his list of honoured guests with great care. He'd have to muster a smile and take Simon Delavallère's every jibe in stride, and yet he was happy, immeasurably happy, to have the chance to see the artist again. He arrived outside the great red awning, took a deep breath and pushed open the heavy door. A luxurious buffet table was laid out underneath the illuminated dome. The guests stood between the pilasters, drinking Champagne. Giovanni looked around at the flurry of silk, furs, feathers and diamonds on display. The women were radiant under the light of the chandeliers. The men were just as elegant, if more discreetly dressed. Only a few of the more daring types like Simon Delavallère or the Beau of Saint-Germain were sporting bright colours and shimmering fabrics. Giovanni edged his way over to the buffet table and procured a glass of Champagne. He turned away when people looked at him, trying his best to stay invisible. Aleksander had not yet arrived; he liked to make an entrance. And yet, nobody seemed to be expecting him, everyone gaily discussing the latest news from around Paris. Finally, it was Ambroise who spotted Giovanni and came over to greet him:

"I'm delighted to see you! I insisted that you be in attendance", he said warmly, shaking Giovanni's hand. "We must make way for reconciliation, my dear Giovanni. Tonight's the night for it!" he added with a wink.

"I agree, but it might take some time."

"Things will work out; Aleksander's not one to hold a grudge. That said, he was profoundly hurt by what happened. He's not as invulnerable as he makes himself out to be."

"I see that our friend Giovanni is eager to turn the page when he should be turning on his heel!" laughed Simon Delavallère, who had slithered into the conversation as was his way.

"Better my feet stay where they are, lest I be tempted to put one of them up your arse," the young Italian parried with a smile.

"You wouldn't be the first!" Simon laughed. "You've grown some moxie since we last saw you! Guilt fits you like a glove...it's almost enough to make you interesting!"

"I think that's the first compliment you've ever given me."

"Enjoy it, then! They don't come often, ask anyone!" he said, moving off.

"That man's mind is as cold as the north wind. Ambroise, sometimes I'm surprised that you're friends with him."

"I find him amusing; his provocations keep things interesting. Besides, is our friendship any more surprising than what you have with Aleksander? Friendships can be more perverse than we care to admit. More often than not we're drawn to people for their faults, not their qualities."

"You always did enjoy a paradox. But I don't think Aleksander has any true faults. Apart from always being late, that is. When's he getting here, anyway? Looks like everyone's been waiting a while."

Aleksander finally arrived, on the arm of an angel-faced young stranger. They wore matching flowers in their buttonholes. Giovanni felt a twinge of jealousy as he applauded the guest of honour's arrival. The artist took a bow and thanked his guests with a short speech, before concluding: "Now let the festivities commence!" A jazz quartet began playing. The young dandy on his arm smiled with satisfaction, proud to have been chosen by the great man. Giovanni observed him simpering by the pianist's side as Aleksander greeted each of his guests with a few courteous words.

"I'm honoured to have you with us tonight!" he exclaimed when he saw the young Italian.

"It's a pleasure to be invited."

Aleksander was happy; he seemed to have forgotten his disappointment in the young man and moved away from Giovanni with a lingering smile. After all, this was not the time to launch into long explanations, thought Giovanni, discombobulated by the pleasantness of their interaction. This done, boredom began to sneak about him. He had little in common with the other guests, and Aleksander couldn't be expected to look after him all night. He should have invited Stella. She'd have helped him have fun; she was in her element at this type of party, always ready with a quick joke or a witty remark. People found her charming and high-minded, whereas he felt gauche and foreign here. Without the pianist's sponsorship, he had no legitimacy and little sense of composure. He stood back and looked on, his Champagne glass staying full. He forgot that he was there and observed the guests like he was at the theatre. A couple was waltzing beside the musicians, disregarding the fact that no waltz was being played. The man stood stiff as a post; it seemed almost impossible that he could turn at all. His partner wore an incredibly elegant and risqué dress in the American style. Her back was completely bare, and a slit up the sides showed off her legs up to the thigh. Diamonds sparkled around her neck. Giovanni was charmed; she reminded him of Marlène Dietrich. "So graceful, my dear!" Aleksander complimented her. She gave him a flirtatious look. Aleksander then went to join in the conversation of four men gathered by the buffet. They were his friends from his early years in Paris; they did not mix much with the other guests and were happy to see him so they could talk about old times. They'd been in their twenties, their lives ahead of them, all their dreams waiting to be achieved many surprises still store. Beside them, the waiters opened a bottle of Champagne and poured the sparkling liquid over the top of a pyramid of glasses. "Aleksander, the first glass must be yours!" Ambroise insisted. Aleksander was being careful not to drink too much. He took the glass to a ripple of applause and dipped his lips into the crystal coupe. "Aleksander darling, you didn't drink anything! I'm watching you!" hissed Marlène Dietrich, who'd finished her waltz. He laughed aloud and moved away, embarrassed. He spied Giovanni talking with one of his most eccentric friends, who was wearing a fur coat over a long dress set with sequins and holding a Venetian mask over her face.

"My dear! To look at you is to be transported; I see before me the Grand Canal and its gondolas, St. Mark's Square, and the Doge's Palace!" he beamed.

"How romantic you are, Spielman," she purred, lifting her mask. "Are you flattering me or implying that I'm in costume?"

"Aren't we all? Some of us just do it with more flair than others."

"I've never seen Venice and its grand canal, but they tell me it's wonderful. I hope it's as beautiful as you are tonight, Madame," Giovanni pandered.

"Finally, a compliment! Tonight everyone's been looking sideways at me!"

"Be very careful of this young Italian, he's a certified skirt chaser!" Aleksander laughed.

"So you're consorting with men who chase skirt now, are you? He must be truly special."

"I'll let you judge for yourself," Spielman answered, making to leave them to their conversation. "Giovanni, I almost forgot to give you this," he added, taking an envelope from his pocket. "It's a letter addressed to you; it arrived at my apartment two days ago."

Suddenly the lights went down, and the brasserie was plunged into darkness as the guests gathered around the pianist. The kitchen's swing doors opened, and a trolley was rolled out gleaming with the light of forty candles. The waiters and chefs began singing 'happy birthday' and were quickly joined by the other guests, some of them famous opera singers who let their voices ring out with grandiloquent volume. Spielman was moved and dabbed his eyes with his handkerchief. "Encore!" cried one lady, and they sang it again before Aleksander Spielman blew out the candles. The applause rang out, and the lights went up again. The pastry chef, dressed in immaculate whites and wearing a stiff hat over his pinched face, climbed onto a stepladder to pour dark chocolate sauce over the pyramid of profiteroles. It was a practised and spectacular move. The sous chef removed the candles from the gateau and began serving the guests. The waiters brought presents, each of which Aleksander opened with impeccable politeness: "How wonderful! You are all spoiling me tonight!"

The Champagne flowed freely until the dawn light crept through the doors, and the guests began to tire. They stumbled out, thanking the pianist for a wonderful night. "You're like a fine wine", "You get younger every day," — Aleksander was spared no cliché, but shook every hand with sincere thanks. He was not in the mood for provocation tonight. His date was asleep in a chair; the boy wasn't used to drinking so much. Aleksander looked at him tenderly; he had a soft spot for sleeping beauties and the innocence of their peaceful faces. He thought of Giovanni sleeping on his chaise longue. Where was he; had he left without saying goodbye? In fact,

Giovanni had been outside longer than he realised, sitting on the steps of the brasserie reading the letter from his mother.

"My son,

I have good news – they let me out of the hospital yesterday. I didn't want to worry you, and so I lied to you or at least failed to tell you everything. I've been in bed for a month. I passed out one morning at the market, and they took me to the nearest hospital right away. They took good care of me here in Livorno. I wasn't on my own – far from it. I had plenty of visitors at the hospital: Valentina came every day, and Marcello and Luca sometimes, and the nurses were very thoughtful. I didn't suffer; I was happy. I wasn't afraid to die; I'm a good Catholic, and when the Lord calls my name, I shall be ready. But this was not my time, and I rejoice because this means I still have time to pray for you and watch over you a little longer. The doctor diagnosed me with a weak heart. I didn't really understand what he told me, or rather I didn't really listen. My only weakness is your absence, my son. Come and visit me; surely you can find the time to come and see your dear mother? Just for a few days, and my heart will be fortified for the years to come. You should see how happy your friend Luca is and how he dotes on his little girl. She's the apple of his eye, and he's a changed man! He often asks me about you and your life in Paris. He asks me to read every one of your letters to him. You're his hero, the adventurer. Isn't that funny? I think sometimes that he's jealous of you, but as I say, he's found his measure of happiness on this earth - a simple, balanced kind of happiness. This is perhaps something you need, my son. I know that you've loved Stella since you were a young boy, and she knows the way to your heart. But she's a married woman; can she give you a family? Time is precious, and affairs should not last forever. You should think about the kind of life you want to build.

All my love,
Your dear mother,
Nina."

The waiters were clearing up the room; Aleksander found himself alone for a moment. He looked at the empty plates and glasses piled up on the trays, and the white tablecloths being stripped away. Sitting at the window, he was sipping a whisky to finish off his evening. He looked at his reflection in the glass: the face was lined with wrinkles and had a grizzled brow, but it was his. How could this be? He did not feel like the man he saw; he did not deserve to see himself so changed. Yesterday, he'd been in his prime, his eyes sparkling and carefree. Yesterday, he'd had the world at his feet and dreamed of proving to his family that he was worth something. Yesterday, he'd been full of wild hope and energy, though he carried his share of rage too. Today, he was tired although satisfied. But he saw his life only in the rear-view mirror, contemplating his memories under the bright lights of wisdom and experience. Novelty bored him; he'd grown fond of habits and repetitive pleasures. His soul was unanchored, and bland as bread. What did life have left for him now? His lover was too young, and he could barely keep up with a twenty-year-old. Music was all that remained. His gaze focused on one of the party guests, still sitting on the steps of the brasserie. It was Giovanni. He seemed worried. Aleksander went out to say goodbye to him.

"I thought you'd left."

"Still here. I had a wonderful time."

"Sitting here alone, in the darkness? It's late; you should be off home."

"I was reading the letter you gave me. My mother was sick, but she's doing much better."

"I'm sorry to hear that."

"I have to go back. I miss Livorno. I've been away for five years. Have I really found anything here in France that's made me better off?"

"I didn't know you were unhappy. You should go back. It's a rare thing to be able to do. It's harder to go back than to leave."

"What about Stella? What about...you?"

"You'll find the answers you need. I'm sure of it.

12.

Aleksander Spielman opened his eyes and watched the first light of the day spill through his bedroom window. The yellowish rays crept over the floorboards, illuminating them like piano keys under stage lights. He let his mind wander, seeing if he could move the light and make it play for him. His lover was sleeping next to him, deeply, as only the young can sleep. Aleksander slept only a few hours per night; he did not like to think of time being wasted and preferred the jitters of fatigue to the sluggishness of too much rest. Age made it easier not to sleep. He enjoyed waking at first light and getting straight to work. But this morning he took some time to think, nestled under the covers. Today, Jews around the world were celebrating the fifth anniversary of the foundation of Israel, and tonight he would have the honour of performing a celebratory concerto at the Paris Opera. The minister had requested he compose a special symphony for the occasion. "France supports Israel and the Jewish people, whom you embody and represent through your talent, your convictions — and your religion of course!" he had joked, buried in his leather armchair like an overfed animal, swirling a Cognac between his fat fingers. Aleksander found him repulsive but had accepted the commission without hesitation. The man did not matter, the cause was too important. He'd been preparing for six months, demanding more of himself each day. He finally got up; the radio was scheduled to be replaying a speech by David Ben Gourion, one of Israel's founders. Aleksander had bought tea and Yiddish pastries to help him revel in the nostalgia. *"The Land of Israel was the birthplace of the Jewish people. Here their spiritual, religious and political identity was shaped. Here they first attained to statehood, created cultural values of national and universal significance and gave to the world the eternal Book of Books. After being forcibly exiled from their land, the people kept faith with it throughout their Dispersion and never ceased to pray and hope for their return to it and for the restoration in it of their political freedom. The catastrophe which recently befell the Jewish people — the massacre of millions of Jews in Europe — was another clear demonstration of the urgency of solving the problem of its homelessness by re-establishing in Eretz-Israel the Jewish State, which would open the gates of the homeland wide to every Jew and confer upon the Jewish people the status of a fully privileged member of the community of nations. The State of Israel will be open for Jewish immigration and for the Ingathering of the Exiles; it will foster the development of the country for the benefit of all its inhabitants; placing our trust in the Almighty, we affix our signatures to this proclamation on this Sabbath eve."* The spell was cast, and Spielman saw himself returned to Warsaw when he and his aunt had lived there in peace and he had studied at the Conservatory, barely thinking of politics. He'd been too busy dreaming of music and Sebastian to worry about his community. When his aunt invited some of her intellectual friends over for tea and they debated the Jewish state, he devoured the pastries, listening with half an ear open. And yet, he recalled some of the things they'd said. They often talked about the famous letter by Arthur Balfour, Her Majesty's Foreign Secretary, who in 1917 wrote to Lord Rothschild, a prominent figure in Britain's Jewish community, to inform him that the government was in favour of the foundation of a national Jewish homeland in Palestine. The letter was submitted to the San Remo conference, which in April 1920 placed Palestine under British control. But the men debated the ambiguity between a national homeland and a Jewish state. For the intellectuals among them, it was clear that the government had not wanted to sow discord among the partially anti-Zionist cabinet. Since then, Jews from around the world had sought refuge in Palestine in their thousands, but the Jewish Agency had been forced to enter into an agreement with the Nazis, and immigration had become clandestine. It was difficult for Polish Jews to return to the homeland. If it had been a Jewish state, things would have been different. They often quoted the works of Théodore Herzl, who'd been a proponent of the idea of an independent Jewish state since the last century: a true visionary! It was by a hair's breadth that the world had changed. Their conversations were often heated. Aleksander had often wondered what pleasure they took from all this empty talk and their notions of political insight. He found them laughable. But after his expulsion from the Conservatory, he began to ask himself questions, to feel angry and to hope. What remained of the emotions and the ideas of his youth? Aleksander smiled; he was far too old to be fighting for a better world. He'd done what he could; he'd honoured his people with his talent and fame. This thought brought him pride. Tonight he must be at the height of his powers, to remind the French people that the war was not long behind them. More importantly, to pay homage to his aunt. Wherever she was, he was sure she would hear him. He sat down at his desk to write his opening speech.

It was a select audience for tonight's performance; tickets had been in high demand, and the seats were sold out months in advance. In front of the Opera, Parisian high society mixed with affluent Jews, journalists and politicians. Giovanni and Stella listened to them with interest. What did they think about the event? "The Minister for Culture is a great fan of Aleksander Spielman; apparently he defended him to the journalists after that article was published," explained one bourgeois to another, who agreed contentedly: "It's about time, my friend, about time we recognised our talent." Beside them, journalists were debating the importance of the event. "An incredibly symbolic event", "No, it's all window dressing and hypocrisy." "France supports Israel, we must remember." "France does what suits it." The Opera bell rang out; it was time to take their seats. Giovanni and Stella were surprised to find themselves seated in the first lodge, facing the stage, flanked by eminent politicians and journalists.

"Not only were we invited, but we're sitting with the elite. What's so special about us?" Stella wondered, uncomfortable.

"I know as little as you do. Maybe it's to thank me for having worked with him these past few years. Even so, he's been very secretive about this concert; apparently there's a surprise in store."

"So you haven't heard what he's going to be playing tonight?"

"Not a note. I've been kept in the dark."

"That's strange. You'd think he'd need more help than ever for such an important performance."

"I'd see him reading his Torah and looking at old photos. He was tormented, as if the past had consumed him. He was more of a perfectionist than ever. He played his scales over and over like a child, played all the great masters again, then he'd suddenly ask me to leave. I'd have no news for days, then he'd call and ask me to bring him a book, a newspaper, flowers, or whatever else he needed to inspire him. Then he'd send me away again. When the article was published, it was the final straw. But he got back on his feet. He always does."

The great red curtain rose. The director of the Opera himself was there to introduce the pianist. "Ladies and Gentlemen, tonight the Opera Garnier is honoured to be celebrating the fifth anniversary of the foundation of the state of Israel. I'm delighted to welcome to the stage the great Aleksander Spielman." The pianist joined him, and the two men shook hands. The flash of camera lenses perforated the darkness and the audience's respectful silence. The weight of the moment hung in the air. Everyone knew the artist had been forced to play on that same stage for his Nazi enemies. They knew that dozens of the Opera's Jewish musicians had been deported. They knew that France's alliance with the Jewish people was in its tender infancy. The moment was no less symbolic, no less moving for its being so keenly anticipated. The director withdrew, and the artist began his speech. "Tonight's performance is a task I can never live up to. There is no homage that can adequately pay tribute to this night. What music could possibly quell the pain my people have suffered? What beauty could possibly emerge from such horrors? You will tell me that joy has brought us together tonight, that the disaster has passed, that crimes have been punished and that the dead are laid to rest. You will tell me that we must not stir up our past mistakes, but rather we must place our faith in the future. And you would be right, in part: the past is the past. But history repeats itself, the dead are never truly laid to rest, and we all carry within us the ghosts of those who suffered. Our mothers, fathers, brothers, sisters, uncles, aunts, children, friends: all taken from us. And the Holy Land offers us protection; Israel has chased away persecutors from around the world through its strength and its solidarity. But Israel is a country born in agony, and this pain shall never be forgotten. I am not a politician, and I cannot speak to you of peace accords or new deals. I can speak only as an artist, as a Pole, as a Frenchman, and as a Jew. Have you heard of Kazimierz? Perhaps the name is familiar. Kazimierz is where I grew up, and that humble neighbourhood in Krakow is where I discovered music. Since I cannot express the depth of my sadness, or the depth of the comfort I take from tonight, and I cannot write an adequate epitaph for our dead, it is to the old accordionist from Kazimierz that I address my speech tonight: that old, poor and piteous musician whose eyes shone like gold when he played in the park beside the synagogue. His pious soul, devoted to his music, has always been a source of inspiration and courage to me. My brothers, my sisters, may you be as compelled as I am by the perseverance of that old Jew. Famous artists like myself are usurpers of greatness, and peace will remain elusive unless we believe in the beauty of invisible, divine things." Aleksander wiped away a tear with the back of his hand. He observed the audience for a long moment. Stoic and impassive, he stared at the crowd gathered before him. His eyes were dark, his gaze cold. Did they deserve to hear what he had to play? He took a bow. The audience hung on his every movement, each gesture forceful and penetrative. He sat down at the piano, cracked his fingers and raised the keylid. He ran his fingers along the length of the keys, finding and inhabiting his space. Finally, he laid his fingers upon the ivory with intent. He was ready to conquer, and the music tore through the Opera like a clap of thunder. It was violent and brutal. Nothing like the genteel Aleksander Spielman harmonies they knew. The audience gasped. The pianist threw his arms around like a bullfighter. His deft hands moved with electrified energy. The rhythm slowed, and the symphony settled down. He led them through a vision of a dream. Giovanni squeezed Stella's hand. He was betrayed. He should be on that stage. Aleksander had stolen a part of his soul, his most intimate creation. But was this not an honour? The artist had taken his scattered crumbs and crafted them into something sublime, lending his piece true grace. And who would have listened to him anyway, the Italian no-one had ever heard of? He could not have dreamed of a more grandiose homage to his dear Maria. Aleksander had lifted him from the pit of his despair, and today he had closed their chapter, in his way. Giovanni was no longer in debt to him; they were even. He was no longer the page-turner who shivered under the wing of the great artist: he was the composer of a piece that was pushing Aleksander Spielman's talent to its greatest heights. Aleksander had taught him that everyone had their own genius, and that to acknowledge the talent of only famous people was poison to the art of creation. Giovanni now saw that it was not his destiny to shine in the spotlight, but tonight he revelled in that vicarious fame. He remembered the dreams he'd had as a child in Livorno, and the type of fame and glory that had seemed to him like the only possible happiness.

He'd wanted his parents to look at him with pride, but more than anything he'd wanted to attract the attention of the unattainable Stella. Was she not by his side tonight? She'd loved and supported him when he was nobody. He had nothing to offer her but himself, and this seemed to be enough for her. His mother was right: his childhood dreams could never compare to all those things his adult self had seen and done. He'd found love without expecting to. The love he shared with Stella was certainly not as innocent as what he'd felt for Maria, but it was a sterner bond. Nothing was holding him back now. He had to go with her.

Acknowledgements

Camille Ferey, Joséphine Fletcher, Simon Averous, Sofia Sadaï, Olmo Beltran, Anastasia Fletcher, Joyce Péronne-Gourdin

Layout by

Alan Alfredo GEDAY

Revisions by

Linda ILDEVERT, John MULLIGAN

Printed in Poland
by Amazon Fulfillment
Poland Sp. z o.o., Wrocław

73141880R00162